# THE GOBLIN GENERAL

## Jonathan Brazee

Acknowledgements:
I want to thank everyone in my editing and beta team who helped whip this book into shape.  All remaining typos and errors are solely my fault.

Geoffrey Morse, Bill Hopkins, Gary Leach, Bob Pederson, Robin Prtichard, Milton Findley, Jim McNeill, Barry Cone, Reed Fallaw Jr., Fred Kingery, William Martinez, John H, Rabbi Fred Natkin, Duane Hallman, John Hyatt, Fraser Butterworth, Norman Blaylock, Dennis Stevens, Rick Bancroft, and Ken Goldstein.


Original Cover Art by Maurizio Manzieri

Dedicated to Nora Faust, Beta Reader Extraordinaire

I just wish you'd been able to read this. I think you would have liked it.

RIP, Nora

# Contents

# THE RACES OF THE WORLD

## <u>The Light</u>

Elves

Dwarves

Sprites

Fauns

Faries

Brownies

Selkies

Centaurs

Gnomes

Peris

Huldefolk

## <u>The Dark</u>

Orcs

Ogres

Trolls

Harpies

Draugrs

Banshees

Ghouls

Satyrs

Pixies

Vurdalacks

Gremlins

Kukudhs

Kobolds
Goblins

## **Unaffiliated**

Humans
Cucullati (Hooded Spirits)
Wights
Mermaids
Minotaurs
Kitsune
Näcken
Will-o-wisps

Jonathan P. Brazee

# THE GOBLIN GENERAL

## Chapter 1

"Keep the line moving, gobby," the orc snarled, accompanied by a hard shove in the back that sent Qod stumbling into the goblin in front of him.

"Sorry, sorry," Qod said to the goblin as she turned around in anger.

Qod was small, even for a goblin, standing just under three feet. The goblin maiden towered over him by at least six inches, and her anger faded as she looked down upon him.

"Don't be in a hurry, small sir. We'll all get action soon enough."

*That's what I'm afraid of.*

Qod bowed his head several times in subservience, and she turned back. The orc kept haranguing the crowd of goblins, urging them to hurry. There was a hint of panic in his voice, something that made the smoke rising in the distance take on a more worrisome implication.

It was hard to believe that only a day ago, Qod was in his small round hovel in Yellow Rock, where he'd lived his entire life, only now getting used to being alone. Father was long gone, lost in the war. At least he and his mom assumed he was lost. He'd been snatched three enlistment sweeps ago, and that was the last either of them had heard of him.

Mother and littermates Leet and Poul had passed away from the skin rot epidemic that had swept through the vale less than two months ago, leaving him the last of his family and in sole possession of their small home. It was small, but comfortable, and the neighbors had cast covetous eyes on it. But the law protected the little guy—at least that was what people said. And the law said that as a full adult of eight years, the home passed to him.

It was just bad luck that the impressers had come through the village. Qod had hidden, of course, but the ogres had unerringly marched to his hiding place down by the creek and grabbed him.

Old man Juut watched the ogres lead Qod away with an eager glint in his eyes. If Qod were a suspicious goblin, he might have thought that Juut had something to do with the unexpected sweep. With seven little sausages and a home half the size of Qod's, he could use the space. That was crazy thinking, of course, but still, Qod was happy that the law protected soldiers, too. As long as he returned within a year, the home would still be his.

The war couldn't last that long, right?

He looked back to the horizon, where the dark smoke was rising. It gave him a feeling of foreboding.

Qod might be the only goblin from the village drafted in this sweep, but there had to be several hundred goblins, kobolds, gnomes, and even a few gremlins in the crowd. In typical Dark race fashion, the new recruits were just milling forward without much in the way of organization, which was why they had the orc soldiers herding them along.

Qod was too short to see what was happening. He stuck close to the goblin maiden's butt, using her to clear the way as they edged forward. Finally, they reached the front, where a line of a dozen tables was laid out, most manned by orcs. Piles of military equipment were behind the tables, while goblins ran back and forth bringing helmets and weapons forward.

Seeing the weapons gave him pause. Qod wasn't an aggressive goblin. His tastes were more towards reading and observation of the world around him rather than physical activities. He tried to melt back into the mass of recruits, but one of the orc shepherds grabbed him by the arm and pushed him toward the nearest table—one manned by a harpy.

Qod stared at her. He'd never seen a harpy before. There weren't many in the Worm Valley.

"Don't just stand there," the harpy said. "We haven't got all day."

Qod took a tentative step forward, his eyes locked onto the harpy's beak. There were tales of days gone by when harpies preyed on goblins. She was easily twice Qod's size, and images of that beak slashing down on him invaded his imagination and wouldn't let go.

"Closer," she said.

"Uh . . . yes, ma'am."

"I'm not an officer. I work for a living," she said with the tired voice of someone who'd said that a hundred times. "Name."

Qod was still staring at her beak, and it took him a moment for the question to sink in.

"Qod, ma'am."

"Qod what?" she asked in a bored voice.

"Oh, yeah. Yellow Rock. Qod Yellow Rock."

Goblins, like some of the other races, only had one name, so when dealing with the government, they added their place of birth as a surname. This was the first time he'd had to do that.

The harpy made a notation on her pad, then turned those predator eyes on him.

Qod gulped and took half a step back.

"Small," she said over her shoulder to the waiting goblin. "As small as you can find. And a spear."

She turned back to him. "Proceed and wait."

He stepped around her, giving her as wide a berth as he could while she asked the name of the next recruit.

The goblin went to the pile of gear, grabbed a few items, then came running back.

"Put these on," he said as he dropped them at Qod's feet. "Then move on to the assembly area."

*These?*

There were three items on the ground in front of him: a helmet, a leather vest, and a five-foot wooden spear with a metal head.

Qod tentatively picked up the helmet first. It was obviously too big for him, and what bothered him most was that there was a half-caved-in gash in the back.

"This one's broken," he said, holding it out to the other goblin.

The goblin just laughed. "Be glad you got something."

Jonathan P. Brazee

Qod gave it a closer look.  There was a dark stain around the gash.

*Is that . . . blood?*

He quickly raised his head.  The other goblin was looking at him with a bemused expression.

"Just hope it serves you better than the last owner.  Now go.  We've got a lot more customers to serve."

He didn't know what else to do, so Qod put the helmet on his head and reached down to pick up the vest.  As he bent over, the helmet shifted, banged his nose, and fell off.

"Cuirass first," the goblin said in a little more sympathetic voice.  "Then the helmet."

"Thanks."

The vest—*cuirass*—was old leather and a little rancid smelling, but at least it was in one piece.  He slipped it on.  The harpy had told the goblin to get a small, but it hung on Qod like a smock, the bottom coming down to just above his knees.

*Well, maybe it's more protection this way*, he told himself as he tried to use the straps to make it fit tighter.

He put on the helmet, then glanced warily at the spear.  It was twice as long as he was tall, and he already felt like he was weighted down.  Trying to keep his head straight so he wouldn't lose the helmet, he squatted to reach for the spear.  To his surprise and relief, it was much lighter than it looked.

*I wish I had a mirror.*

There wasn't a martial bone in his small body, and he'd really rather be home with a good book and a nice cup of nettle tea, but for a moment, he felt, well . . . *studly*.

But he wasn't home, and he didn't have a mirror.  With a sigh, he looked around to find the assembly area the goblin told him about. The new recruits were filing off to the left to where those with their gear were already waiting.  Qod joined them.

The spear was light, but it was awkward, and he dropped it twice.  The bottom of the cuirass was banging into his calves with each step, and the helmet was starting to make his neck ache.

"I'll have to see if I can get these exchanged for something my size," he muttered.

The other recruits were gathering in small groups. With no one else from Yellow Rock here, Qod didn't know anyone. Maybe this was the best time to ask for better gear, while they were still near the equipment.

There was an orc standing to the side just watching with an air of authority around him, and Qod wondered if he was an officer. If he were, then he'd surely want to make sure one of his recruits was properly outfitted.

He cleared his throat, puffed up his chest—which with the cuirass was hard to tell—and marched up to the orc.

"You need something, Private?"

"Um . . . yes, sir. I was wondering if I could get something that fits me before we start training."

The orc snorted in amusement. "Training?"

"Well, yes, sir. Military training. So we can push the Light races back."

This time, the orc laughed out loud.

"OK, Private. Pick up that spear."

Qod was confused, but he picked up the spear and waited.

"Hands farther back," the orc said.

Qod adjusted his grip.

"Now, when an elf charges you, stick it with the pointy end. There, training is over."

"Sir?"

The orc turned and pointed at the horizon. "That, my little goblin, is the battle. In half an hour, that's where we're going. So, if you think you need training, you're just going to have to learn on the fly."

## Chapter 2

The orc was true to his word. Half an hour later, and as soon
as the last of the new draftees was outfitted, he took a moment
to address the company.

"I'm Captain Ryys, and you are now members of the
One hundred and twenty-first Replacement Company."

Qod didn't like the name. Why were they a
"replacement?" What happened to the original company?

The captain half-turned to the smoke on the horizon
and dramatically pointed.

"Over there, the armies of Light have invaded our lands.
They killed our families. They've burned our homes. You—all
of you—have the honor to be called upon to throw the bastards
back to their forests, back to their gleaming cities."

Qod gulped. This was happening too quickly. Sure, he
knew the stakes. The armies of Light had invaded the land of
the good folk of the Dark. It was always that way. The elves,
with their dwarf allies and other enthralled races, thought
nothing of driving off—killing off, more often—the little folk
who struggled on the land just to scratch out a living. And for
what? Ethereal forests for the stately elves to walk around and
contemplate whatever it was that elves contemplated? A
private reserve for a single elf could support an orc village or a
couple of thousand goblins.

But what could Qod do against an elf, a centaur, or a
dwarf in combat? Or even a faun, for that matter? He was
small for a goblin, and goblins were the second-smallest race
in the Dark Coalition.

He was willing to contribute to the defense of the Dark
lands, but how about as a supply clerk? That pile of
equipment could use some help. Qod wasn't particularly good
with his hands, so repairing the helmets and weapons was
probably a non-starter, but he was a whiz with numbers, so he
could inventory the usable and unusable to help each soldier
get outfitted.

And how about singing?  He had a good voice, right?  He could keep up morale, singing songs of victory as the soldiers marched off to battle.

Qod had a vision of himself dancing alongside the column in a satyr's robe, strumming a lute and singing.  Then his imagined image stumbled and fell in the mud, breaking his lute.

That was reality biting him in the ass.  He really didn't have a good voice.  His littermates told him he sounded like a cat with its tail stuck in a door, and he had no idea how to play the lute.

"Right now, your brothers and sisters are over there, dying as they protect our land.  Now, it's our turn," the captain continued.

*Our turn to die?*

Qod wasn't ready for that.  Sure, he knew that soldiering was dangerous work, but the captain seemed to think getting killed was a done deal.  Qod hoped that he would survive and get back home to Yellow Rock.

While the captain went on, stressing loyalty, perseverance, and glory, Qod surreptitiously turned and looked behind the company.  A line of orcs and what had to be a banshee was formed, hands suggestively resting on sword pommels and ax handles.  Qod had no doubt that they were ready to dissuade any of the new privates should they try to slip away.

Not that it seemed most of the draftees had that in mind.  Their eyes were locked on the captain, and they shook their spears and axes and roared with each statement.

It wasn't that Qod didn't understand the existential threat the Dark folk faced.  The elven coalition wanted to kill every one of them.  Their stated goal was to eliminate the "evil vermin" that "infected" the world so that the people of the Light could take over and live according to their vision.

That goal is what brought together the people of the Dark. Orcs, ogres, trolls, goblins, satyrs, and the rest had rarely been allies until the elves forced them to band together for survival.

But what was Qod going to do as a soldier? He was a goblin, and not a very impressive one at that. Small, uncoordinated, and weak, even for a goblin, there was nothing about him that said warrior. That wasn't false modesty. It was just facing facts.

He wanted the elves, dwarves, sprites, and all the Light folk to be defeated. No, *killed*. But he knew he wasn't the one who was going to be able to do that.

The captain continued pumping up the company as the smoke behind him grew darker, while Qod grew more anxious. Once, a flash of light lit up the skyline.

Qod's heart gave a lurch.

*What was that? A wizard? A mage?*

He knew next to nothing about wizards, even less about mages. There weren't any magic masters in the Worm Valley. But if the rumors were anything close to the truth, then Qod didn't want to come anywhere close to one, Light *or* Dark.

The captain's voice started to rise in volume, breaking through Qod's thoughts.

"Now is the time to prove your worth. The Dark is relying on you. Are you with me?"

The company roared in response. Qod belatedly attempted to join in with a sort of yelp of his own. No one seemed to notice that he wasn't as enthusiastic as the rest.

"Then let's go kick some faeby ass! Sergeants, move 'em out!"

The line of orcs behind the new soldiers advanced and started to organize them for marching. There was mass confusion, but with judicial shouting and more than a bit of shoving, the company was formed up and the command to move was given. The 121st Replacement Company started the march to meet its fate.

*************

With a sigh, Qod pushed the crown of his helmet up out of his eyes.  The motion was already automatic.  Take four steps, push up the helmet.  Take four more, push it up again.

He wasn't sure what he hated the most:  his helmet or his cuirass.  The helmet banged around on his head, and his neck was sore from trying to compensate.  There was a welt on the bridge of his nose from each time the edge of the helmet slammed down, and the tops of his ear creases were raw from the helmet's weight. But his cuirass was heavier, and it got heavier with each step as clods of mud kept getting added to it. Qod was in the back of the company, which at first seemed fortuitous—being in the back meant he was farther from the enemy.  However, that meant the ground in front of him was being churned into mud, which seemed to latch onto his cuirass, making it both heavier and stiffer.  Mud was almost an inch thick on the bottom, and it banged into his legs with each step.  He tried to wipe it off, but between holding his spear and pushing up the edge of his helmet, he didn't have a free hand.

Worse than his gear was that the 121st Replacement Company was more of a replacement gaggle with none of the precision of a real military unit. They were a mob eagerly—or not so eagerly—moving forward to face the enemy.  That meant their speed of march varied, which accordioned the company.  In the rear, Qod alternated between standing still while waiting for those in front of him to move and then having to run to catch up.  Each moment of rest was gratefully seized upon, only to have to sprint a moment later.

Rinse and repeat.

To make matters worse, a cool southern breeze kicked up.  With sweat coating his face and running down his back, Qod welcomed it at first.  That quickly changed.  The sweat dried, and the wind started to bite.  Worse, the wind seemed to harden the mud into armor-like consistency, which banged into his legs with ever greater force and weighed him down even more.

Qod's entire existence narrowed down to the butt of the goblin in front of him as he trudged forward.

The owner of that butt turned around at one point.

"Are you doing OK, small sir?"

It was the goblin maiden he'd bumped into in line what seemed like ages ago.

Goblins were relatively egalitarian regarding gender. Males and females were roughly the same size and had the same strength. Maidens had a few of the more subtle curves that set Qod's as of yet unrequited desires afire, but other than that, there weren't many differences. Even when pregnant, the first others knew about it was when a goblinette appeared with a litter of sausages in her arms. Still, Qod was embarrassed and was not going to admit weakness in front of her.

"I'm fine," he tried to say in a confident voice that came out more as a gasp.

He hurried forward a few steps.

"If you need help, let me know," she said before turning back.

*Real smooth, there,* he told himself before starting to fall behind again.

His littermate brother Poul would have come up with some snappy line in the same position. Leet never would have let herself fall behind in the first place. Sometimes—ofttimes—Qod wondered about the fate that spared weakling him while taking his far more capable littermates. The only thing he could come up with was that the gods were assholes who enjoyed screwing with folks.

He was cursing—silently, of course, not wanting any listening god to hear—life in general when he reached the top of the next rise and froze, all thoughts of the vagaries of fate wiped from his mind. He looked down on a valley with a meandering river in the center, rising foothills, and then snowcapped mountains rising behind them on the far side. In another situation, he would probably find the vista picturesque, but none of that registered. Instead, he couldn't tear his eyes from the chaos before him.

First, was the smoke which rose from what looked like a destroyed village and numerous other fires scattered about the landscape. Second, and more disturbing, were the thousands, if not tens of thousands, of figures locked in combat with each other. A phalanx of dwarves crashed into a much smaller platoon of orcs, scattering them like lawn pins. Axes rose and fell with almost mechanical precision, dropping orcs with each blow.

Less than a mile away, a large group of what looked to be mostly goblins was wheeling to face a smaller group of what might be fauns who were ensconced on a small hilltop.

"Kill the bastard faebies," someone in the center of the company shouted as the goblins oriented themselves and faced the battlefield.

Qod tore his eyes away to an isolated troll near the ruined village who was swinging a massive club, trying to hold a mob of gnomes at bay. He'd never actually seen a troll before, and it seemed impossible that anything could stand up to the massive fellow, but like hounds on a bear, the gnomes attacked. One sliced across the back of the troll's thigh, hamstringing him. The troll fell and was swarmed under. Pikes and spears flashed as they plunged into the prone body.

Qod shuddered. If a troll was so easily taken down, what would happen to him?

"Hearth and home!" one of the other goblins in the company swore.

The nearer goblins attacking the hill were just starting up, and it took Qod a moment to realize what the dark spots heading toward them were. Like flies zooming in on a dead dog, the fauns had unleashed a massive flight of arrows. Seemingly in slow motion, the arrows reached their apex before plunging unerringly down toward the goblin company.

They struck with force, and goblins fell by the score. Already, another volley was heading toward them.

There was a sudden shift in the wind, and for a moment, Qod could hear the cries of the dying and wounded before that second volley hit, and then the cries were cut off. He stared slack-jawed. One moment several hundred goblins were rushing to attack, and now most of them were dead. The fauns had suckered them into bow-and-arrow range, then fired their deadly volleys.

And that was just what was happening nearest to them. Across the valley floor, units maneuvered and attacked, and bodies fell. Dark or Light, the carnage was fearful.

Then, the order he feared came.

"Company, ADVANCE," the captain shouted.

The sergeants swung into action, pushing the privates forward, who suddenly seemed less sure of themselves. Several tried to retreat, only to be beaten and driven back.

But most of the goblins and kobolds took up the call and started down the slope, following the captain, their gravitational pull enough to get the entire company moving. In the rear of the company, Qod just tried to keep to his feet, hyperaware of the sergeants who were coming up behind. He caught a few glimpses of the battle as he struggled forward, his helmet constantly falling over his eyes. There was a line of ogres crashing into some centaurs. A flight of harpies dove into the attack against a foe he couldn't see, only to be dropped out of the sky one by one until there weren't any left.

The closer they got, the more carnage he saw. Half hidden in the grass, Qod spotted a very tall goblinette on her back. She couldn't have been more than seven, and she would never see eight. Her face was serene, almost peaceful, as if she were just taking a nap. But as he came up alongside her, he realized that she wasn't tall. There was a gap of six inches between her hips and legs and the rest of her torso. Something had torn her in half.

Qod's stomach churned, and bitter bile rose in his throat. He bent over and retched. One of the orc sergeants came up alongside, put his arm around Qod's back, and straightened him out.

"Just keep up, gobby," he said in a surprisingly understanding tone.

"Yes, sir," Qod managed to stammer out.

He meant it, too. They might be mostly a goblin company, but being with them was better than being alone, where he'd have no chance of survival.

They ran past and over more bodies, but Qod refused to look directly at them. If he didn't acknowledge them, then they weren't there. They hadn't been killed in the very battle he was running to join.

Then, seemingly coming out of nowhere, a company of elite elf huscarls appeared, their white armor so bright it hurt his eyes, even at this distance. They barely paused as their formation ran through the ogres as if they were sausages' toys. Low hoots of despair reached across this section of the battlefield as the ogres died, and the hoots seemed to catch on among the rest of the Dark folk. The huscarls wheeled with precision. For a moment, it seemed to be aimed right at the company, and Qod knew he was about to meet his end. Evidently, though, a single company of goblins wasn't enough to warrant their elite attention.

Goblins went through their short lives with a constant chip on their shoulders. Everyone, even their Dark allies, thought them a useless, incapable, and somewhat worse, a *silly* race. But for once, Qod thanked the gods for that as the huscarls kept wheeling before orienting on a more worthy foe and galloping off.

The complete annihilation of the ogres, without a single elf casualty, had a drastic effect, though. The Dark forces, at least in the immediate area, stopped their advance and started to form defensive positions. Captain Ryys slowed the company to barely a crawl while he scanned the nearest forces. Qod was grateful for the chance to catch his breath.

A pixie in wicker armor appeared out of nowhere, alighted on the captain's shoulder, and whispered into his ear. The captain listened for a moment, nodded, and said something back to her. The pixie took off like a hummingbird, and the captain brought the company to a halt.

"Company, listen up. We're retreating."

"Thank the gods," Qod said aloud.

There were a few shouts of despair, but Qod could feel the relief, even from the orcs.

*Maybe I can go home?*

That hope was quashed when the captain said, "It's not forever. High command wants to step back and reorganize for a final, concerted push. Tomorrow, we're going to kill every faeby invader or send them running. This is going to end, one way or the other."

## Chapter 3

It was a somber army that gathered back at Camp Defiance, where Qod and the rest had been issued their gear. Only, this time, there were five or six times as many of the Dark folk: orcs, ogres, and goblins, of course, but also harpies, trolls, kobolds, banshees, and more, a few races that Qod didn't recognize.

Captain Ryys called the company to a halt, and Qod collapsed onto the ground. If the march to the battle had been exhausting, the march back had been even worse. The fear of imminent death and seeing the carnage had taken an emotional toll that sapped the goblins' strength.

"Look sharp," the captain said. "Don't let the others see any sign of weakness. Show them we're ready for tomorrow."

He called in the senior sergeants for a meeting, then strode off, leaving the company in the charge of the rest of the NCOs.

"Everyone stand easy, and we'll see what we can scrounge up to eat," one of them told the soldiers.

Qod couldn't be the only one who wondered why they hadn't any food in the first place. The command must have thought they wouldn't need any. Being killed in battle meant that the Dark logistics force had one less mouth to feed.

The mention of food made his belly rumble, though. But as tired as he was, he wasn't sure he could get up to receive whatever was brought.

He sighed, took off his helmet, and rubbed his nose. The rim of the helmet had fallen down so many times that by now the bridge of his proudly large nose was raw and weeping.

If he was going to die tomorrow, then why torture himself? He placed the helmet in the mud beside him and tried to kick it away, but after it bounced a few feet down the slight slope, the orc sergeant who'd helped him caught it mid-bounce and brought it back.

"Close, there, private. You don't want to lose this."

*Yes, I do.*

"Thank you, Sergeant," he said with a forced smile.

"Stand up."

Qod managed not to roll his eyes at the command, but he couldn't hide the grunt of pain as he stood up.

*Now what?*

The sergeant looked at him with a critical eye for a moment. The orc was typical of his kind. Twice as tall as a goblin and three times heavier, his face was thin and somewhat wolflike with the trademark protruding lower yellow-stained incisors.

What caught Qod's attention more was the orc's falchion, or rather the pommel and grip that were visible protruding from the leather scabbard. A falchion was a wicked-looking, no-nonsense weapon, but this one had what looked to be blue and gold intertwined filigree woven into the grip. It didn't seem too *orc-like* to Qod, and he wondered how it had gotten there.

An orc lass somewhere, sending her lover off to battle? Qod was a sucker for a good story, and sometimes his imagination could go a little too far.

"That cuirass is way too big for you," the sergeant said.

Qod tore his gaze away from the sergeant's sword and widened his eyes in surprise. No one else had seemed to care that his cuirass didn't fit.

"I tried to tell the captain that, sir."

"I'm a sergeant, Private. I work for a living, so don't call me sir."

That was the second time in less than four hours he'd heard that, so it must be a standard saying, and he probably should pay heed to it.

"The captain?" the sergeant continued. "He ain't gonna rock the boat. And it ain't like the command thinks we're gonna be around long enough for it to make a difference."

He suddenly reached out so quickly that Qod jumped back in fear, but the orc sergeant grabbed one of the straps on the cuirass's side.

"Well, this can be tightened, sure enough."

He pulled it out, which knocked some of the mud off, then turned Qod slightly to the side as he searched for the opposite strap. He had to knock off a bit more mud until he uncovered it, then jerked both to the front, almost knocking Qod forward to his knees.

There was a loop at the end of one of the straps, and the sergeant ran the free end of the other strap through it.

"The tighter the better, but not so tight that you can't breathe, OK?"

Qod just nodded.

"Here goes."

The sergeant pulled, and Qod thought he was getting squeezed in two. He had never been this close to an orc before, and the sergeant's strength was more than a surprise. He was a monster!

And he was too strong for the leather strap. On his second pull, which Qod thought was going to push his guts out of his mouth, the strap snapped.

Qod gasped for breath, glad for the moment the strap had given out.

"Dwarf shit!" the sergeant snarled, fully revealing his three-inch incisors as he tossed the broken end of the strap away.

Qod stepped back in fear. He hadn't been around orcs very often in his life, and this was the first time he'd seen their infamous temper in action.

The sergeant didn't seem to notice Qod's reaction, and just as quickly as the anger had appeared, it was gone.

"Damn military surplus."

Qod gathered himself. "Military surplus" caught his attention, but he wasn't going to question just what that meant right now.

The sergeant looked him over for a moment, then shook his head.

"Well, that didn't work, but at least we can clean you up some. You're caked."

"I tried to get the mud off, si . . . Sergeant."

The Orc put a big meaty paw on Qod's shoulder to steady him and then started to beat the lower half of the cuirass. Except for that hand, each blow would have knocked Qod on his spindly butt. As it was, Qod thought the cure was worse than the symptoms as his legs were beaten.

Finally, the orc sergeant seemed satisfied.

"Sorry, Private, but that's the best I can do.  Uh. . . if you sorta see sumthin' tomorrow, you know, smaller like, I'd grab it."

Which meant if he saw a smaller cuirass on a dead goblin or gremlin.

The sergeant started to turn away when Qod asked, "Why are you helping me?"

The orc seemed surprised at the question.

"Because I'm an NCO.  That's what we do."

Orcs and goblins were not the closest of races.  They were allies only because of a common enemy, and all goblins knew that orcs were vile, dangerous creatures.

But flash of temper or not, this orc seemed nice. Civilized, even.

Before he could consider if this was a good idea, Qod asked, "What is your name?"

"My name?  You want to know my name?"

"Yes, sergeant."

"Sergeant Hjami, Private," he said with a chortle.

The orc spun on his heels and stalked off.

"I'm Private Qod!" he shouted after the sergeant, who didn't acknowledge him.

Qod stared at the orc for a few moments before he collapsed back down onto the ground.

**************

"Here.  Eat up, small sir."

Qod looked up.  The goblinette was standing in front of him, hand outstretched.  He eyed her hand with suspicion.

"What is it?"

"They said rat cracks."

He sat up higher and eagerly took the smallish wafer. Rat crackers were a much-loved treat for young goblins, and although a full-fledged adult, Qod wasn't going to pass up on one of his sausagehood favorites.

Except this didn't look like any rat crack he'd ever had. It was thin, hard, and colorless without a hint of greasy goodness. Qod took a tentative nibble and almost choked.

"This is as dry as a **dwarf's butt**," he said.

"I never said they were good rat cracks," she responded as she plopped herself down beside him.

She took a small bite of hers. "They didn't let the rats age enough."

"I think they forgot to *add* the rats."

She shrugged. "Maybe they just waved a single buck over the batch and left it at that. Still, it's something in our bellies. Be grateful for that."

Qod grunted and took another bite. She was right, of course.

"I'm Pani," she said.

He had to swallow a piece of cracker before he could answer. "Qod."

"Where are you from?"

"Yellow Rock."

"Don't know where that is."

That surprised him. Yellow Rock wasn't very big, but Worm Valley was the next one over.

He took another small bite of the cracker. Maybe there was just a hint of rat to it.

"I'm from Mud Geyser," she offered when he didn't ask.

Somehow, it didn't seem worth the effort of revealing that, seeing as how they'd all be dead tomorrow. Still, he'd heard of Mud Geyser, and that piqued his curiosity.

"Does it really spout mud there?" he finally asked.

"Every eighty-six minutes, small sir," she said with obvious pride. "Thirty, sometimes forty feet high."

"Qod. Not small sir," he snapped.

"Sorry. Habit."

*Weird habit.*

That aside, he'd like to see the geyser. Mud, shooting up like a volcano. Not that he ever would, he knew. He wasn't going to have the opportunity to see much of the world.

*At least I got out of the Worm Valley, which is more than most goblins I know, even if the reason is less than ideal.*

He took the last bite of the cracker, then wiped his forearm across his face. The cracker had been far from good, but he wondered if he could scrounge another one.

"What do you think is going to happen tomorrow, small sir?" Pani asked.

Qod was going to snap about the "small sir" again, but something in her voice stopped him. She was scared.

*I'm scared, too.*

Except for him, it wasn't fear, per se. It was more a fatalistic acceptance tinged with anger. That might change tomorrow when they faced the enemy, he knew, but for now, the anger was prevalent.

He glanced at her out of the corner of his eye. Even sitting down, he could see she was taller than he was. Bigger, too, but a hundred percent female. Her green skin was unblemished, and the end of her nose had the cutest hook.

In other words, she was very far out of his league, yet it seemed that she'd sought *him* out.

And he felt a rush of protectiveness—and that made him feel . . . well, he didn't have words to describe it as it was something brand new to him. He had no illusions as to what was going to happen tomorrow, but he wanted to give her comfort.

So he started spouting the first thing that came to his mind.

"The faebies were all over the place. There were the fauns on the hill, for example."

"Which fired on the other goblin folk," she said in outright despair.

"That's because the goblins attacked head-on, Pani. If they'd encircled that hill and, I don't know, spread out more? Then the fauns wouldn't have been able to mass their arrows. There were orcs nearby, too. They could of, like, *coordinated* their attack."

Qod had just been spitballing, but as the words came out, he knew they were the truth. It was the piecemeal attack that had allowed the fauns to focus their arrows on the goblin company.

Pani seemed to consider it for a moment before she asked, "But what about those elves in that formation?"

"Them? Same thing. The orcs tried to meet them head-on. They should have spread apart and let the elves come, then hit them from the sides."

Pani finished the last of her cracker and delicately licked her fingers clean. Qod had to avert his eyes before *thoughts* could form.

"I hope you're right," she said.

"It's not me who's being right. The generals saw how unorganized both sides were. That's why they pulled us back. You heard the captain. They want to reorganize."

She sniffed, then asked, "You really think so?"

"I *know* so."

Of course, he knew no such thing. But it made sense. If he, with no military training, could see that, then the orc and ogre generals who'd witnessed battle after battle would have seen the same weakness in both sides. And if the Dark army could attack as one tomorrow, maybe they could overcome the elves and their Light allies.

Qod had been trying to give Pani a degree of hope, but he'd ended up giving himself a glimmer of hope as well. It was still likely that none of them were going to survive the morrow, but maybe it wasn't an absolutely foregone conclusion.

She turned to him and smiled. "You're pretty smart, small sir."

He puffed up his chest and let the "small sir" slide again.

"One Twenty-first Company, get some sleep. You're gonna need it," the sergeants started shouting. "We're moving out at zero-dark-thirty."

"Can I sleep here, next to you?" Pani asked.

"Sure, if you want."

She turned to her side, her back to him, and curled into a ball.

"I just hope they don't have a battle mage with them," she mumbled before she drifted off and started snoring.

*Battle mage?*

He shivered at the thought. It was bad enough that they were fighting elves, and there were probably wizards with the enemy, but no one had mentioned a mage. Still, he'd like to talk some more with her about that possibility, but evidently, he'd done too good a job in comforting her, and now she was asleep.

She hadn't returned the favor. Her worst-case comment was hard to dismiss.

A battle mage, even if they were only a fraction as powerful as they were rumored to be, would upset all Qod's conjecture. Even the best military maneuvers could be defeated by the pure power of one of those fearsome creatures.

*They don't have one, right? The generals would have told us.*

Battle mages were rare, and nobody ever wanted to see one across the battle lines. Because of their rarity, they were mostly deployed way down south on the fertile plains where the main battles were fought.

Wizards were far more common. Qod had even seen one today—at least he assumed the gremlin was a wizard, given the purple robe and pointy hat. But while wizards might be able to assist in a fight, they didn't have the power to shift the course of the battle on their own.

Qod didn't *think* there was a battle mage up here in the Fanciful Highlands, but there had been that flash of light yesterday, and the mere thought kept him awake far into the night while Pani snored in peaceful slumber beside him.

## Chapter 4

"They could have waited until daylight," one of the others said as the goblins stamped their feet and blew on their hands.

Qod wanted to explain the early start, but no one liked a know-it-all, and it wouldn't matter much in a few hours anyway. Despite what he'd told Pani the evening before, he was slipping into a pessimistic frame of mind that only grew by the minute.

Goblins were a daylight race, like most of the Light folk, which made them somewhat suspect to more than a few of their allies. Trolls, ogres, ghouls, and others preferred the night. Orcs didn't care and could operate equally well in either.

But the Light liked daylight, so if the Dark army could use the cover of darkness to advance unseen, then that was an advantage that would be stupid to waste.

The only problem was that they'd soon lose that advantage. It had taken the army so long to get ready that the faint hues of rose were already lightening the eastern horizon.

Qod wasn't sure what he'd prefer. Sure, anything to tilt the odds in favor of the Dark was good, but he was a goblin, after all. And with the unseasonable cold snap that had swept in overnight, the sun's rays would bring a welcome warming.

The oncoming dawn revealed more of the Army of the Mist, which was what a sergeant had told them was the name of their force. As a Yellow Rock goblin, Qod had led a rather isolated life. He'd seen orcs, of course. Talked with them, even. The occasional pixie flying in with messages. Ogres. Once, a family of ghouls stopped in Yellow Rock for a day. Then there was the human trader who came through the village on his **vardo** wagon every three months. Heck, before the latest war had broken out, there'd even been dwarves, fauns, and once an elf passing through.

Now, over the last two days, he'd met a harpy and seen trolls. Despite the dire situation facing him, he had a schoolboy excitement to see races he'd only read about.

The trolls were fascinating—in a scary way. He'd watched the one get pulled down by gnomes during the battle, but another had lumbered by the company fifteen minutes ago, not even twenty feet away. Qod felt the ground shake as it passed, and his imagination couldn't let go of the image of one of the huge, hairy feet smashing him flat. The troll probably wouldn't even notice that it had left a Qod-sized smear on the cold ground.

He slowly rotated as he tried to spot where the troll had gone, hoping that with the growing light, he'd have a better look.

No troll—how could something that big be out of sight?—but down the hill by some large rocks was a group of—

Qod bolted to where the NCOs were standing together as they waited for the order to move out.

"Sergeant Hjami! Sergeant Hjami!"

All of the NCOs turned toward him.

One of the Orcs nudged Hjami with her elbow and said, "Here comes your project."

Qod caught the dismissive tone, but what he'd seen was too important for him to get upset.

The sergeant sighed and said, "What is it, Qod?"

"I just saw some fauns! Here!"

That sure caught the attention of the sergeants. They immediately snapped to, hands going to sword hilts as they formed a small defensive circle.

"Where, gobby?" one of the sergeants shouted. "Where?"

"Over there!"

Qod pointed down the slope. The fauns were still there, acting nonchalant.

*They must be trying to blend in before they attack.*

The orcs looked in that direction, but they didn't react.

"Can't you see them?"

Everyone knew that goblins had good sight—one of their few advantages over most other races—but surely the orcs' eyesight wasn't that bad.

"Where, gobby? I don't see shit!"

"By that tree. There are at least thirty of them."

As if they could feel Qod's attention, one of them stopped to stare at the sergeants and him.

"He's looking right at us!" Qod said, and in his excitement, he pulled on the orc sergeant's arm.

The sergeant finally seemed to spot the fauns, but instead of rushing into the attack, he snarled and shoved Qod to the ground.

"Damn gobby," he said as he stepped forward to stand astride him. "You're either a smart ass or a fool."

The orc started to withdraw his sword from its scabbard, and Qod almost fainted as he watched his impending doom come at him.

"Either makes you a liability."

Qod was on his back, and he tried to scramble away, but the orc stepped on his thigh, effectively trapping him.

The sergeant raised the sword, and Qod's eyes were locked onto the wickedly hooked tip, designed to gut the victim like a lake trout.

He squealed in fear, but even that was a poor effort, barely audible.

Sergeant Hjami stepped up and grabbed the other orc's forearm. "Come on, Blakamo. You know what the command says about wasting gobbies."

The orc turned to Hjami, his eyes blazing black with anger.

Qod stopped struggling, wishing he could fade into the ground like a dwarf.

"Don't dirty yourself. Let the elves take care of him."

It didn't look like the sergeant was going to heed the plea, but then, with a derisive snort, the sergeant's eyes lost their obsidian depth of soullessness, and he re-scabbarded his blade.

"Take your pet, then," he said as he turned his back to Qod and joined the others, who'd been silently watching the confrontation.

From their expression, Qod thought that more than a few would have liked to see their fellow orc shorten Qod by a head's length.

Sergeant Hjami reached down and jerked Qod to his feet.

"Thank y—"

"Shut up, gobby!" Hjami hissed as he dragged Qod away from the other sergeants and toward the fauns.

Panic started flooding Qod anew. Was he going to be turned over to the enemy? Nothing made sense, so everything remained a possibility.

They stopped well short of the fauns, however, and Hjami roughly jerked Qod around to face him, then shook him like a ferret on a rat.

"What in the Dark Lord's asshole were you trying to prove there, Private?"

"I . . . you . . ." he tried to say as he was jerked back and forth.

He managed to broadly gesture to the enemy and gasp out, "Fauns."

The shaking stopped, and Hjami looked confused. "Fauns? Why do you think they're fauns?"

Grateful that his neck hadn't separated and his head was still attached, Qod took a moment to glance at the fauns, several of whom had noticed the two of them and were watching with interest.

Goat horns. Check. Naked torso, furry from the waist on down. Check. Goatlike hoofs.

Now it was his time to be confused.

"Those are fauns, sergeant. I've seen them before. Four years ago, before the war, some came through Yellow Rock on their pilgrimage."

Sergeant Hjami let go of his arms only to smack Qod on the side of the head. The much smaller goblin was staggered, but he didn't go down.

"Those aren't fauns, gobby! Those are satyrs."

"What?"

Qod looked again. He wondered if his memory was playing some sort of perverted trick on him, but no. It was said that goblins never forgot, and if anything, Qod thought his mental abilities were on the upper range of goblinhood.

"Sergeant, those are fauns. Look at the horns. Their goat bodies."

The sergeant's anger seemed to have faded, and he gave the fauns a longer look. One of them waved.

"Well, they look a little alike, I guess."

*Exactly alike.*

"But you've seen satyrs, right?"

Qod shook his head, which sent a jab of pain down his neck. Evidently, the shaking he'd received had tweaked something.

"From what they say, satyrs live down on the plains, and we don't get many tourists in Yellow Rock."

"You really are from the boondocks, aren't you?" he asked, but without noticeable malice.

Qod began to hope that he might escape the predicament he'd gotten himself into.

He gave the satyrs another look. They looked exactly like the faun pilgrims he'd seen before the war. Which posed a problem. He was going into battle, so it might be nice to be able to tell friend from foe.

"Uh, Sergeant? How do I, you know, tell the difference between them? Fauns and satyrs.

Sergeant Hjami laughed. It wasn't a pleasant one.

"That's easy. If they're trying to shoot you with an arrow, then they're a faun."

Qod just stared at the sergeant, who seemed pretty pleased with his answer. He was about to press the question when the orders to move out started to be passed through the mass of the Dark army.

"That's it, gobby. Get your ass back to the others. Like now."

Qod gave one last look at the satyrs, who were forming up as well.

"I said, now, Private. And word to the wise. Steer clear of Sergeant Blakamo."

Qod was about to thank the sergeant when the orc added, "I was serious about letting the elves kill you. Maybe your sacrifice will keep them occupied, and one less orc will die today."

# Chapter 5

Qod stared at the ground, just trying to keep to his feet. After the army had marched over the same route three times, the ground had first turned to mud, then it had frozen overnight. Not entirely, though. A hard crust had formed, but a thin one. So every other step broke through, which made the going even harder.

To make matters worse, the cold wind bit at his nose, ears, and hands while the exertion, while wearing the leather cuirass made him break out in a sweat—which rolled down his back and onto his legs, where it froze.

*By the **Dark Mother**, just let me die here and get it over with.*

He guiltily looked up ahead where the army's wizard was trudging along, just like the rest of the peons. He didn't think the wizard could read thoughts, but then again, he'd never even seen one before and had no idea what a wizard could do.

The gremlin didn't seem too impressive. The edges of his purple robe were rather tattered, in fact, and the bottom was caked with muddy ice.

Still, it was probably a good idea to watch what he was thinking. Better safe than sorry.

*I'm so glad I'm fighting for the Dark*, he thought with as much force as he could muster.

The wizard didn't seem to notice, and Qod sighed with relief.

A very short-lived relief. The brim of his helmet settled on the bridge of his sore nose again, and he pushed it up, which sent a lance of pain down his neck, through his back, and then out through his right leg.

Sergeant Hjami was marching right in front of him, so he felt brave enough to give the orc a mental curse for shaking his neck out of alignment.

Qod had never been so sore, tired, and beat up in his life. Cold, too. His face was numb. Snot made ropes that hung from his nose and froze. He couldn't feel his hands anymore.

All of that fed his anger. He had pretty much come to the conclusion that the command was doing this on purpose. If the soldiers got mad enough, when they did meet the Light army, they'd be so pissed off that nothing could stand in their way.

"Look sharp," Captain Ryys shouted. "We're almost there."

All his anger fled, to be replaced by anxiety. The final ridgeline was just ahead. Already, scores of soldiers were cresting it in a massive wave. It seemed impossible that anything could stand up against the huge numbers, but that didn't give Qod any comfort. He'd seen what the army of the Light could do yesterday.

They crested the rise, and Qod struggled to see something through the orcs blocking his view. They steadily advanced, and Qod caught glimpses of, well . . . *nothing*.

For the first time since they started marching, he felt a glimmer of hope. Had the Light retreated? There were *a lot* of soldiers of the Dark, after all.

*Maybe they left and the war's over. Maybe I can go home!*

He let himself hope, and that gave him new energy. He broke off the snotsicles hanging from his nose and tried to march with more purpose.

But instead of speeding up the advance, the massive army slowed piecemeal to a halt, the leading edge halfway to the river.

"What's going on?" one of the other goblins asked.

Qod risked stepping between two of the sergeants, and in a gap between those in front and down the slope, he got his first glimpse of yesterday's battlefield. Pockets of bodies were scattered in clumps, but they had just turned into part of the landscape. What riveted his attention was the far side of the valley where the floor gave way to the mountains.

The Dark wasn't the only force repositioning itself. Arrayed against them, the Light had moved into a massive line a few hundred meters up the foothills.

*Elf snot!*

Qod was no General Kantus, the orc hero who'd taken the elf fortress of Isladaan, but even he knew that if the generals still wanted to attack, the Dark army would have to attack uphill into the teeth of the Light defense.

***************

The two armies stared at each other, separated by about two miles, while pixies flitted like mayflies as they carried messages among the Dark commanders. The wind whipped across the open ground, freezing Qod's bones. The sun was well over the horizon, but so far, it had only brought the promise of warmth.

As the wind shifted, it occasionally carried the taunts of the Light bastards. They had the upper hand, they knew it, and they wanted the Dark soldiers to know it, too.

The mood among the Dark was souring. They'd hoped to catch the Light army in the same positions as they occupied yesterday and run over them with overwhelming numbers.

That was pretty much the way of the Dark, which almost always had more soldiers in the field. What was the life of a goblin or kobold when there were always more of them to conscript? If a hundred goblins were killed for every elf, the Dark command would consider that a win.

All of the Dark soldiers knew that, but they always clung to the fact that with so many of them, it might be the other soldier whose number came up, not theirs. Looking up at the huge array of Light soldiers facing them, though, even the most gung-ho Dark soldier had to know they were facing their mortality.

"Are we still going to attack, small sir?" Pani asked him.

Qod thought he was probably the least qualified soldier in the entire army, but he knew his fellow goblin just wanted comforting words. Unfortunately, he didn't have any for her.

"The command knows we can't win," he said, which didn't answer the question but was about the best he could do.

Between the armies, a gust of wind kicked up a dust devil, which headed toward the Light as if full of righteous fury, but it quickly petered out, as if it never existed.

"Appropriate," Qod muttered.

That was what was going to happen to them once the orders came to advance.

He took a moment to survey this side of the valley, where the entire army was now visible in the morning light. Despite the situation facing them, he had to admit it was pretty impressive, especially for a goblin lad from Yellow Rock.

"You ready, Private?" Sergeant Hjami asked him.

Qod hadn't even noticed that it was Hjami that he'd stepped up beside. He hesitated for a moment as he tried to take in the scope of the Light army.

"Are we still going to, you know, attack them when they've got the high ground like that?"

"It doesn't matter what the enemy does. When our command has something in their head, they hold onto it like a troll baby with a dwarf's leg bone."

The orc didn't sound full of martial enthusiasm. Resigned, was more like it. And that was scary. To make sergeant, the orc had to have survived battles before, and he knew what was what. If *he* didn't think they had a chance, then what hope was there?

About twenty yards to their left, the wizard was standing, alone in a sea of Dark soldiers. His face was expressionless as he stared across the valley floor to the Light army.

Like most goblins, Qod had a slight affinity toward gremlins. They might not have a proper hooked nose, and their ears were too small, but they were similar in size and temperament, and more importantly, were right there with goblins on the lower end of the Dark hierarchy.

Deerhorn Rapids was a gremlin village about a two-hour walk from Yellow Rock, and once a year, the two villages had a combined festival that alternated between them. With food and abundant mead flowing, things could get a little rambunctious—gremlins were a testy race, after all—but it was mostly a good time.

Qod had been surprised to see a gremlin wizard, but it gave him a little lift to see one of the small folk in a position of power. And the fact that the wizard was so close to the company felt like a security blanket.

"What about the wizard, Sergeant?  Can't he blast a hole in the Light lines?"

The orc NCO gave a short, dismissive laugh.

"The wizard?  Iffen you want pretty colored lights dancing over our heads, or maybe make our farts smell like fried sweet dough, then the gremlin might handle that. Anything else? Don't count on it."

Qod frowned as he stared at the gremlin.  Wizards might not be mages, but they were still, well . . . *wizards*. They controlled magic. Wasn't it the great wizard Ptomolon who broke the elf Prince Sylana's charge at Tail End Creek during the Third Elf-Orc War?

"Iffen we're gonna come out of this with our skin intact, Private, it's gonna be up to us. No use hoping for no wizardly miracles. 'Sides, you can bet your bottom gildr them faeby assholes got themselves a wizard, too.  Maybe even a mage."

A cold wave washed over Qod.

*A mage?*

He'd already forgotten Pani's comment from the night before, but the fear came rushing back like a tidal wave.

"Do they have one?" he asked in a querulous voice.

The sergeant shrugged.  "No sign of one, but you never know with those tricky bastards."

"They don't got no battle mage," Sergeant Blakamo, on the other side of Qod, said.

He didn't sound too sure about that.

Battle mages were the bane of the Dark folk. By a cruel twist of the gods, only the elves had true battle mages.  Even Ptolomon, the greatest hero of the Dark, wasn't considered a mage.

The only saving grace was that they were rare.  Very few elves with the potential to become one survived the maturation of their powers.

"Vesa's a mage," Hjami said.

"And he's down at Bonderland, now, ain't he? And as far as I'm concerned, that bastard of the Light can keep his shiny ass down there, far away from us."

Qod was rather isolated from what was going on in the rest of the continent, but he'd heard of Prince Vesa.  And if even a tenth of what he'd heard was true, then he was going to agree with the sergeant. Keep him in the south and out of the highlands. It was bad enough with upwards of two thousand elves in the Light army facing them. Add another four thousand dwarves and all the rest, and a battle mage would make the Light army nigh on undefeatable.

They were pretty imposing now, especially dug in on the high ground. Qod took another moment to sweep his gaze across the Light line, then compared it with the mass of the Dark army. The word circulating among the soldiers was that there were ten thousand of them ready to attack the Light.

*Not enough.*

A pixie flew across Qod's line of sight and came to a stop at Captain Ryys's shoulder. All eyes locked on the two as the pixie relayed her message. The captain nodded several times before the pixie darted away. The captain stared across the valley to the Light army, then sighed.

Qod had a sinking feeling in his belly.

The captain turned to face the bulk of the company.

"Sergeants, get your soldiers ready to move out. We launch the attack in five minutes.

The company was dead silent for a long moment before Sergeant Hjami shouted, "You heard the captain. Get your asses in place."

That opened the dam gates. The other sergeants burst into action and started herding goblins, kobolds, and the rest into a semblance of order. Qod rushed back into position.

All around them, units broke into motion. The air was electric. Qod couldn't tell if it was fear, excitement, or a sense of duty.

He was sure about what *he* was feeling, though. That was fear, pure and simple.

"What are we going to do, small sir?" Pani asked.

"I don't know."

"You were talking to the sergeants, right?"

"They didn't tell me anything."

She nodded and scrunched her bushy brows together. Qod knew she was worried and that he should say something, but what? If history were any indication, there just weren't enough Dark soldiers to absorb the enemy's weapons so that the elite orc **Black Smoke** force could get close enough to use their falchion **elf gutters**.

Qod turned around to the ridgeline behind him, where the **Black Smokes** were smashing their wicked-looking weapons against their halberds as they shouted and psyched themselves for battle. They were the key to winning the fight. If the Light forces expended their arrows, lances, and other projectiles, if they tired themselves by smashing goblin heads with their maces and swords, then the **Black Smokes** might prevail.

Or might not.

Still, Qod would much rather be with them than with the 121st Replacement Company. If the lead elements didn't deplete the Light forces enough, then the command might not even commit the **Black Smokes**, choosing to save them for another day.

"Eyes front, Private," Sergeant Hjami said. "You don't need to worry none about them. You worry about the Light bastards in front of us."

Before Qod could respond, a single discordant blast of a ram's horn washed over the massed army, followed almost immediately by a hundred more. The front ranks of the mob started to advance.

The battle against the Light army was on.

## Chapter 6

Qod's mind was numb as he stumbled down the hill toward the creek. He knew he needed to be at his best, but it was all he could do to keep his feet moving. The sun had done little to warm up the day, yet he was sweating, which made his helmet slide down even more.

He couldn't tell if the wetness running off his nose was sweat or blood from where the edge of the helm was slamming into it, and he didn't have the energy to lift his hand to check.

"Keep moving," one of the sergeants kept saying every ten or fifteen seconds, and that echoed in Qod's mind.

His neck was on fire, his nose hurt, and the hand holding his spear was numb with the cold. If he could focus on that, he could forget what was waiting in front of him. Pain meant he was still alive.

They reached the creek, and the cold water shocked Qod into the present. The water was waist-deep to a goblin, and he had to fight the current to keep upright. A troll splashed by, the water barely over its bare, hairy feet. It created a wave that splashed Qod's face, making him cough for breath. Two strides, and the troll was climbing up the other side, but not before the wake he made dislodged a body killed the day before and sent it floating down the creek. Qod tried to ward it away with the butt of his spear, but the headless body bounced off him before it was pulled farther downstream. He wasn't even sure what kind of body it was. Maybe a gremlin. Maybe a kobold.

*At least it wasn't a goblin.*

He reached the far side of the creek, but after so many Dark soldiers, the bank was muddy, and Qod kept slipping until a hand pushed him in the butt.

"I've got you, small sir," Pani said, and between the two of them, they got him to level, if still muddy ground.

"Thanks," he said as shouting broke out from ahead.

He craned his head as he tried to see what was going on. All he got were some brief glimpses between the bodies, but it was enough to tell that the lead ranks had joined the battle. They were surging forward, screaming their battle cries.

Arrows arched through the air—not as many as had hit the goblins yesterday, but enough that Dark soldiers fell. They didn't falter, though, and Qod felt a touch of pride at their bravery.

At that moment, Qod swore that he wouldn't falter, either. He'd slowly accepted that he was going to die today, but if the ghouls and gnomes in the company ahead of him could do it, then he had to make goblinhood proud.

A second volley of arrows reached out from the high ground, but this time, a bubble of light blue expanded to meet it. Half of the arrows turned to ashes.

"The wizard!" Qod said.

In his physical misery, he'd forgotten about the gremlin, but there he was. The quiet, almost emotionless wizard had changed. He was animated, and a pale blue aura seemed to surround him.

Hope surged through Qod. This wasn't just "light tricks." This was honest-to-goodness magic.

The wizard squared his feet, and the air around him crackled with energy. He drew back an arm, then made a punching motion in the air. Another bubble of pale blue light— a little less intense this time—reached out to the arrows that were now plunging into the ghouls. Qod couldn't tell for sure, but he didn't think as many were ashed this time.

The wizard didn't seem fazed. He strode forward with purpose for several steps, and Qod started to edge closer to him to hopefully fall under the wizards' protection.

"Come on," he told Pani.

The wizard suddenly stopped, and some of that confidence seemed to vanish. He made an intricate motion with two hands, and the blue aura intensified and expanded outward a couple of yards. He seemed to brace himself, and Qod stopped just short of the magic master.

Out of nowhere, a blinding light smashed into the gremlin wizard. Qod's nose hairs stood on end as the air crackled with power. The wizard raised both arms, hands clasped together to ward off the light washing over him.

Pani yanked Qod backward and instant before the light intensified and the wizard's bubble collapsed with a loud snap of displaced air.

Qod was blinded for a moment, and when his sight returned, the wizard was gone. Not dead. Not even a mangled body. Gone. There was a patch of scoured earth, ringed by charred and smoking grass.

"Let's go," Pani urged as she tugged on his free arm.

Qod let himself be pulled away, but he kept his eyes over his shoulder at the spot where the gremlin wizard had been just a moment ago.

Sergeant Hjami might have demeaned the wizard's power, but the gremlin had been able to burn arrows in midair, making him far more powerful than a mere goblin. If something had been able to—

The realization hit him. "Something" was another wizard. A wizard of the Light. Of course, he knew the Light army had wizards, but somehow, despite the talk earlier about a battle mage, despite the light from over the horizon the night before, he hadn't really considered that a wizard might actually be facing them—one evidently stronger than the gremlin.

He finally broke his gaze from the spot and turned his head to look up at the foothills. Amazingly, Light wizard or not, the lead ghouls had covered most of the distance to the Light lines. Arrows were still being fired at them—not just at the lead ranks, though. A lone arrow came whistling down to pierce the cuirass of a goblin just a few yards to Qod's left. The goblin—Qod had never even gotten his name—gave a soft, rat-like mewl and collapsed face-first on the ground.

This was all too much for him. Nothing was registering. All he could do was follow Pani as they pushed forward.

"They're breaking!" an orc voice called out excitedly.

It was like an electric current passed through the company. Every orc, goblin, and kobold turned to the voice.

"Shift left! Into the draw," Captain Ryys shouted. "Reinforce the ghouls!"

With a surge of renewed confidence, the company quickened the pace. Kobolds started trilling their *uran*. They were hardly the most martial of the Dark races, barely better fighters than goblins, but their **haka** had to instill a sense of foreboding in the dwarves and brownies they faced. Qod was on the kobolds' side, yet the high-pitched warbling ran a shiver down his spine.

The surviving ghouls broke into a run as the Light line started to collapse. From somewhere out of sight, another volley of arrows flew over the Light lines and dropped them, but still they kept charging.

The ghouls and the 121st Replacement Company weren't the only ones who realized what was happening. From behind the company, ram horns sounded, and the **Black Smoke** sprinted into action.

"Don't let those assholes take your glory!" Captain Ryys shouted.

The sergeants urged the company to move faster. Qod tried, but the bottom of the cuirass, now wet from the creek, was like a hammer on his thighs, and he had to use his free hand to keep his helmet in place.

A ghoul, all bony arms and legs, reached the first breastwork. She turned and made a dramatic "Follow me" motion before disappearing on the other side. The rest of the ghouls flowed after her, and a few moments later, the first of the replacement company followed. Qod was one of the slowest in the company, so he, Pani, and one of the sergeants were the last to reach the Light trench. Qod tried to leap it, but he didn't clear it and instead fell inside. Once again, it was Pani who reached back and lifted him to his feet on the other side.

The Dark soldiers were in full killing mode, but the Light soldiers, mostly sprites, weren't cooperating. They were in retreat up the draw, keeping just out of reach of the pursuing ghouls.

It made sense to Qod now. Sprites were the Light army's goblins, so to speak. The Light generals had made a mistake, putting them on the line without heavier reinforcements, especially as the draw seemed made to be a logical Dark avenue of approach.

41

And now, the long legs of the orcs in the Black Smokes gave them speed the goblins and kobolds couldn't hope to match, and they were vaulting the creek in short order as they rushed forward to break past the old Light line.

Qod heard their battle cries and turned to see when he stumbled and went down, losing his grip on his spear on the way. His helmet fell off, and he lunged to grab it before it was kicked away by running orc feet.

He was kicked several times as well before he had it and twisted to grab his spear a moment before an orc stepped on it. There was a crack, and the shaft, just short of the spearhead, bent.

Still on his hands and knees, Qod tried to check the damage when his eye caught movement to the flank. Dwarves were moving into position, and his heart skipped a beat. But the dwarves weren't charging down into the draw to hit the Dark force. They seemed to be . . . *watching?*

With a sense of foreboding, Qod twisted his bent body around to look between his legs to the other flank. He could see a dozen fauns, armed with bows. They held their bows ready but were not engaging.

*What's happening?*

Those fauns had the slight high ground, perfect conditions for them to fire down on the ghouls, orcs, ogres, and the replacement company.

An orc captain from the Black Smokes vaulted the trench and ran at Qod while waving his elf gutter in the air over his head.

"Uh, sir? I think something's wrong."

The orc never even looked at him as he ran past.

The company sergeant bringing up the rear snarled at Qod.

"Private, get up and move your gobby ass!"

"Sergeant! I think it's a tr—"

An impossibly bright light scythed through the air, passing just inches above Qod's head. It cut through the sergeant like a supernaturally sharp sword. The top half disappeared, and the legs stood for a moment as if they didn't realize their former owner was gone before they toppled over.

Qod shrieked in surprise.  He spun around on his hands and knees to the most horrible sight he could imagine.

The battle cries of the Dark had been cut off, and most of what had been hundreds of warriors were simply gone. Others were charred lumps on the ground, a few still smoking. Some were still alive, either feebly crawling away or in full racing retreat.

As bad as that was, it barely registered to him. What had his full and undivided attention was the elf striding confidently down the slope.  He was clad in gold and white armor that shone so brightly that it hurt Qod's eyes, yet he couldn't break his stare.

Somehow, the light bursting from the figure was in two colors:  the white of elf royalty, and the blue of . . .

It was like the paler blue of the gremlin wizard, but much, much brighter, much more intense.  And it seemed alive.

This wasn't a mere wizard, if "mere" could be used in reference to any practitioner of the arcane arts. Just as a baby rabbit understands what a lynx is, Qod didn't have to be told that this was a mage.  A battle mage.

And like a baby rabbit, Qod froze as the mage steadily advanced.

Dwarves and fauns cheered the elf's progress.

A few arrows and a javelin flew through the air, but the mage didn't even bother with them.  They hit the blue aura and fell to the ground.

Almost as an afterthought, the mage flicked a finger here, a finger there, and tiny balls of blue light flew to hit those who had dared attack him.  Not just them, but also wounded ghouls, goblins, and orcs.  An ogre with seemingly half of his head gone struggled to his feet, raised his mace, and staggered toward the mage.

A couple of the dwarves raised their axes and started to rush to the ogre, but the mage flicked a wrist, and the ogre dropped to the ground. The spectators cheered.

Qod watched in horror as the apparition approached. He was in shock, so much so that for a few moments, he hadn't really realized the danger he was in.  Slowly, he started to

Jonathan P. Brazee

crawl backward into the Light trench behind him.  Before he could reach it, the mage seemed to make an imaginary snowball, then, with a dramatic flourish that had to be aimed at the Light army, mimed bowling, complete with the approach.

A small ball of whirling lights shot from the bowling hand and immediately started growing as it flew toward the Dark forces.  Qod jerked back and fell into the trench as the ball bounded overhead.  Shouts of warning rose from the Dark side, shouts that were cut off as the devil's ball wreaked havoc.

Qod shivered at the bottom of the trench.  He'd never felt so helpless in his short life.

He realized this had been a trap, pure and simple, one that the Dark command had walked right into.  The sprite position hadn't been a mistake. The Light command had used the sprite's reputation to make their "retreat" more believable. And in doing so, they'd sucked in the **Black Smokes**, who were, without doubt, the most capable of the Dark forces.

The enemy commanders knew the **Black Smokes** would be frothing at the mouth to be part of a victory, and they'd used that aggressiveness against them.  Concentrated in the draw, they'd been sitting ducks for the battle mage.

Anger overshadowed the fear that kept his heart pounding.  He was still petrified, but the sense of wasted lives was overwhelming, all because some high and mighty elves wanted their forest glens, all because the dwarves wanted the minerals under the feet of goblins, orcs, and kobolds. The mage's steps got closer.  Qod could hear the elf mutter something under his breath.  There was a pattern to it.  An incantation?

"Ammee tel amah!" was said from almost on top of him, and a bolt of lightning emerged from the clear morning sky to strike somewhere down in the valley.

With a curse aimed at **Juut**, who he knew would take over his house in Yellow Rock, Qod forced himself to stand. The mage was ten feet away.

"You're . . . *bad!*" Qod shouted as he tried to scramble out of the trench.

The helmet fell down over his eyes, smashing into his raw nose, but with his hands busy, he couldn't adjust it, and he was blind.

He expected to feel the might of the battle mage, and he almost welcomed the embrace that would send him to the Sleep Kingdom, but nothing happened. Somehow, he gained the top, and still on his belly, he pushed back the helmet and looked up.

The mage, standing less than ten feet away next to what was left of an orc body, was watching him. His nasty-looking pale blonde hair was long and perfectly aligned, and the soulless, icy blue eyes drilled into Qod. But it was the mage's sardonic smile that infuriated him.

"I'm going to kill you," he screamed.

"I'm sure you want to," the mage said in the calm, melodic voice that powerful elves favored. "But I've got a little much on my plate to allow that."

He raised a little finger, as if that was all it was going to take, and looked back to where more dwarves were crowding closer to watch.

"Kill the gobby!" was the most common response.

The mage looked back at Qod and raised a single, thin eyebrow. "Well, you heard them."

He made a show of examining his little finger, then said, "I don't need my power to take care of one very small gobby, though."

The mage mimed sheathing the finger, then drew a ten-inch, rapier-like dagger from a gold and silver scabbard at his belt. Like everything else about the mage, the blade glowed with light as if alive.

He started to step over the orc body, which Qod only then recognized had been Sergeant Hjami, and toward Qod, when he suddenly swung around at the sound of orc battle cries.

His complacent attitude disappeared, and Qod had a brief flash of hope. The Black Smokes might be gone, but there were still thousands of orcs, and he knew that for as much as they could be arrogant assholes, they weren't cowards, and they would swarm to avenge their brethren.

The mage glanced back at Qod, and then with a dismissive sniff, sheathed the blade, stepped back, and started chanting while weaving his hands in the air.

Qod had had enough. He hadn't wanted to be conscripted. He hadn't wanted to leave home. He hadn't wanted to be given inferior equipment, and he sure the hell hadn't wanted to be facing an elf battle mage with most of his company dead.

More than anything else, though, he wanted to be taken seriously. He was a goblin, for the Dark's sake. A living and breathing soul who deserved more than this.

He pushed the helmet back on his head and stood, gripping his spear shaft so hard his green knuckles turned white.

Captain Ryys had told him to point the spear at the enemy and jab.

The mage finished his spell, and a pressure wave flew outward toward the orcs who'd just appeared in Qod's sight. The orcs went flying like **broken toys,** their battle cries cut short.

A small side lobe must have hit Qod, and he stumbled back a step, almost falling into the trench. He recovered while the mage took a moment to look upon the results of his blast.

Qod started forward again, hoping the mage had forgotten him. Foolish hope.

"And now to my little friend," he said as he pulled out the dagger again and turned around.

Qod broke into a charge, and for a moment, the mage's eyes got big, which gave Qod a small sense of satisfaction. It wasn't going to make a difference, but at least he'd surprised the bastard.

With his second step, the helmet came down again, this time with the added force of running, and the pain in his neck shot down through his body all the way to his left foot. He started going down, and he thrust out his spear in an attempt to keep his feet.

At the same moment, the mage flicked a quick, one-handed spell at Qod that, because he was falling and at such short range, missed and went over his head. The mage continued his lunge toward him, blade raised, and his back foot stepped on the forgotten Sergeant Hjami's body. His foot slipped on the sergeant's splayed intestines, and he stumbled forward, hands outstretched.

The gods, either in their infinite wisdom or pure perversity, had chosen to give the children of the Dark the short shrift. Every advantage seemed to go to the Light. But still, on rare occasions, things went along a different path.

As Qod tried to keep himself upright by bracing the butt against the ground, the spearhead was tilted forward. Against any possible probability, the tip of the spear happened to momentarily occupy the very same spatial location as the elf battle mage's pristine silver and gold cuirass.

Nine hundred and ninety-nine times out of a thousand, that intersection of time and place wouldn't matter. The elf had the finest armor that elven and dwarven smiths could make, and Qod's spear was not only the lowest quality, but it was also damaged.

Instead of the spearhead catching on the armor and breaking off, the damaged shaft flexed, and with the mage falling, the tip skittered down the elf's body until it hit the edge where the plackart met the fauld. The tip drove in the tiny gap where the elf's own weight drove the spearhead home.

The spear shaft was ripped from Qod's hand, and he used the freed hand to throw off the helmet, only then seeing the battle mage kneeling on the ground in front of him for an impossibly long moment before he toppled face-first to the ground. Everything moved into slow motion.

The cheering from the Light soldiers went silent as shock at what they were seeing set in. Qod was in shock, too, not understanding what had just happened. The blue aura surrounding the battle mage was flickering, and the normal white elf-light seemed weaker.

The elf groaned, then turned on his side. Uncomprehending eyes looked up at Qod as the mage struggled to sit up.

"I'm so sorry!" Qod said. "I didn't mean to."

47

Except he had, of course. It was just that he'd never killed anything in his life. He wasn't a violent goblin, and this shook him to his core.

The mage tried to speak, but bright golden blood erupted from his mouth. Not just blood. Blue light seemed to be fleeing from his body like rats on a sinking ship.

The elf seemed to notice the spear for the first time, and he reached to grab the neck with both hands. With a grunt, he pulled it free.

Just the shaft. The spearhead had broken off inside the elf's body.

He stared at the bloody shaft for a long moment before tossing it aside.

"You!"

"I'm sorry," Qod said again.

The battle mage raised a hand and made unsteady motions. He mumbled a few words that were lost while he coughed up blood, which splattered the unmoving Qod.

Too much had happened that hadn't sunk in yet, and he was frozen in place.

The mage managed to get a few incantations out, but then fell back on his side with a clatter of armor.

"Are you dead?"

The mage groaned. Light, both blue and white, was fleeing his body in wavering streams. His blue eyes lost their vivid hue and started to dull, but not before, with one last flick, the mage raised his little finger and coughed out his last word.

A small ball eked out from the tip of the finger and wavered as it slowly floated to Qod. The last of the light reached for the heavens, and the battle mage seemed to deflate.

Qod watched in fascination as the ball, blinking on and off, reached him. At the last moment, he tried to duck, but the edge of the ball brushed his shoulder, and his world went dark.

## Chapter 7

"There he is."

He couldn't see anything. Couldn't feel anything, either. He wasn't numb. He was just nothing.

"By the Dark Mother, it's true."

The voices gave him something to grasp at, though. Like a drowning goblin, he grasped at the thread and hung on.

"A fucking battle mage, dead. I thought that was impossible."

*Battle mage.*

The thread expanded to a rope, and he started pulling himself up. Images flashed in his mind, and the universe started coalescing around him.

With a start, he gasped, and suddenly, Qod knew who he was. He knew where he was.

He opened his eyes. Two orcs were standing over the battle mage's body. They spun around at Qod's gasp, weapons ready, then just as quickly dismissed him. One of the orcs held his falchion out, then prodded the elf mage with his booted foot.

"Dead, I'd say."

"Mages can come back, you know. Death ain't no thing to them."

"Should we, uh, cut off the head?"

"Wait for the colonel."

"But if it can come back . . ."

Qod looked around while the two orcs argued. The shaft of his spear was within arm's reach, the broken part covered in gold elf blood. He clasped his hands around it and drew it to his chest. It made him feel much better.

The mage certainly looked dead. The light that had glowed from him was gone, and even the armor looked dull.

He didn't understand what had happened. One minute, he was falling, and the next, the battle mage was pulling the shaft out of his body. Then there was the light—

*Am I dead?*

The two orcs certainly weren't paying him any attention. But no, they'd both turned around to look at him. He had to be alive.

As hard as it was to believe, somehow, the mage had gotten himself killed, and Qod was still with the living.

He tore his gaze from the dead elf and looked around. Dark soldiers were on the run, but toward the enemy, not away. Farther up the mountain, Light soldiers were in full retreat. Even from a distance, Qod could see their panic. Helmets and weapons were being discarded so as not to slow them down.

And the Dark soldiers were in close pursuit. As he watched, a group of ogres trapped a dozen elves who turned to fight, but were almost immediately bowled over.

"What's happening?" Qod asked.

The two orcs turned at the question.

One of them sneered and looked away, but the other one said, "The faeby bastards are running, gobby, praise the Dark."

"But why?"

The mage might be dead, but he'd killed hundreds, maybe thousands of Dark soldiers, including **Black Smokes**.

The orc gave a short, barking laugh.

"'Cause some hero killed their battle mage, that's why. He's probably up there chasing them right now. Hey," he said, changing the subject. "Did you see who did it? Was it an orc?"

Qod frowned, then pointedly stared at the elf blood on his spear. "Uh, I di—"

"There's the colonel!" the other orc shouted, pointing down the hill. "Up here!"

She jumped up and down, waving her arms. A moment later, a pixie buzzed into view, tiny major's pips on her collar. She made two quick circles around the dead mage.

"That's him," she said. "You two, don't let anything happen to the body. I'll bring the colonel."

"Yes, ma'am," the orcs said in unison.

Qod hadn't realized that a small folk could be officers. He'd assumed that all officers were orcs or ogres. Then he shook his head. That didn't matter, not with a dead battle mage and the Light army seemingly in retreat.

"Um, I think I killed the mage," he said to the orcs' backs.

They were excitedly wondering if they would be getting a reward for finding the body, and they didn't seem to hear him.

"I said, *I* killed the mage."

It wasn't really true. The elf had sort of killed himself, if he was being honest. But being ignored was making him angry. He didn't somehow survive an elf battle mage bent on killing him, only to be dismissed as a non-person.

But then the pixie major was back, quickly followed by assorted orc officers. All of them crowded around the mage's body. Two of them bumped into Qod, who had to back up out of the way.

Orcs were fast runners, but it was only a moment before the ogres, then a banshee showed up.

"Who killed him?" was the running question.

Qod tried to speak up, but no one was paying attention.

It was hard to miss a gathering of officers. Their high-quality armor alone was like a beacon. Soldiers of all types started to converge on them, eager to see what was happening.

And then the great one himself arrived, and the others parted to let the worthy approach the body. Qod had never seen a colonel before, and he was cowed into silence.

The ogre looked down at the body for a long moment while the others waited for his words.

"It's dead," he finally said.

The rest nodded and patted each other's backs.

His attention shifted to Sergeant Hjami's body.

"Did this orc kill the mage?"

The staff officers exchanged looks with each other, obviously not wanting to speak up. Finally, an orc major said, "Doubtful, sir. That's a banji."

The orc's tone was dismissive, and that pissed Qod off. She was right, of course. Hjami hadn't killed the battle mage. Qod didn't know what a banji was, but the way the orc said it was a pretty good indication that the sergeant wasn't high in the orc hierarchy.

"Well, then who did?" the colonel asked.

Qod barely knew the sergeant, but Hjami had tried to look out for him. The way the major referred to him gave Qod courage he hadn't known was in him.

"I killed the mage," he shouted at the momentarily silent staff.

At least fifty sets of eyes turned as one.

The colonel had to step to the side to see him. Qod raised his spear shaft, the sun catching the gold blood.

No one said a word until the colonel broke out into a deep, bass guffaw.

"No, really. We need to find the hero who killed the mage. You two," he said to the orcs who'd found the body. Did you see what happened?"

"No, sir. He was already dead when we found him."

"I said, I killed the mage," Qod said as he pushed his way through the staff to stand in front of the colonel.

The ogre wasn't laughing now. "Careful, Private. It was funny the first time, but now you're skating on thin ice."

"Small sir did kill the mage," a voice cried out.

Pani limped forward. One arm hung motionless to her side, and her face was swollen and oozing blood.

"Pani! You're alive!" Qod shouted.

"What in the Dark **Mother's ass** is going on with these gobbies," the colonel asked. "Somebody get these two out of here before I have them killed."

"It was a gobby that killed the mage. A goblin," a ghoul said in its reedy voice. "I saw it."

The colonel spun around, his anger evident.

"This . . . this gobby killed an elf fucking battle mage?" the colonel roared.

"I don't know if it was this one. I can't tell them apart, and I lost sight of them once the dwarves started running."

The colonel shook his head. "Impossible. I don't know what you three are trying to pull, but I won't have it. Take them into custody. We'll get to the bottom of it later."

It took a moment, but an orc stepped up and roughly grabbed Qod's arm, which tweaked his neck, making him cry out.

"Sir!" a voice cut in. "It was this goblin."

"Who is that?"

An orc in the obsidian armor of a **Black Smoke** sergeant forced her way forward. She was breathing hard, as if she'd been running, and blood had flowed down from her nose and across her face. Qod saw what looked like brown dwarf blood on her **elf gutter** before she sheathed it.

"I was with the company when the battle mage hit us with **a fire ball**. Just six of us survived. Honor, sir. That said, I had to avenge my brothers and sisters, so I goes and runs at him. Then I seen this goblin rise from the trench and challenge the mage to single combat."

That wasn't quite how Qod remembered it, but with an orc's claws locked on his upper arm, he wasn't going to argue.

"Before they could get at it, the Smoke resumed the attack, and the mage created a **bouncer spell** that rolled down the mountain."

There were nods of agreement from the staff officers at that. They'd probably have been well out of range, but they would have seen the mage's spell devastate the army.

"Then the two, the mage and the goblin, they go. The mage, he goes down, but hits the goblin with what looked like a **sleeper**."

She turned to Qod. "I thought you were dead, but I'm happy to see you are among the breathing."

The colonel was staring at her in frank disbelief.

"Anyways, I seen the mage. His lights were off. He was dead, so I goes and attacks the dwarves. That's my duty. But then I seen you arrive, so I think I better go report."

"You said he got hit with a **sleeper spell**? Yet he's alive right now? You expect me to believe this shit?"

The sergeant frowned, then drew herself up to her full height before spreading her arms and kneeling, head bent to expose her neck.

"Honor or death, sir."

The colonel rolled his eyes, and his hand went to the hilt of his sword, but stopped at the sharp intake of breath from orcs in the staff and the troops who'd gathered.

Qod had no idea what this "honor or death" was, but the orcs didn't seem to like the colonel's reaction. He also had no idea about the politics of the situation. Command was always held by an ogre or orc, but things hadn't always been friendly between the two races. They were allies now only because the Light races were a mutual enemy.

All eyes were now on the colonel, and Qod could sense that things could go either way. Finally, the colonel smiled at Qod.

"We are in debt to you, Private."

It looked like it pained him to say that.

"I think we need to take you to see the general."

He had a calculating look in his eyes that Qod didn't trust.

"Thank you, Sergeant, for your report."

The orc sergeant stood and asked, "Can I go kill more dwarves now?"

That calculating look turned into satisfaction, and he said, "By all means, Sergeant. Do your duty."

She nodded first at the colonel, and then, to his surprise, to Qod, before she spun around and broke into a run as she unsheathed her **elf gutter**.

"As I said," he addressed the group, "I want Private . . . what's your name?"

"Private Qod. Qod Yellow Rock."

"Of course. I want Private Yellow Rock taken to the command post. The other gobby, too. And the ghoul. The rest of you, the faeby bastards are running, but the battle isn't over, so go!"

He gave Qod an intense stare that only increased his unease before the colonel spun on his heels and started to stride back down the slope.

The orc released Qod's arm.

"I guess that's me. Let's go," he said in a neutral tone. "You, too," he told Pani, who looked like she was wavering on her feet.

Qod jumped to her side and put her good arm around his shoulders.

"Can you walk?" he asked.

She started to nod, then grimaced.

It took her a moment to gather herself.

"I can do it, small sir."

"Just lean on me, Pani. I'll help," he said as they started to follow the orc.

Qod would never have imagined that he'd meet a general. At the moment, he wasn't sure if this was something good or something bad. He was sure, though, that he'd rather not find out.

## Chapter 8

"Are you OK?"

Pani shrugged.

"I'm breathing."

Goblins had a high tolerance for pain, but she looked horrible. Fluid was oozing out of half her swollen face, and the left arm looked broken as it hung limply from her shoulder. One ear was torn and barely hanging on. Worse, she smelled of burnt flesh, like a skewer of rats forgotten on the fire.

"Does it hurt?"

"Yes," she said.

With the left side of her face swollen, her words weren't very clear, but she might as well be describing what was for breakfast. She didn't seem particularly concerned.

That was when he noticed the dark, squishy substance splashed across her right arm and cuirass.

"What's that?" he asked as he pointed.

She glanced down, then calmly said, "Used to be ogre, I think."

Qod grimaced. That wasn't the way a person reacted when an ally was splattered over her.

*Maybe she's in shock.*

Qod, on the other hand, was buzzing. Everything was settling in, and the relief of being alive, even if he didn't know what was next, was almost too much to bear. He wanted to talk about it, but she didn't seem to want to engage at the moment.

He looked at the ghoul who was walking just ahead, but then shook his head. Ghouls were taciturn in the best of times, and this one looked like he wished he'd kept his mouth shut. Qod thought it would be prudent to leave him alone.

That left the orc, who was leading them down the hill with purpose. Another one Qod decided to leave alone.

He looked across the battlefield. There was still sporadic fighting higher up the range as Dark soldiers chased the Light, but it was over in the immediate area. Relatively few bodies were scattered about, far fewer than out on the valley floor from yesterday's butcher's bill, and that puzzled him for a moment until he blanched as he realized why.

The mage's spell hadn't just killed soldiers. It had vaporized them. There were survivors. Wounded soldiers wandered about if they were mobile, cried for help if they were not.

Grey-robed **genii cucullati**—commonly called "hooded spirits"—were already moving among them. The unassuming race supported neither the Dark nor the Light, and they never lifted a weapon in anger, but their skill in the healing arts made them welcome, and once a wounded fighter was in their care, they were off-limits to the enemy.

Qod shuddered to see them, though. It was bad enough that their robes and hoods concealed their bodies and faces, but rumor was that their healing skill came from being able to manipulate the victim's life force, and they absorbed some of that force as payment for services rendered.

Still, as he spotted one of them working on an orc with horrible burns, he figured it was a fair price to pay.

"Do you need a **hooded spirit?**" he asked Pani, who shook her head.

He turned back to the burned orc, who was whimpering as the **healer** plied its craft, tripped over a twisted mass of metal, and landed face-first on the ground with a loud thud.

The orc wheeled around, then rolled his eyes as he waited for Qod to get up.

Qod rubbed his ankle and looked at what had tripped him. It took a moment to recognize the lumpy metallic object. It had once been a maul. A troll-sized maul. Yet there was no troll.

He swallowed hard. A troll generally used their massive fists or a club. A maul was something to be prized among them, and there was no way it would have been abandoned. And that meant the battle mage's power had been enough to erase all sign that the troll had even existed.

*Yet somehow, I'm still here.*

The maul was a massive hunk of forged metal, and it had only partially survived complete destruction. From the looks of it, this area near the Light trench line had borne the brunt of the battle mage's two spells and had been scoured clean.

"Are you OK, small sir?"

The seriously wounded Pani was standing to his side, her good hand outstretched to help him up. It was with a sense of shame that he took it and got back to his feet.

"Be careful."

"If you're ready, Private," the orc said with a slight downturn of the corner of his mouth.

As they moved farther down the hill and crabbed somewhat to the left, more bodies and weapons managed to survive complete destruction. And with that, soldiers were already poking around, looking for something of value.

A two-wheel ox-drawn vardo was crossing the creek, driven by a—

"Hey, there's a human!" Qod shouted.

The orc looked back before following Qod's finger pointing to the cart. She sneered but kept walking.

This was only the second human Qod had ever seen, and it was just like the trader who rolled through Yellow Rock.

Qod thought humans had to be the ugliest race on the planet. No nose to speak of, dull, soulless eyes—their flat, almost featureless face seemed to hide an uninspired if cunning mind. Clumsier than an elf and weaker than an ogre, the sneaky humans had almost no redeeming capabilities other than cheating the other races, Dark and Light alike.

It was commonly said that if a human shook your hand, check to make sure you still had all your fingers.

The vardo came to a halt, and the human jumped off. It ran to an ogre body and flipped it over, then pounced before standing and holding a relatively intact war axe aloft. It rubbed a spindly thumb along the edge, then tossed it into the cart.

"It's stealing weapons!"

"That's what scavengers do," the orc said with a scowl.

Qod didn't know if the scowl was for him for asking or the human scavenging, and he wasn't going to ask. But his sense of outrage at what the human was doing was too strong for him to be quiet.

"We need those weapons!"

The ghoul opened his mouth for the first time since they left the colonel's party. "And the human will repair them and bring them back. For a price, of course."

"Or sell them to the Light," the orc said.

"Do you really think the Light wants our weapons? They've got dwarf metalsmiths, in case you've forgotten," the ghoul said. "Anyway, humans gonna human."

A human would sell its own offspring to either the Dark or Light, Qod knew. But this just seemed wrong to him. Those were Dark weapons and equipment it was taking, weapons made by the Dark. Surely, they could be repaired by kobolds or **gremlins**.

He looked down at his cuirass. It had seen a lot of wear before it had been issued to him, and he wondered if a human had ever touched it.

The thought gave him the willies. He kept looking back as the human guided its cart from one spot to the other as it looked for something else it could steal.

They reached the creek a few minutes later. The water had risen somewhat, and with Qod's stature and Pani's condition, both the ghoul and orc had to help the two goblins across.

There were far more Dark soldiers on the other side, and something strange started happening. All eyes turned to the foursome as they walked past. Orcs, ogres, goblins, satyrs—all races moved out of their way.

Qod felt extremely uncomfortable. He didn't like to be noticed, as a rule, and he didn't know what was going on. It felt as if the four were going to be rushed.

A pixie flew right at Qod, who squeaked and ducked out of the way. The pixie came to a hover in front of his eyes.

"Thank you," she said before darting off.

"Thank you?" Qod whispered as she disappeared.

"Word travels fast in the army," the orc said.

Qod looked back up the mountain where the battle had taken place. The four of them had come straight down from where they'd met with the colonel, and he hadn't seen anyone pass them. So, how would they know what had happened?

But with the orc's statement, Qod looked at the soldiers from a different perspective.

He was used to being demeaned, to always being less-than, so he'd assumed the looks of the growing mass of Dark folk were aggressive. But now, he could see something he'd never experienced before.

It was respect. Tinged with fear, maybe, but still respect.

And that floored him.

More and more Dark soldiers gathered, all pushing forward to see the mage killer, yet giving him space as if they were afraid he was going to turn his power on them.

He couldn't help it. He broke out into a laugh.

Fear him? No matter that the battle mage had managed to kill himself. In reality, he was still Qod, a small, weak goblin.

More than a few of the soldiers jumped back at his laugh, trying to get out of the way, and that made him laugh even louder.

Others pointed in awe at the mage killer. Not just awe. A goblinette blew him a kiss—another first. Before he could respond, though, Pani "accidentally" stepped up between him and his admirer.

The command post—three large, interconnected tents— was on the top of the next ridge, where the staff could view the entire battle. The middle tent was guarded by two draugrs, resplendent in black and silver, beaded battle axes at their sides. Qod could feel their piercing stare as the four climbed the rise.

"Mage killer!" someone shouted, and a moment later, a thousand voices picked up the chant.

Qod's blood started pounding to the beat, and he was afraid he'd burst an artery. This kind of thing only happened in dreams, not in real life.

The draugrs subtly shifted their feet as the crowd got louder. Rumored to guard the dead in the far north, the skull-faced beings were a rare race of warriors and were favored as bodyguards. They were reputed to be the most dangerous beings of the Dark, and a tiny tremor of fear went down his spine.

"They have to know we're not challenging the general, right?" he whispered to Pani.

"A goblin? In a challenge?" she asked. "No. We're just reporting in."

Still, Qod kept his eyes locked on the two as they closed the distance.

"Colonel Manticoz sends his respects, and he told me to escort the goblins and the ghoul to the general," the orc said.

Qod noticed that she'd stopped just out of axe range.

Without a word, the two conducted opposing facing movements, creating a path for the four. The orc pushed forward through the flap. Qod kept expecting to see the axe slash down, but the draugrs were statues as he entered the tent into a small waiting area.

"Take a seat," the orc said. "Wait until you're summoned."

And then she disappeared through the next flap, leaving the three alone.

## Chapter 9

The two goblins sat on the rough plank bench as they waited. Very rough. Qod shifted his weight, and a splinter jabbed his thigh above the edge of his cuirass. He yelped.

Are you OK, small sir?" Pani asked and then opened her eyes.

Qod reached down, grabbed the edge of the splinter, and pulled it out with a whimper.

"It's a big one," he said, holding it up for her to see, and then immediately felt embarrassed given how badly she was hurt.

"You should see a **hooded spirit** for that."

He was concerned with Pani. She was trying to hide it, but he could tell she was at the end of her rope. If anything, her face was swelling larger, and any movement of her arm elicited winces.

She was the one who needed one of the healers, but each time Qod suggested it, she shook her head and said she was fine. Concern warred with pride in Qod. Here he was, crying about a splinter, yet this goblinette was fighting to make light of her serious wounds.

*Respect, Pani.*

He quietly dropped the splinter to the ground, then looked around the waiting area while hoping she'd forget his lack of martial fortitude.

The ghoul had remained standing and was now so still that he could have been a statue. Qod was grateful to him for speaking up, but except for the comment about the human selling weapons, he'd been silent, and to Qod, he was now just part of the background.

With the ghoul not interacting and Pani sitting with her eyes closed again, there was no one for Qod to talk to. So much had happened that his nerves were as tight as **dried marmot intestines.** Waiting to see a general only heightened his unease. He leaned his head back against the wall of the tent and sighed.

"I don't believe it. A gobby?" a deep orc voice said.

The words were a little muffled coming through the tent walls, but they were clear enough for goblin ears.

The CP wasn't a quiet place. There'd been a low murmur of noise from the moment they'd entered it. But hearing "gobby" caught his attention, and he focused on separating the speaker from the background rumble.

"We have witnesses, sir."

That was their orc.

This conversation suddenly took on a much greater import.

"Who. Another gobby? They lie, you know."

"One gobby, yes, sir. But also a ghoul. Colonel Manticoz wanted me to bring him, too."

"Can't trust one of them, either."

"Then there's the Black Smoke sergeant, sir."

There was silence, then a "Dwarf shit. An orc saw this gobby kill an elf battle mage? A Smoke at that?"

"Yes, sir."

"That's a little harder to cover up."

*Cover up? Why does the general want to cover up anything?*

The voice hadn't identified itself as belonging to the general, but it was pretty obvious to Qod.

There was a long moment of silence, and Qod turned his ear slightly to press up better against the tent wall.

"You said the gobby's hurt. It'd be a damn shame if he didn't survive his wounds, hero and all like he is."

"Not this gobby, sir. I brought in the gobby witness. She's the one who's hurt."

"Damn it all, Lieutenant. You're just full of good news, aren't you?"

The orc didn't reply.

"Sir, this doesn't look good. Almavoy won't like it when she hears that a gobby saved our asses," a different orc said.

"A gobby? I won this battle. Me!" the general shouted.

The ghoul finally stirred and looked at the tent wall. Even ghoul ears could hear that.

"I'm the commanding general. If a gobby killed the mage, that's because *I* put him there."

There was a crash, as if someone had thrown something to the ground.

No one spoke for a long few moments before the general finally said, "But you're right. Almavoy won't like this. An ogre, maybe. But not a fucking gobby. It's embarrassing, but if she gives me any shit, I swear I'll challenge the bitch now."

*Oh, rot.*

Orc hierarchy, and in reflection, the entire Dark's hierarchy, relied on challenges to take the leadership, thus ensuring that the strongest always led. This was all above the heads of the small folk who had no say, but when elephants fought, it was the rats under their feet who got smashed.

Qod didn't even know the name of his general, but he could be sure the orc had challenged his way to the top, killing the previous general to take their place. He knew who **Almavoy** was, though. The Empress of the Dark's name brought shivers and prayers alike.

**Almavoy** became the empress of the orc race after fighting to reach the top and had become the de facto leader of the Dark since they'd coalesced into an alliance to meet a previous Light threat. All of this was well before Qod was born, so her on the Misty Throne was all he knew. A challenge for the throne now would be just begging the Light to destroy all the Children of the Dark.

Qod hoped the general was just venting, but with orcs, it was sometimes hard to tell what was real ambition. All he knew was that this was getting too deep for a goblin from Yellow Rock.

"Well, who's to say that this gobby wasn't wounded, too. I think we can squash this. Get rid of the gobby and put an orc in his place. Who'll know?" the general asked, but with the tone of someone who wasn't really looking for advice.

Qod glanced at the door opening into the tent. He could make a break for it, scoot past the draugrs and head for the hills. But Pani wasn't in any condition to run, and as much as he feared for his life right now, he couldn't abandon her.

The general might not have wanted advice, but the orc was going to give it to him.

"Begging the general's pardon, but the small folk have already seen him. They surrounded us as we came up, cheering him. I think they're still out there."

"The Dark Mother's stinking ass!"

There was the sound of movement, and Qod sat straighter as he tried to look innocent. A moment later, the general, followed by the orc and a banshee, rushed out. Neither gave him a look.

"Do you know what's going on?" Pani asked.

For a moment, he thought she'd known he was eavesdropping, but she'd been looking to him for guidance even before this.

The ghoul, on the other hand, was staring at him, dead eyes looking into his very soul. Qod shifted on the bench, sure the ghoul was going to say something, but thankfully, the lieutenant remained silent.

Qod was numb, his emotions whipsawing at each turn. He'd gone from regret for killing the mage to anger that no one would listen to him to pride when he was greeted by the other soldiers and now to fear. The general wanted to do away with their inconvenient existence. All it would take was one word, and Qod knew the draugrs would make them disappear.

*Think!*

There had to be some way out of his predicament, but for once, his mind was blank. Nothing held any promise.

The flap at the entrance blew open, making him jump to his feet. The general stormed in, his face purple with fury. Once again, he ignored the three. The banshee, however, slowed down slightly as she gave Qod the once-over before following the general.

Qod couldn't tell anything by her expression, but he was fearing the worst. Dragurs or not, he started considering bolting for the entrance. Most races couldn't, or just wouldn't bother, to tell goblins apart. He was pretty sure he could lose himself in the thousands of Dark soldiers.

But once again, he couldn't leave Pani. She was barely keeping conscious. There was no way she could bolt between the two guards and get away. And if he, by some miracle, was able to evade capture, she would pay the price, and that was something he just couldn't do to her.

Less than a minute later, an ogre colonel, looking quite worried, rushed past them and disappeared inside. Voices were raised, and this time, Qod didn't try to listen. He was afraid he'd hear their death sentence. Still, it was hard to miss some of what was going on. Much of it was cursing and the general deriding goblins as a race.

That caught Pani's attention, and she scooted closer to Qod. He wasn't sure if that was for comfort or to protect him.

After four or five minutes, the next room went quiet, and that was somehow worse. Qod tried to gulp, but his mouth was too dry.

The silence dragged on, and he'd had about enough. Whatever was going to happen, he just wished they'd get on with it.

The flap to the inner room was pulled back by the orc, and a moment later, the general walked out. For the first time, he looked at the two goblins sitting on the bench. Both of them automatically came to attention.

The general's face was impassive as he approached and stood in front of Pani.

The orc cleared her throat and said, "He's the small one, General."

The great one looked surprised, and Qod subconsciously took a deep breath and tried to puff out his scrawny chest.

"This one?" the general asked.

"Yes, sir," the ghoul said, the first words spoken since they arrived inside the tent. "That's the battle mage killer."

There was a hint of warning in the ghoul's voice. Nothing overt that he could be called on, but it was there all the same.

And it worked. The general gave a tiny start as if he only then realized that he was facing a killer. An accidental killer, to be sure, but he didn't know that.

Then a smile exposing his canines came across his face. A forced smile.

"Private Kud. I am pleased to meet you."

"Qod, not Kud," Pani said.

The general ignored her.

"You've done the Dark forces a great service."

He turned to the colonel. "Make sure we give this young gobby a medal or something."

"Right away, sir."

"Come with me, son," the general told Qod.

This was going better than Qod had hoped. It didn't look like he was going to be killed, at least right away. But he was wary.

He didn't have a choice, though. As the general started to leave, Qod followed.

Pani started forward, too, but the banshee captain said, "Not you."

"Small sir!" the goblinette called out.

"Stay here. I'll be back."

*I hope.*

She wrung her hands, but she stayed put.

The two stepped up to the entrance, where the general stopped and faced him. The forced pleasantness disappeared, and in a command voice, he told Qod, "You shut up and don't say a word."

"Sir?"

"You just stand there. That's all. Understand?"

"Uh, yes, sir. Yes, General, sir."

The orc stared at him for a long moment, then took Qod's hand and pulled him forward. Qod's uncertainty kicked in, and he tried to pull back. He might as well have been fighting a troll. The general might be older, but he'd gotten his moons by defeating another in mortal combat, and he was still strong. He bodily dragged Qod through the entrance, past the two draugrs, and to the front of the tent.

A cheer rose from several hundred throats. Orcs, kobolds, sprites, trolls, and yes, goblins were screaming. Still being alive must have given them a burst of energy.

The general stood in front of the troops, a smile plastered over his face. After a few moments, he raised Qod's hand, almost lifting the smaller goblin off his feet while wrenching Qod's shoulder.

"Fellow soldiers, I give you Private Kud, Hero of the Army of the Mist, Killer of the battle mage!" the general bellowed as the gathered soldiers went wild.

# Chapter 10

Qod had been shocked at the level of acclamation that washed over him like a physical blow, and he soaked it in. For once, he was the center of attention, and not even the piercing pain in his shoulder from how the general was yanking on his arm could spoil his elation.

Something else could. He raised his free hand to wave at the shoulders, and the general subtly twisted his arm in a way that escaped him except that it increased the pain enough to make him gasp.

"Don't let this go to your head, gobby," the general hissed out of the corner of his mouth, never letting his smile change.

The two of them stood there for another half minute before the general turned and half-dragged Qod past the draugrs and into the tent.

"Get my staff now," he told the banshee.

The general didn't release his hold on Qod until they were inside a large space with an ornate conference table that would have been more at home in the empress's castle than on the battlefield. He gave Qod a small shove toward a chair, then moved to the head of the table and sat, staring at him with emotionless eyes.

With just the two of them in the tent, Qod nervously shifted his weight in his chair. The mood inside the conference space had decidedly shifted from the cheering of the army.

"How did you do it?" the general finally demanded.

"Sir?" Qod said in a voice that was more squeak than anything else.

"Come on, Private. Don't play coy with me. The battle mage. How did you do it, if in fact, that's what happened? I'm still not sure I accept that."

"Yes, sir. I did it."

"I asked how."

"Well, sir. I, uh . . . my captain . . . Captain Ryys, he told me to point the tip of my spear at the enemy and stick them."

"Do you take me for a fool?" the general asked, his voice quiet but full of lethal danger.

"No, sir!"

"You just stuck the battle mage, one of the deadliest fighters that exists?"

A perverse sense of **fuck-it-all** almost made him correct the general to "existed," past tense, but a strong desire to remain breathing made him bite his tongue.

"Yes, sir. With my spear."

The general was silent for a long moment before he asked, "Have you ever been to Taxian?"

The question completely took Qod off guard.

"Taxian? Where the empress lives?"

"Is there another Taxian, Private?"

"Uh, no, sir," he said, before he added, "No, sir, there isn't another Taxian, and no, sir, I've never been there."

He swallowed hard. Qod could read fellow goblins well enough. Orcs, not so well. But he could tell the general didn't believe him. He didn't know why the question, though. Taxian? What did that have to do with the battle?

The general rose quickly to his feet, which made the tautly strung Qod jump in fear. But the orc strode to the entrance and stuck his head out. Qod couldn't make out what the general was saying, but it only took a few moments before he returned.

"We'll see about that. And if you're lying to me . . ."

Qod gulped again.

"Now, tell me what happened. Tell me everything. Don't leave out a single fact."

"Yes, sir. Everything. Um . . . well, when the impressors came to Yellow Rock, I was the only—"

"I don't give a shit what little village you crawled out of. The battle mage. I want to know about him."

"Oh. Yes, sir."

It took him a moment to regain his bearings, but he started to recount what happened. He told the truth—mostly. For some reason he couldn't quite put his finger on, he didn't relate that it was all luck.

He knew orcs respected strength. Orc leadership relied on it. So, instead of saying that his helmet fell down and he stumbled, he left the impression that every step had been planned, based on the training Captain Ryys had given him.

At one point, he almost believed it himself, and he added that he did it for the empress—and that got such a reaction that he knew he'd overstepped, even if he didn't know why.

He quickly wrapped it up, saying it was the army's leadership, especially the general's, that put him in the position to kill the mage.

"Charging up the hill, sir. That was genius, sir. It forced the battle mage's hand and got him into the open, where we could attack. Well done."

He winced at that last. The charge had been falling into the Light army's trap. And now, kissing the general's ass, it was too groveling, too fake, and he expected the general to call him out on it. Instead, the orc nodded and puffed up his chest just a bit.

At that moment, the banshee stuck her head inside the flap.

"General? Everyone's here."

"Give me a minute, then bring them in."

"Yes, sir."

The general turned back to Qod.

"I don't know if you're the weak, bumbling gobby that the gods unfathomably decided to favor, or if you're part of some imperial plot. If it's the latter, well, don't think you've got protection."

"Yes, sir. I mean, no, sir. I'm not part of any plot."

The general stared deeply into Qod's eyes, then grunted.

"We'll see. But if you're for real, I can use you to help with my soldier problem."

Qod didn't know what "soldier problem" the general had, nor how he could help with that, but he kept quiet."

"Keep your mouth shut and do what I tell you to, and I can make things comfortable for you. More than comfortable. But cross me—"

"No, sir!  I would never!"

The general grunted again.  "We'll see."

An orc colonel entered, followed by an ogre, then more of the staff.

The general stood and moved to where he could put a big hand on Qod's shoulder, which still hurt from where he'd jerked on in front of the soldiers.

He leaned in to Qod's ear.  "Don't give yourself airs, little gobby.  Always remember, I can crush you without trying.  Now, go, sit along the wall and don't say a word."

The general stood while the staff filed in.  Qod scurried to the far corner of the room and tried to make himself small.

This was rarified atmosphere for a goblin from Yellow Rock.  Another general, nd ogre, this one with only one moon on his collar and clearly subservient to the commander, along with no fewer than five colonels and other lower-ranked, but still powerful officers, took their places around the table.

The general looked relaxed, and he good naturedly teased one of the colonels as they took their positions, but Qod could feel the tension.  All the staff officers were tighter than lute strings.  A few stole sidewise glances at him, but none met his eyes.

The general waited until everyone was in position before he sat, to be immediately followed by his staff.

"Colonel Manticoz, let me begin by offering my congratulations.  The faeby bastards are on the run, thanks to your diligence in following orders."

The colonel who'd ordered Qod to the CP relaxed ever-so-slightly, but he was still tense, his hands clasped on the table in front of him.

"Thank you, sir.  But it was your foresight that had my troops in position to pursue your plan."

The general gave a slight, humorless smile, but he nodded in acceptance of the praise.

"The enemy is on the run," the general said.  "But the battle is not done.  We need to chase down every last faeby coward and put him to the sword.  They need to be taught a lesson that they will never forget."

*So, why are you here in the CP instead of chasing the Light army?*

Qod didn't know who the other colonels were, but Colonel Manticoz, at least, was a combat commander. He thought the colonel should be out there commanding his troops instead of sitting here.

"Colonel, if you would, please brief the staff on what you accomplished. I want them to see what I expect from my commanders."

"Yes, General. Of course, General."

The colonel started hesitantly, but once he got going, he warmed up to the process. He started with his preparations, caveating everything with "As General Yare planned," or "As General Yare ordered me to." His tone shifted to what could be scolding the others, which wasn't lost on Qod—or them, judging by the narrowing of eyes among both the other colonels and the junior general.

From how Colonel Manticoz told it, he specifically called up the 121st Replacement Company and sent them into the fight to confront the battle mage, then, knowing the Black Smokes would move quicker, committed them to then bound over the replacement company to flush out the elf prince.

Two things stood out to Qod. First, while it wasn't exactly stated as such, the implication was that the 121st was some sort of highly trained special operations group, moving incognito to fool the Light forces.

Qod thought back to the disorganized company, which had been formed only the day before.

Second, there was no mention of marching into a trap, nor of the casualties suffered because of that. Listening to the colonel, it was as if every step of the way was in accordance with a carefully choreographed operations order.

All the while, General Yare sat there like a toad on a silk pillow with a satisfied look on his face as if he already knew every detail.

And just as the Light trap was never mentioned, something else was glaringly missing. When it came to the battle mage's death, Qod was ignored. It was the 121st that killed the elf prince.

It wasn't fooling anyone. Every officer there was hyperaware of the goblin sitting along the tent wall, even if none actually looked in his direction.

Qod knew there was command politics going on—he'd already seen that. But still, he didn't like being erased from the battle, and he had a perverse inclination to stand and say, "That was me! I killed the battle mage."

The colonel ended his brief, then deflated somewhat as he looked to the general, probably to see if the great orc approved of his version or not.

The general leaned forward. Qod knew the orc was aware of the colonel's apprehension, and like a cat playing with a mouse, he didn't say anything for the longest time.

Finally, though, he said, "Thank you, Colonel Manticoz. Your service to the Dark Coalition is appreciated. And for the rest of you. That's what happens when you dedicate your efforts to crushing the faeby invaders. You've been failing during this campaign, so, for your sakes, I hope you follow Colonel Manticoz's example."

The colonel's chest visibly swelled, and the others vigorously nodded. An orc colonel shouted, "Long live Empress Almavoy!" which made several of the other officers flinch.

"Yes, of course. The empress will be most impressed with what we've accomplished," the general said.

It sure didn't sound to Qod that the general's heart was in that statement.

"Chef Bnt has prepared wolverine for lunch. I want all of you to join me. Maybe that will instill a fighting spirit in you," the general said.

Qod perked up. He'd never had wolverine. When he did eat meat, it was almost always rat.

The only ghoul colonel, who wore the scarab collar device of command, looked for a moment like she was going to argue, but she bit back whatever it was she was going to say.

"Before we eat, though, I want to introduce you to Private Kud."

*Qod.*

All eyes finally turned to him with frank curiosity and even a hint of fear?

"The private was the dagger I used to kill the battle mage. Now that he's a known entity, you'll be seeing more of him in the coming campaign."

There was some polite applause. Qod knew it was all ratshit, but still, he couldn't help feeling a little bit of pride. That was a general officer who'd just mentioned his name, even if he'd gotten it wrong again.

The general lifted a hand and signaled. Within seconds, a kobold rushed in, holding a platter high where a whole wolverine was surrounded by snaggleberries and mud fungus. A wonderful, almost musty aroma immediately filled the tent. Qod's salivary glands went into overdrive.

The chef placed the platter in front of the general with a flourish, and the staff and commanders broke out into applause with far more enthusiasm than when they'd clapped for Qod.

Qod didn't care, though. His entire attention was on the wolverine, which had been mounted in attack mode, teeth bared.

But if he thought he was going to be able to taste the feast, that was rudely crushed when the banshee captain slithered around the tent wall to him.

"Come with me," the captain said quietly.

The two circled around the table to the entrance. Qod gave one last, longing look at the meal before he followed the banshee out and into the waiting area. Pani wasn't there. Hopefully, she was getting treated by the hooded spirits.

"Take a seat and wait," the captain ordered.

"What happens now?"

The banshee didn't seem to be upset that she was being questioned by a private.

"I don't know," she admitted. "No one does until the general decides what to do with you."

She spun on her heels and went back inside.

Alone, Qod sighed. The aroma of roasted wolverine made its way through the seams of the tent to tickle his nose.

## Chapter 11

Qod had sat in the CP waiting room for hours while the wolverine feast dragged on and on—all while the fight with the Light forces continued. Chef Bnt—Qod didn't know if he was a soldier or a civilian—had taken pity on him and brought him a sandwich after an hour. It wasn't wolverine but pork, he thought.

Still, it wasn't rat.

It was hours before the banshee captain came to fetch him and, for the first time, let him know her name.

"The general's decided that you need armor suited for a hero," Captain k'Ree said in a flat voice.

Qod still thought he detected a trace of sarcasm when she said, "hero," but he let it go. Not that there was much of anything he could do about it, even if he wanted to.

She led him out of the tent. The sun was already dipping toward the horizon, but there was still enough light to see. Not that there was much to look at. If the battle was ongoing, it was well out of sight. Groups of Dark soldiers were scattered across the valley and up the lower reaches of the mountain range. Smoke from a hundred campfires wafted to the sky.

It was . . . *peaceful*. A far cry from the death that had cut through Dark and Light soldiers alike. When they first emerged, the two of them were ignored. That didn't last long. First one soldier, then another, realized who was walking among them. They stopped and stared. A few gave him a thumbs up or a fist pump. Pretty soon, it was as if his presence was billowing out like some sort of messenger cloud.

Soldiers of every kind gathered, which slowed the two to barely a crawl. Captain k'Ree had to shanghai a troll to run interference for them as they made their way to the creek—the same one Qod had trouble with that morning—where a group of mostly kobold armorers were working, making minor repairs to weapons and gear. The ringing of hammers on metal was continuous.

The head armorer was not happy when the captain gave her the general's orders.

"We don't have much here, ma'am," the armorer said. "The damn human scavengers already snapped up most of what didn't get melted by the battle mage."

"You don't understand, sergeant. The general doesn't want used armor. The goblin needs to *look* like a hero."

The kobold gave Qod a long, appraising look.

"Did you really kill the elf prince?"

"Yes, Sergeant."

The armorer shrugged and scratched the scar that ran across his scaled face. "I guess the gods work in mysterious ways, as they say. Wait."

He put down the hammer and walked over to a wagon off to the side. He waved his hand through an intricate pattern, and the door swung open.

Qod looked on with interest. Wizard locks weren't high magic. The kind that could be keyed to non-magic individuals had a limited shelf life, so they were rare enough that Qod hadn't ever seen one in use.

The kobold disappeared inside, leaving the two of them alone in the middle of the camp. There might be a hundred soldiers around them, but with the troll still standing by, it was as if there was a bubble of nothingness surrounding them.

If he had a choice, he'd really rather have someone else with him at the moment. It was common knowledge that banshees could sense death. Qod didn't know how accurate that was, but with the captain not talking, the death aspect was giving him the creeps.

After a few moments, Qod had to break the silence.

"Did the general say what will happen to me?"

For a long moment, he thought the captain was going to continue to ignore him, but finally, she said, "You're going to be used, Private."

He didn't know what that meant.

"How?"

She sniffed and said, "General Yare has a . . . less than optimal relationship with the . . . *conscripted* soldiers. He thinks you can be of assistance in that regard."

Qod frowned. The general had mentioned a problem before, but it hadn't really registered. What kind of problem could he have? Generals were all-powerful, and the conscripted soldiers, especially the small folk, were pawns in the games of war. They had no power at all.

If a general had an issue with a soldier, all they had to do was snap their fingers and the draugrs would eliminate that problem.

Furthermore, what could he do to help the general?

He wanted to ask for clarification, but the kobold was emerging, his arms full. He walked up and dumped a load of armor at their feet.

"This is what I've got, ma'am," he told the captain.

She frowned and then said, "Well, let's try it on."

The armorer looked at Qod, then at the armor on the ground, then back at him. With a sigh, he picked up a cuirass. Qod's heart started beating a little quicker.

It was beautiful. Obsidian black with intricate designs across the front, it might be the finest worked object he'd ever seen.

*I'm going to look so studly!*

He held his breath as the kobold put it over his head—breath that rushed out as the weight settled over his shoulder.

*It's heavy!*

Qod didn't know what he expected, but this wasn't it.

The kobold stepped back and frowned.

"'E's too small," he told the captain.

Qod looked down. He wasn't an expert in armor, but he was pretty sure a cuirass was supposed to stop at the waist. The bottom of this one ran across his thighs.

"Just put on the rest, and we'll see how it goes."

"You're the boss, Captain."

Piece by piece, the kobold put on the armor, and piece by piece, Qod sank under the weight. Pauldron, rerebrace, vambrace, suisses, greaves . . .

The kobold actually discarded several pieces, telling the captain that there wasn't enough room on Qod's body. Finally, the last greave was fastened, and the kobold stepped back.

"How does that feel?" Captain k'Ree asked.

"I can't move," Qod said.

The banshee gave the armorer an exasperated look, but the kobold just shrugged and said, "We don't get a call for armor so small."

*You can put armor on a pixie. Why not me?*

"Can you, uh . . . make something?"

"Not without no forge, ma'am, no way. Not even a Light-worshipping dwarf could."

She stared at Qod for a moment before saying, "Try to take a step forward."

Qod was having a hard enough time just standing, but an order was an order. Taking a step was more of lifting a leg and trying to thrust it out. Qod failed and fell to the ground with a crash. He was stunned, and as far as he was concerned, he'd be happy to just lie there.

Both the captain and sergeant rushed forward, however, and lifted him back up to his feet.

"This isn't going to do," the captain said, stating the obvious. "What are our options?"

"Aside from going back to Haejeklford? Not much."

"The general isn't going to accept failure, *Sergeant*."

The kobold paled.

The crowd that had been watching started to quickly melt away, and as if summoned by their conversation, the general strode toward them with several other officers pulled along in his wake.

Qod froze.

"What do you think?" the great one asked without preamble.

Qod was about to answer when a kukudh major stepped around the general's bulk to stare at him.

A shudder ran through him. Kukudh were rare, and Qod had never seen one. But he sure knew what it was. And judging from the raised lip of the captain, she was not a fan, either.

Rumors abounded, but Qod didn't actually know what a kukudh was, except undead. He didn't think that was actually true. Dead was dead, at least without sorcery. But he couldn't shake the thought as the major stepped closer.

"The armor doesn't fit," the major said, its voice a whisper in the wind.

General Yare frowned, then stepped back to get a better look.

"No goblin looks good," he said. "But I see what you mean."

He turned to Captain k'Ree. "Get something runt-sized."

The captain nudged the reluctant armorer, who looked like he wanted to melt into the soil, forward.

"Sir, beggin' the general's pardon, sir, but we don't . . . we don't have anything smaller, 'cepting a pixie set. I mean, general sir, 'e's a goblin, and a tiny one at that," the kobold said as if that answered everything."

"Well, make something, *Sergeant*," the general said.

Qod was about to collapse under all the weight, but he winced at the venom in the general's voice.

"Beggin' the general's pardon, Sir General, but we ain't got no forge. Not that I'm complain', I mean. We're in a battle. 'Ow can we have a forge 'ere. That'd be stupid. I don' mean anyone's stupid. I—"

The general raised a hand, cutting the panicking kobold short. He stared at Qod for far too long, and Qod thought he was going to pass out.

"Sir?" Captain k'Ree asked.

"What?"

"I was just wondering, sir. If you want to use Private Qod as an emissary, so to speak, with the conscripts, then would a bespoke suit of armor be the best way forward? You said you wanted them to relate to the private and give them hope."

Qod did not want to be around a general whose plans were being stymied, but suddenly things began to gel. He started to understand how the general wanted to use him.

"What do you mean?" the general asked.

"If the private was outfitted like the run-of-the-mill grunt, wouldn't that serve your purpose better?"

The general snorted, then was quiet for a moment before he turned to the major.

The kukudh didn't hesitate.

"The captain is right. I do believe that the small folk would be more conducive to someone who looks like them, not an elite."

Qod feared the general was going to stick to his guns as many in power do, but he turned to the armorer, who was visibly ashen-faced.

"Can you put together something along those lines, but make him look like a warrior?"

For a moment, Qod thought the armorer was going to say something along the lines of, "He's a goblin. Nothing will make him look like a warrior."

But the kobold just nodded his head so hard it looked like it was going to fall off.

"Yes, General. Of course, General. If I—"

"Don't tell me how. Just do it. I want this private outside my CP at dawn."

To the banshee, he said, "As always, Captain, I don't know what I'd do without you."

The general wheeled around and stalked off, the major and two colonels following behind. Qod didn't know which one he was happier to see leave— the general or kukudh. The captain waited until they were out of sight before she asked the kobold, "You're an armorer. How are you going to outfit the private?"

Confidence was returning to the sergeant.

"Sometimes, Captain, it's just best to let the NCOs do what NCOs do and not ask questions."

Captain k'Ree gave a short, barking laugh.

"Point taken, Sergeant. And I'll get out of your hair. For now. You take our private and make him shine. I'll be back an hour before dawn to pick him up."

She marched off, and the sergeant turned back to Qod.

"Now, what the 'ell am I going to do with you?"

## Chapter 12

As the sun's rays just started peaking over the horizon, Qod was standing in front of the CP. He was tired—bone tired. But at the same time, he felt *martial*.

He glanced down at the cuirass, the black leather making the two hammered copper dragons facing each other on his chest stand out even more. An iron link belt slightly drew his waist in, and from it hung a wicked-looking burnished iron dagger. A simple gray tunic under the cuirass, matching gray tights, and black leather shoes with copper buckles finished the look.

It had taken a team, working through the night, to get him outfitted. The sky was already tinged with rose and purple before Captain k'Ree was satisfied.

Well, not exactly satisfied. She gave the assembled team further orders on adjustments, but she said that his appearance would do for now.

Qod had thought that the idea was to keep him looking like a normal grunt. This wasn't it. Not that he was complaining. No one would ever mistake him for a Black Smoke, but he thought there was a definite legacy from that elite unit in his outfit.

He stood there, hand resting on the hilt of the dagger, very conscious of the covert looks being flashed his way. The blade was a relief. It might be small for most soldiers, but for him, it was a short sword. Best of all, it was light. No real sword. No ax.

And the dagger was beautiful. Perfectly balanced and sharp as winter ice, he'd never seen anything of the same quality. He'd been admiring the blade when Captain k'Ree ordered him to sheath it and never take it out.

"You're likely to cut off a finger with it," she'd told him. "Not the image the general wants to project."

Qod carefully sheathed it, but not carefully enough. He didn't even feel it at first, but then the blood flowed from the thin line along the inside of his forefinger. He guiltily looked around, but no one seemed to notice. With what he hoped was a surreptitious movement, he pressed his finger, which was now beginning to burn, against the leather cuirass, hoping that would stop the bleeding.

*My first wound as a soldier.*

Even if this thought was in jest, he felt a twinge of guilt. This was nothing like what happened to Pani while facing the enemy. He'd done the same thing often enough, cutting thistle roots for dinner back at Yellow Rock.

At the thought of his friend, he glanced at the captain. Several times during the night, he tried to work up the nerve to ask her if he could check on his fellow goblin. Each time, though, he'd backed down.

*Maybe now's a good time?*

But he knew it wasn't. It would be just his luck to leave when the general wanted him. Pani was going to have to wait until after he was done with . . . well, he wasn't quite sure what he was going to be doing.

*Should I ask, though? All she can do is say no, right?*

Qod cleared his throat when the flap to the CP opened, and he snapped to attention. But it was the kukudh major, who gave Qod a long look with eyes that pierced his soul before he spun around and went back inside.

Qod shuddered. His heart was pounding, and he tried to will it to slow. He had a feeling that if he messed up, there would be consequences.

"Ma'am? May I ask you a question?"

The banshee had been up all night just like he had, but she seemed fresh and ready for anything.

"Go ahead, Private."

"What will I be doing? I mean, what am I *supposed* to be doing. No one has told me anything, and I don't want to screw up."

There was a flash in her eyes, and Qod thought that's what he'd just done—screw up. Privates didn't question captains.

The fire faded after a few moments, and she said, "Don't say anything, for one. The general will probably want to show you off, so let him." She paused, and in a slightly softer tone, added, "Just remember, Private Qod. You are a tool, a prop, nothing more. You have no hopes, no dreams, no ambitions. If you remember that, then you'll be fine. More than fine, I'm guessing."

Qod gave a slight frown. Maybe it was the leather armor. Maybe it was the fatigue. Or maybe it was that he *had* just killed an elf battle mage, even if it was all a weird accident. The fact was that he didn't want to be a prop. He wanted . . .

Other than being back in Yellow Rock, asleep in his comfy bed in his comfy, if small, hovel, he didn't know *what* he wanted.

Before he could come up with something, the two draugrs, who hadn't flinched when the kukudh came out, stiffened, and their eyes darted back and forth as they scanned the area for danger. A moment later, the general, in bronze and charcoal armor, stepped out, stretched mightily, and hawked a huge glob of spit onto the ground.

He looked around until his eyes locked onto Qod.

The kukudh filled Qod with unease, but he feared the orc general from the pit of his stomach. It wasn't so much that the orc could order his death. What was worse was that Qod knew in his bones that he was nothing to the general. Captain k'Ree had said Qod was a tool, but as he stood in front of the orc, he knew he wasn't even that. Qod was no more consequential than a flea.

And that cut Qod to the quick.

The general grunted and asked, "That's our goblin?"

"Yes, sir," Captain k'Ree said. "Private Qod."

He turned to where the kukudh was hovering.

"Do we really need to do this?"

"It would be beneficial, sir," the major said.

The general let out a sigh that would put a two-year-old goblin sausage to shame.

"Let's get it done, then." He paused and then said, "Staff, get on the Berking Valley plan. I want a full brief when I get back," he said before striding off.

Qod froze, unsure of what to do.

Captain k'Ree frantically gestured at him to follow the general. Qod broke into a sprint, but before he made two steps, the general said over his shoulder, "You, too, Captain. He's your gobby."

The banshee's eyes flashed . . . something. It wasn't good, Qod knew, and he shuddered as he brushed past her to hurry after the general. A moment later, he heard her start to follow.

He caught up to the general after a dozen strides and, not knowing what else to do, fell alongside the orc.

"I don't need a damn miniature bodyguard, Captain," the general said. "What would the troops think?"

Captain k'Ree grabbed Qod's shoulder and yanked him to a stop.

"What in the name of the Dark do you think you're doing?" she hissed.

"I'm sor—"

"Just stay invisible until he wants you seen."

*How do I know when that is?*

He fell in behind the captain. The two followed the general as he made his way through the camp. Outside the CP, about a dozen of the senior staff watched with sharply honed focus as the three of them descended into the camp.

It was very different with the troops, though. The common soldiers made no overt notice of the three, but Qod knew they were very aware of them. They were being too studiously ignored for it to be anything less than intentional.

Not every soldier was going about their daily tasks. Qod hadn't seen them fall into place, but six draugrs were flanking them as they made their way down the slope. The other soldiers quietly got out of the general's way, but they moved with a little more alacrity to avoid the six bodyguards.

They were in the command camp with the might of the Army of the Mist around them, and the Light army was on the run. Qod wasn't sure why the general needed bodyguards here. Unless it was a formal challenge for command—and that was done under strict protocol—no one would have the brash courage to confront a general.

Rumor had it that by mutual agreement, not even the Light forces would assassinate a general officer. Whether Dark or Light, generals could only be felled in battle. Qod didn't know if that was really true, but if he were a betting goblin, he'd wager on it being the case.

The general reached the bottom of the slope, then hesitated for a moment before he shrugged and turned to the left. He strode into the middle of a kobold camp and stopped.

All around them, the kobold soldiers froze and stared until a lieutenant rushed forward and saluted. The general's flick of his left hand was hardly a return salute.

"Everything OK, Lieutenant?" the general asked.

The lieutenant's mouth dropped open, and he looked at Captain k'Ree for rescue, but the banshee stayed silent.

"Sir?" the lieutenant croaked in the deep rumble of the kobold—they might be only somewhat larger than goblins, but their voices were almost as deep as a troll's.

"Is everything OK?" the general repeated. "Uh . . . are your troops ready to take it to the faeby bastards?"

"The captain, he . . . uh . . ."

"Damn it, Lieutenant. I don't need your captain. I'm asking you a simple question," the general barked.

The kobold lieutenant paled and took a half-step back before he managed to get out, "Uh . . . yes, sir. Yes, General. We're ready?"

That was more of a question than a statement. Qod felt a wash of empathy for the stumbling lieutenant, but he was glad it was the kobold in the crosshairs, not him.

The general grunted. "Good. I'm counting on you."

Then the general turned and nodded at Qod.

"You know Private Kud, right?" the general asked the lieutenant.

*So much for being out of the crosshairs.*

Qod took a deep breath and tried to draw himself up.

"We've heard of him, sir," the lieutenant said warily, as if he was afraid of what might be coming next.

His eyes darted from the general to the draugr bodyguards and back several times.

"Good, good. Well, he's just an example of what a sma . . . *conscript* can do in a battle if he's loyal to me and follows orders. Even the most insignificant private can help achieve victory if they do their duty without question or hesitation."

*What?*

If that was supposed to be a pep talk, then it was obvious that the general had no idea how that was supposed to work. Generals ordered, and the troops obeyed, usually getting killed in the process. Once again, Qod wondered what was going on that the kukudh major thought this was necessary.

He glanced at Captain k'Ree, but her face might as well be carved in stone.

The lieutenant didn't respond—he hadn't been asked a direct question, after all.

An awkward few moments of silence followed until the general said, "Well, I'm expecting the same from you and all your troops. Carry on."

He suddenly was in motion again. The kobold soldiers seemed relieved as the general—and draugrs—made their way out of their camp.

The next thirty minutes were more of the same. The general wandered with seemingly no clear plan while flanked by the draugrs. Qod and the captain followed. They stopped seemingly at random, where junior officers rushed to greet him, and the general gave his less-than-enthusiastic endorsement of Qod and how the soldiers could emulate him.

Either the general got bored or he realized this wasn't doing much, because after his fourth little speech, he said, "This is dwarf shit. I'm a general, by the Dark blood, and I don't kiss small folk ass."

Without another word, he turned and headed back to the CP. The general staff, who had watched their every move from afar, stirred as they got ready to welcome back their leader.

Qod wasn't sure if he was supposed to follow, but the Captain said, "Go back to the armorer. I left a few adjustments on your leathers that I want them to make."

She paused for a moment, and her voice got slightly softer.

"Did you get any sleep last night?"

"No, ma'am."

She sighed, then rubbed her forehead. Qod wondered how much sleep *she* had gotten.

"They don't need you to work on your leathers. Go drop them off, then tell Sergeant Lissif that I want him to find you a rack. Understood?"

"Yes, ma'am."

"I'll get word to you when you're needed next."

She turned and started back up the hill to the CP when Qod said, "Ma'am?"

The captain stopped and stood there for a moment. She didn't turn around but asked, "What now, Private?"

Qod almost faltered, but his need was too great.

"Private Pani. She was with me, and she was hurt pretty bad. After I drop off my leathers, can I go see her first? I mean, before I find Sergeant, uh, Lissy, I mean, Lo—"

"Lissif."

"Sergeant Lissif. May I see Private Pani first, to see if she's OK?"

Qod hoped that he hadn't pushed the captain too far.

But she said, "Permission granted. *After* you deliver your leathers."

A huge load dropped off his shoulders. He'd been worried sick about his friend.

"Thank you, ma'am," Qod said to the captain's retreating back.

## Chapter 13

Finding Pani wasn't as easy as he'd thought it would be. There wasn't a central field hospital, and even with all the dead, there were still thousands of soldiers in and around the camp.

Medical care among the Dark folk was rudimentary at best. Without the hooded spirits, Qod thought that the wounded conscripted troops would be left to their own devices.

It didn't help that in his simple smock and without any officers around him, no one seemed to realize who he was. He was brushed off more than a few times as he asked for help. It ended up taking him almost two hours of asking and several false leads before he found Pani along the creek, almost where they'd crossed it during the battle. She was with a dozen other goblins and gremlins on the bank.

"Pani!" he shouted with relief as he hopped down to the creek side and ran over to her.

"Small sir!" she said with a smile as she struggled to sit up.

Qod started to hug her, but he backed off at the last moment—he wasn't sure if that was because of her injuries or because he was too shy.

"Are you OK?"

She nodded.

"We goblins are tough. You know that."

Which was true. It was taken as a fact that if you didn't kill a goblin in a fight, they'd probably recover from their wounds. Qod wasn't sure that was a hundred percent accurate, and Pani had been badly hurt, but he was relieved to hear her say that.

She was still moving gingerly, and the side of her face was a mess, but her color was getting back to the pallid green of health.

"What did the hooded spirits say?"

"We haven't had one," Pani replied. "I found the others here, and we're sort of taking care of ourselves."

"What?  No healers? But I've seen them all over the place."

"I'm sure they'll get to us, small sir," Pani said.  "But how are you?  I was worried about you."

A gremlin limped up to Qod.  His right arm was gone at the elbow, which was wrapped in a dirty piece of torn cloth.

"Is this him, Pani?"

"Yes, this is the mage killer."

Qod was suddenly aware that each set of eyes, except those of the unconscious soldiers, was locked onto him.  Their intensity was frightening as they closed in on him. His hand drifted to his non-existent belt and non-existent blade.

Qod yelped as the one-armed gremlin lunged at him, and it took him a moment to realize he was being hugged.

"You saved our lives, you did, sir," the soldier said in a half sob.  "Thank you."

The group became a scrum with each of the soldiers wanting to hug, shake his hand, or pound his back.  Pani stood at his shoulder, pride beaming from her still swollen face.

Qod had felt the adulation and cheers the day before, but this was different.  This was more real, more personal.  Hidden by the raised creek banks, they could almost forget that just steps away was the bulk of the Dark army.

One of the gremlins removed a small leather flask from under his jerkin and handed it to him.  All against Army regulations, of course, but Dark folk tended not to be too concerned with those.

Qod wasn't much of a drinker—no goblins were—but he was intrigued.  Gremlins were renowned for their skill in distilling spirits.

He took the flask, which was much heavier than he'd expected, and gave it a tentative sniff.  His eyes grew wide.  Whatever was in there was powerful, but there was an undertone that piqued his curiosity.  Qod wanted to take a tiny sip, but while he'd been told often enough by his sibs that he lacked social skills, he could tell by the eager look of the other soldiers that he had to goblin up.

Qod popped the cork, raised the flask, and said, "Here's to friends who wish us well, and may all the elves go to hell," before downing a big swallow.

His head almost exploded as liquid fire burned his throat. He staggered a step, and Pani had to hold him upright.

"Wow!," he managed to get out through his tears. "That's sure a conversation starter!"

The soldiers erupted into laughter, and Qod passed the flask to Pani, who took a sip before handing it to the next soldier.

The burning settled into a warm glow in his belly as he looked at the soldiers. Each of them was wounded. None of them knew what was in store for them. But for the moment, all was well in the world.

"Can you tell us how you killed the elf battle mage, sir?" one of the goblins with a Crooked Forest accent asked.

Both legs were crudely splinted, and she'd dragged herself on her butt to get close to him. She looked at him with hopeful eyes.

Qod glanced at the sun's progress across the sky. Captain k'Ree hadn't told him when to return to the armorer and cordwainer who were adjusting his leathers. He probably should be getting back, but the fact was that he wanted to spend time with Pani. And it was pretty nice to be with just small folk. No orcs, trolls, or ghouls. No banshee captain telling him what to do.

More than that, though, was that these small folk didn't look at him as a tool in the bigger games afoot. He was one of them, and there was a camaraderie and a sense of belonging, something that had been missing in his life since the skin rot took his family.

*Screw that banshee. She can take it up with the general.*

He plopped down beside the goblin.

"What's your name?"

"Jama, sir."

"Well, Jama. I think I can do that, if you want."

The others jostled closer for position as they sat.  They had the eager faces of Yellow Rock's sausages as they listened to the storyteller weave their tales.

Pani was shoved a little closer as she sat beside him, her leg pushing up against his.  Qod was very aware of her presence, and that gave him a moment of pause.

He shook it off, cleared his throat, and started.

"It's like this . . ."

\*\*\*\*\*\*\*\*\*\*\*\*\*\*\*

"As soon as you can, you find me.  OK?"

"Of course, sir."

"I told you, Pani.  It's Qod."

"Yes, I know, sir."

Qod shook his head.  Pani was agreeable, and she was not treating him like a superior, so why the "sir" all the time?  He was feeling more and more uncomfortable with the deferential honorific.  No matter if he'd been saved by a miracle, he was still a lowly private in the Army of the Mist.

He glanced at the sun, which was just about to slip behind the line of mountains to the west.  Qod had spent much more time with the group than he'd expected.  He was already undoubtedly late.

"Well, uh . . . I need to go.  "You're sure there's nothing I can do for you now?"

"We'll be fine, sir," she said, waving her good hand to indicate the gathered goblins, gremlins, and even two satyrs who'd wandered by and joined them.

The soldiers nodded their agreement.

"I don't know if anyone will listen to me, but I'll ask that you get some better food," he said.

"Thank you, sir," Jami said before stepping up to him.

He offered his hand, but she brushed past it to give him a hug, which took him by complete surprise.  Goblinettes just didn't do that with him.

That opened the floodgates.  The rest of the wounded soldiers crowded forward to shake his hand.

Most said something along the lines of kicking the Light's collective asses, and several called him "Mage Killer." Even the two satyrs seemed impressed as they shook his hand.

He bent down to Jama to shake her hand, but she grabbed him by the neck and pulled him in for a hug and kissed his cheek, much to the delight of the others. He felt his face flush. Pani was staring at him as he stood back up, and she gave him a second hug before he said goodbye to the group.

Qod was feeling pretty good as he turned and hurried back toward the CP with a spring in his step and a much lighter soul.

His elevated mood didn't last long.

"Where in the damn Light have you been, Private?" someone shouted as Qod approached the CP.

Qod spun around to see an ogre, a sergeant, striding toward him with what looked like evil intent.

He gulped and asked, "Are you Sergeant Lissil?"

"Who in the reaches of the Great Demon's hell do you think I am? Little Private Sunshine?"

"I was . . . the captain told me to find you."

"Hours ago. And now Captain k'Ree is looking all over for your sorry ass, and she's blaming me for losing you."

"She said I could go see my friend," Qod said, his voice cracking.

"That was this morning, you fool. You're a soldier, and this is war. This isn't the time for an afternoon social."

Qod winced. He knew he'd been gone too long. He just hoped the consequences wouldn't be too serious.

"Um . . . if you can tell me where my bed is, I'll just sit there until I'm needed. I promise," he squeaked out.

"Fat chance on that now. Corporal Cyrena needs to see you like now. Asses and elbows, private. Asses and elbows."

*Ass and elbows. I've only got one ass,* he thought as he turned to get away from the sergeant.

His habit of correcting folk, even just in his mind, made him forget that he didn't know who this corporal was.

He turned back and asked, "Excuse me, Sergeant. Who's Corporal Cyrena."

"Oh, by the Dark Mother," the ogre said as he rolled his eyes. "He created your leathers, right?"

"Oh. Yes, Sergeant."

The cordwainer who worked with Sergeant Tark never introduced himself to Qod.

"Then get your ass to him like an hour ago," the ogre said.

Qod was happy for the excuse to get away from the sergeant. He'd deal with the cordwainer when he got there.

"See me when you get done, Private, and I'll get you set up with berthing," the sergeant shouted to his retreating back with a slightly more reasonable tone.

Qod hurried back down the slope. Sergeant Lissif might have recognized him, but to the rest of the soldiers in the camp, he was just one more goblin, hardly someone who deserved special notice.

And after the—not adulation, but maybe *approval* of Pani's fellow wounded soldiers—it was nice to be able to fade into the background of anonymity. He was nervous as to what the leatherworking corporal was going to say, but after dealing with a general and a captain, he was a little inured to a mere corporal.

*Steady there. You're still a private, and a corporal has your balls in their grasping hands.*

Qod slowed down as he approached and rehearsed what he was going to tell the corporal. He crossed the last rise and stopped dead in his tracks. It wasn't the large number of spectators of all types, including a huge troll, who dominated his view.

His attention was focused on the goblinette being attended to by Corporal Cyrena, who was working on the leathers. *Qod*'s leathers.

At least he assumed they were his. The two facing dragons on the chest were the same, but there were some modifications. Shiny copper filigrees adorned the shoulders, and the goblin had black leather sleeves on her thighs and shins. Metallic thread ran along all the seams in a simple, but pleasing pattern.

The left side of the cuirass was open, and Corporal Cyrena was working on closing it with the metallic thread.

Qod's heart fell. Had he been replaced because he'd been hanging out all day with Pani and the others?

For a moment, he was almost relieved, but then his sense of righteousness took over.

"She didn't kill a battle mage," he quietly muttered as he pushed and wove his way through the spectators. "And she's a goblinette. Can't they see she's not me?"

It was almost a joke among the others that no one could tell one goblin from another, so if the general wanted this goblinette to play the part, Qod knew that no one would be the wiser—at least no one who mattered.

The corporal was grunting as he pulled on the edges, which jerked the goblinette around. She didn't look like she was enjoying herself. Corporal Cyrena didn't look happy, either, which made Qod pause.

So, instead of walking up to him, he tapped one of the assistants' shoulders.

"I think that's supposed to be me?" he asked.

"You're the mage killer?" the kobold said.

Qod nodded.

"Then where have you been? The corporal, he waited as long as he could to do the refitting, but finally, he grabbed another gobby to stand in so he could be done in time."

The private stepped back and looked at Qod with an appraising eye.

"I told him that this gobby was bigger than you."

"Not that much," Qod objected.

"Wait. Let me see what Cyrena wants to do."

The kobold left Qod, approached the corporal, and whispered in his ear.

Corporal Cyrena whirled around and locked blazing eyes on Qod for a moment. He whispered something to the private, then returned to his task.

*Am I out?*

The kobold returned and said, "'E can't take it off 'im right now . . ."

*Her. Can't you see she's a goblinette?*

". . . 'cause the resin 'as to set first. So 'e'll finish with that gobby, and as soon as 'e can, 'e'll take it off 'er and make sure it fits you."

Qod didn't know the first thing about leathersmithing. Leather was expensive, and any detailed leather work was beyond the reach of most. But what the kobold said seemed reasonable. The twin dragons on the cuirass chest had taken a while before they were firmly attached, after all.

Partially soothed, Qod just took in the scene. He had to admit that the improvements added more than he'd initially thought. The metallic thread was a step up without being gaudy. And it might not be just decoration. He suspected that it gave the leather just a bit more protective ability. With heavy iron armor out of the question, this might be bridging the gap between iron and the rough, untreated leather he'd been issued before that first battle.

Finally, Corporal Cyrena was finished, and he stood back to take a look, one hand stroking his massive chin. He motioned for the goblinette to turn, and she spun on one leg like a Hoar's Eve dancer.

Several of the onlookers hooted and clapped, and the goblinette beamed in pleasure.

Qod frowned for a moment before he relented.

*Let her enjoy it for a moment. It's not often that we get approval from the other races.*

The corporal called his assistants in, and they huddled together, occasionally pointing at her while they conferred. They pulled and poked at the leathers while still in discussion. They also looked back at Qod more than once as if picturing him in the gear.

Every ten minutes or so, the corporal kept poking at the filigree on the shoulders. With nothing going on, some of the crowd that had been hanging about started drifting off. Qod's belly growled, and he would have wandered off himself to find something to eat if he thought he could get away with it.

At last, the cordwainer seemed satisfied. He motioned to his three assistants, who started to unlace the cuirass, then beckoned Qod forward.

*Finally.*

Qod watched the late afternoon sun's rays glint off the filigree as he approached. It might not be tactically sound, but he had to admit it looked pretty cool.

"Let's get it off this gobby and onto you," the corporal said. "And hope the captain's satisfied."

Qod knew that last part wasn't aimed at him, and he could empathize with the cordwainer. He'd only been in uniform for five short days, but he already had the instinctive wariness that enlisted had around their officers. The less they dealt with them, the better.

The goblinette saw him approach, and he could see her demeanor change, like she was a sausage caught with her hands in the rat tail jar. She knew who he was and that she was wearing his leathers.

Qod smiled and gave her a nod to put her at ease—he knew she'd been shanghaied into being a modeling dummy.

Just as she smiled back, a satyr on the other side of her stepped up from the others and approached. No one paid him any attention, and for a moment, neither did Qod—until he glanced at the satyr's face.

It was fixed in determination, and Qod felt a chill.

"Hey!"

The assistants were unlashing the leg sleeves, and the goblinette was looking at him. The corporal didn't seem to notice anything.

Qod took two steps forward without realizing what he was doing when the satyr silently pulled a white dirk from under his cloak and raised it in a sweeping motion.

"No!" Qod shouted as he lunged forward.

The thin blade slashed down, catching the goblinette at the side of her neck before cutting through leather and opposite shoulder alike.

Blood sprayed out, catching Qod in the face, half-blinding him as the goblinette's head tumbled to the ground with a thud.

Two of the assistants struggled to hold her body upright, but the third, the one who'd been speaking with Qod, fell back, his hands clutching the slash in his belly. The blade had cut clean through the goblinette and hit the kobold.

Qod hadn't known something like that was even possible.

The satyr wheeled about and faced the stunned onlookers, the bloody blade raised high.

It was as if time froze for far too long. Qod attempted to wipe the blood from his eyes while his mind tried to make sense of what had just happened.

Then the satyr was in motion, as lithe as a yearling buck. A banshee stepped up to stop him, but the satyr cut the soldier down without pausing.

"Stop him!" rose from the crowd.

A gnome slashed at the satyr with his ax, but the nimble creature ducked under the slash while scoring on the gnome's thigh.

Anger replaced confusion in Qod, and he started chasing the satyr. He wasn't sure what he would do if he caught him, but he was acting on instinct.

The satyr was quick. Really quick. And as he reached the edge of the area, it looked like he might be able to blend into the camp and escape.

Until a huge form lumbered past Qod, covering the ground in giant strides. The satyr must have sensed it at the last moment, and he tried to dodge before the huge fist came down like a hammer of the Dark gods and crushed him.

The troll had too much momentum and ran half a dozen steps past the crumbled form of the satyr.

No, not crumbled. Crushed. The body was barely recognizable.

Qod skidded to a stop, joined almost immediately by more soldiers.

The satyr was a mess of blood and guts, but the blade was remarkably whole and unblemished. Qod instinctively reached down to pick it up—and immediately dropped it. His entire arm echoed with an intense ache.

"It's a **Dragon Tooth**," Corporal Cyrena, who'd come to a stop beside him, said. "Elf crystal, dwarf-made, mage-enchanted. We Dark folk can't touch them."

The troll returned and nudged the mess on the ground with a huge, hairy toe.

"I'm so sorry, Mage Killer," it said to himself in a low rumble. "I was too slow."

"It's not your fault," Qod said automatically.

Then he realized what the corporal had just said.

"If we can't touch it, then how did a satyr carry it?"

The corporal gave Qod a confused look.

"Satyr? That was a faun. An assassin."

The confusion hit him again, this time harder. A faun? This whole thing about satyrs and fauns was getting to be too much for him to fathom.

"But why?"

This time, there was pity in the cordwainer's voice.

"It came for you, Private Qod. You were the target."

## Chapter 14

"How did that Light-spawn faun get so far into camp?" the general fumed. "It could have hit the CP!"

Qod tried to back into the corner of the tent. So far, the general hadn't aimed any of his anger at him, and he wanted to keep it that way.

An ogre major was the current target of the general's ire, and the officer looked like he would rather be in the elf's notorious Ice Prison than here at the moment.

"He had on an authentic battle kit from the eighty-ninth, sir," the orc said.

"He was a Light-cursed faun, not a satyr," the general shouted so hard that spittle smacked the major on the forehead. "You're in charge of security here, and you can't tell the damn difference?"

Qod stared in awe at the glob of spit. It hung there like some obscene grub for a full twenty seconds before it started oozing down the officer's face. The head of CP security's hand twitched as if to wipe it off, but the ogre held his hand while the general ranted on. The spit reached his left eye, and the officer blinked several times, but all that seemed to do was spread it around, making it look like the orc had cataracts.

Arteries pulsed on the general's head while he screamed and paced. Qod didn't know how they hadn't burst under the pressure. Just as he was sure they were about to give out, the general stopped mid-rant. Somehow, the quiet seemed worse than the yelling.

The hapless major raised a hairless eyebrow with faint hope, hope that was crushed when the general asked, "Who is your second in command?"

"Ma . . . Captain Bane Ca," the ogre officer stumbled out.

"Well, let's see if Captain Ben Caw has more than the single brain cell you've shown me."

General Yare flicked his left hand, and two draugrs appeared at the major's side. The ogre's shoulders slumped, and without a word, turned to be escorted out of the CP.

None of the other officers showed any sign of sympathy for their former fellow staff member. A few showed nervousness or even fear, but more than half had a glint of what seemed to be satisfaction. The fear made sense. Qod didn't know what was going to happen to the former head of camp security, but he knew it wasn't going to be good, and any Dark soldier, officer, or conscript was subject to the whims of the general.

The satisfaction some of the others exhibited floored Qod, though. Were things that cutthroat at the top?

No one said a word, though, as they watched the general, who stood there without speaking for a long moment.

It was Captain k'Ree who finally broke the silence.

"General, about Private Qod?"

Qod's heart skipped a beat, and he shuffled his feet as all eyes locked onto him.

The general's gaze was the worst because Qod couldn't tell what was behind those vapid eyes.

Finally, the general turned to the kukudh major.

"What do you think, Pishlyss?"

"Making him a martyr could take care of a number of your problems."

This time, Qod's heart stopped still, and his eyes widened.

*You have to be dead to be a martyr.*

He mentally measured the distance to the door and wondered about his chances should he bolt. Slim to none, to be sure, but still . . .

The general gave an almost imperceptible nod, and Qod was about to take the chance when Captain k'Ree spoke up again.

"Or he could be a banner, a symbol of the danger the Light poses to all of the Dark races. That could rally the troops. Fill them with patriotic fervor."

The general seemed to consider her words. Qod watched him with bated breath, knowing that his very existence hung in the balance.

"The faebies will just send another assassin," the general said. "And another, and another."

"Give him a security team. Make it obvious, clear to both the troops and the Light spies."

When the general didn't respond, she added, "Elissia will know you prevented the attempt to kill the goblin. If you remove Private Qod now, she'll think she won."

The general's eyes hardened. "Fuck that bitch if she thinks she can just send some damn faun into our camp."

*Well, she did. And the faun almost succeeded.*

Qod wasn't going to point that out, though. If the thought of this Elissia "winning" pissed the general off, all the better.

He didn't know for sure who Elissia was, but he'd be willing to bet she was the opposing Light army commander.

The general grunted, then asked, "What would this team be?"

"I would suggest that a mixed-race team, so all of them have a buy-in."

The orc general glanced at Major Pishlyss, but to Qod's surprise, the officer gave the slightest of nods.

The general grunted, then said, "I've wasted enough time on this. Captain, you take care of it. Kud belongs to you from now on. And the rest of you, get back to work. We've got a battle to plan."

The staff shifted into motion while Qod let out a huge breath. He was safe, at least for the moment. And it looked like he'd actually have security, which was almost unfathomable.

Then a hand descended to painfully clamp on his shoulder.

"I can't believe I'm stuck with you," Captain k'Ree said. "Shut up and come with me. And by the Dark Mother, if you cause me any grief, you'll wish that faun had done his job.

# Chapter 15

"I heard you were creating a security team, small sir," Pani said as she limped up to him. "I should be part of it."

Her face was still swollen, and the bruise was turning a nasty shade of orange that clashed horribly with her normal lovely green, but aside from the limp, she seemed alert. Goblins were quick to heal, but this seemed too soon for her to be up and about.

"Are you OK?"

"Good enough."

He glanced over to the captain, who was arguing with Sergeant Lissif, who, in turn, had his face screwed up in defiance. Qod didn't know that was even possible—a sergeant arguing with an officer—and from the look on the captain's face, she was getting pretty angry.

"I said, I want to be in your security detail," Pani insisted.

"It's not up to me," Qod said. "The captain is putting it together."

"Can you tell her?"

He quailed. This didn't seem like a good time to ask k'Ree for any favors.

"Like I said, it's not up to—"

He stopped at her look of . . . *desperation*?

"The One-twenty-first has been disbanded, and they're folding the survivors into the Three-oh-sixth before we move out. They'll be the lead element in the assault," she told him.

"Assault? But we won."

"You don't know? The faebies are reforming at the Long Caldron, and the general wants to hit them before they can dig in or bring up reinforcements."

Qod spun around to stare at the CP. How did Pani know about this new push when he was right here in the shadow of the command, and he hadn't heard a word?

He didn't really think that winning one battle meant the end of the war. Of course, the Light would react. He just didn't expect it this soon.

"Are you sure about this?" he asked before he scanned the area.

There did seem to be a sense of purpose among the Dark troops around him.

"Yes, small sir."

Now he understood her concern. No matter that she was walking around, she was still wounded with only one fully functional arm. If she were in the lead unit for the entire Army of the Mist while so handicapped, her chances of survival were minimal. As a member of his security, she'd have a better chance of surviving until that old goblin resiliency was able to heal her back into fighting trim.

But that left a big problem. He didn't know what criteria Captain k'Ree was using to form this team, but chances were that a one-armed goblin wasn't going to make the cut.

The thing is, he realized he wanted Pani with him. He was being pushed back and forth like a chess piece, and he felt extremely alone. The few hours he'd spent with her and the other wounded had been the only time since he'd left Yellow Rock that he'd felt like he belonged.

Sergeant **Lissif** spun around and stalked off. Qod could feel Pani's eyes drill into him, waiting.

He made a small sigh, puffed up his chest, but then turned back to Pani.

"Um . . . can you turn to the left?"

"Turn?"

Qod reached over and turned her so that her arm and bruised face were out of the captain's line of sight. He stepped back, gave her a discerning eye, then adjusted her position a little more. It wasn't perfect, but if the captain wasn't looking closely, she might not notice that Pani was a walking wounded.

"Don't move."

He marched over to the captain, then faltered when she glared at him.

"What, Private?"

"Ma'am, uh . . . you said that you're . . . uh . . . a security team for when we . . . different people . . ."

"Spit it out, Private."

"If-it's-OK-with-you-not-that-I'm-telling-you-what-to-do-but-could-Private-**Mud-Geyser**-be-part-of-the-team?"

"Who is Private **Mud Geyser?**"

The captain had seen Pani before, of course, but Qod didn't think her village name had been used. And then there was the fact that others had a hard time telling goblins apart.

Qod pointed to where Pani was standing, a statue staring off into the distance.

"A goblin? I don't think we need another one of you."

"Sh . . . *He* already saved my life twice, ma'am. I would feel safe with *him*."

He held his breath, sure that the captain was going to see through him.

"Saved your life twice?"

Qod swallowed. Helping him out of the creek was hardly saving his life, but if she hadn't, would the stars have aligned just right, resulting in him killing the elf prince and still being among the living?

It was a stretch, to be sure, but goblins weren't noted for being wedded to the truth.

"Yes, ma'am."

She considered it for a moment before saying, "I guess that's one less I'd have to pull. Who's he with?"

"The Three-oh-six."

The captain grunted, and the corner of her mouth actually tilted up—barely, but it was an actual smile.

"And now you're saving his. I can appreciate that."

*So, it's true. We are going right back into battle.*

"I'll take care of it. And since we're on the subject . . ."

She turned and beckoned a kobold who'd been standing off to the side.

"Private Qod, this is Corporal Maoileanach. He's the NCO in charge of the team. You pay attention to him, do what he says, and you might actually make it back to Yellow Rock someday."

Despite just asking the captain for Pani to be part of the security, Qod was expecting to have more, well . . . *lethal* soldiers to protect him. Not draugrs, but orcs, maybe. Or ogres. Kobolds were larger than goblins—just about everyone except for pixies were—but not by much, and they were known more for their tool skills than fighting ability.

"You've got that goblin up there," the captain said as she pointed at the still frozen Pani, "and I'll round you up some more bodies before nightfall."

She strode off as kobold and goblin took stock of each other. The corporal's ear tufts were the silver of age, something rare among the junior ranks of the Dark military. His body reflected a hard life, but there was nothing hinting at weakness.

"So, you're the mage killer?"

"Yes, Corporal Mao . . . Mal—"

"Mac."

"Yes, uh, Mac. That's me."

"There must be more to you than meets the eye." He glanced up at Pani. "What's with 'er arm?"

The captain might not have caught Pani's injury, but that didn't slip past the kobold.

"Got hurt in the battle, Corporal. But goblins heal quickly."

"Mac," the kobold repeated. "You expecting to get yourself a little nookie?"

"What? No!"

Qod felt his face flush with both embarrassment and guilt. He hadn't outright fantasized about a romantic relationship with her. She was out of his league, for one. But still . . .

"Don't panic, Mage-killer. I'm dinnae gonna rat you out to the captain. But if she puts you in danger, or if she can't pull her weight tomorrow, I'll off 'er myself. You good with that?"

Qod's mouth dropped open, then closed again. There was no animosity in the kobold's tone, but there was also no doubt in Qod's mind that the corporal was serious. He'd kill Pani without hesitation if it came to that.

*Can I risk that?*

Pani was still standing there, and he could see how tense she was. Her good hand, the one nearest to them, was slowly clenching and unclenching.

If she was still incapacitated, then Qod might as well be signing her death warrant. But if she was still incapacitated, then leading the charge with the Three-oh-six would *certainly* be the last thing she'd do.

*It's not like the general is going to be sending me into the brunt of the battle. Right? She won't have to fight around me, and then she can heal up.*

That decided it.

"Yes, Mac. I'm good with that."

"You go get 'er, then, so I can see 'oo you and the captain stuck me with."

\*\*\*\*\*\*\*\*\*\*\*\*\*\*\*

"I'll be seeing about getting some chow," Mac said. "And, you're getting what you be getting and be thankful for it. No damn special meals, Nataly. No blood."

The vurdalack lowered her hand and scowled.

Qod thought it just as well. He'd never seen a vurdalak before. As far as he knew, they didn't even live on the continent but on the scattered islands in the far north. She had a passing resemblance to the draugrs, and in some ways, she seemed the most dangerous among the team, even more than Tulip.

Vurdalacks weren't the only blood drinkers among the races, of course, and Qod didn't want to judge, but the thought still gave him the willies.

"Lymon, keep everyone ' ere. Especially the package. 'E doesn't get out of your sight," Mac ordered.

The gremlin, who was a PFC and the second highest-ranking-member of the team, flipped a wrist in acknowledgment.

Qod didn't like being referred to as "the package," even if that was the case. He was the very reason the team had been formed.

But as he looked around at the others, he wondered just what kind of priority was being given to keeping him alive. To him, he felt it was more lip service than anything else.

A corporal was the team leader, and aside from the gremlin, everyone else, except for Dulce, was a private. There was Pani, of course, who was sitting beside him. She was exhausted, but she was putting up a strong face.

Standing about as far away as he could and still be part of the group was Yannis. The satyr was armed with a slender bow, and he'd assured Mac that he could use it.

That left Dulce and Tulip. Dulce was a pixie wizard, so she was not technically a soldier. Qod had been surprised and grateful to have a wizard on the team, but it was becoming obvious that her powers were limited, and her position was much like most other pixies he'd seen so far. In other words, she was a messenger.

He shifted his vision to Tulip, who was sitting on the other side of Pani and in deep conversation with her. The troll had to be fourteen feet tall and pushing eight hundred pounds. She was quiet and had barely said a word to him, but at least she had the size and strength to fight.

This was a mixed crew, to be sure, and one he thought had been selected primarily to give the races on the lower end of the social ladder some visibility. No orcs. No ogres.

Qod was not a huge fan of orcs—or ogres, for that matter—and his short time in uniform hadn't changed that. But he couldn't deny their martial prowess, and he would have felt more secure with an orc sergeant, like the late Hjami, in charge. Mac seemed competent enough, but a kobold was not a Black Smoke orc.

With Pani in conversation with Tulip, Qod didn't feel comfortable enough with any of the others to start a conversation. He sighed and stared out across the area where soldiers were a beehive of activity. The plan was for the entire army to move out shortly after dusk.

*For how many of them will this be their last night alive?*

Qod had survived two battles, and that gave him a pretty good idea of what was coming up. Even if they managed to surprise the Light army, even if they managed to carry the field, Dark soldiers were going to die. The Three-oh six, to which Pani had been slated to join, was going to be devastated.

It seemed like such a waste. If the thrice-damned elves would just be satisfied with what they had, the world would be a better place.

The only saving grace was that Qod wasn't going to be facing death again. He wasn't going to be charging the enemy, waving his little **dagger**.

There could be another assassin, of course, but now he had a team around him.

"Who's with Mac?" Lymon asked.

Qod turned around. The corporal had only left a few minutes ago to get food, and now it looked like he was returning with an orc but empty-handed. Qod's stomach growled in protest.

As they got closer, he could see the orc was a lieutenant.

"Gather up," Mac said. "This be Lieutenant Glascock. 'E's our new OIC. 'E's been looking for us all afternoon."

*An officer?*

Qod had just been wishing for an orc sergeant to lead the team, but a lieutenant seemed to be an unwelcome overkill. So far, his experiences with officers hadn't been the best. And as he took in the lieutenant, his "orcness" didn't fill him with confidence.

Orcs moved with a shifty grace, like rat grease on a skillet. This orc had an odd, halting impression, and his eyes lacked the assuredness orcs seemed to broadcast.

"Dae you want to address the team, sir?" Mac asked.

"Well, uh . . . which one is the mage killer?" he asked, his voice sounding uncertain as his eyes locked on Tulip, who shifted uncomfortably under the gaze.

*There're only two goblins here, and I'm the only one in the fancy leather armor. Who do you think?*

"Me, sir."

The lieutenant broke his lock on Tulip and shifted to Qod.

"You? OK. Well, uh . . . rest assured, Private, that we'll keep you safe for whatever the general wants. Yes. That we will."

He shifted his feet, then seemed to take stock of where they were.  Qod thought he was trying to lock the location in his mind.

"Now that I've located you, I need to, uh, get back to the CP, you know, to find out our orders for tomorrow.  We're taking it to the faeby assholes, you know."

Behind him and one step to the side, Mac rolled his eyes.

"Well, yes. I was told we have a pixie?"

Dulce rose from the ground ten feet away and hovered at eye level.

"Can you get a lock on me?"

"I can try, but since this is the first time I've met you, so it might not be a strong one."

"Good.  I'll need you to come get me before we move out," he said, seemingly not hearing that it might not work.

"Dinnae worry, sir.  We'll make sure you find us," Mac said.  "Now, as I told you, I need to get some chow?"

"Yes, yes.  Of course.  Always make sure the troops can fight, right?  So if you can point me back to the CP, I'll leave the team to you."

The CP was hard to miss, up the hill and only a hundred yards away.  If that was where the lieutenant was going to be, then why did he need Dulce to guide him back?  Qod's misgivings about the officer were growing.

"How did that one survive the culling?" Lymon asked Mac as the officer headed off.

Qod snorted.  Evidently, he wasn't the only one questioning the lieutenant's capabilities.

Orc litters could number as high as a dozen.  Soon after birth, the culling started, with the stronger, more focused killing off their weaker siblings, with one, two, or in some cases, three surviving into childhood.  Qod was more than happy that goblins didn't cull, but orcs took an almost religious pride in the practice, believing it was the reason for their racial primacy within the Dark races.

The lieutenant, at least at first glance, didn't seem to have that nasty streak that was necessary to survive the culling.

"'E's a Glascock," the corporal said with a sneer.

"Shouldn't make no difference," Lymon said.

Qod wasn't an expert on orc dynamics, but just like everyone else, he had heard of the Glascock clan. The empress herself was a Glascock.

"Right. And elves fart sunshine."

Mac looked around to see if anyone was listening in, and Qod diverted his gaze and took an interest in his claws.

"It's obvious 'e's been stashed with us to get 'im out of the way. So we make the best of it. And if 'e wants to spend 'is time at the CP, all the better. You get me?"

"Got it."

"Good." The corporal stretched, and his back made an audible crack. He then added, "Now, to get back to my task and try to rustle up some chow."

Qod quit the pretense of examining his claws as he watched the corporal head back up the hill. First with the general's comments about the empress, then with the disdain the other orcs had used when demeaning Sergeant Hjami as a banji, and now with what Mac had just said, it was getting obvious that orc politics were far more convoluted than he'd expected.

Orcs had very little impact on the folks of Yellow Rock. But Qod was now inextricably intertwined with the orc leadership, at least here in the army. If he was going to navigate these waters in hopes of actually getting back to Yellow Rock someday, he'd better learn more about the rapids he was rushing down.

## Chapter 16

"Snap your collar, Private. Remember, you're on display," Captain k'Ree hissed as she strode past Qod.

He sighed and fastened the clasp. He wasn't sure how he'd ever thought his new leather armor was comfortable. Maybe in comparison to his initial issue—and at least it fit. But it was getting heavier with every step, and where the last few weeks had been cold, today it was unseasonably warm. Too warm for a mountain goblin, especially one heavily clad in leather.

Qod glanced at the sun, which was already baking the ground, not two hours since it rose. Just like last time, the Dark army had been late in actually moving, and instead of hitting the Light forces before dawn, this would be a daylight battle. At least the sun would be in the invaders' eyes, which would give the Dark races an advantage.

His helmet was acting like a small oven, baking his bald skull, and sweat ran in rivulets down his brow. He wiped a leather-clad forearm across his face, which didn't do much good.

"This sucks dwarf ass," he muttered just as Pani grunted.

He immediately felt guilty for feeling sorry for himself. He might be hot and tired, but she was suffering. Goblins might heal quickly, but there were limits.

"Are you OK?" he asked.

"I'll make it," she said in a weak voice. "I have to. The lieutenant's been watching me."

Qod immediately started to swing toward the officer when she stopped him. "Don't look now. But he's been staring at me."

He nonchalantly swept his gaze around. They were surrounded by the Three-oh-six, who'd seemed pretty pleased when they realized the Mage Killer was among them. Tulip was to his right, lumbering along with three-yard-long strides. Yannis, his bow at the half ready and arrow notched, was leading the group. Lymon was on his left, Dulce was flitting over them, and the rest were following.

Qod let his gaze pass over the lieutenant. Pani was right. The orc seemed particularly intent on watching her. A slight frown, which revealed his incisors, was not a good sign.

*But what can he do? We're almost there.*

He hadn't seen it with his own eyes, but there were rumors that orcs sometimes killed their wounded, but even if that was true, it didn't make sense in this situation.

*Right?*

No one ever knew with orcs, though, and Qod really didn't want to find out the answer to that.

"If you need a break, tell me," he whispered to Pani. "I'll figure out something."

"I'll make it, small sir."

He didn't have to do anything, though, as less than a minute later, the mass of soldiers came to a halt. Soldiers from the 306th immediately flopped down and took off their helmets before the NCOs went crazy, screaming at the soldiers to face outboard, weapons at the ready.

There was some movement in reaction, but it really didn't do much good. The battalion was more of a mob than a well-trained force.

*Which is why they're the sacrificial lambs*, Qod noted with sadness.

Three days ago, that was him, and most of the others in his company were now dead.

Captain k'Ree came striding back down the column and stopped to say something to Lieutenant Glascock before moving on.

"Why are we stopped?" Qod asked Mac.

The kobold nodded ahead. "The faebies be just over that rise."

Qod followed with his eyes. The ground sloped up for another half mile before it got steeper to the top. He knew that the Light forces occupied the valley on the other side. He just hadn't been paying attention to the terrain.

His heart started racing with the knowledge that the Light was so near. He might be considered a hero by so many, but he knew how close he'd come to dying during the last battle, and he was under no illusions that the Light couldn't succeed in killing him this time.

And despite being told he wouldn't be in the heart of the fight, he was pretty darn close to the front of the army. Even the Black Smokes were behind them.

But as he watched, things were shifting. Dark units were beginning to spread out to either side of the 306th. The Army of the Mist was moving into its assault formation.

The plan was simple. The Light army had ceded the high ground and occupied a rock formation on the valley floor. With a lake on the other side, they were effectively trapped, which would seem to put them at a huge disadvantage. But to reach them, the Dark army would have to cross relatively open wetlands. In typical Dark fashion, the command was relying on waves of soldiers to cross the wetlands, absorbing the Light's fire, which would allow the more seasoned orc and ogre troops to close with, dig out, and destroy what was left of the Light soldiers.

Qod thought the plan was reasonable on a strategic level, even if it would come at a cost, but he refused to accept it as a done deal. The Light were tricky bastards, as they'd shown in the last battle. And if it weren't for the lucky course of events that turned the battle, it would be the Dark survivors who were preparing for a last stand.

From what he could tell, Qod's cautious pessimism was the exception rather than the rule. The general mood among the Dark forces was high. The Light army had been routed with huge casualties. One more push, and the invading army would be gone from Dark lands, an outcome that had been all too rare lately. The Light might respond with another campaign, but for the moment, there would be peace in the Fanciful Highlands.

And possibly—just possibly—Qod and the rest could go home and forget about the fighting.

The Dark army might have won the last battle, but it had been decimated as well, losing thousands of dead and wounded. There were still more than 7,000 soldiers, though, and even with NCOs haranguing and pushing, that took a long time to crowd into position. So long that the sun crossed its zenith. Now, the sun would be in the Dark force's eyes.

That wasn't a dealbreaker, but it would make the Dark army's task that much harder, and more soldiers would pay the price.

The delay had one benefit, though. The rest was doing Pani a world of good. Her breathing settled down, and her skin regained a healthier shade of green.

Finally, ram horns sounded and signal flags unfurled along the massive line of the army. Soldiers stirred into motion and started to advance. The final battle for the Long Caldron had begun.

## Chapter 17

"Hold up," the lieutenant said as the 306<sup>th</sup> started forward. A few of the soldiers of the replacement company looked back and seemed disappointed, but most of them had their eyes locked forward as they marched.

Guilt battled relief within Qod. On the one hand, he felt that he owed it to the soldiers to go into the fight with them. On the other hand, though, he was glad that they were hanging back, and not by his choice.

More troops passed them, including several platoons of Black Smokes, who were chomping at the bit. They lived with one purpose—to kill the Light. If this battle went their way, there might not be any more killing in the **Fanciful Highlands** for the foreseeable future, and they didn't want to miss out on the fun.

Surrounded by shouting soldiers, Qod could feel the strength of the force, and despite his earlier misgivings, he started to feel more confident. How could the Light stand up to the righteous fury of the Dark?

Another pixie flew up to the lieutenant and whispered in his ear before taking off.

"That's us," the lieutenant said. "We're to follow the command group."

"You 'eard 'im," Mac said. "They'll be coming up on the left, so Tulip, make a hole for us."

The troll nodded, then started crabbing through the mass of soldiers. Qod stuck right on her heels. Without the big body running interference, he didn't think he could have managed it.

Tulip had no problem pushing through the mass of common soldiers, but even she had to stop for the line of a dozen draugrs marching lockstep. She might mass nearly as much as all of them combined, but their focused lethality would make anyone hesitate.

The command group followed the draugrs, a gaggle of officers and staff with pixies buzzing around like flies on shit. Qod immediately banished the analogy—or tried to—replacing it with "wolves on an elk." He still didn't know if wizards could read minds, and he didn't want his **imagery** reported to the general, who was just now coming into view astride a magnificent ox.

Dark folk generally didn't ride beasts, but Qod had to admit that it was an impressive **picture**. Following General Yare, also on an ox, were the other general and a colonel Qod had seen in the CP.

He watched the slow progression for a moment, then shifted his gaze to the ridgeline ahead of them, which was essentially a gap in the surrounding high ground. Over that ridge was the enemy, soldiers who would love nothing better than to bag a flag officer. Qod had assumed that the general wouldn't actually join the fighting, but the command group didn't seem to be slowing down.

Something else about what he was watching seemed wrong, though, and it took him a moment to figure out what was bothering him.

"Corporal Mac."

"Yeah?"

"Should both generals be that close to each other?"

"What do you mean?"

"Well, if the elves have another battle mage, then they could take out both generals at the same time. Shouldn't one of them be, like, somewhere else so we can fight on if that happens?"

The corporal snorted so hard that something flew out of his nose and whizzed past Qod's shoulder.

"First thing," he said, then lowered his voice to just above a whisper, "Our fearless leader don't care what 'appens to us if 'e get's zapped. And likely 'e wants to keep an eye on General Tillmus, so 'e keeps 'im close, you know."

Qod frowned as he realized what Mac was saying. They were about to head into battle. Orc politics and leadership struggles had no place here and now.

"Second, 'e ain't going into battle. 'E's gonna be far from the killing and dying. So, dinnae you worry none about your own skin."

Qod had been worried about losing the chain of command, and he started to protest that he hadn't been thinking about his own safety.

But right then, Mac pointed and said, "See?"

The line of draugrs came to a stop just over the crest, orders were shouted, and the massive command group started to slow down and spread out.

The rest of the army split around the command to continue its advance, and a company of kobolds sprang into action, erecting tents quicker than Qod would have thought possible.

The general tried to dismount, but the ox had other ideas and kept moving forward despite a few orcs and ogres trying to stop it.

He could have just jumped, Qod thought. Instead, the general glared at his officers, waiting for them to do something.

"Tulip, stop that thing," Mac said, but just as the ox started down the other side, a draugr stepped forward and sank his axe into the beast's neck.

The animal collapsed, and the general slid off as if that was the normal way to dismount and shouted for his staff. Qod was impressed with the orc's aplomb.

The flow of soldiers continued unabated while the support team buzzed with activity. It was only then that Qod noticed what looked like a platoon of Black Smokes taking security positions around the command group. A few looked wistfully at their brothers and sisters as the rest of the elite force kept advancing to meet the enemy.

"They seem upset," Qod told Pani.

"I understand them. They're missing out on history, small sir."

"Do you want to keep going?" Qod asked in surprise. "Be part of history?"

She'd been the one who'd wanted to be in his security detail, after all, instead of the 306th.

"I'm a goblin, not an orc," she said as if that hadn't needed to be asked.

With the Black Smoke platoon and the draugrs setting up security, the footprint of the command group became evident.

"Where dae you want us, Lieutenant?" Mac asked.

The junior officer looked around for several moments, and Qod thought he was going to go ask someone else, but then his expression firmed. "We're fine here. Just move forward so we can see what's going on."

"You 'eard 'im," the corporal said. "Right up there next to those Smokes."

The small group edged ahead, right to the crest of the rise. The entire battlefield opened up below them.

Qod wasn't great with distances—he'd never left Yellow Rock before this, so it hadn't been important. Still, he thought the narrow oval-shaped bowl had to be five miles across before surrounding mountains soared into even higher jagged peaks. The ridgeline they were on curved around to the right, getting steeper the farther away it was, until it was a sheer cliff. Directly below them, the descent into the bowl was more gradual and not as steep. A growing number of Dark soldiers were marching down the approach. The farther away, though, the rougher the terrain. Boulders were scattered across the bottom lands, probably knocked free from the adjacent high ground by seasons of frost and sun.

This wasn't some pastoral valley with a serene river running through. It looked as if some giant god had slashed the rough terrain with a claw and gouged it out.

All of that was secondary, though, and Qod locked onto the lone hill on the far side. It looked like an afterthought, rising as it did from the floor of the basin. Goblins have excellent eyesight, and even at that distance, Qod had no problem seeing the Light army arrayed in defensive belts laddering up the slope. There were a lot of them, but not as many as he'd expected. He thought that there were already more Dark soldiers descending into the bowl with more still on the march.

At the very top of the hill, a huge flag fluttered in the light breeze, a single gold figure standing next to it.

"Is that the Elf general?" he asked Mac.

"Where?"

"On top of the hill.  In gold.  Next to the flag."

The kobold squinted his eyes for a moment before saying, "I see the general's flag but no gold.  But probably, yeah.  Elves are big on appearances and all, so that's where she'd be waiting for us."

He paused a moment before adding, "Elves dinnae take to failure, so she's probably making this 'er last stand."

Qod grunted.  Scuttlebut was that losing elf generals were killed.  Killed in battle or executed—he didn't care.  They deserved it for invading Dark lands.

"Why do you think it's a last stand, though?  They've got the high ground."

He remembered the fauns on the hilltop in the last battle and the devastation they unleashed with their bows."

"There's no retreat, Qod," Tulip said from beside him.

Qod jumped.  For such a large person, Tulip could move in relative silence when she wanted to.

"What do you mean?"

"Where can they go?  They're trapped.  Their only hope is to beat back our advances."

Qod studied the terrain.  The slope behind the hill looked formidable.  The sides of the valley were also much higher and steeper than they were right here.  Still, he didn't think they were insurmountable.

"Can't they climb out?"

Yannis patted his bow.  "That's where we come in.  We'll pick them off like rats in a silo."

It was only then that he noticed the companies of satyr bowmen passing by and into the valley.  Maybe he'd heard wrong, but he thought the archers would take the high ground along what was left of the intermediate ridgeline above the hill and provide plunging arrow fire onto the enemy.

He glanced to the right to the high ground above the basin.  None of the Dark units were moving to occupy the area.  The entire force was entering the valley.

Once again, the image of the fauns decimating the **goblin company** force during his first battle captured his mind.

"Did we, uh . . . did we check all that high ground? For the enemy, I mean."

The lieutenant chuckled, joined by Mac.

"Don't worry about that, Private," the officer said. "Scouts overflew it while we approached. It's clear."

Qod frowned. None of this made sense. The Light force, or what was left of it, had a defensible position, true. But now that Mac and Tulip had pointed it out, it was a trap for them. They *had* to hold out against a much larger foe. So, unless the corporal was right and this was some sort of last stand thing designed to eliminate as many Dark soldiers as possible before falling, then this was a lousy battlefield for the Light. Why would the Light commander choose it?

*Forget it. You were reading cozy mysteries at home a week ago. What makes you think you're some sort of military genius now?*

The stream of advancing soldiers was relentless for ten or fifteen minutes, but the Dark army had suffered significant losses in the previous battles, and the supply petered out. Still, there had to be six thousand soldiers with the 306th, only now reaching the basin floor.

Facing what looked from this vantage to be only three or possibly four hundred Light soldiers. Qod pushed aside his misgivings. Even if there were another few hundred hiding on the other side of their hill, that still meant the Dark had a ten-to-one advantage. The 306th was being sent into the meat grinder to absorb the Light's first blows, but the final outcome seemed to be pretty much set.

The CP was finished, complete with a raised platform for the general and his principal staff to observe the fight, and they began to take their positions.

The dead ox was gone—Qod hadn't seen them move it, and the kobolds who had erected the camp started to form up to join the fight. On the other side of the CP, a small platoon of harpies was milling about, stretching their wings. Qod had only seen a few harpies in his life, and this was the most he'd seen gathered in any one spot. They jostled each other like so many crows until four suddenly took to the air. Two flew along the high ground to the right, and two flew to the left.

Qod felt a bit of relief as he watched them fly. Evidently, the general wasn't completely trusting what the scouts had reported.

"Now we wait," Corporal Mac said as the army started to snake its way in a long column to the hill.

"That's going to take a while," Lymon said, the first words the gremlin had uttered since they stepped off that morning.

Seeing how long it took the army to do anything, Qod had to agree. The column still had to cross the length of the basin, then shift into their battle formation as they moved into Light weapons range. Where that was exactly depended on what the Light had. The general feeling was that they didn't have siege weapons, and their battle mage was dead, so it was going to be arrows and light wizardry, but the Light had surprised them before, so Qod was expecting anything.

He took a couple of steps toward Pani. "Are you still OK?"

"I'm fine," she snapped.

She gave Qod a sidewise glance and, in a quieter, softer voice, said, "If I hadn't been hurt, I would have gone with the Three-oh-sixth."

"No one's doubting your courage," Qod said. "You're not at full-strength yet."

She didn't look like she believed him.

The eight members of the team stood in silence for a couple of minutes before the lieutenant said, "I'd better check with the CP," and hurried off.

Lymon and Mac exchanged glances, but no one said anything. The politics of Dark high society were so alien to Qod that he might as well try to understand the dead ox, so he didn't give the lieutenant a second thought.

Instead, he asked Dulce, "You never told me why you are here."

"To fight the Dark, just like you."

"But you aren't in the army. You're a civilian."

She shrugged her tiny shoulders.

"Most wizards are. Civilians, I mean."

That was news to Qod.  Pani, too, if her expression was any indication.

"Why?' he asked.

"Unless you're very powerful, there's something about being a soldier that makes it harder to cast spells.  No one knows why, so most of us wear the purple and do our thing outside of the formal organization."

That made no sense to Qod, and he wondered if there was something more to it.

"During the last battle, there was a gremlin wizard who got killed."

"Wonto," she said.

"I didn't get his name. Was he a civilian?"

"He was wearing the purple," she said, which Qod decided to take as a yes.

She didn't seem to want to go further into the subject, but their conversation opened up the others.  For the first time since the team was formed, they started chatting among themselves as the Dark host continued its advance.  Qod learned more about his security team over the next thirty minutes than he had over the previous two days.

Nataly surprised him. He'd been wary of the blood-drinking vurdalak. But she was turning out to be the friendliest and *funniest* of the team.  Deadly and funny seemed a strange combination, but he warmed to her.

Her tale describing her first walrus hunt had the rest laughing so hard that the Black Smoke soldiers on security duty glared their displeasure at them. None of them cared, nor did they quiet down, which seemed to upset the orcs even more.

Qod was already close to Pani, but what had been a loose group of soldiers and a wizard was beginning to gel into a real team.  Along with the day with the other wounded small folk, this was the second time since he'd been conscripted that he felt like part of something larger than just him.

*Maybe this soldiering isn't all that bad.*

Qod reached into the cleverly designed pocket in his cuirass, pulled out a rat crack Pani had scrounged, and absentmindedly started nibbling on it.  He felt more than saw someone staring at him and turned to see Nataly looking at him in obvious disgust. He held up his hand, offering her a bite, and she visibly shuddered in disgust. Qod smiled and turned back to the battlefield below when a flash of light lit the enemy hill. His heart dropped as a ball of fire arched out toward the 306th.

"They've got wizards," Qod said.

"No shit. You only killed the battle mage, not every damn **spellcaster**," Mac said. "No offense, Dulce."

"None taken."

The fireball seemed to fly in slow motion, but it was quickly obvious that it would fall short. It landed in a burst of sparks a good two or three hundred yards from the nearest Light soldiers and quickly fizzled out.

"Just a premature ejaculation," Nataly said, earning a huge elbow in her ribs from Tulip.

The fireball might not have been much to see, but it had a major effect. The army's orders were to deploy into their assault formation upon receiving fire. Evidently, that didn't mean *effective* fire.

Immediately, the 306th halted in place, and the follow-on unit essentially ran up their butts. Six thousand soldiers had a lot of momentum, and they couldn't turn on a pinhead. Adding to the fact was that those in the middle and rear of the column started speeding up as if they were afraid of being left behind. The result was more of a cluster than of a precise military maneuver.

"I keep telling the brass that we need to rehearse these movements, but dae they listen to a twenty-three-year vet? No," Mac said.

Qod slowly turned to the corporal. He knew the kobold had been around for a while, but twenty-three years? And he was just a corporal? Qod wanted to get to the bottom of that after the battle.

One more fireball flew out, but if anything, it impacted even shorter of the 306th. The Dark army had not yet demonstrated to Qod the ability to move quickly, but goaded by the urgency of the coming battle, the mass of soldiers started to achieve some semblance of order. They were still packed closely together, but the Black Smokes started to shift into position while battle cries reached those on the ridge. The Dark soldiers were ready—Qod just hoped they would wait until everyone was in position before starting the assault and not let their battle fever take over and attack the hill piecemeal.

The army was slowly spreading out into their assault formation, but with those in the back rushing forward, the core mass kept getting larger—and denser. The faun attack on the goblins during his first battle had made a big impact on Qod, and any arrow fired into the Dark army was going to find a target.

"Yannis, can their fauns reach the army?" Qod asked.

"Those with a kyna bow might be able to. A longbow? Too far," the satyr said.

"Do they have that kee . . . kyna bow?"

"There should be some. Centaurs are partial to them."

*So why aren't they firing?*

Qod stared at the hill, waiting for the arrows to reach out and start taking a toll, all while mentally urging the army to start their assault.

It wasn't arrows, though, that changed the course of the battle. A giant clap reverberated across the basin, and the air above the high ground to the right shimmered.

"What the—" Qod started when his mind froze.

One moment, the high ground was empty, the two recon harpies making slow circles above. The next, it was filled with soldiers. Light soldiers.

There were shouts of alarm from the command group, followed by the same rising from the army below.

Dulce rose ten feet into the air and stared, while Mac muttered, "Dwarf shit."

"What happened?" Qod asked.

"Cloaking spell. Powerful. It had to be almost mage level," Dulce said. "Or a meld."

The harpies wheeled about and tried to gain altitude. Too late. Arrows hungrily reached up, and the harpies tumbled to the ground.

Qod didn't think that the Light archers could reach the entire army from their position, but they could reach the right flank, and the slope was too steep for the soldiers to make an effective charge uphill. Dark soldiers were going to die.

And then the Light plan was revealed. The boulders that littered the area around the ridgeline started to roll over . . . and down the slope, faster and faster as gravity took over. Most hit other boulders and started them down as well.

This was the real Light plan, Qod realized, and once again, the Dark army had stumbled into a trap.

The soldiers down below realized it as well. They tried to run, but the bodies were packed too tightly. The first boulders hit with devastating effect, flattening orcs, ogres, and small folk alike. Not even the trolls could stand up to that.

Qod tore his eyes away from the carnage, and that's when he saw the dwarves, centaurs, and others moving to still more boulders which had been staged and ready. This attack wasn't over.

He spun around, but to his surprise, while the command group was pointing and shouting, no one was doing anything. Without a conscious decision, Qod bolted.

"Small sir!" Pani shouted, but he ignored her.

The Black Smokes on this side of the CP were staring in horror at what was happening, but they remained in place, and that infuriated Qod. He charged them, spotted a lieutenant, and rushed up to yank on the orc's arm.

"You've got to attack them," he shouted, waving his other arm to point toward the enemy. "Go!"

"We can't," the lieutenant said guiltily.

"Why in the **dwarf king's ass not**?" Qod screamed. "Our soldiers are getting killed!"

The lieutenant pulled back, and seemingly forgetting that he was an officer and Qod was a private, whined, "This is our post. We can't abandon it."

"The hell you can't!"

"No . . . I . . ." he spun away from Qod and looked to the CP.

"Lieutenant?" an orc sergeant who was close enough to have heard Qod asked.

For a moment, Qod thought the lieutenant was going to give the order to attack. He was a Black Smoke, after all, the best that orcdom had to offer.

But after a moment, he shook his head. "We've got our orders, Sergeant Uuginni. We stay here until the captain says differently."

The anger that had been building up in Qod broke like a tsunami. He pulled his dagger, and the lieutenant recoiled a step. Qod might be a quarter his size, but he was the Mage Killer.

Qod had already dismissed the orc, though. He spun on his heels and started charging back to his team, who were staring at him with a what-the-hell-is-he-doing-look on their faces.

"Dulce! Can you get their attention?" he shouted as he approached.

"Yes. Probably. Why?"

"Just do it," he ordered as he ran past them. "Let them know the Mage Killer is coming!"

Part of his mind was going, "Whaaaaaat?" as it tried to will his legs to stop, but something had taken over him. In a short week, Qod had found his tribe. He'd become part of something much bigger than him. Than Yellow Rock. Than even goblinhood. And he wasn't going to stand by while his brothers and sisters were slaughtered.

He had no idea what one small goblin could do, but he had to try.

"Stop, Qod!" Mac shouted. "Private Qod, you stop your ass!"

He ignored the corporal and focused on the enemy. They gave him no attention at all, and the first vestiges of sanity started to force their way into his foremind. He started huffing—his leather cuirass might be lighter than the first one he had, but it was still heavy. Feet pounded behind him, and that goaded him faster. He was not going to let the corporal stop him, not until he . . .

*Until I what?*

Qod didn't know exactly what he was going to do. He couldn't take on a couple of hundred Light soldiers.

There was another flash in the sky, and Qod instinctively ducked, but he wasn't under attack. An image formed in front and above him—ghostly and ten yards high, it formed into a . . . goblin waving a flaming sword. Words in elven script formed. Qod knew enough elvish to spell out the sounds, but he was behind the words, and it took him a moment to make them out.

*MAGE KILLER*

*Rat tails, Dulce. I didn't know you could do that.*

He laughed. Cackled, more like it. He probably wasn't going to survive the next few minutes, but if he was leaving this mortal plane, he was going out in style.

"Qod!" Tulip shouted as she lumbered up.

"I'm not going back—"

"Behind me," she said as she thundered past, her club raised high.

Between the floating image and the troll, the enemy finally took notice. The nearest team of dwarves stopped leveraging yet another boulder over the ridge, pointed in awe, and scrambled for their weapons.

It wasn't just the Light soldiers. From down below, the shouts of fear and anger shifted to something more like a cheer.

The rest of the team reached him.

"You're crazy, gobby!" Mac shouted as he ran past, a war hammer in one hand.

Like a wave coursing the shore, more and more of the Light soldiers realized what was happening. What they should have done was to let the nearest of them take up a position against what was just a handful of Dark soldiers, even if one of them was a troll, while the rest continued with the rock barrage. What happened instead was that well more than half left their assignment to face the Dark Mage Killer.

Dulce's wizardry was paying dividends. And if this disruption in the Light attack allowed more soldiers to get out of the way of the boulders, then whatever happened up here was worth it.

Two fauns stepped up and launched arrows. Tulip batted one to the ground, and the other passed over Qod's head and landed behind him somewhere—being small could be an advantage. If he were an orc, that might have taken him in the throat.

The faun archers paid the price, though. One took an arrow in the shoulder, and Yannis gave a little shout of victory. The second fell back behind a line of five brownies, an arrow half-nocked.

A centaur stepped up to face them. Centaurs were the largest of the Light folk, so it made sense they were helping push the boulders. Yannis had said that the centaurs used the bigger bows, but this one was armed with a club almost as large as Tulip's. And the centaur's attention was locked onto the charging troll.

That didn't escape her, and she bellowed out her own challenge and adjusted course to meet him.

The centaur galloped into its own charge, club raised high. A centaur was shorter than a troll, but longer from chest to tail, and they massed about the same. The two behemoths collided in a crash that made Qod wince. Tulip staggered to the right, and Qod's heart stopped until she regained her balance. A flap of skin was hanging from her shoulder.

The centaur was down hard, his equine back broken. His obscenely human arms weakly tried to push himself up, but it was hopeless.

Tulip let out a victory roar just as the team caught up to her, and together they charged across the last hundred meters to the lead enemy.

At the same moment, the Mage Killer apparition started to swoop down at them. More than half of the soldiers broke and ran, and hope sprang eternal. But that still left upwards of a hundred facing them.

"Stick with me," Nataly said.

Qod wasn't going to argue.

With his initial rage cooling, he was realizing what he'd gotten himself into, and the knowledge that he wasn't the fierce Mage Killer but a rather small, untrained goblin was slamming home. If he was going to survive even the first thirty seconds, then it was going to be because of his team.

Tulip hit first, a massive sweep of her club taking out three brownies. Then the rest hit. Nataly was death in motion, moving quicker than Qod thought possible, he tried to follow her, his dagger awkwardly held out in front of him as he looked for a target.

He had no idea how . . . *chaotic*, fighting would be. He'd seen fighting from a distance, and he'd had this standoff with the battle mage, but that was nothing like this. It was almost too hard to take in. He had kaleidoscopic glimpses of what was happening, but nothing as a whole.

Tulip let out a bellow as two arrows slammed into her. She wheeled, and one foot knocked Qod in the back, slamming him into the ground. He lay there stunned for a moment. A gnome darted forward with a long spear, but she wasn't looking at him. She wanted Tulip. As she rushed to thrust her spear, Qod swung his dagger through her foot and into the ground.

The gnome screeched in pain, twisted to face him, and tried to stick him with her spear. But he was too close, and with her foot pinned, she couldn't step back. The shaft smacked him on the head.

The gnome shifted the shaft back further, but before she could use it again, her head flew off.

"I said stick with me," Nataly shouted as she finished the follow-through and spun to face the next Light soldier.

The pressure was collapsing the team. Lymon was down, and Tulip was bleeding freely from a dozen wounds. Pani was ashen-faced with the effort, but her face was locked in determination.

They'd given Qod that extra thirty seconds, but he could see where this was going. Hopefully, it was enough for the Dark army to maneuver out of the killing field.

Mac and Yannis maneuvered apart for a moment, creating a small gap, one that a dwarf took advantage of. He darted through, axe raised, and Qod knew he was the target.

"Mage Killer, my ass!" the dwarf shouted when an arrow went through his shoulder from above and deep into his chest. He went to his knees and started gurgling.

But Yannis was down to his sword. Qod looked up to a wonderful sight. A platoon of harpies was plunging in from on high, their short recurve bows deadly at this range.

The enemy saw them too, and the pressure immediately lightened as they shifted to face the death from above.

The harpies swooped in, striking from above. Nets were thrown in their paths, and several were entangled. Deadly from above, they were weak fighters on the ground, and those were quickly dispatched.

The gurgling from the dwarf stopped, and Qod dropped his eyes from the sky just in time to jump back. The axe missed him by an inch. The follow-through took the dwarf to the ground.

"I'll kill you, demon spawn," the dwarf hissed, spitting blood with every word as he struggled to get back up.

Qod jumped forward without conscious thought. The tip of his dagger caught the dwarf right above the collar of his armor. He was shocked at how easily it pierced the Dwarf's neck.

The enemy gave one last shudder before he collapsed. Qod pulled back his blood-covered hand, leaving his knife in place. He stared at the hand for a moment in shock before Nataly yanked him to his feet.

"Damn it! I can't protect you if you don't stick by me."

"I . . . I will."

He looked around to where the fighting was in full swing. Dwarves, brownies, and gnomes were locked in battle with . . . orcs?

It took him a moment to realize that the Black Smokes had arrived. He recognized the lieutenant he'd yelled at. The orc was a demon, crushing those facing him. The Black Smokes were pushing the enemy back.

Not just Black Smokes. There were officers from the command group, too. He saw an ogre colonel fighting until he took a dwarf ax in the chest.

Even General Yare, surrounded by his draugr guard, was in the midst of the fighting. Qod caught several glimpses of him as he battled the Light.

A familiar figure was cutting a swath through the enemy. Captain k'Ree was almost beautiful to see as she danced her ballet of death. He watched her for a moment before she moved out of his sight.

His team tightened their little defensive circle around him, facing outboard. Lymon was dead, and Dulce was wavering on her feet. Tulip, Mac, and Yannis were wounded, but still combat-effective. Pani looked like she was going to collapse.

Through Tulip's legs, Qod could see the rest of the Dark soldiers coming, and even if those would outnumber them, he felt a sense of accomplishment. His team—and the command group—had bought the army time. They could withdraw and regroup. Qod counted that as a win.

Shouts of "Mage Killer!" rolled over the group, and Qod twisted to see. Orcs—regular, not Black Smokes—were cresting the ridge from below. And then kobolds, even goblins. More and more poured into the fight. Hundreds. A thousand.

And they wanted blood. With Dulce's apparition still hanging in the air, they shouted "Mage Killer" as they rushed the enemy.

The general tried to control the group, shouting at them to follow him, but the army was beyond control. They slammed into the Light soldiers.

It was too much. The Light had a good plan, and they probably expected an easy victory. The way it had fallen apart was just too much for them. With the mass of bloodthirsty Dark fighters descending on them, they broke and ran with the Dark chasing.

There were pockets of fighting, but the battle had been decided. Lieutenant Glascock, his uniform sleeve slashed and his sword caked with dwarf blood, finally found them.

"We've got to get Private Qod out of here," he said with a wild look in his eyes. "General's orders."

"I think we're fine 'ere, sir," Mac said. "Seeing as the Lights be on the run."

"Oh, yeah. I guess so. Wow. Some fight. Uh . . . is everyone OK?"

"Lymon's dead," Mac said.

'Oh," was all he said.

The lieutenant's eyes started to return to normal. He sheathed his sword without wiping off the blood, then looked around until he spotted the gremlin's body.

"That's too bad. He was, uh . . . a good soldier, I guess."

"What about Dulce?" Qod asked. "She's unconscious."

Corporal Mac stepped over to the prone pixie and knelt beside her body.

"Let it go," he whispered as he cradled her head. "Come on back."

She didn't move.

"Let it go. You did good."

Her eyebrow twitched, and Qod felt a little rush of hope.

"You can dae it," Mac said in a quiet, soothing voice.

Dulce groaned, and above Qod, the apparition started to fade.

The wizard's eyes opened, but they took a moment to focus on Mac's face.

"I'm alive, and I'm looking at your ugly face," she said. "Does that mean we actually did it?"

"You bet your tiny **pixie** ass we did," Mac said. "We won."

## Chapter 18

Qod watched somberly as Lymon's body was laid out with the other dead. He'd only known the gremlin for a couple of days, but he was part of their team. He felt like he'd lost a brother for the second time.

The Dark might have won the battle, but it was a Pyrrhic victory at best. The Light trap had been defeated, but at a cost of over a thousand Dark soldiers. The fact that it could have been worse—almost *certainly* would have been worse had not half of the Light soldiers stopped rolling boulders, which allowed the Dark soldiers to charge up the slope—didn't do much to assuage Qod's sense of loss.

He seemed to be an outlier of sorts, though. Most of the army was in a celebratory mood. Word was circulating that 2,000 minions of the Light had been killed. Qod had a hard time believing that. From what he could see, there hadn't been that many in the battle in the first place, and the bulk of them had retreated once their plan had been stymied. If he were a betting goblin—and he'd been known to wager a gildr or two— he'd say there were about 200 Light bodies strewn around the high ground.

Down on the hill in the basin, there were more Light bodies, but not that many. After the onslaught of boulders, some of the Dark army had continued with the planned attack, but the coordination had been disrupted, and most of the enemy had managed to withdraw and climb to safety. The elf general—if that had even been her in the golden armor—was one of those who got away.

Qod was beginning to suspect that the entire Light disposition had been a ruse. It had never been the last stand that the command staff had said it was. It was merely a delaying tactic designed to attrit the Dark army while the Light army reorganized and resupplied itself. And if that was true, then what did that say about the Dark leadership?

He stared down the ridgeline to the CP, which was now a hub of activity. The elf general's flag had been captured and presented to General Yare, who had placed it on the ground and invited the cheering soldiers to walk on it. The general, to his credit, had been a force in the fighting, personally accounting for several Light deaths. But was it a general's job to wield a sword? Qod wasn't so sure. Wouldn't it have been better to have more accurate intel and make better decisions so as not to walk into the trap in the first place?

"Why so serious?" Corporal Mac asked him. "We won."

"At what cost?"

The kobold sniffed, then ran a forearm across his face, smearing the dust and grime there.

"There's always death in a battle. It comes with the territory. You just gotta accept that you're alive and move forward. 'Sides, a lot more woulda been killed without you going charging like some crazed 'uman."

The corporal was right. Soldiers had been killed, but the fight wasn't over. Too many Light soldiers had escaped, and now, after two defeats, they'd be even more determined to extract revenge.

"What now?" he asked.

"We sit 'ere and wait for the lieutenant," Mac said hooking his thumb back to the CP.

Qod scowled. Mac had told them that this was their leader's first actual taste of combat. For someone who seemed what could be generously called "less than capable," he'd acquitted himself well. He'd regaled the team with his two one-on-one fights with the enemy in great detail, and he was holding his slashed upper arm as a badge of honor.

His excitement had been too much, though, and he'd told Mac to take over while he rushed to the CP "for orders."

"He's probably over there dancing on the flag," Qod said.

"Give 'im a break, Private. First blood can pump up the adrenaline." He paused a moment and gave Qod a close look. "You're beat. Sit for a while."

Qod nodded, and as he stepped away, the corporal said, "You did good for an undersized gobby, Mage Killer or not."

"Thanks," Qod said, and a small blossom of warmth bloomed in his chest.

He started toward Pani, who was sitting with her legs spread and her head down between her knees. Qod decided to let her rest, so he diverted to where Dulce was sitting in the shade of a small rock, her eyes closed. She was awake, though. Every few moments, she raised a small flask and took a sip of whatever was inside.

"Are you OK?" he asked as he sat beside her.

"No."

Alarm blasted away the satisfaction Mac had raised in him. "Should I get a **hooded spirit?**"

The healers had already started to arrive and were plying their craft.

"They can't do anything for me. Only time will."

"Time?"

The pixie opened her eyes and turned to him.

"I need time. I depleted **my aether** down to the bare bones."

"I don't . . . what do you mean?"

She gave him a critical look and asked, "Just what do you know about magic?"

He shrugged. "Not a lot. Just that you wizards can, uh, do things."

That even sounded dumb to him the moment he said it.

Dulce gave a tiny chuckle. "Yeah, magic can 'do things.' Lots of things. Make pretty lights. Create an image of a Mage Killer. Blow through the ranks of orcs. But all of that takes power. Lots of it. We call that aether. And I used up all I had. So no hooded spirit can help. Only time. Time and this," she said, hoisting the flask.

"What is that? Booze?"

She chuckled again. "Booze is the enemy of wizardry. This is infused pear nectar."

Qod let that sink in. He'd never thought about magic much. Other than the little spells that could be bought, there wasn't much in the way of wizardware in Yellow Rock. No wizards or mages, that was for sure. But since wizardry was part of warfare, he realized he needed to know more about it.

He knew that Dulce just wanted to rest, but his curiosity was piqued, and he wanted information.

"The elf battle mage could kill with balls of light. You made an image that floated in the air. During my second battle, the gremlin wizard ashed arrows that were shot at us."

"So?"

"Well, how many types of magic are there?"

"Types? One, of course."

Qod wrinkled his brows together. That didn't seem right.

"No. The battle mage, he killed soldiers. What you did, that was just an image. I don't mean 'just,'" he hurriedly corrected. "That put the fear into the faeby bastards and made them turn to us."

"It's all the same. Just a matter of power."

"That doesn't make any sense. How can what a wizard does be the same as what a battle mage does?"

Dulce sighed.

"Look, if I said I wanted to punch you in the face, would you let me?"

Qod looked at her tiny arms. "Um . . . well, if you really wanted to, I guess so."

"What if Tulip asked you the same thing?"

He gave the troll a quick glance. She was sitting stoically while a hooded spirit was removing one of the arrows from her massive arm.

"No! She'd kill me if she did that."

"Yet both are still a punch in the face. The only difference is in the power of the delivery."

Qod wasn't convinced.

"Magic is a natural force. A battle mage is skilled in manipulating it and has the power to maximize its effect. A wizard had either less ability to bend it to their will or less power behind the manipulation."

"What about you?"

There was a long pause, and Qod thought he'd trodden on her toes and she wasn't going to answer.

But finally, she said, "I **understand aether** far better than most. I just don't have the strength to do much more than what you saw today, and holding it that long was almost the death of me."

Jonathan P. Brazee

"Death? You don't mean that literally, do you?"

But this time, Dulce did ignore him. She closed her eyes and leaned her head back in an obvious dismissal.

Qod stared at her in shock. The Mage Killer image had been vital in interrupting the Dark soldiers. But he had no idea that keeping it going almost killed her. He shook his head. There really was a lot more he had to learn.

He probably should start with Corporal Mac, but before he could ask, the corporal shouted, "On your feet. Brass inbound."

Qod twisted around. The activity at the CP hadn't slackened, but now, five draugrs abreast were marching toward them, followed by General Yare, Major Pishlyss, Captain k'Ree, and Lieutenant Glascock.

"About time," Nataly said. "We did turn the battle, after all."

Tulip helped Pani up to stand on unsteady feet as the seven faced the approaching party.

"I guess the general got tired of the lieutenant bragging on 'imself," Mac whispered out of the side of his mouth. "'E dinnae look too 'appy."

It was true, Qod noted. Their team leader had lost the post-battle excitement he had when he left them.

The draugrs stopped a couple of yards from them and left a gap that the general stepped through to stand in front of them.

"You created the floating image?" he asked Dulce.

"Yes, sir."

The general grunted before he swung to face Qod while bending slightly at the waist as if trying to come down to goblin eye level.

"I've been informed that you were the one who started the assault on the Dark position."

Uh . . . kind of, sir. This was a team effort. Everyone did their duty to save the soldiers below."

"But you were the first to move."

"Well, yes, sir."

The general was silent for a long moment before he straightened and said with a voice as sharp as ice, "And in

138

doing so, you almost ruined my plan. Luckily, I was there to minimize your damage and turn disaster into victory."

Qod heard the words, but his mind couldn't understand what the orc was saying. The next words were crystal clear, though.

"Arrest those two," the general told the draugrs. "They are charged with treason."

## Chapter 19

"Don't worry. We'll get this sorted out," Qod told Dulce, who was perched on his shoulder while clinging to his neck.

She was still too exhausted to fly, and she didn't want one of the draugrs to carry her.

"You've got more confidence than I have."

"He just doesn't realize what happened."

That's what he thought must be going on, at least. Once the general was brought up to speed, this would all be forgotten.

Things had almost gone to hell, though. As the draugrs moved in to take Qod and Dulce, the rest of the team stepped forward to oppose them. It had taken fierce pleading from Qod and the lieutenant for them to stand down.

Ahead of them, a mass of jeering soldiers was crowded around the viewing platform the general had built so he could watch the battle. With the draugrs shoulder to shoulder in front of him, Qod couldn't see, at first, what had their attention. But as they got closer, he got a glimpse of a fairy being restrained by two ogres. One of the prisoner's wings was obviously broken, and he glared evil malice at the Dark soldiers.

Despite the seriousness of his and Dulce's own situation, Qod winced. The fairy—who was easily twice as large as any other Qod had seen—was being held up as red meat to the crowd, which somehow didn't seem right. But maybe it didn't matter in the long run. His time was probably limited. Once a prisoner was sucked dry of information, they were usually dispatched. This was true with both sides.

With the general leading, the group started crabbing behind the mob, and it struck Qod.

*He's using the fairy to pull attention away from us.*

That pissed him off, and he was tempted to shout to the soldiers, but his rational self stepped forward just in time. Whatever was going to happen to the two of them, it wasn't a good idea to anger the general even more.

Qod didn't have to shout, though. Just before they slipped into the CP, someone shouted, "Mage Killer!"

It took a moment before the rest to spot him, but the chant of "Mage Killer, Mage Killer" reverberated into the very rocks themselves. The mob abandoned the fairy and surged to surround them.

The draugrs stepped up to the general, and there was a flash of pure hatred from the orc's eyes before he controlled it and changed to a forced smile. He raised a hand and waved, all the while attempting to keep moving forward. It was like trying to swim upstream as the chanting soldiers tried to move closer.

A pixie flew between a draugr's legs and up to Qod. She hesitated a moment upon seeing Dulce on his shoulder, but then she swooped in and placed a kiss on Qod's cheek before darting away.

The draugrs shifted from protection mode to clearing and began to force the soldiers to either side.

Major Pishlyss stepped up to Qod and put a fatherly-looking hand on his free shoulder—but with an iron grip.

"Keep moving," he hissed through grinning lips.

Qod didn't resist. He still thought this was all a mistake, one the general would correct. He couldn't help waving back at the soldiers, though, and a moment later, Dulce joined in.

It took a few minutes, but they finally reached the entrance to the tent. The draugrs pulled aside while the general, Major Pishlyss, and Captain k'Ree led the two into the empty conference room.

Outside, the chants of "Mage Killer" continued, even if deadened somewhat inside the CP.

The moment the flap closed, General Yare wheeled so suddenly on him that Qod jumped back, causing Dulce to clutch at his neck.

"Just what the hell possessed you?" he asked with a snarl.

Qod's mouth gaped open. He had no idea what the general was asking.

"Sir?" he finally asked, his voice quavering.

Jonathan P. Brazee

"Sir?" the general parroted in a falsetto.

He grabbed Qod by the collar of his cuirass and yanked him within inches of his face. Fetid orc breath washed over Qod.

"You abandoned your post without orders. That's punishable by death in a war zone."

"I . . . no, sir. I mean, I didn't run away. I saw the enemy, and I thought I . . . I mean, we . . . uh, had to do something to disrupt—"

"Oh, you thought? Who are you? The second coming of General Kantus?"

"No, sir. But it worked. The enemy stopped—"

The general jerked Qod so hard his neck snapped back, and Dulce was thrown to the ground.

He gave an inarticulate roar before asking, "Did you know that your little adventure almost ruined my plan? That because of your screw-up, I had to personally step in to rescue the operation?"

*What is he talking about?*

"I had the faeby bastards lured into my trap, but you revealed the trap before we had all of them inside it."

The spark inside Qod wanted to say, "You had no trap. You walked us into *their* trap!" but self-preservation kept his mouth closed.

The general suddenly let go of Qod, who stumbled back. "You almost cost us the battle, and you would have if I hadn't taken over."

The general had fought and fought well, Qod had to admit, but he hadn't "taken over" anything. By the time he had arrived, the fighting was a melee down at the individual level.

"What you did was treason, and there's only one punishment for that," he said in a suddenly calm voice.

His hand drifted to the blade at his belt, and he glanced at the major.

The kukudh raised his whip-thin eyebrows and tilted his head to the walls of the CP, through which the chants of "Mage Killer" could still be heard.

142

Qod froze, his eyes locked on the general, whose mouth was clenched so hard in anger that one of his protruding fangs pierced his cheek. No one moved for a very long moment until the orc drew a hook-tipped blade.

Qod's heart skipped a beat, and he took a step back, but the general wasn't looking at him. Instead, the orc stepped forward to stand over Dulce, who was still on the ground.

"And you! Why didn't you just create giant arrows telling them where we were?"

The pixie gave a soft little mewl of fear.

The general shook his head and raised the knife.

"I gave her the order, sir!" Qod screamed as he rushed to grab the general's arm. "It was my fault!"

The general shook Qod off like an annoying fly.

"Sir. The Concord!" Captain k'Ree said in a flat monotone.

Qod didn't think that would have any effect, but the general froze in place for way too long.

Finally, he lowered his arm.

"I will be reporting your treachery to the Wizard's Guild. Let them deal with you," he said, obviously forcing each word past protesting lips.

"Get that thing out of here," he told the major. "You, too, Captain."

Captain k'Ree hesitated.

"Do you have something else to say, *Captain*?"

She shook her head. "No, sir."

"Then get out."

Qod was slowly backing away, but when the major, who was holding Dulce like a sausage's toy, and the captain started to leave, he tried to follow.

"Not you," the general barked.

Qod winced and froze.

The moment the flap closed again, the general slowly turned to Qod. There was anger in his eyes. Anger and something else. Pleasure?

The orc reached out and placed the tip of his knife under Qod's chin and raised it. Qod could either lift his head or be pierced.

He raised it to stare at the general's face, sure that was the last thing he was going to see in his short, miserable life.

"I don't know what your game is, gobby."

Qod didn't respond.

"If what witnesses say is true, you somehow killed a battle mage.  I still don't know how you managed that.  But then you try to give victory to the enemy by disrupting my plan."

Qod's vision seemed to tunnel down to the general's mouth.

"You say you aren't working for the empress, but do I believe that?  Maybe yes, maybe no.  Maybe you are a loyal gobby, or maybe you're an agent for the Light.  The safest thing for me to do is to kill you now and be done with it."

Qod gulped, and the knife bit in a little more.

The general turned to the tent wall.  The chants were not as strong, but they were still there.

"*They* believe you.  The small folk. Maybe I can still use you for now."

His voice suddenly hardened, and he pushed a little harder with the blade. "But listen to me, gobby. I'm watching you.  You cross me, you make as much as one step out of line, and all the small folk in the world won't save you. Major Pissy Face won't save you.  I'll gut you like the rat you are.  I promise you that.  Do you understand me?"

"Yes, sir," Qod squeaked.

The general's eyes bored into Qod's.  All Qod saw was hatred in them.

With a quick motion, the orc snapped the blade away and wheeled around.

"You're on borrowed time, gobby," he said as he pushed through the flap.

Qod stood in silence for a moment before he slowly sank to his knees.

Blood dripped down onto the copper dragons on his chest.

# Chapter 20

The mood was festive outside the CP. The elf general's banner had been hoisted over the platform, and a steady stream of soldiers was drawn to it. They elbowed each other to get close enough to spit on it.

Barrels of mead appeared as if by magic and cracked open. Racial lines evaporated as the celebration grew. An orc major with a goblin astride his shoulders stumbled into Qod. The major grabbed his arms, then swung him around like a doll before letting go and moving on into the crush.

That wasn't the only odd pairing. All around, goblins and gremlins were riding orcs and ogres like battle steeds.

A small part of him wondered if the celebration was a big mistake. A large number of Light soldiers had escaped, after all, and the main body might be just over the next mountain. A drunk army would be easy pickings.

But even that couldn't get a rise out of him. He was emotionally numb. He barely acknowledged the congratulations of those who recognized him. After the Black Smoke lieutenant from the CP security tried to hoist Qod to his shoulders, Qod squirmed away and took off his cuirass.

He wasn't sure just how things had changed. Or why. One moment, he was proud of what he and his team had done. The next, the general was accusing him of treason.

Now more than ever, he wished he were back in his little home in Yellow Rock, his nose buried in a book, a cup of warm nettle tea in his hand. The wider world was just too confusing for him to understand.

More soldiers were climbing out of the basin to join the party, and it took Qod ten minutes to finally reach a relatively open area. He stopped to catch his breath and looked out over the scene of the fight in the highlands.

Not everyone was at the CP celebrating. Soldiers and hooded spirits were tending to the wounded. A team of five trolls was collecting the Light dead and tipping them down the slope, where they rolled and slid out of sight. A human had already arrived, scurrying in from whatever hole it had been hiding in to start scavenging.

The first time Qod had seen one do that, he'd been both angry and disgusted. Now, he didn't even care.

"Help?" a voice weakly called out.

Qod looked around. Everyone near him was dead, and his heart gave a flutter.

"Uh . . . hello?"

"Help me, please."

Qod knew that ghosts wouldn't ask him for help. *Right?*

But all he could see near him were dead. The orc at his feet would never need water again—his body had been hacked in two.

He carefully stepped over the orc's guts and asked, "Where are you?"

The slightest motion caught his eye, the flick of a filthy hand.

He took a step closer. The hand was connected to a gremlin lying on her back, eyes closed. None of her skin was visible. The dirt that caked her had been turned to mud with the blood. Both of her legs were gone at the knee.

The wounded in the immediate area had been gathered, but the gremlin must have been mistaken—understandably so—for one of the dead, beyond help.

Qod's stomach churned, but he hurried over to her and knelt. His leg brushed against the gremlin, and she opened her eyes, impossibly amber staring out from her mud-encrusted face.

"Can you help me?" she asked, barely above a whisper.

Qod tried not to blanch as he ran his eyes down her body. It wasn't just her missing legs. A chunk of her left side had been sliced away. He could see ribs, and some of her organs had spilled out onto the ground.

He was at a loss as to what he could do for her. She needed a hooded spirit. He spotted one about forty or fifty yards away.

"I'm going to get you a healer," he said.

He started to stand when the gremlin shot out a hand and locked it onto his wrist with surprising strength.

"Stay," she croaked.

"But you need a healer," he told her as he tried to avoid looking at the void where her legs used to be.

"Stay. Please."

With a sigh, he knelt again and took her hand in his. Not knowing what else to do, he softly sang "The Bright Star," a standard goblin lullaby.

Qod didn't know exactly when she died. He quit singing and stared at her for a long moment.

*I don't even know her name.*

He replaced the hand on her chest and stood. A group of wounded had been gathered a hundred yards down the ridgeline, where they were waiting for their turn with a hooded spirit.

The dead sure didn't need him, and he was too small to help gather the bodies. He might be more useful over there. He made his way over to the healer.

"Can I help?" he asked.

The healer pointed a skeletal hand to a cask on a small cart.
"Water."

This was something he *could* do, and he ran to the cask. He pulled the lid and dipped in his flask to refill it, then returned to start down the line of the wounded.

The first was a kobold who was propped up in a sitting position. Qod couldn't see any obvious wounds. The soldier dully watched his approach. Qod uncorked his flask, cupped the back of the soldier's neck, and held the flask to his lips. The kobold took a small sip, or rather tried to. Immediately, his body was wracked with spasms.

"Easy, sir," Qod said.

He tried again, and he managed two swallows before the spasms returned.

"Do you have any more water, gobby?" the ogre lying next to the kobold asked.

"Yes. Yes."

He gave the kobold one last look, then let the ogre drink. And the next two orcs. Then a goblin who kept thanking him. Two times, three times, he had to go back and refill his flask.

Each soldier he helped, each kind word of encouragement he made, gave him a tiny sense of calm, of worth.

And that's where his team found him an hour later.

"Small sir? Are you OK?"

Qod stared at Pani, then the rest. He grunted and returned to his task.

"Here," he told an ogre who had a rag tied across his eyes.

He placed his flask in the ogre's hands and let him drink.

"Thank you," the ogre said after drinking, then, "Am I blind? Can you heal me?"

"I'm just a goblin, sir. But the healer's coming."

Mac pulled Qod away from the ogre.

"What did the general say? What's gonna happen?"

Qod shook his head and said, "I've got work to do here," and stepped to the next wounded soldier.

The team watched silently for a moment until one by one, they moved in alongside him to help.

# Chapter 21

Tulip and Pani gave Qod a suspicious look before breaking into peals of laughter.

"What's so funny?"

"Oh, nothing, nothing," Pani insisted, and both laughed even harder.

Tulip rolled onto her back with so much force that he felt the ground vibrate.

Qod frowned. Sometimes he didn't understand those two. He looked to Corporal Mac for help, but the kobold just rolled his eyes.

The last day had been different, to say the least. After helping with the wounded well into the night while most of the army got shitfaced, the team had collapsed in exhaustion until daybreak.

Dulce had briefed them on what had transpired up until the time she was kicked out, but Qod had kept tight-lipped on what the general had told him. He spent the day continually looking over his shoulder, worried that the draugrs would appear to whisk him away. The general had already shown a propensity to change his mind on a whim, and the comment about it just being easier to eliminate him was cemented into Qod's thoughts.

The further the day progressed, though, the more confident he became that nothing was going to happen, at least today. He was able to relax just a bit more and engage with his teammates.

Even with the **Goof** twins making comments about him behind his back.

He wasn't really upset with them. Both, but Pani in particular, had been particularly protective of him all day. A steady stream of soldiers had tried to approach him, but Tulip's looming stance had been enough to deter most of them. There wasn't much she could do about officers, though, and more than a few had come to offer observations or congratulations.

One had been the Black Smoke lieutenant who had nervously tried to explain why he hadn't acted when Qod first asked him to. Qod had felt decidedly uncomfortable about that. He was a private, after all, and the Black Smoke was an officer.

Qod took a bite out of his pampam roll and closed his eyes in bliss. He might not like the attention—and he worried about how the general would take it—but he couldn't complain when one of the cooks had shyly presented the team with a pack of the tallow-ladened treats. Mac said they were filched from the officer's mess and that maybe they should return them. That lasted all of three seconds before they all snatched a handful of rolls and sat down to eat them.

The twins stopped laughing, and Tulip sat up. She looked longingly at his last two rolls. Each of the team had grabbed five of them, but the troll was a big, big girl, and five didn't do much for her.

Qod, on the other hand, was full after only three. And as he looked around, his final two were the only ones left.

He made a show of preparing to eat another, though, and Tulip's eyes dropped.

"Oh, go ahead," he said, unwilling to tease her anymore.

She snatched his last two before he could change his mind.

Corporal Mac walked over and sat down beside him.

"Nice, that. Taking care of your troops."

"You guys aren't my troops, Corporal. I'm just the package."

The kobold snorted. "You *were* the package." He was silent for a few moments, then asked, "Are you doin' OK now? It's been a pretty stressful twenty-four hours."

Qod knew Mac wasn't referring to the battle itself.

"To be honest, I don't know. The general . . ."

He let that train of thought die.

"Why doesn't he like me?" he asked instead. "What have I done to him?"

This time, the corporal laughed out loud, and when Qod frowned, he said, "Sorry. I'm not laughing at you."

*Except you are.*

"It's not what you've daen, it's what you *might* dae."

"Me? What I might do?"

Mac nodded. "That's right."

"Give me a break. Like he's afraid I might challenge him for the command? That's really going to happen. General Qod," he said.

"You can't challenge him. You're not an officer."

Qod had zero-point-zero desire to challenge the orc general. He wasn't a fool. But the statement surprised him.

"I can't?"

"Of course, not. Haven't you ever wondered why there are no troll officers?"

Qod shifted his gaze to Tulip, whose head was leaned into Pani's as they chatted. He hadn't wondered, to be honest. But no matter how powerful the general was, a troll was more so. If what Mac was saying was true, then by not commissioning a troll, the system was almost certainly assuring that a commanding general was always an orc or ogre.

He shook his head.

"So, the great fearless Private Qod of Yellow Rock can't challenge the general. What is he afraid I might do, then?"

The corporal shook his head. "Sometimes, I forget 'ow much of a boot you are." He sighed, then pointed to the vast camp that had risen from the celebrations of the night before.

"Over there somewhere is the Three-oh-sixth."

"And?"

The unit, which had been expected to be wiped out in the first wave of the attack, had actually fared quite well. The Light forces on the rear had waited until the bulk of the Dark army was in the path of their boulders, so the 306th was past the main killing zone. And being in the fore of the army, they had farther to run to join the fighting in the high ground.

So, it was reasonable that most of the soldiers had survived and were with the bivouac.

"Do you know what they call themselves now?"

Qod shook his head while he wondered where this was going.

"The Broken Spears."

Qod frowned. Some of them were survivors of the 121st Replacement Company, and since Qod had been a member when the battle mage had stuck himself on Qod's spear, there might be a tenuous connection.

"Oh."

Qod hadn't known that the fact his spear had been broken was known, but it was obvious now that the word had circulated.

"That's right. They're claiming you as one of them. They're also saying they're your personal troops."

Now it became clearer. If the general heard about it, then it wasn't just him trying to avoid blame for getting caught in the Light trap and taking credit for fighting their way out of it.

The military—Light or Dark—existed on a strict hierarchical structure with an iron-clad chain of command. A unit, even a unit of untrained small folk, could create a stress point that a general didn't want.

"I'm not part of that," Qod said.

"And if I was a smart little gobby who wanted to get back to Yellow Rock someday with his skin intact, I'd keep it that way," Mac said.

Qod nodded his head. He fully intended to do so.

Still, a blossom of warm pride filled his chest that anyone would really care about him.

# Chapter 22

Qod might have intended to steer clear of the 306th, but the 306th had other ideas.

The same goblin cook who'd brought the pampam rolls had returned before sundown, this time with a pot of scorpion stew large enough that even Tulip had enough.

The six gorged themselves, then lay back around a campfire. The horrors of the last battle were lost in the darkness, and for a brief slice of time, they could be ignored as if they'd never happened.

Yannis let out a loud burp before saying, "You're a big beast of a girl, Tulip. I saw you crush dwarf heads yesterday."

"I'm a soldier."

"Yeah, and a good 'un. But as such a beast, who in their right mind named you 'Tulip'?"

All eyes shifted to the troll. Qod had wondered the same thing himself. The last thing he was reminded of when he saw the powerful being was a flower.

He thought she might pass on the question, but without hesitation, she said, "I did."

"You named yourself?" Mac asked.

"Of course. We all do."

"Why?"

"Who else? No one knows a person better than themselves."

"You don't know yourself when you're a sausage. Uh . . . a child, I mean," Qod said.

Tulip shrugged. "And so we remain nameless until we decide."

That elicited a small uproar of protest from the others that she ignored. Instead, she threw a log onto the fire, which sent a burst of sparks up into the darkness.

"Why 'Tulip,' then?" Yannis asked.

"I like them. I grow them. What else would be more meaningful?"

"Food. Sex. Killing elves," Nataly said.

Tulip ignored the comment and continued, "A tulip is the very manifestation of perfection. I believe any flower is an analogy to the journey all of us make. All seeds are the same, but the potential is there. With the right environment and nurturing, that seed can grow to a bud."

Just like people," Pani said. "We need nurturing, too."

The troll turned her gaze to her and said, "Without it, we will shrivel on barren ground. But love and care will take us only so far. A bud is merely what a flower *can* be. All of the parts are there. Each individual must make the decision to blossom and reveal the beauty inside all of us."

Qod stared at her. People often assumed trolls were on the stupid side, given their slow tempo of talking. He'd been around Tulip long enough to know she was far from dumb, but still, this huge troll, who'd crushed Light skulls with abandon, raised flowers and could come up with an observation like that?

"I like the name," Pani said. "It fits you."

"My name means 'Gift of the Gods,'" Yannis suddenly offered.

"Oh, you're a gift all right," Mac said to the laughter of the others.

But before anyone else could chime in, a shape silently entered the ring of firelight.

The soldiers immediately jumped to their feet.

"Private Qod. Leave your leathers and come with me," Captain k'Ree ordered.

"Ma'am?" Qod asked, his voice cracking as a tsunami of potential reasons he was being summoned swept over him.

The others closed in on him, like yaks protecting their young from wolves.

"Now," she ordered in a calm but steel voice.

"Does the lieutenant know about this, ma'am?" Mac asked.

"He does."

The corporal exchanged looks with the others and then said, "We'll be going along with Private Qod, if that's OK."

"No, that's not OK, Corporal. Private Qod, and he alone, will come with me."

Nataly muttered something that not even Qod, with his goblin hearing, could make out, but the tone was clear. Tulip took half a step forward.

The captain didn't flinch.

Qod was sure that even if the team kept the captain from taking him, things would go wrong. They couldn't take on the entire army, and assaulting an officer was one of the most serious offenses a soldier could commit.

No matter what was going to happen to him, he couldn't let them be at risk. Before he could second-guess himself, he pushed past Pani and dropped his leathers as he marched up to the captain.

"Let's go, ma'am."

Her eyes narrowed as he approached. She had to have seen the team get ready to resist, and for all Qod knew about the military, that might be enough to warrant action. If it was, though, she ignored them. Instead, she spun on her heels and stalked off into the darkness toward the lights of the campfires. Qod hurried to catch up.

She was walking quickly, and with his short legs, Qod was almost running.

He was getting out of breath, and finally, he had to ask, "Can you please slow down?"

The captain turned around and stared at him for a second. She didn't respond, but when she started off again, it was at a more reasonable pace.

Not having to focus on just breathing, Qod could wonder what was happening. Emboldened by the captain actually slowing down when he asked, he decided to push his luck.

"Are we going to the general, ma'am?"

"No."

That gave him a moment of relief until he realized she could be delivering him right to the draugrs. The fact that he had no armor was worrisome, not that his leathers would even make a draugr pause.

He screwed up his courage once more and asked, "Please, ma'am. Can you tell me where we're going?"

"Not here. Wait."

They walked in silence, and a few moments later, they were at the outskirts of the bivouac, making their way between campfires. None of the soldiers around them gave the two a second glance as they passed by. They were headed toward the CP, and despite the captain's assurances, Qod was getting nervous until she entered a tent. Qod hesitated a moment before he followed her in.

The tent was empty—no furniture and no one else. A single small lantern hung from the center pole.

She turned to him and said, "Listen up, Private. The Three-oh-six—"

"The Broken Spears," Qod automatically interrupted.

Her eyes narrowed for a moment, and Qod winced while mentally scolding himself.

"Yes, that's what they're calling themselves."

"I don't have anything to do with that," he blurted.

"Yet you know of them."

"Word, uh, gets around, ma'am."

She studied him for a long moment before continuing.

"As I was saying, the Three-oh-six, along with a small number of others, has expressed a loyalty to you. That's a problem."

Qod didn't say a word. He didn't want to get himself into more trouble with his runaway mouth. Instead, he just nodded.

"The army cannot have two generals. I know you understand that."

She waited in a pregnant silence. Qod knew she was expecting something, but he wasn't sure what.

Finally, he said, "I am not a general, ma'am. I am just a private."

She rolled her eyes. "You are hardly *just* a private. And that's where the general has himself a conundrum. He knows now that eliminating you might cause more problems than it solves."

The matter-of-factly way she said "eliminating you" made him gulp.

"And simply breaking up the Three-oh-six and ordering them to rescind their sworn loyalty to you might further exacerbate his little problem with the small folk. So, to get around this, he wants you to renounce the Three-oh-six. Reject their vow."

*That's all?*

"Of course, ma'am. I renounce them."

"Not to me, Private. What good would that do? Just wait."

Outside, the sounds of a bivouac reached them. Laughter, shouting, the murmur of soldiers who knew they might not ever make it home again. Inside the tent, neither spoke, isolated from the life out there.

Finally, more to break the uncomfortable silence than anything else, Qod asked, "Is it true that only an officer can challenge for the command?"

She raised a single eyebrow, and he could tell that the question surprised her. Somehow, that pleased him.

"Don't tell me you want to challenge General Yare?"

"Oh, no, ma'am. Never, ma'am. I was just . . . I mean, I heard that, and I was, you know, curious. I'd never challenge him."

"Well, I'm sure he'll be relieved, but yes, only an officer or a member of royalty—you're not some royal goblin, are you?"

He wasn't sure if she was being serious or not with the question, so he treated it like she was.

"No, ma'am. Not me."

"Well, then, the general's safe from you, right?"

This time, the sarcasm was clear. He shut his mouth and turned away.

It was probably close to twenty minutes before the flap opened and a satyr captain entered. He stopped for a moment to let his eyes adjust, then looked from the captain to Qod and back to the captain.

"Is that him?"

"That's Private Qod."

Qod couldn't help but to frown. Sure, he wasn't wearing his leathers, and sure, most races had a hard time telling goblins apart, but in his pride, he thought he should be recognized.

"Not what I expected," the satyr said.

"He can be surprising."

"And you're the general's shadow," the satyr said.

"Captain k'Ree."

"Captain Kritikos. Three-oh-six. But you know that, I'm sure."

"And you know why I'm here."

"I can guess." He gave Qod a longer, more intense examination. "I don't see how he killed the battle mage."

"He did."

Qod didn't like the way he was being ignored by the satyr as if he wasn't there, but he was also fine with letting Captain k'Ree take this.

"Whether he did or didn't, my troops think he did. They also think he was the one who broke the ambush, and that's why we're still alive to talk about it."

He gave k'Ree a questioning look as if he wanted her to confirm or deny it. She remained stone-faced, but that was evidently enough for him.

"So it is, true, by the Dark Mother."

K'Ree just stood there.

"And let me guess. The general wants the Three-oh-six to disavow their, uh, patronage of the gobby."

Captain k'Ree nodded.

"That's easier said than done. You know the small folk. Especially the ones in the company. A week ago, they were farmers and craftsmen. They don't have a military background. And they think that this gobby saved their lives, which is evidently true. Saved my life, too, I might add."

For the first time, he addressed Qod. "Thank you for that, Private."

Then he continued. "I don't think you telling me to tell them is going to have much effect."

"It's Private Qod who will do the talking. Did you bring them?" When the satyr nodded, she said, "Get them in here."

The satyr captain stepped back to the flap, opened it, and ordered someone inside. A few moments later, five soldiers entered and blinked their eyes. The senior was an orc

sergeant. The rest—a kobold, two gremlins, and a goblin—
were privates.

Qod understood what was happening now. If he was
supposed to address the mass of the entire company, things
could go sideways quickly as emotions fed on emotions. With
only a small group, the two captains could control the
situation and have them report back to the others.

"Soldiers," Captain k'Ree said, "This is Private Qod
Yellow Rock, who you call the Mage Killer."

The soldiers' eyes got wide, and Qod could see their
excitement—except for the kobold.

"With all due respect, Captain, 'ow do we know 'he's the
Mage Killer?"

"That's him, Frydle," the goblin said.

He seemed to take the goblin's statement as fact.

"In that case, sir, I gotta thank you." He dropped to a
knee. "My family thanks you."

"Stand up, Frydle," the sergeant ordered.

"I think Private Yellow Rock has something to say to
you," Captain k'Ree said. Then, "Private?"

Qod probably should have rehearsed something, but it
was too late now. He cleared his throat.

"Well, uh. I'm honored for all your support, but it's like
this. I mean, we've got the general—"

"Who's a dumbass orc dick," the goblin muttered under
her breath, probably too quietly for anyone other than Qod to
hear.

Or maybe not. The gremlin next to her fought back a
smile.

"What I mean is we have a general. And only one can
give orders. So, you guys, if you can stop with the Mage Killer
stuff and just, you know, follow orders?"

"Your allegiance is to the Dark through the empress,
and through them, to the army and General Yare," Captain
k'Ree said. "I know you appreciate what Private Yellow Rock
has done. *I* appreciate it. The general appreciates it. But as
Private Yellow Rock just said, now is the time to focus on the
upcoming battle—"

*Upcoming battle?*

"—and remember that we can only win if we're all in this together, one unit, with one commander. Any questions?"

The satyr company commander then made a few comments that Qod didn't listen to. Instead, he watched the five soldiers. He could tell they weren't convinced, but they were also smart enough to keep their mouths shut.

The satyr dismissed them, and after the flap closed, Captain k'Ree asked him, "Do you think we made any headway?"

"Not a chance."

"I think you're right."

"I'll try and get them to tone down a bit, not that I think it'll do any good. They're pretty pumped, and I don't blame them. Not really."

He sighed and then said, "Screw it. What's the general going to do to us? Shave our heads and send us out first as the tip of the spear? He's already done that, and yet we're still here."

With that, he stalked out of the tent.

"Go back to your team, Private. Get some rest."

"Ma'am? You said 'upcoming battle.' Is that true?"

Outside the tent, a chorus of voices broke out into a ribald, but fan-favorite song about a dwarf maiden and a dragon.

The tiniest of smiles cracked the corner of her mouth, and she listened for a moment before she said, "We move out in three days. But don't tell your team just yet. Let them have one more night to relax before things get hot."

With that, she left him alone in the tent. Qod just stood there for a long, long moment. He'd obey that order and give his team this night, even if he would be stressing out.

He took a deep breath, then stepped out into the night.

# Chapter 23

"Are you Corporal Maoileanach?" the gremlin asked as the team donned their gear.

"Who's asking?"

"I'm supposed to report to you," the gremlin said as he looked around before his eyes locked onto Qod. "I'm to be part of the Mage Killer's security."

"Oh, for the love of the Dark Mother. Now? As we're stepping off?"

Qod shifted uncomfortably under the gremlin's gaze.

"You got experience?" Mac asked.

"Nine months," the gremlin said, never breaking his lock on Qod.

"At least that's something," Mac conceded. "What's your name?"

"Private Faulnom, Corporal. And I'm proud to be with you to protect the Mage Killer."

"Belay that. 'E's Private Qod, and until I tell you different, you're New Guy."

New Guy finally broke his stare from Qod and asked, "Where's the team leader? I need to report in."

"The lieutenant's up at the CP, but 'e'll probably be 'ere by and by. Consider yourself reported. Now stand over there until we're ready to move."

"But I . . ." the gremlin started to say to Mac's turned back before he trailed off and stepped to the side.

"We lost Lymon, so they've got to stick us with another gremmie to make all the small folk happy?" Nataly muttered.

Qod didn't mind having another in the team, and with Lymon dead, it made sense to replace him with another gremlin. The Dark was really pushing the narrative that this war was going to be won with all the Dark races, each contributing their own special capabilities, after all, so why would the team be any different?

Of course, that didn't explain why the only orc was the lieutenant, who was rarely even there, and there wasn't an ogre or even a harpy on the team.

Qod didn't care if New Guy was another gremlin, but he was put off by the staring. It was almost . . . hero worship?

*No, not that. Don't let it go to your head.*

The others took New Guy's appearance in stride. Nataly was the only other one who actually greeted him. Yannis barely nodded, and Tulip was still happily engrossed with polishing the hammer Sergeant Tark, the armorer, had presented to her that morning to replace her old beat-up club.

"Inspection time, boys and girls," Mac said. "Let's get ready."

Qod and Pani checked each other's gear, yanking to make sure it was secure. His fellow goblin seemed to have mostly recovered from her wounds, and she seemed eager to get going.

"Don't push it, Pani. Conserve your strength."

"I'm fine, small sir. Really."

The horns started to sound.

"That's us," Mac said. "Move out."

The team settled into their formation: Yannis and Nataly leading, Mac and Qod next, and Pani and Tulip behind them.

"Where do you want me, Corporal?" New Guy asked.

"Bring up the rear."

All over the high ground, soldiers converged from their scattered bivouacs into a single mass. Pixies flew like swarming wasps as they located and directed units to their assigned positions. It was mayhem, but traces of organization started to surface.

Qod didn't think this was the most efficient way to form the army. Having previously assigned positions relayed to the officers might improve the process, or marking the positions with signal flags would help, but no one was asking him for input.

No pixie flew to them, though, and the lieutenant hadn't appeared yet, so the team was somewhat at a loss. Corporal Mac brought them to a halt just at the flanks while he waited for orders.

Qod watched the army assemble. It had been depleted during the last two battles, from reportedly 10,000 to what might be 4,000 soldiers, but it was still an impressive show of force. The question was how many Light soldiers were out there. The command staff might know, but if so, that hadn't trickled down to the rank and file.

Not that all 4,000 would be moving together. The Army of the Mist was broken into three groups. Qod and two replacement companies were in Team Lightning, along with some satyrs, a line company of orcs, and the "Motivation" Company—a group of mostly orcs and ogres who had run afoul of military order and discipline and were subject to extra duty.

Qod was leery of what was essentially a convict company, but one thing was for certain. Team Lightning wasn't going to be the Point of Main Effort.

Team Thunder, made up of mostly Black Smokes, was the other advance group, and Team Hammer was the main body of the army.

Groups of soldiers spotted them and called out as they passed. But that was nothing compared to the 306th. Shouts of "Mage Killer" thundered over them. A group of ten broke off and ran over.

"Mage Killer? Are you coming with us?" a sergeant asked as the others looked at him with eager eyes.

"We're awaiting our orders, Sergeant," Corporal Mac said.

"We'd be honored, sir, if you would," another soldier said as if she hadn't heard a word Mac just uttered. "With you leading us, we'd be invincible."

"You've got Captain Kritikos commanding you. I met him," Qod said.

"He wants us to change our name," a private said, as if that answered everything.

The 306th stopping in place created a logjam, and pixies started converging on the company while other NCOs headed over.

Qod was very sensitive to the Broken Spears nickname and the general's perceived slight, and he didn't want to give the orc any excuse to take it out on the company or him.

"He's still your commander. A good commander, too. I've got full confidence in him."

He mentally winced.  Here he was, a private with very little experience giving his blessing to an officer combat vet. But if anyone else took issue with it, they didn't say so.

"As Corporal Mac just said, we're awaiting our orders, but I'm sure we'll be close by."

"We'll take care of you, sir!" another sergeant said.

"And I'd be honored.  But let's wait until things start to shake out. Why don't you move to your position so I can know where to find you?"

"At the front of the army, of course," a private said with some pride.

An officer was making his way to them, and Qod said, "I think that's one of your lieutenants.  Go back to your company, OK?"

They hesitated, but with the lieutenant closing in on them, the ten soldiers agreed.

"We'll see you at the fight!" one of them yelled as they returned to the company, which started moving again.

"Smooth talking, that," Mac said. "You did good."

All of the team knew by now what the general had said, and they were very aware that they were skating on thin ice.

"There're more of them now," Pani said. "Did we get more replacement conscripts in since the battle?"

"Not that I heard.  But it 'appens.  Units get depleted so much that the survivors 'ave to go join other ones," Mac said.

"But to a replacement company?  One that's going to lead the attack?" Yannis asked.

Mac shrugged and said, "A unit that's getting a rep."

"One favored by the great Mage Killer," Tulip whispered.

Qod glanced up at the troll.  He wasn't sure if she was joking or not.

They watched the army slowly form until Lieutenant Glascock showed up.

"I finally found you," he said. "Dulce, you need to keep me informed of where you are."

Dulce had told the lieutenant more than once that she wasn't able to get a good lock on him, but that hadn't seemed to sink into the orc officer.

"No matter.  I found you.  Follow me."

"Where's our position in the movement, sir?" Mac asked.

"Right behind the lead elements.  The Three-oh-six and the Eight-one-one."

"The Broken Spears are going to be happy about that," Tulip said.

"The who?"

"The Broken Spears."

"Oh, yeah.  Them," the lieutenant said. "I don't think the general likes that name."

Qod and Pani exchanged glances.  The two of them had wondered why it had been Captain k'Ree taking him to the general instead of the lieutenant.  Now, Qod was wondering just how seriously their team leader was being taken.

That was definitely something to stash away for further thought.

Dulce took off to locate where they were supposed to be, and the team followed.  There was less confusion, but it still took half an hour to make their way through the soldiers to take their position.

There was an immediate cheer from the Broken Spears, and Qod gave a little half-wave.  But their cheer was almost drowned out by the company to their flank.  Qod didn't know anything about the 811th other than they were a replacement company just like the 306th—untrained soldiers whose mission was to absorb the first blows from the enemy.

Qod looked them over.  Most, if not all, the soldiers had turned back to look at the team, and they were now cheering.  A makeshift banner was being waved, a black background with a brown . . ."

*Oh, dwarf shit.*

He started heading over to them.

"Qod, where the 'ell do you think you're going?  Get your gobby ass back 'ere!"

He ignored the corporal and kept on, much to the delight of the soldiers.

A moment later, the team coalesced beside him.  Corporal Mac asked him one more time what he was doing, then muttered something under his breath about stubborn gobbies and just followed.

They reached the rear of the company, and Qod asked, "Who are you?"

"The Eight-one-one," several shouted out in uniform.

Qod waited, and a gremlin reached up and pulled the banner out so all could see.

The Copper Dragons!" the entire company screamed.

Qod stared at the crude, brownish dragons on the banner, then glanced down at the matching hammered copper dragons on his chest.

*Oh, the general is really going to love this.*

The horns blared, ordering the army to move out.

# Chapter 24

"Keep moving," Captain Kritikos shouted as they slowly retreated back toward the canyon.

Qod stepped around the charred husks of two orc bodies, smoke still rising from the corpses. The smell of burnt orc cut through the naphtha and made him gag.

It was difficult to believe that the Dark army had stepped off just that morning, full of patriotic fervor. Now, it was in full retreat with a sizable Light force advancing on them.

Qod took a moment to look, but he wasn't tall enough to see much.

"Tulip! Lift me."

Without a word, the troll picked him up and placed him on her shoulder.

A mile away, elf infantry was marching forward in their perfectly aligned ranks, hundreds of them. Dwarves and centaur cavalry flanked them in their steady push.

Despite their discipline and numbers, Qod didn't think they could stand up to the entire Dark army in a massed battle. The problem with that is that the entire army wasn't here.

Who even knew where it was?

With the brief warming spell gone, the cold of the coming winter had returned before Team Lightning started out from the bivouac. It was supposed to take two days to march to the suspected Light position at the edge of the Whispering Forest, where Intel said they were hastily constructing a strong point. The accepted opinion was that they intended to hold out until reinforcements from the Light stronghold or Elmiria could arrive.

The general wanted to crush them into dust and rid the Fanciful Highlands of their presence before that could happen. And that meant moving quickly, something that seemed genetically impossible for any of the Dark races to do. Even while they were crossing the basin, they got strung out, and large gaps appeared in the column. At the far side, the army split into two groups. Team Lightning, with the Broken Spears and Copper Dragons leading the way, was ordered to march along the dry Bounding River bed through the canyon while the much larger Team Thunder climbed up to a pass high in the mountains a dozen miles to the south. Team Hammer, the main body of the Army of the Mist, would follow the next day. According to the plan, Thunder and Lightning would meet up tomorrow and move together, while Hammer would link up the next day for the actual assault on the Light position.

That was in the future, though. First, Team Lightning had to move alone through the canyon, and Qod's nerves had been on high alert.

With images of the boulders from the previous battle, he looked suspiciously at the tops of the high canyon walls, but death didn't come tumbling down to crush them. A sharp bend created a perfect choke point, but they passed through it without a problem.

After several nervous hours, they emerged into the lowlands with no sign of the enemy.

There was also no sign of Team Thunder, which was supposed to link up with them there. The colonel in command held up his column and sent a pixie messenger back. He returned an hour later, relayed the message to the colonel, who then ordered the unit forward. Not in a column, though. Without the Team Thunder, their flanks were vulnerable, so he deployed quickly-moving orcs and satyrs to the flanks to screen the main body.

Which made perfect sense to Qod, who had been beginning to wonder just how tactically sound the Dark command really was. At least this colonel seemed competent.

The enemy also had a firm grasp of tactics. And as the group advanced across the grasslands, a string of ten fireballs suddenly arose from a concealed draw. Soldiers scattered in fear. The balls seemed to be flying in slow motion until the end, when they hit and splashed their deadly fire, engulfing the slow and unlucky. The main orc company was especially hard hit, and that included the command. The screams of those who weren't immediately consumed made Qod shudder.

Qod had seen fire before.

"They have a battle mage?"

"Mother-cursed naphtha," Mac hissed. "Launched by trebuchet."

A distant horn, as pure and high as the Dark ram horns were low and guttural, sounded, and in the distance, the empty grassland shifted into lines of elf soldiers. It was the same cloaking spell that had hidden the dwarves and centaurs with the boulders.

The Dark forces were in chaos, and that only increased when another volley was fired, this time from a different draw. Soldiers started running back toward the canyon. Others tried to drag the wounded out of the line of fire.

"Pull back, Broken Spears, but keep your order," Captain Kritikos ordered.

Other units, especially those that had felt the touch of naphtha, were in complete disorder. The Broken Spears and Copper Dragons kept unit integrity, but Qod sensed that they could break at any moment.

He forced himself to keep to a walk until he'd stepped over the two dead orcs and asked Tulip to lift him.

A ball of fire rose from behind the elves to arch toward the Dark army. Qod thought the range was too far for it to be effective, but the ball somehow kept going and going. It passed close enough over his head that he thought he felt the heat before it smashed down among the Copper Dragons.

That was it. He knew the two replacement companies were going to break.

Not just them. Where the colonel and his command group had been was now a black, smoking ruin, and the survivors from the line company were starting to run.

"Let me down," he told Tulip.

He wasn't sure what he was going to do, but he knew the companies had to retain order. If not, the enemy would run them down, one by one.

"Stop!" Captain Kritikos shouted as Tulip started to lower Qod.

The troll froze at the command.

"Stay up there. Let the troops see you!"

*He's right.*

Jonathan P. Brazee

Qod stood on Tulip's shoulder and shouted, "Keep your position. Discipline! For your families!"

Meanwhile, the captain was running, shouting, "To the Mage Killer. Rally on him."

A few soldiers broke and ran. But the two companies and even some of the misfit Motivational Company soldiers pulled in to surround Qod and his team.

Some shouted, "Mage Killer," but most stayed silent, their faces a mixture of fear and determination.

"Dulce!" Qod shouted. And when she flew up, he said, "See if you can locate Team Thunder. We're going to need them."

"I'm not leaving you."

"You have to. Go!"

She looked like she was going to refuse, but she said, "May the Dark Mother guide you," before she took off.

Qod looked back at the enemy. The elves were steadily chewing up the ground with their long strides. The centaurs were looping to the left—why, he wasn't sure. They had the mass to plow through the scattered Dark soldiers. The fireballs had largely passed over the two replacement companies, and they were moving to face the enemy.

And not just the two companies. A platoon of satyrs closed in on the other side of the Copper Dragons, their bows ready for the moment the enemy came within range. The Motivational Company, along with some of the mostly orcs and ogres from the main line company—those who weren't dragging the wounded along—merged with them.

Captain Krikios and Captain Lura, the orc Copper Dragon commander, were everywhere. So were the NCOs as they urged the soldiers along, all while maintaining control. Qod kept looking toward the canyon entrance, then back at the elves and centaurs. If they could speed up, he was sure they could get into the canyon and maybe to that choke point before the enemy caught them. The problem was all the wounded. They couldn't move quickly enough. Speeding up would be sentencing all of them to a brutal death at the hands of the Light.

Which, he swore an oath to himself, wasn't going to happen.

He was just turning back when something slapped him hard on the thigh, and Tulip stumbled and went down. Qod hit the ground hard and had the breath knocked out of him.

The soldiers shouted in alarm, and Pani immediately rushed to his side. It took a moment for his head to clear. Tulip was just sitting up. An impossibly **large arrow** was protruding from her shoulder.

"Are you OK, small sir?" Pani asked, her voice filled with concern.

He ignored her and tried to reach the troll, but his leg screamed in pain, and he stumbled.

Tulip slowly stood, then turned her head to look at the arrow. All around them, soldiers were crying out in alarm, asking what had happened to the Mage Killer.

Qod pulled himself to her and asked, "Can you still pick me up?"

She reached around with the other arm and snapped the immense shaft off where it met her flesh, leaving the rest inside. She flexed the arm slowly a few times, opening and closing her hand, then lifted him to her good shoulder. Cries of relief rose from the soldiers as they spotted him.

"Are you OK?" Qod asked her. "That's a big arrow."

"The cost of being a big target," she said, "But I'll live."

"Qod!" Pani shouted from the ground below.

He looked at his thigh, which was on fire. But the leathers weren't cut, which meant he must have been hit with the shaft of the arrow, not the head.

It still hurt, but he probably wasn't badly injured.

He looked back at the elves. They were closer, but he thought they were still out of arrow range. The satyrs pacing him hadn't fired yet, either.

*Is that the kyna arrow Yannis told me about? I didn't think it would be that big.*

One massive arrow, though, and it just happened to hit Tulip? Either that was the unluckiest shot in the world, or they were targeting him.

Or, then again, maybe it was just as Tulip said, they were targeting her as a formidable opponent.

*How much farther?*

Ahead, all the soldiers who had broken were already in the canyon and probably still running. The wounded were scattered between them and the canyon mouth, which was still six hundred or seven hundred yards away. Meanwhile, the centaurs had pulled up about two hundred yards out and the same to the side, where they were milling about but not advancing. They were waiting, but for what?

The Copper Dragons' commander was busy shifting both his company and what was left of the Motivational Company to meet that threat.

Qod glanced once more at the canyon mouth and was surprised to see an orc emerging and running at him. It took him a moment to realize that it was Lieutenant Glascock.

"The lieutenant's coming," he shouted down to Corporal Mac.

"The lieutenant? By the Dark Mother, 'e's gone all day, and now 'e shows up?"

The orc officer pushed through the soldiers while shouting, "Where's Qod?" before he spotted him on Tulip's shoulder.

"Why is he still here? Take him back now!"

The Copper Dragons around him were startled and paused as they looked up at Qod.

Tulip started to react, but Qod tugged on her ear and said, "Hold up," before shouting back, "We can't leave these soldiers."

There was a cheer from those close enough to hear.

"That's an order, Private. You *will* retreat," he said as he finally reached the team.

Qod was about to tell him to get stuffed, but Corporal Mac said, "Not smart, sir. If we leave these soldiers, we lose their protection."

Which was complete BS, but it sounded reasonable to Qod. He waited for the lieutenant's response.

Once again, the soldiers within earshot were listening, and it didn't look like they appreciated what they were hearing. They started crowding closer. The lieutenant wasn't dumb. He could see the same thing, and he made the smartest decision he could.

"Dwarf shit," he muttered before asking one of the soldiers, "Where's your commander?"

A sea of arms pointed to the left.

He took a lingering look at the broken shaft of the arrow still sticking from Tulip's shoulder, then hissed, "Do *not* let him get hurt," at the corporal before he pushed his way toward the captain.

Corporal Mac gave Qod a small nod before turning back and telling the soldiers to keep moving.

From his vantage point, Qod had a good view of the area. He kept shifting from the centaurs, who were anxiously stamping their hoofs, to the canyon mouth, and then to the Light soldiers approaching from the rear. Still, he missed the volley of arrows—normal-sized ones—that suddenly appeared. Soldiers dropped around him, and the screams of the wounded and just plain startled filled the air.

Being a tight group gave them some protection from the centaurs, but it also made them a target that was almost impossible to miss.

"Pick up your buddy if he can't move on his own!" a sergeant shouted. "And pick up the cursed pace! Go!"

The satyrs on the right wheeled about, raised their bows, and fired their return volley. That was a magnet for the Light archers, who fired back. Several of the satyrs were hit. But while their fellow soldiers surged ahead, they took whatever meager cover they could and kept up their fire.

"What are the centaurs waiting for?" Qod muttered.

"The elves, I think," Tulip said. "They want to hit us at the same time the elves do."

Qod hadn't actually been asking the troll, but she might be right. He didn't think it was a particularly good strategy, though. Already, Dark troops had reached the canyon, and if they could get to the choke point, they might have a defensible position.

A better move would be to release the centaurs so they could pin the satyrs and Copper Dragons in place, which would allow the elves to close in.  And if they could overrun them, then the rest of the Dark soldiers could be swept up piecemeal.

Not that he was going to tell them that, of course.  Let them discover their mistake on their own.

He surveyed the field once more.  Team Thunder was outnumbered, their command leadership dead, and they couldn't survive a melee in the open.  Qod hadn't experienced much of centaurs in battle yet, thank the Dark Mother, but their reputation as berserker monsters preceded them.  And from what he could see, they carried the bulk and warrior mindset to simply overrun the two companies of Dark soldiers.

As if summoned by Qod's thoughts, the centaurs couldn't hold back any longer.  With a deafening roar, they broke into a gallop, heading right for the retreating Dark forces.

"Hurry!" Qod shouted into Tulip's ear.

She surged forward, which made Qod lose his footing on her shoulder.  He only stayed up by grabbing that same ear and hanging on for dear life.

"Tulip!  This way!" Corporal Mac said, waving his hands so she could spot him.  The big troll adjusted her course toward him as she tried to pick her way through the running soldiers at her feet.

"Captain Lura!" Captain Krikios shouted above the din.  "Take the convicts and stop them!"

Somehow, the Copper Dragon commander heard.  He shouted his orders, and Lieutenant Veemor, his XO, led the company in retreat.  The captain took over the Motivational Company.  Within moments, they were in position, standing fast and facing the charging centaurs.

The satyrs loosed one more volley of arrows before they, too, turned and bolted for the canyon mouth.

Qod shifted his grip on Tulip's ear, then turned on her shoulder so he could get a better view. Lura and his soldiers were too few.  They couldn't stop the herd of centaurs, who could just flow around them to attack the main body before returning to mop them up.

It was one of the bravest things Qod had seen, but it would ultimately fail.  It had to.

Except, to his utter amazement, the centaur charge collapsed inward, and like a faun's arrow, headed directly to the formation.

"For the Dark!" Captain Lura screamed before the centaur charge plunged into the formation with a crash of bodies and weapons.

Tulip slowed and started to turn around, but Qod said, "Keep going," as he winced, expecting total annihilation.

But somehow, the first of the centaurs were pushed back, and that kept more of them from reaching the convicts. Dark soldiers fell, but so did the enemy.

Qod immediately understood.  Captain Lura had packed his soldiers as tightly as he could, making their frontage as small as possible.  The larger centaurs, with their big, four-legged bodies, could not bring their full strength to bear.

When one of them got to the defensive line, they faced four or five orcs.  While their big sabers slashed down, spears, pikes, and **billhooks** reached out to pierce legs and chests.

And that seemed to enrage the centaurs.  Instead of bypassing Lura and his convicts, they fought among their own fellow soldiers to get at their Dark foes.

Arrows whistled through the air to land among Lura's soldiers.  Qod shifted his view to the elves.  They'd stopped to support the centaurs with their bows while one of the big kyna arrows flew over their heads but fell short, piercing a centaur through the back.

The fight was one of utter violence, one where the Dark soldiers couldn't hope to prevail.  But their bravery, coupled with the centaurs' bloodlust, had given the rest of the Dark force the thing they needed most:  time.

Qod wasn't overly fond of the race, but if he survived this fight, it would only be thanks to Lura and his fellow orcs.

There wasn't much he could do to help them.  But he could do his best to make sure their sacrifice wasn't in vain.

Qod twisted back, almost losing his footing again, and only just hanging on. To his surprise, they were less than forty yards from the canyon mouth. A squad of Broken Spears was at the entrance, weapons facing outboard, while the first of the Copper Dragons and satyrs were streaming past them.

Qod felt a surge of hope. "Maybe—" he started to say as he shifted back to Captain Lura and his group.

One look cut that hope off.

The Dark soldiers were being cut down like wheat. Not just cut down. In a killing frenzy, the centaurs were hacking at fallen orcs. As Qod watched, the last three—two orcs and a kobold, all standing back-to-back—were dropped in a flurry of saber blows.

It took a few moments, but the centaurs slowly stopped violating the dead. One leaned back, opened its mouth, and bellowed like a bull ready to mate. Immediately, the others joined in as they waved their bloody sabers in the air.

That was the moment that Tulip entered the canyon. The winter sun had warmed the open area, but in the growing shadows, the wind coming down the canyon bit with winter's teeth—but Qod didn't care. The cold was a small price to pay for what could be their salvation.

If they could set up a defensive position.

Lieutenant Glascock was everywhere, yelling, screaming, and physically pushing soldiers up the canyon. He spotted Qod on Tulip's shoulder and gave him a quick look of relief before he continued haranguing the soldiers to keep moving.

One goblin, not much larger than Qod, collapsed right in front of them, an elven arrow protruding from his hip and burns along his side. Tulip dipped and scooped the goblin up with her bad arm as she continued forward.

The goblin hung limply in her massive hand, but Qod thought he was still alive. For now, at least. He whispered a small prayer to the Dark Mother and tried to make sense of the flight.

But it wasn't as chaotic as it seemed. As soon as Captain Krikios entered the narrow canyon, he grabbed a satyr sergeant and placed a dozen of the archers to the side of the canyon wall.

Krikios was not just Broken Spears commander anymore. With the colonel's death, he had assumed command of the entire Team Lightning, and that included the satyr platoon. And being a satyr himself, he was probably more attuned to their capabilities.

He rounded up another dozen and, as Qod watched from his perch, positioned them behind a pile of flash flood debris.

It didn't take a genius to understand what he was doing. The first group of archers would fire at the enemy, then retreat while being covered by the second group. Simple and direct, but it showed more tactical proficiency than Qod had seen so far among the Army of the Mist.

"Slow down, Tulip," Qod said as they came abreast of the second group.

The troll stopped, then bent slightly at the waist, her breath sounding like a steam engine. She was struggling, and Qod felt a rush of guilt.

"Put me down," he said.

Tulip didn't argue. She dropped her new hammer, then reached back to grab him and lower him to the ground.

He winced at the pain in his thigh and almost stumbled, but Tulip didn't seem to notice. Not so a couple of the satyrs.

"Are you OK?" one asked as the rest looked on.

The satyrs weren't members of either the Broken Spears or Copper Dragons, but they still seemed concerned.

"I'm fine. I just wanted to, well, tell you that you're, you know, doing good."

Qod thought that was about the lamest thing he could have said, but to his surprise, to a satyr, they puffed up their chests in pride.

"Don't you worry none, Mage Killer," a sergeant said. "You can count on us."

Qod was only sort of used to the deference from the soldiers in the two companies, but to have a satyr sergeant say that was hard for him to fathom.

Before he could respond, a roar sounded from the canyon mouth.

"Here they come," the sergeant said. "You'd better get a move on."

Jonathan P. Brazee

Qod watched as the first group of satyrs fired the arrows. Beyond them, the roars increased in pitch and anger. The satyrs let loose another volley, then turned and started running back, passing a few stragglers as they came.

One went down to an elven arrow, but Qod couldn't yet actually see the enemy.

"It's our turn," the sergeant told his archers. "Get ready."

"We'd better move," Tulip said.

She picked up her hammer and, with the unconscious goblin in her other hand, started trudging up the wash. Qod watched for a few more seconds before he turned and limped after her.

Qod forged on, encouraging Dark soldiers to keep moving. Captain Krikios continued placing his archers where they could cover the retreat. Lieutenant Glascock was everywhere as well, doing everything he could to push the wounded or merely tired soldiers along. He didn't think the satyrs could keep the Light soldiers at bay indefinitely, even with the coming darkness. He just hoped they could make a stand at the choke point.

His hopes took a huge leap when he reached the bend. It was better than he could have hoped for. Lieutenant Veemor, the Copper Dragons' new commander, had somehow come up with a miracle.

The choke point had accumulated a significant amount of flood-stripped trees, and the lieutenant, along with his NCOs, had managed to keep control of what looked like the majority of the surviving soldiers. Instead of retreating pell-mell up the canyon, the soldiers had stopped and, like a nest of army ants, were frantically creating a barricade, one that already almost spanned the entire choke point. Satyr archers were moving into firing positions.

Qod knew that it might be too little too late, but it was something. And the fact that the soldiers weren't in a panic-stricken flight filled him with pride. They might not be the best-trained fighters, but no one could doubt their heart.

His team slipped through the gap in the barricade, and Tulip handed off the wounded goblin before she collapsed, back against the canyon wall.

"Catch your breath," Mac told her. "I think we'll be needing you soon enough."

The soldiers noticed Qod, and that seemed to give them a boost. With renewed energy, they attacked the barricade, adding more and more flood detritus.

"Make yourself seen, Private," Lieutenant Veemor told him.

"Yes, sir."

He walked behind the barricade, trying not to limp, and offering encouragement. It was only a few minutes, though, before the last of the satyrs, along with a couple of gremlins, burst through the gap.

The last one to enter was Captain Krikios, who shouted, "Close it!"

Five kobolds pushed the last pile in place while gremlins and goblins jammed cross-branches to sure it.

Despite seeing them fall, Qod was hoping against hope that Captain Lura and his orcs would somehow appear, but that act put an end to that.

"Copper Dragons, to your weapons. Broken Spears, keep working on the barricade."

The captain said something to the satyr sergeant, who nodded and started checking the positions for the archers. Some of the Dark soldiers carried spears and even pikes that could be thrown, but were better kept for stabbing. That meant the archers were the only ones who could reach out and touch an elf or centaur beyond the barricade.

Qod had to see what was happening, so while the captain conferred with his two lieutenants, Qod started climbing the barricade.

"You should keep your 'ead down," Mac said.

Qod ignored him. He pressed his belly against the branches the best he could with his head just high enough for him to see down the canyon. A single body, which looked to be a gremlin, was face down and motionless in the dry river bed.

His heart skipped a beat, and he pulled himself up higher.

"There's still someone out there," he shouted.

A voice behind him said, "She's already dead, Mage Killer, and I couldn't carry her no more."

He turned around to see a goblinette staring mournfully up at him.

"I just couldn't carry her no more," she repeated.

"It's OK, son," Mac told her. "You couldnae done anything else."

She didn't bother correcting him, but got back to shoring up the wall.

Qod watched her for a long moment. He knew she wasn't the only one suffering, but still, it hit him hard.

He turned back to the front, just as the first elf appeared around the bend. Immediately, five or six satyrs fired. The elf jumped back as the arrows struck the ground.

"Save your arrows!" one of the sergeants shouted. "Make every one count."

Captain Krikios was much taller than Qod, so he could just see over the top of the wall without climbing it. An elf stepped out and loosed a single arrow at him. The captain stood, seemingly unconcerned, as the arrow flew just over his head and skittered across the river bed.

"Go fetch that and give it to an archer," he told a gremlin who hurried off to obey.

He studied the area for a few more moments, both downstream the dry riverbed and the canyon walls, then turned to this side of the barricade.

"We've scrounged up almost everything here. I don't think this wall is going to get much bigger." He stood behind it and judged its height against his own. "Good thing centaurs can't jump well and they're shitty climbers. Give me ten soldiers to keep working on it, and get everyone else armed and ready," he told the two lieutenants. He paused a moment, then added, "Start the wounded going back. Have the walking wounded carry those who can't move on their own."

It was a long way back to the camp, and Qod didn't know if many of them could make it, but at least now they had a chance, no matter what happened here.

Pani crept up and flattened herself next to him.

"I guess this is it," she said.

"Looks it."

"You think they have a wizard?" she asked, with a hint of worry. "A wizard, he can just burn our wall."

Qod knew that was true, but if there was a wizard with the Light forces facing them, then there was nothing he could do about it. Dulce was Team Lightning's only wizard, and he'd sent her off to Find Team Thunder.

Not that she was a particularly powerful wizard.

"I don't think so," he said, preferring to say that and keep her from worrying.

She watched for a moment before asking, "Why don't we just get out of here?"

"Not everyone here is an orc," Qod told her.

"Of course, we aren't. But we can still run, right?"

"What 'e means is that with no one 'ere to stop them, the elves and centaurs can catch up to us before we get back," Mac said from where he'd crawled up beside Qod.

Orcs were probably the fastest runners among the dark races. On the Light side, Elves were reportedly almost as fast, and with their four legs, Qod would guess that centaurs were faster yet. Even if the orcs could outrun them in a race to the main body of the Army of the Mist, there was no way the rest of them, especially with their wounded, could.

The barricade wasn't much of an obstacle unless it was defended. It would barely slow the Light if Team Lightning chose to run now.

The wall they built could protect them from a full-on Light assault, but it was also an anchor that kept them trapped to the spot. Their real hope would be that Dulce could bring Team Thunder to the rescue. The question was whether they could hold out that long.

## Chapter 25

"Here they come again!" a voice cried out.

There was a general stirring of anticipation as the Dark soldiers readied themselves.

"This is their big push," Captain Kritikos shouted. "They want to finish us before full dark."

Qod hoped that was true. Not that they were about to attack, but that they didn't want to fight at night. They *could* fight if they wanted to. Some of them, like dwarves, had decent enough night vision.

But if they didn't want to fight on in the dark, then that meant Dulce had more time to bring Team Thunder. With the sun setting, that potentially meant that if they could hold back this assault, they'd be safe until morning, at least. And at the moment, that was good enough for Qod.

The enemy commander had stepped out in the open early on and demanded their surrender, promising that there would be no retaliation. Even if the elves followed through with that, Qod was pretty sure the centaurs couldn't hold back.

In response, Captain Krikios unslung the bow that had been strung across his back since forever. He climbed to the top of the wall and fired a single arrow. The elf stood there until the last second, then twisted as the arrow passed through the space his head had been a moment before. The two commanders stared at each other for a long moment before the elf stepped back out of sight.

The first assault started a minute later. It seemed a little tentative to Qod. Mac said it was a probe, but Qod wasn't sure. Their barricade and the choke point seemed to have pinpointed their position pretty clearly.

That assault died off quickly. One gremlin had been killed, and two elf bodies were left behind as the Light pulled back.

The second assault was similar to the first, but that all changed with the third. The enemy must have figured that the satyrs were running out of arrows. Tulip thought that was because the satyrs were shooting back the elven arrows they'd recovered. Whatever the reason, that assault was different. Most of the elven infantry were stopped by an array of pikes and billhooks, but a dozen made it over before being swarmed by the Dark soldiers.

Qod managed to stab one of them in the calf before he was knocked to the ground and trampled. He got back to his feet, his adrenaline surging, and he looked for another target, but as quickly as it started, the elves were fading away.

This time, though, they left twenty bodies, which would be cause for celebration if not for the thirty-eight Dark soldiers who were dead or too wounded to continue fighting.

The dead elves were stripped of their weapons and pulled to the side while the Dark soldiers waited to take their revenge on the Light. And it looked like the wait was over.

"Elves again," Yannis said, almost sounding disappointed.

He had four arrows left, which was more than most archers, and the order had gone out to all of them not to use their dwindling supply on elves.

That wasn't meant to shortchange the elves, who were easily the match and maybe more to an orc in skill above and beyond their better weapons and armor. But the centaurs hadn't made an appearance yet, and they were bigger and stronger than any of them but the wounded Tulip. The centaurs were coming, and the Dark needed something in their quivers to meet them with.

"Steady," one of the sergeants said as the elves filled the canyon as they moved forward without fear of the Dark archers.

"Look at the smug bastards," New Guy said.

"Just be ready for them. Dannae let your contempt be your downfall," Mac told him.

Instead of steadily advancing, though, the elves started splitting and moving apart at about a hundred yards out.

"What are they—" New Guy started to say, only to have the enemy answer his unfinished question.

The elves sheathed their swords and unslung their bows while a thunder of hooves filled the canyon.

"Finally," Yannis muttered as he nocked an arrow a moment before the centaurs stampeded into sight.

Their war cries echoed off the canyon walls, and Qod's blood ran cold.  They seemed too big to hold back.

"Tulip, get ready," Mac told the troll, who'd been told to lie down and out of sight during the first three assaults.

Qod hoped she'd recovered, but even at full strength, he didn't think she could stand up to what was closing in on them. He clutched his blade to his chest, wishing he had his old spear, the one he'd killed the battle mage with, but he swore his much smaller **dagger** was going to taste Light blood once more.

More than a few soldiers quailed, and officers and NCOs alike said, "Hold the line."

A goblin near Qod dropped her spear with nervous fingers, then hurriedly picked it up a split second before the first centaur smashed into the barricade in front of her, bending the wall in.  She raised her spear, but one swipe of the centaur's saber sliced it in half.

That was all Qod had time to see as the entire barricade shuddered as tons of centaur flesh collided with it. Right in front of him, a centaur attempted to jump over the wall, but the horse-like part of his chest struck it hard.  The initial shock pushed Qod back while the centaur's legs struggled for purchase.  Immediately, soldiers closed in around the centaur, spears, billhooks, and pikes seeking purchase.  But while the lower body was tangled in the wall, the upper body was free, and he was wielding his saber with lethal strength.

Anger coursed through Qod, and he pushed forward, looking for something to stab, when a kobold pushed him aside in his eagerness to spear the centaur.  The saber sliced down, whistling past Qod's head and cutting the kobold in two.

Something grabbed Qod's collar and yanked him out of the way of the return stroke.

"Stay back, Qod," Nataly said before she stepped in front of him and swung her sword.

The centaur, who was now bleeding from multiple wounds, parried her blow a moment before one of his hoofs gained purchase, and he got most of his body to the top of the wall.  He roared something in Centaur, and his eyes blazed with a killing fury . . . for all of two seconds before a hammer crushed through his attempt to block and crushed the Light soldier's skull.

Tulip had joined the fight.

The shaft in her shoulder had started the bleeding again, but if anything, her countenance outdid the centaurs'.  The gentle troll had turned into something terrifying.

If her appearance alarmed the centaurs, they didn't show it.  All along the wall, the centaurs were pressing, reaching over to cut down Dark soldiers as they attempted to breach it.  Meanwhile, the elves were firing their arrows at the defenders, who had to weigh taking cover against repelling the centaur assault.

Being the biggest target and unable to take cover herself, three arrows hit Tulip in rapid succession, but the much smaller bolts didn't seem to give her pause.

Qod tried to wipe centaur blood and brains from his face when a shape completely hurdled the wall, hind legs clipping a branch as the centaur came over, belying the captain's contention that the creatures couldn't jump.

The centaur's hoof's skidded for purchase in the dry river bed before it turned around to face the Dark fighters.

"Take it down," Lieutenant Veemor screamed at the shocked soldiers.

He charged the centaur, followed by a mob of screaming defenders of the Dark.

With freedom to move, the centaur bugled a cry to the Light gods and rushed to fight.  The saber swung, which the lieutenant dodged to the side.  With two orcs engaging the saber, he moved in to hamstring the centaur, only to take a kick from the hind legs to the chest that sent him flying back.

Qod hadn't realized the hoofs would be a weapon, but with room to maneuver, the centaur was using everything at her disposal to wreak havoc among the Dark.

The swarming of the Dark soldiers created a gap in the wall, and more centaurs were managing to climb it.

"Tulip, Mac! Plug the hole!" Qod shouted.

Tulip had started to the centaur already over the wall, and for a moment, Qod thought her bloodlust would make her ignore him, but she shook it off as the team rallied to the gap. With fighting behind them only a few yards away, they beat back the three centaurs who had almost managed to climb to the top. Yannis fired three arrows at point-blank range, each perfectly finding their mark in three centaur eyes. He fired his last arrow at an advancing centaur, then drew his sword. More centaurs took the fallen enemies' place while Nataly struck with lightning-quick strokes that slashed centaur flesh. Pani speared anything she could reach.

New Guy climbed to the top of the wall to join Mac, and then the thunder blows of Tulip's hammer began to take a toll. But again, she was a magnet. More arrows were aimed at her, and the remaining centaurs were converging on the troll. They seemed to Qod to be eager to test themselves against her.

It was a test they were failing. Tulip was gasping for breath, but still her hammer rose and fell with machine-like precision. And with the team protecting her side, they were able to keep the centaurs at bay.

Qod tried to climb the wall to help, but New Guy was knocked off, and he fell on top of Qod and pinned him to the ground.

He tried to climb out from under New Guy's groaning body, but it was Yannis who yanked him free. Once more, he tried to mount the wall. This time, he made it to the top, but there wasn't a centaur to engage. No living centaur, that is.

Not just immediately in front of him. Across the entire front, centaurs were pulling back, some shouting threats about returning. As the assault retreated, the elves collapsed on their allies and followed in the growing shadows.

Several centaurs were still fighting, including the one immediately behind him. The Light soldier looked like a porcupine with the spears and pikes sticking out of him, but with a crazed grin, and while shouting curses in a mix of Old Centaur and Lingua, he kept swinging his saber, keeping the Dark soldiers at bay.

Tulip's chest was heaving like bellows, but Qod scrambled along the top of the barricade.

"Tulip. The centaur," he told her.

Her bloodlust was gone, and when she turned around, she sighed. But once more, she lifted her hammer and stepped forward, using her bad arm to push soldiers to the side. It took a moment, but the Dark soldiers got out of the way, leaving a clear path to the enemy.

The centaur's eyes lit up when she spotted her. She flexed both arms, lifted her head, and bellowed her challenge to the sky.

Tulip had had enough with the dramatics. With one swing, she smashed the centaur in the chest mid-bellow. With the head of the hammer buried in her chest, the centaur looked down in surprise and then up at Tulip with an accusatory expression that Tulip didn't follow some centaur code of honor before the two hind legs collapsed first, followed by the forelegs. A moment later, the centaur tipped over, snapping a few of the spears sticking in her as the body hit the ground.

Tulip didn't try to retrieve her hammer. She simply sat down where she was and breathed in huge gulps of air while the soldiers around her cheered and offered congratulations.

It was only then that Qod tore his eyes away and looked around. There were no more living centaurs still in the fight. The Light soldiers, centaurs and elves alike, were still retreating, and most were already around the bend and out of sight.

A few of the Dark soldiers tried to raise cheers, but it was a half-hearted attempt. The pent-up fear and excitement of the battle had left most of them drained.

Pani clambered up the barricade to join him, and together, they slowly took in the scene.

The barricade itself had been pushed this way and that, but it was still basically intact, which was saying a lot for something that had been hurriedly erected from flash flood debris. What grabbed Qod's attention, though, were the bodies strewn in front of, on top of, and behind it.

On the Light side, he could see one elf and about twenty centaurs. On the Dark side, however, there had to be fifty dead or dying soldiers and more wounded. Between the number who had been cut down out in the open and here, Qod thought Team Lightning had lost half of their soldiers.

It was a sobering realization, and Qod might have gone numb except for the groans of the wounded.

"Come on," he told Pani. "We've got to help them."

Together, they half-slid, half-jumped off the wall. Qod turned over New Guy first, but the gremlin was gone.

"New Guy" was too impersonal for a companion who'd died fighting beside him, but for a long moment, Qod forgot his real name. He struggled before he was able to dredge it up from the recesses of his mind.

"Faulnom," he said. "Private Faulnom."

"He didn't do too badly," Yannis said from behind him. "None of us did."

"Tulip," Pani reminded him.

Qod had to tear his eyes from Faulnom. Tulip was sitting motionless, ignoring the soldiers who were thanking her. His heart skipped a beat in concern, and he ran the few steps to her side.

The troll was slumped with only the constant expansion and contraction of her chest her only sign of life. Four more arrows had pincushioned her. One looked like it had been snapped in two during the fighting, but three were whole, their obscenely white fletching seemingly mocking everything the Dark stood for. Blood seeped from those entry points, from a gash along her side, and from the original kyna wound on her shoulder.

It wasn't until Qod put his hand on her thigh that she looked at him.

"Can you get my hammer?" she asked.

He'd been about to ask her if they should break off the arrows, and her question took him by surprise.

But he said, "Uh . . . of course."

When he looked at the dead centaur, though, he had second thoughts. Even in the best of conditions, he doubted he could lift it. And now . . .

A centaur's lower ribs were massive, and now, the head of the hammer was buried behind them. If he was going to pull it out, he needed help.

Captain Kritikos, with blood running down the side of his face, and Lieutenant Glascock were reorganizing the soldiers for another possible assault. Between that effort and the care being given to the wounded, there weren't many left to help him. But after calling his team over and shanghaiing two ogres to hold the centaur's body in place, they were able to jerk the hammer free. It took both Nataly and Yannis to drag it to Tulip and place it beside her.

Tulip gave a slight smile and put a possessive hand over the shaft.

"I'm ready for when they come back," she wheezed.

Qod looked around as some soldiers tried to shore up the barricade while a much-diminished group of satyrs scavenged elven arrows. Most of his fellow soldiers were untrained conscripts, just like he was, but they'd stood firm against the Light, and he was filled with pride.

But bravery and spirit would only go so far. The Light still outnumbered them. With night rapidly approaching, he didn't think the Light forces would launch another attack soon. He also didn't think that the Dark could survive another full-on assault. Their only real hope was that Dulce was able to bring Team Thunder, with their Black Smokes, before morning.

"We're ready, too, Tulip," he said with a bravado he didn't quite feel for real. "Let the bastards come."

## Chapter 26

Three hours later, a very tired Dulce flittered up through the dark to Qod.

"Where's Thunder? Are they close?" he asked as he looked up and down the canyon, trying to spot them.

"They're not there. Anywhere," the pixie said as the team, minus Tulip, who was asleep, crowded around her.

"What do you mean, they're not there?" Nataly asked. "They can't just disappear."

"Water? I need water," she said, her voice cracking.

Pani tipped her leather flask and let Dulce take a few swallows.

The pixie sighed, then said, "I mean, they weren't anywhere."

"No sign of them?" Mac asked in a subdued voice.

"I found their tracks. But they just ended. I broadened my search, but I couldn't see anything. I even went back along their trail, but then I figured I'd better get back here to let you know."

The team exchanged concerned looks. Their survival depended on being reinforced with the Black Smokes in Team Thunder.

The last three hours had been full of determined purpose as soldiers tended the wounded, worked on shoring up the barricade, and ate their field meals, all with the understanding that Thunder was on their way.

Qod thought that the news that their reinforcement was missing might be too much to take. But they couldn't keep it to themselves.

"We need to tell the captain," he said.

"You and me," Mac said. "The rest of you, keep working."

The two made their way to where Captain Kritikos—the now-dried blood still on his face—was taking a breather while nibbling on some rat cracks.

"What is it?" he asked with an obvious lack of interest in what either of them had to say.

"Team Thunder isn't coming," Qod said.

That changed his demeanor. He choked on the cracker and stood up.

"What do you mean by that? And how do you know it?"

"I sent Dulce to go find them. She couldn't. Their tracks just ended, and they're nowhere around."

"Dulce? Who in the Dark Mother's bed is Dulce, Private?"

"Dulce. Our wizard."

"She's a pixie," Mac added.

"And you just sent her off to find Thunder? Without telling me?"

Qod winced. He probably shouldn't have done that, but in his defense, things were rather hectic at the time.

"It seemed like the right thing to do."

The captain glared at him for a few moments before he whispered, "I should have thought of that myself," probably forgetting just how acute goblin hearing was.

"I want to talk to her," he said.

He summoned Lieutenant Glascock and Sergeant Voran, the senior surviving enlisted soldier, while Mac fetched Dulce. All three listened to her repeat what she'd told Qod and the team, then stood silently for a few moments after she was done.

"We can't stand up to another assault, sir," Sergeant Voran finally said.

"Maybe the Light won't come," Glascock offered.

The look the other two leaders gave him was a response enough.

If it were just elves, Mac had told the team shortly after the last assault, then they might turn back. Elves were easily the match of orcs, even better fighters in some ways, as much as the Dark hated to admit it. But they liked to rely on the other races and overwhelming numbers. In an even fight, they often withdrew to seek out more favorable conditions.

But too many of the centaurs were still alive, and they were like honey badgers in their lust for battle.

"Will the main body be coming?" Qod asked hopefully.

Captain Kritikos shook his head.  "They have a different route, Private."

It sounded like a dismissal to Qod, captain to enlisted peon.  But Qod wasn't going to shut up, not with the stakes so high.

"Even if Team Hammer has left, there's still the rear party at the bivouac, sir.  Isn't that right?"

Probably several hundred of them at least, Qod figured.  They might be armorers, quartermasters, and the like, but they could all wield a weapon.  Even the wounded.

The captain frowned and then said, "They won't be coming, either."

"But there're a lot of them, and they can still fight."

Kritikos seemed to consider it for a moment, but then he shook his head.

"As soon as we leave the barricade, the Light will come, nighttime or not.  And we can't move fast enough.  They'll run us down in the open.  No, it's better that we stay here."

*Which only delays the inevitable.*

The captain turned back to the lieutenant and sergeant, which was absolutely a dismissal, but Qod wasn't done.  The rough idea he had had just solidified into a plan.

He grabbed the captain's elbow and pulled him around.

"What if they don't know we've gone?  We can gain a seven or eight-hour head start."

"Private Yellow Rock," Lieutenant Glascock said, "Thank you for relaying the message, but leave the planning to us."

"How would you do that?" Sergeant Voran asked.

Qod chose to ignore the lieutenant and answer the orc.

"Leave behind a detachment.  They keep fires going, they keep talking.  Some can climb on top of the barricade, let them be seen by any watchers," he said while keeping his eyes locked on the captain, trying to see how the suggestion was being received.

The captain didn't seem to be receptive, but he wasn't flatly dismissing it, either.

"They won't be watching closely, sir.  Not at night, and if they see and hear activity, they'll assume we're all still here."

As if on cue, a centaur bellowed an obscene and physically impossible challenge from around the bend and out of sight.

"It'll be suicide for whoever stays behind, once the Light bastards figure it out," Sergeant Voran said.

It didn't sound like a rejection to Qod.  What he had to say next might be, though, he knew.

"Not if they're orcs, Sergeant."

The orcs were the fastest runners among the Dark races, and they could run almost as far as elves.  Qod didn't know how they'd fare with centaurs, though.

Both officers waited for the sergeant to respond.

"Possible," he said.  "But that's a long way, and we're pretty beat.  We'd be more so after staying up all night making noise."  After a moment, he added, "And there's our armor.  It's much heavier than the elves'."

Like most Dark soldiers, the orcs had kobold armor—utilitarian, strong, and heavy—while the elves had elven or dwarf-made armor, which was just as strong, but much lighter.

Qod had an answer for that.

"Before you leave, you drop your armor and weapons."

"No fucking way!" the sergeant shouted loud enough for soldiers to turn and stare.

Qod knew this was going to be the sticking point.  Orcs had an unreasonable—to him—attachment to their weapons.  Some of them had been passed down from generation to generation.  To lose their weapon was almost a fate worse than death.

"Without your armor," he said, leaving out the weapons this time, "You can outrun them until you reach the bivvy.  You can get more armor there."

The orc sergeant turned to the captain and said, "Sir, can you tell this gobby that will never happen?  An orc, leaving his tools of battle behind?"

But the captain was quiet for a long moment.  He stared at the barricade, then turned toward the bend 120 yards behind them.

"If we can get most of our soldiers that far without being noticed, this might work."

"But our weapons," Sergeant Voran said. "We won't abandon them to the thieving elves."

Captain Kritikos was quiet for another long twenty seconds before Qod could see him make up his mind.

"Swords and short blades are up to you, but your armor goes. Otherwise, you won't stay ahead of them."

Qod felt a rush of victory.

"But—" Voran started.

"That's an order, Sergeant."

The sergeant looked gutted. It was probably worse having a satyr give the order. Qod wondered if Kritikos had been an orc, would he have agreed?

The captain turned to the lieutenant. "I want us gone in ten minutes. Once anyone starts moving back, I want utter silence. Go."

"Yes, sir," Glascock said.

"And you, Corporal," he said to Mac. "You get your troll moving, crawling on her belly, if she has to. If she can't make the bend without being spotted, then she stays."

Which would be a death warrant. There was no way Tulip could keep ahead of the pursuing elves or centaurs, even if she wasn't wounded.

"Were you going to fill me in on your plan?" Mac asked as they rushed back to the team.

"I didn't have a plan, Corporal, not when we got there. It just sorta came to me."

Mac shook his head. "You're something, you know, for a damn gobby."

Which, from the kobold, was pretty high praise.

As the word spread, Team Lightning shifted into determined, if silent, motion.

It went beyond what the captain had said. Qod watched in confusion as dead orcs and centaurs were dragged out into the open. The orcs were propped up and positioned over the centaurs as if they were stabbing them with spears.

And then it hit them. In the rush to get over the barricade, the centaurs, with their focused bloodlust, might mistake them for an active battle. It probably wouldn't work if the elves came over first, but after seeing the centaurs completely lose it fighting the Motivational Company, it could delay them just enough to give the orcs a bigger head start.

They reached the waiting team and told them what was happening. Tulip looked apprehensive when Mac told her she was going to have to crawl.

"I'm pretty big," she said. "I don't think the barricade's going to hide me from prying eyes."

Qod hadn't considered that. But he wasn't going to abandon her. Never in a million years.

*If we can camouflage her, she might be invisible in the dark . . .*

Then it hit him.

"Dulce, up above Long Caldron, the Light used some sort of shield so we couldn't see them. Can you do that?"

"I know how, but I'm not very powerful, especially when it's just me with no one to meld with, and I've been flying all afternoon."

"But you can do it?"

"Sort of."

That was good enough for Qod.

"I want you to put it behind Tulip as we go."

"I don't think I can hide her. Like she said, she's pretty big."

"Just do what you can. Let's go."

Tulip groaned as she went to her belly, but slowly, with the team at her side, she inched her way along the canyon wall, one painful yard after one painful yard. By the time they were halfway, others had started to pass them.

Somehow, though, whether the elves weren't paying that much attention or Dulce's spell had worked, they reached the corner of the bend. Tulip pulled herself out of the line of sight and gratefully stood up.

Qod, however, stopped just short and looked back. There were still soldiers quietly making their way toward him, but at the barricade, the stay-behind orcs were making a show of it. Campfires glowed like demon eyes. One orc was standing on top of the barricade, exchanging obscene challenges with an unseen centaur.

"Good luck, comrades," he whispered before joining the rest of the team for the long march back.

# Chapter 27

"It was a communications problem. Word got to Thunder to abort, but not to us," Lieutenant Glascock said. "The command had no idea we were still advancing or that we were in contact."

Most of his righteous anger, which he had when he left to find out why they'd been abandoned, was gone, but he seemed troubled.

"We didnae get the word? Every single pixie somehow coudnae find us, sir?" Corporal Mac asked. "And why was the operation aborted in the first place?"

It was a very good question—two good questions—and the lieutenant didn't offer an answer to either. The command had been hellbent on hitting the Light before they could erect full defenses. But then the general decided to abandon the entire operation?

Intel could have discovered something that changed the calculus, Qod had to admit, but Intel had not been giving anyone a reason to trust them lately.

He gave the lieutenant a penetrating look. That was something else that didn't make sense to him. The lieutenant had been back with the command group—getting the latest in preparation for the battle, he'd said at the time. Somehow, he had been able to charge forward to join in the fight, yet no other troops had been dispatched to help the lead elements retreat?

It wasn't until the Team Lightning survivors had reached the end of the canyon after a long night movement, carrying their wounded, that other troops took over.

The only bright spot was that the orc stay-behind party, the ones who'd kept up the activity through the night, managed to reach the fresh troops steps ahead of the pursuing elves, who, when faced with a larger Dark force, retreated back down the canyon.

The Dark army, while full of courageous and dedicated soldiers, had not shown much in the way of tactical unit expertise. That could account for the major screw up that had ended up with so many dead, and all for naught. They were right back where they'd started the previous morning.

"What next, sir?" Mac asked.

"No firm word yet. But the talk is that we're heading back to Defiance."

"And leave the Light bastards in Dark land?" Nataly blurted out.

"I don't think so, Private. I think it's just to regroup and resupply."

"And give them more time to prepare," the vurdalak muttered.

Qod had seen a lot of death in his short time as a soldier, but he wasn't inured to it. And he realized that the Dark faced an existential threat to their very being, and to counter that, lives were going to be lost. He didn't know why the operation was called off. That was way above his pay grade. But if the general changed his mind, then it should have happened before Team Lightning came into contact. Even a boot private could understand that, and that was what had him angry.

"What do you want us to dae today?" Corporal Mac asked.

The lieutenant looked around at the little plot of dirt the team had claimed, then shifted his gaze to the packed Broken Spears and Copper Dragons who had surrounded the team like castle walls before settling in. Several hooded spirits were working their way through the two companies.

"Just sit tight until I get more word," he said before he turned to Tulip.

"Have you been seen by a hooded spirit, Private?"

"Not yet, sir."

"I'll see about sending one of them over to you. I guess you've got them, Corporal," he added before he turned away.

He'd only taken a couple of steps before he stopped and turned back.
"I almost forgot. Captain k'Ree told me she's sending over a replacement gremlin, so expect him today sometime."

*Another gremlin?*

If Qod had any doubt that the team had been assembled with anything other than politics in mind, that banished the thought. It wasn't that he'd choose anyone else for the team. They'd all bonded, and each of them was capable, but to the general or Captain k'Ree or Major Pishlyss, that wasn't important. They had to present a representative team to the enlisted troops.

Qod watched the lieutenant pick his way through the Broken Spears. He might have come up with the plan that saved their asses, but he knew his place, at least according to the brass. And he didn't like being just some sort of mascot. But if there was any weight he could pull to make sure the small folk weren't being abused, he swore he would use it.

## Chapter 28

The entire army abandoned the Long Caldron highlands and marched back to Camp Defiance, where Qod had first joined it. The CP was erected and immediately turned into a hub of activity for the next three days while the rest of the army sat on their respective butts. No one was complaining, though. The fighting had been going on for weeks before Qod showed up, and the soldiers took the opportunity to rest and maintain their gear.

Qod had a wicked-looking bruise on his hip and upper thigh from the kyna arrow shaft, and he walked with a small limp, but he wasn't about to complain, not with Tulip having suffered the head piercing her shoulder.

Trolls didn't heal as quickly as goblins did, and the wound was festering. But she acted like it was nothing. And she was still refusing treatment, saying there were others more hurt than she was. That might be true, but Qod kept a very close eye on her.

Lieutenant Glascock was right about a replacement for Faulnom. Private Castor showed up on the second day and was immediately christened as "New Guy." Qod wasn't too sure about that. It didn't seem quite right to give him the same name as their departed teammate.

Whatever his name, the gremlin was happy to be part of the Mage Killer's security, calling it an honor. Nataly said the obvious—gremlins hadn't fared too well so far with the team. New Guy just smiled and said the odds were against three gremlins being killed.

Qod knew that wasn't how statistics worked, but he let it go. If it gave Private New Guy solace, then why spoil it?

Truth be told, while Qod was glad he had his team, he wasn't sure it was really necessary. Both companies stayed close to Qod, always watching him. He couldn't even go to the jakes without an "honor guard," as they were referring to themselves.

Captain Kura's body hadn't been recovered after the battle, and Lieutenant Veemor had been killed at the barricade, but Captain Kritikos came by to check on him several times each day.  Other than that, there wasn't much for the team to do but sit and wait.

Qod took another rat crack from his pocket and idly chewed on it as he watched the human make his rounds.  The rat crack was the same as he'd gotten that first evening, and it would never be accepted back in Yellow Rock, but either the soldier life had ruined his taste buds or he just didn't care.

One thing sure hadn't changed.  He still couldn't look at a human without shuddering in disgust.  This one didn't have a vardo wagon. He was walking, a bundle of gear on his back as he moved from group to group.

"What does it expect to get?" Qod asked Pani and Nataly, who were sitting on either side of him.  "We don't have any money."

"*You* don't," Nataly said.

Qod gave her a sidewise look.

"And you do?" Qod asked.

"Sure.  I'm getting paid, just like the orcs."

"And goblins don't get paid?" Pani asked in sudden indignation.

"They would if they're volunteers.  Not many do that, though.  You're all conscripted."

"That's not right.  You get paid.  We don't."

"Oh, you're earning a salary.  And if you survive until you're released, you'll get it."

"Fat chance of that," Qod said, "with as much as they use the small folk as fodder."

"How much is it?" Pani asked.

"I'm not sure.  I think half a gildr."

"Half a gildr a day?" Qod asked.

It wasn't much, but it was more than he'd expected.

"A month."

"What?  Half a cursed gildr a month?  I haven't even earned that yet?"

Nataly shrugged.  "You should have volunteered.  We get fifteen, and they pay us at the end of each month."

"If I wanted to be here, I would have.  But since I wanted to stay back home, they had to drag me here.  Half a gildr. So, if I survive a year, I can buy myself a nice table setting for one. Or a sleepshirt. Yay."

"Come to Mud Geyser. You can buy two for six gildrs," Pani said.

Qod just shook his head and watched the human try to sell his salvage. To his surprise, Captain Kritikos passed him something and received what looked like a small dagger instead.

"Where's its wagon?" Qod asked, not that he really cared one way or the other.

"Those are for the authorized scavengers. This guy's probably picking up the scraps and doing all of this under the table," Nataly said. "But sometimes, they've got something nice the authorized scavengers missed. A couple of months ago, a buddy of mine got a dwarf axe in almost new condition."

The only axe Qod had seen had been in the hand of a dwarf who was trying to kill him. But he wouldn't mind getting a closer look.

"Where's this friend now?"

"Dead," she said with a shrug. "Some other human probably sold it back to another dwarf by now."

Qod still couldn't come to terms with humans scavenging weapons. They were made by kobolds and other Dark people and given to soldiers who were then killed in battle. It didn't seem right that humans, who never contributed a single thing to the world, could just scoop them up and charge the rightful owners for their return.

"What's that?" Pani asked, breaking his train of thought.

Qod turned to see where she was pointing. Something was approaching from high in the sky. Somethings, plural. Not just one.

His heart skipped a beat, and he jumped to his feet, fearing a fairy attack, but goblin eyes are sharp, and he was able to make out that they were harpies. Four of them. What was strange was that they were flying in a square, and they looked to be carrying something.

"What is it?" Nataly asked—vurdalak's eyesight was as notoriously bad as goblins were good.

"Four harpies," Qod said.

"And it looks like they're carrying a gremlin in some sort of sling," Pani added.

"Oh. Just a palanquin."

"A what?" Pani asked.

"A palanquin. The harpies are carrying someone to us. Probably from army headquarters. Maybe we're getting new orders."

Nataly was acting like this was an everyday occurrence. Maybe it was, but Qod had never heard of it, much less seen it."

"Why don't they just send a pixie with the message?" Pani asked.

"Long way for a pixie to fly. You need harpies."

"OK, then. Just send a harpy."

"Because whatever this is has to be delivered by an officer, and there are no harpy officers," Qod said.

He didn't know that for sure, but he thought it was a reasonable guess, given what he now knew about officers and challenging for the command. Harpies weren't trolls, but they had wicked claws and that dangerous beak. In a fight with an orc, a harpy certainly stood a fighting chance.

Nataly didn't correct him, so he was sure he was right.

That wasn't what was important, though. The fact that the orders were being delivered in person had to mean they were too important to send by wizardry, and that meant that they were going to have a big impact on the soldiers in the division.

Corporal Mac joined them, then Yannis. All around them, soldiers stopped what they were doing to stare into the sky.

"What's with the harpies' uniforms?" Qod asked.

"What do you mean?" Mac asked.

"They're black and red."

"Are you sure?" Mac asked as he and Yannis turned to stare at him.

"Yeah. I can see them."

"Dwarf shit," both soldiers said in unison.

"Why? What does that mean?"

"The messenger isn't from Army HQ," Nataly said. "Those are imperial guards flying them."

# Chapter 29

"They're massive for harpies," Nataly said.

It was true. Qod had only seen a relatively few harpies during his short time in uniform, and these four were much bigger than any of the others. They were standing silently in front of the CP in their black and red leather half-armor. Right behind them were six draugrs. Qod and the others might be fifty meters from the CP, but the tension in the guards was palpable.

They might all be allies against the Light here, but that didn't mean there was absolute trust.

The harpies had come down in a slow hover until the slung chair reached the ground, and their gremlin passenger, in what Pani called a "resplendent" uniform but Qod thought ostentatious, climbed out. A waiting colonel escorted the gremlin inside, and the harpies came to light on the ground while ignoring the draugrs.

That was almost an hour ago. Since then, there'd been nothing, at least from the inside of the CP. Outside, there'd been a slow creep of soldiers edging closer and closer. Everyone knew that whatever the imperial messenger had to pass was going to have an impact on each one of them.

Dulce had even flown closer to see if she could hear anything, but she came back with nothing new.

As the time crept on, some of the soldiers drifted off to return to whatever they'd been doing, but for the most part, it was a captive audience who remained surrounding the CP.

"Any chance the empress is going to disband the division, small sir?" Pani asked wistfully.

"The Light's still here on our lands," Qod gently told her.

She sighed. "I'd really like to go back to Mud Geyser. You could come, too."

"I'd like that."

He'd said that just to be polite, but as he thought about it, he really *would* like to see more of the Fanciful Highlands, especially another goblin village. He'd only seen two villages in his life before getting conscripted, Yellow Rock and Deerhorn Rapids.  Since then, he'd seen more of the land, but not exactly as a tourist.

"When's the best time to visit?" he asked.

"Oh, next month, when the—"

She was cut off when an undercurrent swept through the crowd.  A figure finally emerged from the CP:  Captain k'Ree.

Qod felt a twinge of misgiving as she scanned the soldiers, and that spiked when she spotted the team and started pushing her way forward, the soldiers parting before her path.

Up until the Broken Spears, that is.  For a moment, Qod thought the soldiers were going to stop her.

"Get ready to move, Tulip," Corporal Mac said.

But Captain Kritikos was already on the scene.  He barked a few things that Qod couldn't make out, and the soldiers moved out of the way.

The team took positions around Qod as the captain approached. Qod knew they couldn't defy her, but their mere presence was a warm blanket on a cold night.

"Private Yellow Rock, come with me," she ordered.

Pani took half a step forward, and Qod said, "It's OK. Just wait here until I come back."

The captain wheeled around and started back, and Qod had no choice but to follow.

"Mage Killer!" a few of the soldiers shouted as they made their way through them.

Qod tried to smile and put up a brave face, but the fact that both they and his own security team seemed to have misgivings only fed into his own.

*This doesn't have to be bad*, he tried to tell himself.

It was a little easier to move once they made it past the Broken Spears and Copper Dragons, and Qod couldn't take the suspense anymore.

He hurried to come abreast of the captain and asked, "Do you know what this is about?"

"The minister wants to see you."

He wasn't quite sure what a minister was, but it must be the gremlin, he figured.

"Do you know why?"

She gave him a sidewise glance and said, "Do you really think I'm privy to imperial dealings, Private?"

*You seem to know everything else.*

They walked in silence the rest of the way to the CP. The harpies gave him condescending looks as he passed between them. The draugrs didn't even seem to notice him, so intent were they on the harpies.

Given the word, Qod was sure they'd happily take the four imperial guards down.

*Just don't get me caught up in the middle.*

And then they were inside. What had to be most of the command staff were packed in the entrance and anteroom, and they were all staring at him. Maybe glaring—Qod couldn't tell.

Captain k'Ree led him back to the conference room and held the flap open, then stepped partially aside.

Qod hesitated, and she said, "What are you waiting for? Go."

Qod steeled himself and stepped inside.

The general and the gremlin were waiting. No one else.

"Minister, this is Private Kud," the general said, obviously fighting to keep his voice calm.

His face was a wooden mask, but his entire posture screamed anger. Qod was petrified—an angry general was a dangerous general—but the gremlin seemed nonplussed.

"Thank you, General Yare. That is all."

The wooden mask slipped for a moment, and Qod thought the orc was going to explode, but with an obvious fight to regain control, the general said, "Very well."

He spun around, and as he passed Qod, he gave him a glare that didn't need a gorgon of legend to turn him into stone.

It wasn't until the general barged back out past the flap that Qod exhaled—and then tightened up again. Anyone who could make a general—an orc at that—bow to his will was his own kind of dangerous.

"Is it Kud or Qod?" the minister asked.

"Uh, Qod. Private Q . . .Yellow Rock, sir."

"We'll use Qod, shall we? Gremlins don't bother with surnames, either. Not like the big folk."

Which Qod knew, of course.

Qod was still nervous, but the comment gave him a brief moment of courage.

"Who are you, sir?"

"Why, I'm Minister Plenipotentiary Moran, young gobby. Here on orders from the empress herself."

Qod heard the words. He understood them all, except for "plenipotentiary," but he couldn't grasp what the minister was saying. The empress sent him? And he wanted to talk to a goblin private? It was beyond reason.

"Let's sit," the gremlin said, "Although I sat long enough during the flight from Taxian."

"Taxian?" Qod couldn't help himself from blurting. "You came from the imperial city?"

Qod wouldn't have been more surprised had the minister said he'd come from the moon.

The gremlin laughed. "Where else would I have come from?" He rubbed his butt and said, "Eleven-hour flight, too. One of the prices I pay for being among the smallest ministers in the imperial court."

Minister Moran asked him if he wanted water, which Qod accepted.

The gremlin waited until Qod had finished before he said, "Tell me about yourself, Private Qod."

"About me? What do you want to know, sir?"

"Start at the beginning. That's usually the best place for that."

"Well, sir. I'm from Yellow Rock, from a litter of three . . ."

For the next forty minutes, Qod essentially told the minister everything from his sausagehood to today. The minister deftly steered the conversation with tiny course corrections, barely noticeable. But Qod soon realized that this wasn't just a casual get-to-know-you conversation. He was being interviewed—and by someone skilled in the process.

That quickly came with the realization that, despite the folksy, us-small-folks demeanor, Qod was skating on thin ice. The gremlin didn't get high in the imperial court by being a nice little small folk.

If Qod said the wrong thing, those harpies might have another job than just flying the minister around. The problem was that Qod didn't know what the right thing and what the wrong thing was.

That knowledge made him hedge his bets. He was as honest and thorough as he could be in response to the gremlin's nudging of the direction of the telling—except he was a little vague in how the elf battle mage actually died, pleading confusion in the heat of the battle. He didn't know if the gremlin bought that, but he didn't call Qod out on it.

He also made sure to give credit to the empress. He might have laid it on too thick, though. And when he recounted giving credit to the empress in front of the general, he almost recounted that worthy's reaction, but Qod cut that off. For all he knew, loyalty to his commander was something that the minister was looking for.

More time than he'd have thought was spent on the battle in the Long Caldron highlands. The gremlin seemed curious as to why he'd acted as he had. Qod had treaded lightly here. He didn't want to be seen as a wild card that couldn't be trusted to follow orders.

Finally, though, the interview was over. The gremlin had seemed friendly throughout, but Qod was sweating, and he felt as if he'd gone through the wringer.

"Well, that's been enlightening," the minister said. "Thank you for your time."

*I didn't have much of a choice.*

"And Empress Almavoy wants to thank you for your service."

"The empress? She knows who I am?"

The idea was just too preposterous to even consider.

"Of course, she does. It's not every day that a battle mage is killed. She knows the name of the warrior who did the deed."

He leaned in closer, smiled, and said, "And the fact that it was a small folk who did it. Well, that's precious. You should have seen the orcs in the court when we got the word. It was wonderful."

Qod gave a chuckle. He was way out of his depth talking to someone in the imperial court, but he could still appreciate the image.

"Especially a gobby, by the Dark Mother. No offense, Private. I mean, I even have friends who are gobbies, so I'm not prejudiced."

*There it is.*

"But that reminds me. There's one more thing."

Qod had been expecting the blow, and maybe this was it after being lulled into a sense of safety. He tensed back up.

"What's that, sir?"

The minister shifted the short cape-like whatever, reached into a side pocket, and withdrew his closed hand.

"Come closer."

His hand wasn't big enough to hide a blade, but still, Qod reluctantly stood and moved closer.

The minister opened his hand, revealing a small black crescent moon.

"Sir?"

"You recognize it, right?"

"Yes, sir. That's a lieutenant's insignia."

"And?" the minister prompted.

"Why are you showing that to me, sir?"

"For a bright young gobby, *Lieutenant* Qod, you sure can be pretty dense."

*Lieutenant?*

His heart fell into despair.

As the minister affixed the moon to his collar, all Qod could think of was that now that he was an officer and not some powerless private, the general could consider him a threat, no matter how improbable that might seem.

## Chapter 30

"General Yare, I do have a few more messages from the empress, so, if you please?" Minister Moran said as the two emerged from the conference room.

The general stared at Qod with cold, dead eyes for a long moment before he pushed past Qod with a hip to the shoulder that sent the smaller Qod stumbling back a step.

If there was any doubt as to the general's opinion of Qod's sudden rise, that dispelled it. Qod was on dangerous ground now, and he knew it.

He wasn't the only one. From the stares of the rest of the staff, they didn't give him much hope of a future. They moved out of his way, giving him a large buffer as if they feared catching some of his bad luck.

*I didn't ask for this.*

To be honest, Qod didn't have the foggiest notion as to how officers were selected. He'd never seen a goblin officer—he didn't even know they existed. But odds were that the Misty Throne didn't often reach down and elevate privates, and when they did so, there were political repercussions. That meant that private or lieutenant, Qod was a pawn in a much bigger game being played.

And pawns were often sacrificed.

Qod stood there a moment, wondering what was next, when Captain k'Ree stepped up to him.

"Go back to your team and wait there. Do nothing. Do you understand?" she told him in a low voice.

"Yes, ma'am," he said, just happy to leave the CP.

He could feel the staff's eyes boring into him as he passed through the entrance. The draugrs didn't give him a second look, but one of the harpies caught his eye and gave him the slightest of nods.

That was an unexpected boost. Qod had been feeling like a mouse in a cat hotel, but that tiny gesture reminded him that he did have someone in his corner. A pretty powerful someone.

Even as a pawn, the empress wouldn't want *her* pawns casually eliminated.

*Right?*

Qod stopped for a moment as he surveyed the sprawled camp while he reached up to touch the single crescent moon of a lieutenant. It wasn't very big, yet it seemed heavier than a miller's wheel. He was worried as to the consequences, but a part of him was bursting with pride. He took a moment to imagine strolling back into Yellow Rock as an officer. Surprise would be the order of the day.

*I only wish Leet, Poul, and Ma were alive to see it. Pa, too.*

Heeding Captain k'Ree's orders, he started back, but then diverted his path. Too much had just happened, and he didn't want to make his way through the mass of the Broken Spears and Copper Dragons. Instead, he started a slow loop that would bypass the bulk of them and come in through the far side.

Still, soldiers recognized him and shouted a hello or gave him a wave. No matter how much he thought his moon collar device was like a beacon, no one seemed to notice it. At least, it wasn't mentioned.

"Maybe the idea of a goblin officer is so unbelievable that their brains just refuse to comprehend it," he muttered facetiously under his breath.

But the more he thought about it, the more he realized there was probably a grain of truth to the statement. It wasn't really a good reflection on what the other races thought about goblins.

It took him longer, but he stepped into their little camp. The others were all staring back toward the CP, and he had to clear his throat to get their attention.

They wheeled around, and Pani said, "Small sir!" Then her sharp goblin eyes dropped to his collar, and her brows furrowed together. "*Sir?*"

"I sorta got promoted," Qod told her.

"What are you two . . ." Yannis started to say until he saw Qod's moon. "Oh!"

"A lieutenant?" Nataly asked.

Trolls had notoriously bad eyesight, especially during the day. Tulip got to her feet and lumbered closer. She bent at the waist to put her head closer to Qod-level before she could make out the insignia.

"Congratulations, Lieutenant. I guess we should be saluting you now."

The minister had called him lieutenant, but here, among his team, that somehow made it real. And the thought overcame him. His knees got weak, and a wave of dizziness washed over him. He sat down on the log Tulip had dragged up from somewhere and took several deep breaths.

The others, except for Corporal Mac, crowded in to congratulate him. The corporal hung back for a few moments, then asked, "Did the general promote you?"

"No. It was the empress. I mean, she's not here. One of her ministers, a gremlin, he was the one."

A dark cloud passed over the corporal's eyes. "Why don't you tell us exactly what happened."

"Well, uh . . ."

Qod spent the next dozen minutes relating what happened. He closely watched Mac's reaction to what he was saying. The others were greedily lapping up each detail, but the corporal seemed concerned, and that only added fuel to the fire that was Qod's misgivings.

When he was done, Mac shook his head and said, "I thought we'd be able to get you out of the spotlight given time, but that was before you decided to lead the charge down that ridge."

"Wait. You want the Mage Killer out of the spotlight?" New Guy asked.

Mac ignored him. "But this," he said with a sigh. "We cannae keep you low profile now."

"Why would we?" New Guy persisted. "The soldiers love him."

He was getting angry now.

This time, Corporal Mac faced him, but Tulip beat him to the punch.

"It wasn't the general who promoted him. It was the empress. That puts Qod—Lieutenant Qod—on the opposite team."

"But we're all on the Dark side. The Light is the other team," Pani said.

"Remember what we were talking about yesterday?" Tulip asked her.

"Yes. We were talking about how . . . oh!"

Qod made a mental note to find out about that conversation, but what Corporal Mac and Tulip had said crystallized the fears that the general's glare and the reactions from the command staff had grown. He didn't have to be an expert in court intrigues to see that.

It was more than just being a pawn. He now had a target on his back.

"So," Corporal Mac said. "Our mission is the same. It just got more difficult. I'll be making some changes, though, starting now. Twenty-four-hour watches, for one."

"No one's hurting Qod. I'll die first," Pani said with fervor, before she added, "I mean, no one's hurting Lieutenant Qod."

"Just Qod's fine," he said. "This promotion is all politics. We're the same team we've been."

Mac raised one bushy eyebrow, but he didn't object.

"And you," he told Qod. "No wandering off. You dannea go anywhere alone. Right?"

"Nowhere alone. Got it."

Qod took a moment to catch the eyes of each of them. They were ready to fight for him, he could see, and that almost made him choke up. But the fact of the matter was that there were only the seven of them. Even with Tulip, there wasn't much they could do if the general sent, say, a platoon of draugrs.

His eyes lifted to the two companies who'd attached themselves to him, and a thought came unbidden.

*How loyal are they? Would they fight for me?*

A wave of guilt swept over him. The war with the Light wasn't about him. And if the Dark coalition started infighting, then the Light had already won.

"Here comes the lieutenant," Dulce said. "I mean, the other lieutenant. The old one."

The team spun around. Lieutenant Glascock was striding through the Broken Spears on a beeline to them. The other team members shifted to put themselves between Qod and the lieutenant.

In a low voice, Mac said, "Easy. Nothing 'appens unless I say so."

Once again, the team's loyalty filled Qod with warmth, but he also knew that any action against the lieutenant would result in all of them getting killed.

"And you're not going to say so," Qod said.

The corporal glared and opened his mouth, but Qod said, "That's an order. From an officer. Me."

Qod wasn't sure where that came from, and he looked at Corporal Mac in surprise tinged with trepidation, fearing an explosion. But Mac took a moment before nodding.

"Roger that, *sir*."

If the lieutenant noticed the protective wall in front of Qod, he didn't show it.

"You. Come with me."

Qod walked under Tulip's legs and stopped.

"You sure about this?" Corporal Mac asked.

"I'm sure. Everything's OK."

Lieutenant Glascock frowned while he waited. Qod stepped up, and Glascock motioned him to follow. But instead of heading back to the CP, he led Qod to the edge of the high ground to where they could look down over the Upper Anemia River Valley, which had been the site of a large battle before Qod joined the army there. Vultures were still hopping around as they looked for food. It might have been several weeks, and most of the bodies had been recovered, but bits and parts of bodies were undoubtedly still scattered about, which was drawing the birds.

They weren't the only scavengers. There were no fewer than four vardos as the humans searched for anything they could sell back to the army. And to Qod's surprise, it wasn't just humans. He spotted a group of three raggedy kobolds close to the base of the drop-off, and farther out were a scattering of shapes in tattered cloaks that hid their identity.

Lieutenant Glascock watched for a few moments before he muttered, "Scum."

He let out a sigh and turned to face Qod.

"I guess congratulations are in order."

It sounded more like a surrender rather than an actual congratulations.

"But I need to get some things straight. I'm senior to you, so I'm still in command. You will obey my orders just like before. Understand?"

Qod gave the lieutenant a long, appraising look. This wasn't what he was expecting. This wasn't Corporal Mac, with his long time in service, understanding some of the political and practical ramifications surrounding Qod's sudden ascension into the officer ranks. This was someone worried about a loss of position. It was about him, not Qod.

The lieutenant was a very difficult puzzle to figure out. On the one hand, despite being orc royalty, he did not instill a sense of confidence in his soldiers, and he was always at the CP hanging around the center of power. The rest of the team assumed he was trying to ingratiate himself with the senior officers—"brown-nosing," to use the soldiers' slang. But on the other hand, when push came to shove, he was a fierce fighter, skilled and unafraid.

"Do you understand?" he repeated.

"Yes, sir."

Qod wasn't sure if lieutenants called each other "sir," but it just came out.

"I am the commander. You are the package. That means, you don't give the soldiers orders. *I* do."

*No, Corporal Mac does. Or Captain k'Ree.*

His mind went to the last fight, where the lieutenant had tried to get Qod to safety and the entire team refused. Warrior? Yes. Leader? No.

"Understood," Qod said.

Anything to just get the orc to leave and disappear to wherever he spent his time.

"OK, then. I just wanted to get that cleared up. Don't worry. We'll take care of your safety. You just keep showing your face where the general wants, and he can make sure you go far."

Qod had to fight to keep his face neutral. Every member of the staff who'd seen him emerge with the minister as a brand-new lieutenant understood how things were playing out. General Yare was not going to make sure he went far.

For someone littered into a political family, the lieutenant was painfully oblivious to the obvious.

He put a hand on Qod's shoulder and said, "I'm glad we had this talk. I think everything's cool. I'm going to head back to the CP, but if you need anything, just let me know."

Lieutenant Glascock started to turn away when he said, "Oh, I almost forgot."

He handed Qod a small leather pouch.

"What's this?"

"It's your pay, of course. One month."

Qod hefted the purse. "A month? I have only been an officer for an hour."

"It's advanced pay, of course. You're an officer now."

*So, conscripts maybe get paid at the end of their tour, if they survive. But an officer gets paid in advance?*

Somehow, that didn't surprise him.

He loosened the drawstring and looked inside. There was a glint of gold, and he quickly pulled the purse closed.

Qod had never seen a gold coin before until this moment.

"What am I supposed to do with this?"

"I know. It isn't much, right? It doesn't amount to anything decent until you're a major. But it's better than nothing, I guess."

He gave Qod one more pat on the shoulder and walked away.

Qod just stood there. He'd had quite a few shocks today, but in some ways, this was the strongest one. This was concrete.

He slowly opened the purse again.  Inside were five gold imperials. Lieutenant Glascock might not deem it much, but he could feed half of Yellow Rock for a year with it.  And this was one month's pay?

*What now?*

Not to belabor a point, but this was pretty far outside Qod's life experience.  He knew what a pound of rat cracks cost. He knew the price a traveling trader charged for a tin pot, or how much a sack of seed corn went for. Dealing with this type of wealth was simply beyond his ken.

He looked back to where his team was waiting, all of whom were watching him closely.  When Pani saw him looking, she gave him a questioning thumbs-up, which he returned. Even from this distance, he could see them relax.

It was still hard for him to fathom, but they cared for him.  Really cared.  And that was heady heights for a goblin from Yellow Rock.

He knew what he had to do.  He slipped one coin into his pocket and tied the purse to his belt, then returned to the team.

"What did Glascock want?" Mac asked.

"Nothing much. He wanted to make sure I knew he's still the commander and I'm just the package."

"That's it?" Mac asked.

"Pretty much so," Qod said.  "But can I talk to you for a moment?"

"Sure. What about?"

Qod tilted his head to the side and stepped ten yards away to where they'd have a tiny bit of privacy.  A moment later, the corporal joined him.

"What do you need?"

"Well, the team.  Except for the hammer Sergeant Tark gave Tulip, they all sort of came with what they had.  I mean, look at Pani.  Her spear's in rough shape."

"Yeah?"

"I was thinking.  Is there any way, like, maybe we can upgrade the team?"

Mac's eyes narrowed. "And you're thinking that, you being an officer now, you can just go to supply and requisition better gear?"

From his tone, the corporal didn't sound like he thought that was likely.

"Not me." He looked around, opened his purse, and then showed it to Mac. "You."

The corporal quickly put a hand out and closed the purse.

"Where did you get that?" he hissed.

"From Glascock. He said it was my first month's pay."

"One month's pay?" Mac said, his eyes wide in surprise. "I never imagined . . . I mean, four gold imperials?"

"So, can you?" Qod asked.

"You mean, with this?"

Qod just nodded.

"Are you sure?"

"I'm sure."

A tiny smile creased the kobold's mouth. "With this, I think I might be able to manage something."

## Chapter 31

"Mage Killer!" a gremlin from the Copper Dragons shouted as he lifted his cup.

The call was picked up by the others, starting a round of back-and-forth chants between the company and the Broken Spears.

Qod burped, then took another sip of devil's piss and enjoyed the warm rush that spread through his gut. He raised the cup in acknowledgement.

He was feeling good, and not just because of the devil's piss. After all the trepidation of getting promoted and facing the general's reaction, things had been quiet for the last two days. Not even Lieutenant Glascock had made a showing. Qod was beginning to feel that he'd been overreacting.

It made sense. The Empress Almovoy was the single most powerful figure of the Dark. General Yare might be a god here with the Army of the Mist, but he still answered to her. So, if she wanted to jump up a goblin, was it really worth it to fight her on something so inconsequential?

He, Pani, and Tulip had discussed it at length last night. None of them were very schooled on the goings on in Taxian, but logic was logic. Qod knew he had to watch his step, but he thought he was reasonably safe for the nonce.

The party was in full swing, much to the obvious displeasure of the orcs and ogres who came to see what was going on before turning away in disgust. Maybe this was the devil's piss talking, but screw them, Qod thought.

Corporal Mac had been true to his word. Qod's four gold imperials had been converted first to new weapons and uniforms of black with copper-accented armor. The team might not be to the Black Smoke level, but they looked—and felt—more like a real unit. Qod didn't know who was more excited: Pani or New Guy, but Qod caught the normally more taciturn Yannis admiring the copper dragon on the chest.

Qod was more than pleased. He asked Mac how, way out here at Camp Defiance, out in the middle of nowhere, he'd managed to procure the equipment, and he'd been told rather bluntly that officers didn't ask NCOs how they did their business. They just accepted the mission being accomplished.

But the armor and weapons weren't all. When Mac brought back the change—eight silver imperials—he mentioned a "wetting down," almost as an afterthought. Qod had never heard the term, so he asked what it meant.

It turns out that since time immemorial, whenever someone in the military was promoted, they would "wet down" the new rank with alcohol, provided by the soldier getting said new rank.

Qod asked him if he knew how much booze eight imperials would buy, and of course, the corporal had the figures at hand.

Officer wetting downs were usually held with other officers, and while Mac wasn't sure how much officer-acceptable liquor cost, he guessed they'd expect him to spend his first month's pay on it.

*Ah, that's why Glascock made sure to get me the pay right away.*

If he wanted to have the wetting down with just the team, Mac thought he could "acquire" some of the officers' stash.

The third option was to make it a bigger party and treat both the Broken Spears and the Copper Dragons. It wouldn't be the good stuff. For that many soldiers, it would have to be the infamous devil's piss, and even with that weak, tepid booze, each soldier might only have two cups.

Mac stood there, waiting for his decision. Qod was tempted to ask what he would do, but somehow, he realized two things. First, it was his wetting down. It was his decision. Second, the corporal wanted him to step up, even for something so unimportant.

Qod had heard that one of an NCO's most important jobs was to train officers, and he wondered if this was his first lesson.

He started to consider his options, but then quit. There was only one real choice.

Having it with the officers was a no-go from the beginning. It might be politically astute, but Lieutenant

Glascock was the only officer to congratulate him, and he knew most of the others hated his rise. Even if he did the wetting down with them, he no longer had the funds to fulfill their expectations.

Treating the team would certainly be acceptable. They'd stuck with him. Lymon and Faulnom had been killed, and Tulip had been wounded over his choices.

But the best way to spend his last silver imperials would be on the two companies that had expressed loyalty to him. He told Corporal Mac to get the devil's piss. And from the pleased look in his eyes, Qod knew he'd made the right choice.

The companies thought it was the right choice, too, judging from their reactions. Very few, if any of them, had realized Qod had been promoted, and they were confused when the barrels of devil's piss had been rolled out. Corporal Mac jumped up on one and made the announcement, which was greeted with a thunderous roar.

Tulip put Qod on her shoulders, and he managed a few words from that perch, but frankly, he didn't think it mattered what he said. They were happy and anxious to start the party.

Mac had been right in that with so many soldiers, the booze didn't last long. The most anyone had was probably two cups, and devil's piss was already notoriously weak. But the stress from the last few battles had been building, and this gave them the excuse to let go. None of them, except for maybe a few of the pixies, were as drunk as they were acting.

All three of the officers—Captain Kritikos and Lieutenant Faree from the Broken Spears and acting company commander Lieutenant Pu from the Copper Dragons—made an appearance, either summoned by their NCOs or they heard the commotion and came to investigate.

Qod stiffened when the captain approached, but the company commander just took a moment to take in the scene before he turned to Qod and said, "You're a smart young gobby, Lieutenant."

One of his soldiers rushed up with a cup of devil's piss, which he dutifully drank. He then congratulated Qod, then made his way through the mass of soldiers, stopping to say a few words here or there before he disappeared over the rise.

All in all, it had been a good afternoon, and for the first time in a long time, Qod felt safe. He had no idea what the morrow would bring, but for the moment, life was good.

And that's when Dulce flew to him, hiccuped, and said, "Captain k'Ree's coming."

That peaceful feeling disappeared in a flash. Qod put his hand to his mouth and exhaled. His breath reeked. Two cups for a smallish goblin had a lot more effect than they would for a larger soldier.

He straightened his tunic the best he could and was standing at attention when the captain arrived.

She looked at the team with him and said, "Leave us."

They were out in the open high ground surrounding the Caldron, so it wasn't as if they could actually leave. Instead, they merely backed up fifteen or twenty yards. It wasn't far enough for Pani not to be able to hear, though. Qod caught her eye and gave a short nod before turning to the captain.

"Was this your idea, Lieutenant?" she asked, flicking a finger to encompass the two companies.

"Yes, ma'am. I was told a wetting down was traditional."

"Not like this," she said as she swept her gaze across the soldiers before shifting tack. "You are smart enough to realize that you are in a precarious position, aren't you?"

Qod winced. He'd been very concerned the day he was snatched up and promoted. But since then, he'd managed to convince himself that he was overacting. Now, with the captain's words, he was back to being a target.

"I believe I told you to return here and do nothing. I could be mistaken, but is having a drunken party doing nothing?"

"They aren't drunk, ma'am. No one had more than two cups of devil's piss."

She grunted, then said, "Drunk or not, you're attracting a lot of attention, something that could be quite detrimental to your continued existence."

He knew she was right, but he refused to acknowledge the statement. Truth be told, while there was still a core of fear in him, he was getting a little angry at the course of events

223

that brought him to this point. He was fine and happy—well, maybe not *happy*—back home in Yellow Rock before he was dragged into the army, given shoddy equipment, and thrust into battle.

It was pure luck and perhaps intervention by the gods that he killed the battle mage, but since then, he'd done everything he could to be a good little goblin soldier. And what did he get for all of that? Evidently, the animus of General Yare, the most powerful orc in the Fanciful Highlands at the moment—that's what.

The banshee lowered her voice and said, "Lieutenant Yellow Rock, I cannot stress enough that you are in a dangerous place right now, and you have almost no control as to your future. So it is imperative that with whatever small degree of control you have, you cannot make any mistakes."

"Ma'am?"

She sighed, then said, "Let me rephrase that. You have to remain as invisible as possible. You need to minimize whatever attention is put on you and deflect it somewhere else."

Qod let that sink in. It made sense when she put it that way. He looked away to the top of the rise where orcs and others were looking down at the two companies. He was doing exactly what she had warned him against.

"Ma'am, we all know I'm not a real officer—"

"You are by an imperial order."

"Well, yes. But—"

"No buts, and you need to accept that if you want to survive."

He clenched his jaw, took a deep breath, and said, "OK, I'm a lieutenant. But why are you telling me this?"

It took so long for her to respond that he thought she was going to ignore him.

But finally, she said, "We've fared OK here in the Highlands, but down south, things have not gone so well. The only way we'll survive is if we truly band together. And if there's a challenge for the Misty Throne now, that could be the end of us."

Qod's mouth dropped open in surprise. This was getting to something he hadn't even considered.

"General Yare?"

This time, she did ignore the question. Instead, she said, "You cannot be the catalyst for internal strife. If it gets to that, I'll eliminate you myself. Do you understand me?"

Qod barely squeaked out a, "Yes, ma'am."

He knew he was expendable, of course, and her job was to protect the general. But to hear her so calmly say she'd kill him was rather frightening.

"So, can I trust that you won't have any more parties? That you'll stay out of sight as much as possible?"

"Yes, ma'am."

What else could he say?

She sighed again, this time a little louder. "It might not matter anyway," she said more to herself than to Qod.

"Ma'am?"

She gave him an emotionless stare.

"You'll find out soon enough anyway. The Three-oh-sixth and the Eight-eleventh are being reorganized as the Third Scout Battalion."

It took him a moment to realize she was talking about the Broken Spears and the Copper Dragons.

"Captain Kritikos is being briefed now, but you're leaving on a mission in the morning, and that includes you."

"A mission? What is it?"

"I'll leave that for Kritikos." She swept her gaze across the two companies—across the battalion—and frowned.

"If you still have any of the devil's piss, you might want to cut them off. You're going to want your battalion in their best condition."

"It's not my battalion, ma'am. I'm just a package, as they call me."

"Don't be naïve, Lieutenant. It's unbecoming. It's *your* battalion."

With that, she spun on her heels and marched off. Qod watched her retreating back as he tried to figure out what the change meant.

And then he remembered one of the last things she'd said.

"It might not matter anyway."

*Just what kind of mission is this?*

# Chapter 32

For once, the Dark soldiers left on a mission in a timely manner, even if it was only the "Mage Killers"—the title the soldiers of the newly formed 3rd Scout Battalion were already calling themselves. The battalion, with Captain Kritikos as the acting commanding officer, moved out before dawn, hoping to escape prying Light eyes.

The mood was high and only partially from the last remnants of devil's piss. The feeling of the troops was that General Yare was rewarding them with an important mission.

Qod wasn't so sure. By designating the old Team Lightning—minus the satyr archers and the Motivational Company—as a scout battalion, he could effectively get them out of the camp—as Mac said, far enough away so that they didn't infect the rest of the division with their loyalty to Qod.

Without that reasoning, using the two replacement companies to form a scout battalion was unusual, to say the least. The other two battalions of "Gray Ghosts" were formed from experienced professional soldiers, mostly orcs, but from other races as well. No goblins or gremlins, of course, but pixies and kobolds from the small folk were part of the mix.

Scout battalions were second only to the Black Smokes in prestige. They had to be good as they usually operated behind enemy lines. So, to reorganize two companies of poorly trained small folk as a scout battalion didn't make sense without that ulterior motive.

Whatever the reason, they had a simple mission. The general was concerned that the Light forces might send a raiding force looping around the Mossy Ridge to cut off the Dark army's resupply route from Offerton and Muskrat Crossing. If they were able to do that, it could delay or even jeopardize the planned final offensive against the Light's main force somewhere in the Whispering Forest.

The Mage Killers' mission was to occupy the southernmost Mossy Ridge, where they could watch over the Lower Anemia River marshlands for enemy activity and report any back to the command group so they could react.

They were not to engage. Just observe and report. Whether highly trained soldiers or raw conscripts, that was a job they could do. Captain Kritikos actually welcomed the mission as an opportunity to let the two companies get used to working with each other while not facing certain combat.

It was a little strange that the general left the captain in temporary command. Team Lightning had been commanded by a colonel. Battalions were commanded by majors, and any major looking to make colonel would seemingly jump at the chance to take over—at least according to Corporal Mac. But maybe there hadn't been time to assign someone else. The division was in full planning phase for the final offensive push, after all.

The night's frost was still on the ground when the battalion headed down toward the far side of the valley, where the Upper Anemia plunged down the Barrel Falls Canyon to spread out in the Lower Anemia Delta below. At the edge of the camp, about a hundred Grey Ghosts from the 1st Scout Battalion gathered and stood silently while they watched the Mage Killers pass. Qod couldn't read them, and that put him on edge. It wasn't their fault that they'd been designated as a scout battalion.

But when he caught the eyes of a sergeant major, the senior enlisted gave him a slight, yet respectful nod.

Qod was surprised, and that nod changed the calculus. The scouts weren't looking at them in disdain, but with acceptance.

"Why aren't they going out now?" Pani asked.

"Saving them for the real push," Mac said.

"And that will be when?" Pani said.

It was a valid point. The final offensive was supposed to be the mission of four days ago, the one where Team Thunder had been recalled, leaving Team Lightning exposed.

Pani was still upset about that. Qod was, too, but not to the same degree. He had no idea how that decision had been made. Maybe it was something that the 2nd Scout Battalion— which was forward deployed at the moment—had observed.

Whatever the reason, what Corporal Mac just said made sense. There was no getting around the fact that the 3rd Scout

Battalion was made up primarily of new conscripts. Leaving 1st Battalion free for a more critical mission where their experience would pay off in support of the actual offensive seemed like a rational command decision.

"They'll have their mission," Qod said. "We just need to make sure we do ours."

Pani scowled, then said, "I know, small sir. It's just . . ."

"Just what?"

She shook her head. "Nothing. Forget it."

Qod stared at her for a long moment. He wanted to know what was bothering her, but he wasn't going to push.

They reached the end of the Gray Ghosts, and two pixies from the Copper Dragons took off. From here on out, they were in no-man's land, and the pixies were their forward eyes and ears. Pixies didn't have much stamina, so they'd be rotating every fifteen minutes for the expected eighteen-hour march.

*Eighteen hours*, Qod told himself as he hitched up his cuirass. *This is going to suck.*

## Chapter 33

"Another bridge, Tulip," Nataly said as the team's feet beat a tattoo on the weathered boards, just as she'd announced as they crossed the previous fifteen of twenty along the highway through the Lower Anemia River Delta.

And as with each other time, Tulip rolled her eyes.

But this time, she said a quiet, "That's just a stereotype, you know."

Still, her eyes seemed to light up past her fatigue as they crossed, and her hand reached out to stroke the center support.

This looked to be the last one, though. The highway veered slightly to the right and onto relatively dry land, and after another three hundred yards, Captain Kritikos brought the battalion to a halt.

Qod whispered a quiet thanks to the gods. He was beat. His back hurt, his shoulders hurt, and his feet were screaming. While not terribly far from Camp Defiance as the crow flies, the Barrel Falls Canyon was impassable, so the battalion had to first climb, then descend to the valley on the other side. It hadn't been constant walking. The captain had stopped them every couple of hours for ten or fifteen minutes, but Qod wasn't sure how effective that was. After each break, lurching back into motion was torture.

The cold weather, at least, was a blessing. Qod wasn't sure he could have kept up with the march in the heat of the summer.

The captain and the other three lieutenants were in a huddle as they discussed where they would best have eyes on the delta. Pani, who looked equally as tired as Qod was, had caught his eye and nodded her head in their direction, but Qod stayed put. He was the "package," after all, and although he was technically an officer now, he was still not a member of either of the two companies.

He recognized his personal hypocrisy. As a private, he'd interjected himself and been a major part of the planning for the Team Lightning retreat. Now, as a lieutenant, he was holding back.  But the fact was that he was exhausted.  Let them decide while he rested.

"You surviving?" Corporal Mac asked as he came alongside him.

"All in one piece."

Qod glanced over at Tulip, who was the depiction of exhaustion.  She was sitting, hunched over, on the ground, seemingly oblivious to all else.

"How about her?" he asked the corporal.

"She'll be fine. She just needs rest and food."

Tulip was an immensely powerful being, and Qod had seen her destroy the enemy who tried to stand against her.  This was the second time, though, in just a period of five days, that he'd seen her in a physically demanding evolution over a sustained period of time.

Aside from just having had an arrow the size of a small tree removed from her shoulder along with four smaller arrows by a hooded spirit, just simply being that big took a lot of energy, and stamina was not her—or any troll's—forte.  That was actually news to Qod.  Back in Yellow Rock, he'd just assumed they were invincible beings.  Actually seeing them for the first time made him question everything else he'd heard about the various races, Light and Dark alike.

For her sake, though, he just hoped she would recover quickly and get back to normal. And, if possible, before they climbed into position.

The Mossy Ridge was a massive, tree-covered finger protruding from the Fanciful Highlands, rising about five hundred feet above the lowlands below.  Eight miles to the north, where the battalion had descended to the valley floor, the river broke up into hundreds of small fingers and became a slowly flowing fluvial marsh.  Twenty-one miles to the south, at Muskrat Crossing, where the river reformed once more into something navigable, was Offerton, an agricultural center for the region and through which half of the Army of the Mist's resupplies passed.

Once the battalion was in position, they'd have eyes over the large, boggy area.  There wasn't a possible way for a

Light unit of any size to move over the two main roads through those wetlands without being spotted.

But first, the captain had to decide where to place the two companies, and the longer he discussed it with the two lieutenants, the longer the soldiers had to rest before making the climb.

All too soon, though, the captain gave the order, and the battalion was on the move. The Broken Spears went to the right, and the Copper Dragons, along with Qod and his team, headed to the left. Two weary pixies flew in advance of each company.

"Just a little farther, Tulip," Qod told the troll.

She just nodded as her massive chest was still heaving like bellows.

The lead elements of the company reached the base of the ridge and started up a draw that looked like it would guide them to the top. Qod hoped that the trees growing on the slope didn't hide a rough climb.

At least the mostly evergreens gave a little shade as they started up. It wasn't much, but it was better than nothing.

He skirted a large boulder halfway up when Dulce startled him by flitting up to his ear. "Something's off."

Qod stopped and looked ahead. He couldn't see the lead elements from his vantage, but up above the trees, their scout pixie was slowly watching over their progress.

"Off like how?"

"I feel—"

"What?"

"I don't know."

"Wizard stuff?" Qod asked as he looked up the slope.

In his short time in uniform so far, Qod had seen too much of Light wizardry. Each time, Dark soldiers had died,

"I don't think so, but maybe I should fly on up in case the other pixies—"

She was cut off by a shout of pain off to the right. Both turned in that direction, wondering if someone had tripped and fallen.

A moment later, a voice called, "Incoming," and almost immediately, a flight of arrows that seemingly appeared out of nowhere plunged at the climbing soldiers.

Qod dodged behind a smallish bristlecone a second before two arrows clattered into the branches and stuck.

Others weren't so lucky. Screams of pain rose from the slope.

"Charge them!" a voice called out. "That's the only way."

Qod vaguely remembered one of the sergeants saying after his first battle that charging through an ambush was the best way to survive, but it was one thing to hear that back at camp and another while trying to take cover behind a small tree.

He hesitated, and he wasn't the only one. Just to his right, Corporal Mac was still pushing forward, but most everyone else in sight was either taking cover or retreating.

"What do we do?" Dulce asked him.

Every ounce of him wanted to retreat, but he said, "Follow Mac."

He took a deep breath, drew his dagger, and started to move from behind the bristlecone when a deep roar from above washed over him, followed by the clashing of weapons, and he froze. Ahead, through the trees, he saw a sight that froze his soul. A line of screaming, axe and pike carrying dwarves, their faces and beards painted blue, was charging down toward them.

Some of the lead soldiers, a mere forty or fifty yards from him, tried to make a stand, but they might as well try to stop an ocean wave. The dwarves smashed into them as if they were six-month-old goblin sausages.

The dwarves had surprise, gravity, and massed numbers on their side. The battalion was climbing in its march formation—a column with flank security. It would be impossible for them to make a stand on the slopes.

Qod wasn't the only one to come to that realization. Captain Krtitikos's voice pierced the din, ordering an immediate retreat.

It was too much to hope for a disciplined movement. The moment the order was given, the Dark soldiers broke into a full-out run as they plunged back down the slope they'd just climbed. The battalion quickly outpaced the charging, but slower-running dwarves, who were built for strength, not speed.

His team closed around him as they bounded downhill. Twice, Qod stumbled and went head over heels. Each time, Nataly, in stride, yanked him back up to his feet and got him going again.

Finally, they broke out into the open on the bottom, joined by more and more of their fellow soldiers emerging from the tree-covered slope. Some turned as if to head back along their route in, while others looked about in confusion, all while the screams of the dwarves reached out to them.

That was before Captain Kritikos appeared and immediately began giving orders to keep moving to the road. NCOs jumped in, and despite the chaos, order was being at least somewhat restored.

Five dwarves reached the open area and charged a group of kobolds, who turned to face them. A sergeant yelled at them to retreat, but they ignored her. Qod tried to watch over his shoulder as he ran, but then he stepped into a muddy depression and went down yet again. By the time Tulip, this time, hauled him to his feet, the dwarves and kobolds, historical adversaries, were locked in combat.

All along the tree line, dwarves were emerging. Some Dark soldiers, too, who were almost immediately set upon. But what looked like the bulk of the Dark soldiers were running across the open area toward the road and marshland.

Satyrs were fast, almost as fast as orcs, and Captain Kritikos sprinted ahead.

"The coward," a gremlin gasped out as he ran.

But the captain wasn't running away. He spun as he reached the road and started shouting orders again. NCOs and Lieutenant Faree joined him, shouting and sometimes physically shoving soldiers into place as they formed a defensive line. Qod, who was slower than most, was still a ways out, but he could see both fear and determination as the battalion faced the dwarves.

Quicker than Qod would have thought possible, a basic line took shape, and as more soldiers reached them, it got stronger, even if haphazardly.

Qod and his team finally reached them, just steps ahead of the pursuing dwarves. The line opened to let them in, then closed just before the clash.

Dwarves crashed into the line, which bent and buckled as soldiers fell, but somehow held. The dwarves, who were unstoppable with gravity behind them, were not as strong after running across the open grass on their short legs, and their assault was just as piecemeal as the Dark's defense.

Qod tried to make sense of the battle. He started to move forward, his dagger in his hand, but Mac pulled him back, and Tulip took a position in front of him, ready to crush any dwarf who came near.

She never had to swing her hammer. Amidst all the fighting, it was as if they were in a little bubble, protected from the mayhem. Blood—Qod didn't know if it was Dark or Light—splattered him from the side, but that was as close as the fighting got to him.

Corporal Mac or not, Qod was going to move forward when the pure tone of a dwarven Gjallarhorn sounded in the chill air, and the dwarves broke contact and pulled back. They retreated to the base of Mossy Ridge, chased by the jeers of the Dark, but then they stopped and turned to face them.

The jeers petered out as the dwarves started reorganizing. They weren't done with the fight.

But the battalion wasn't standing pat, either. While most of the soldiers were poorly-trained conscripts, the NCOs and officers were professionals, and they went into overdrive to transform what had been a hastily set up defense into one with more order and tactical positioning.

They couldn't move back any. The marsh was at their heels, and anyone moving into it would be bogged down. With the water behind and the dwarves to the front, the highway was the only way out. But as narrow as it was, if the battalion tried to use it to retreat, the dwarves would easily tear through the massed soldiers trying to get away.

It was obvious to each one of them that this was going to be their stand. There was no retreat as there had been just five days ago. Their fate was going to be decided right here.

Qod wasn't going to be left out this time. He moved forward to join the line.

"You stay back," Corporal Mac told him.

"No. If the dwarves break through, then it's all lost anyway. So, we might as well join in. We can make a difference," he said, pointedly looking at Tulip.

She was the single most potent fighter in the battalion, and she hadn't swung her hammer in anger during the initial assault while standing guard over him. How many lives were lost because of that?

The corporal was going to say something but then shut his mouth.

He stared at Qod for a moment before he said, "You're right, sir. And if we're going to die, I'd rather do it with my falchion in my 'and sticking a dwarf than cowering in the rear."

Qod led the team forward and tried to push his way to the front. The soldiers there resisted until a gremlin turned back and saw Tulip towering there. He hit the vurdalak next to him in the shoulder, and after she turned, they made a hole, allowing the team to move to the front.

After the battle at the barricade, Qod had sworn to do whatever he could to protect the small folk soldiers. As he stared at the dwarves some 200 yards away, he shook his head. He'd imagined his efforts would have been in line with trying to convince the leadership to make changes. He never dreamed it would be as a fighter.

*But a soldier's got to do what a soldier's got to do.*

He just wished he had his spear again, instead of his small dagger. Officers carried swords, though, and this was about all he could handle for a blade.

"Why aren't they using their archers?" Pani asked. "They can't miss us."

"Too far," Mac answered.

"The elves were a lot farther away when we were Team Lightning," Qod said, looking at Yannis.

He patted his bow. "Elves, fauns, and us, we use long bows. All of us can send a bolt three hundred, three-fifty yards. Dwarves got their shorties. Good for fighting in the mines and maybe in a forest like on the ridge, but they don't have the range."

Qod frowned. It sure seemed that the two volleys that hit them on the ridge had been fired from a distance.

"Those shorties, as you call them, sure killed a lot of us," Nataly said.

"I didn't say they weren't dangerous. They just don't have the range."

"The dwarves made a mistake," Tulip offered quietly.

Every team member turned to her.

"Mistake?" Mac asked.

"They fired too early. Someone prematurely loosed an arrow, which then made the rest of the archers let go without having targets."

"And then their infantry had to break early, too," Qod said once the troll's point sank in. "And that let most of us escape the initial ambush."

"Not most," Mac said. "There aren't that many of us 'ere."

Too many Dark soldiers hadn't made it off the ridge, but without a formal headcount, Qod wasn't sure that it was "most." He wasn't going to argue the specifics, though.

"OK. Maybe not most, but a lot. More than would have made it down if they'd waited a few minutes longer. And if that had happened, we wouldn't have been able to hold them off right here."

Corporal Mac accepted that statement with a nod.

The Dark command had surely made mistakes since Qod was conscripted, but it was heartening to know that so had the Light. Not just here, he remembered. But relying on the battle mage without a good backup plan at Qod's second battle turned out to be a big mistake. The initial plan at the Long Caldron had caught the Dark flatfooted, but they hadn't been able to follow through. Five days ago, they'd positioned their trebuchets too close to the canyon mouth, which, coupled with the centaurs delaying their charge, allowed Team Lightning to regain the relative safety of the canyon.

And now this.

The Light Army was a deadly foe, but they were hardly the invincible force of evil he'd been led to believe as a sausage back in Yellow Rock.

He was about to mention that to Pani when the clear call of the Gjallarhorn reached across the space between the two enemies, its undeniable beauty hiding the utter death and destruction it heralded.

But the dwarves held fast except for a lone faun, clad in pure white, who stepped forward twenty yards and faced them.

"Is that a battle mage?" Qod asked as fear shot through him.

"A wizard," Dulce said.

"What's he gonna do?" Nataly asked.

Dulce just shook her head.

"Can you stop him, whatever it is?" Mac asked her.

"Probably not," she said as she flew up to Tulip's shoulder. "But I'll try."

Qod had been ready to face charging dwarves, but he'd seen what the battle mage had done, and even with Dulce telling him it was a wizard, not a battle mage . . . well, the wizards he'd seen with the Light had been far more effective with their magic than any of the purple-clad Dark wizards.

Only the gremlin wizard had managed any magic to protect the Dark troops, and he'd been killed almost immediately after that.

He wasn't the only one who was nervous. A ripple of concern seemed to spread across the battalion as they waited.

The faun opened his mouth and screamed.

*That's it?*

But then he raised his arms, and a bubble of power spread out, rippling the air as it advanced, and the scream transformed into a thousand fingernails on blackboards, a thousand yowling cats, a thousand wails from the damned in the pits of hell. Every Dark soldier recoiled as the discordant cacophony ate into their brains.

The next blast from the Gjallarhorn was almost lost in the pain, but the roar from the dwarves as they charged managed to register. Soldiers struggled to bring their weapons to bear to meet the threat.

Dulce's shout was barely audible. Someone pushed Qod to the side, and he twisted to see Yannis, his body rigid as a board, step up. Slowly, he raised his bow and drew back the nocked arrow. Sweat was pouring from his brow and into his eyes, and blood was coming from where he was biting his lower lip.

Qod had his hands clasped to his ears, not that it did any good, and he struggled to watch his satyr friend. How he managed to concentrate amazed him. He held the position for too long as the roars of the charging dwarves started to overcome the devil's symphony assaulting them.

Finally, he let loose and then collapsed. Two unbearable seconds later, the aural attack ceased, just like that. The pain was gone. Qod glanced up. The Light wizard had fallen onto his back, Yannis's arrow protruding from his chest.

The wizard might be down, but the dwarves were not. Soldiers had maybe five seconds to orient themselves, mentally and physically, before the wave of dwarves smashed into them.

One dwarf swung his axe just over Qod and the prone Yannis and into the chest of the kobold next to him. His momentum slammed him into Qod, knocking him down. Qod struggled to slash the body with his dagger when the dwarf went limp. Tulip, the head of her hammer now covered with dwarf blood, yanked him free, then stepped forward to take on two more dwarves.

The next ten minutes—or maybe it was a hundred minutes—devolved into chaotic snippets of images. Qod getting knocked over by another dwarf. Qod dodging a kobold sword swung at the enemy and almost taking off his head. Qod stabbing the lower back of a dwarf, right under the edge of the cuirass. Pani latching onto his side, with a demonic-looking snarl on her face as she attacked any enemy who got close to the two of them. Tulip, swinging her hammer with machine-like precision. Captain Kritikos, falling under the slashes of three dwarves.

It was a kaleidoscope of images, all twirling around in his mind, all impactful, but nothing had any degree of continuity. He didn't even try to make sense of it. His entire purpose was centered on killing dwarves. He wasn't succeeding very well with that, but not for the lack of trying. After getting knocked down again, he thought he scored a hit on the back tendons on the leg of a dwarf—but her armor could have protected her. And he stabbed another who might or might not have already been killed. Other than the one he stabbed in the back, that was it when the Gjallarhorn blew three long blasts, and the dwarves started to pull back once more, or at least tried to. Enough of them had broken through the front line of the defense that now they had to fight their way back, and the Dark soldiers were not in a forgiving mood. Five, ten, maybe fifteen of them were taken down by swarms of Dark soldiers before they could break free.

Even then, not all of the Dark troops wanted to let them go. Several started chasing them, and it took Lieutenant Glascock, who once again was unblemished, to scream them into submission and return to the position. Only one, an orc, kept going, and Qod watched with the dull eyes of exhaustion as the dwarves turned and closed in on him. They left his body, just fifty yards away, before running off.

As before, they stopped just short of the ridge's tree line.

"Haven't they had enough?" Dulce asked.

This time, the dwarves formed their own defensive position. Qod knew that now would be a good time for the battalion to launch its own assault. But as he swept his gaze around the position, he knew that wasn't in the cards.

So many had fallen, either dead or wounded. Soldiers were moving among the bodies on the ground, assisting any still-living Dark troops and dispatching the Light. Qod briefly wondered if killing them was honorable, but after all they'd been through, he turned a blind eye to it.

"Your nose."

"What?" he asked as he tried to focus.

"Your nose," Pani repeated, pointing at his face.

It was only then that he realized how much it hurt. He reached up a tentative finger. His big, beautiful nose, his only physical feature that he took hidden pride in, was smashed to the side. Blood was dripping out of it.

He groaned and tried to straighten it, which sent a blinding flash of pain through him.

"When did that happen?" Pani asked.

"I don't know," he said, and he didn't.

Until she mentioned it, he didn't even know it had been broken. He gave himself a quick lookover. His cuirass was slashed, right through the right dragon, the one he'd named Yrid, which gave him a start, but his questing fingers didn't find any blood.

*Thanks, Yrid. I guess you did your job.*

His teammates, who had been somewhat separated from him in the fight, gathered around.

"Are you OK, sir?" Mac asked, his eyes latched onto his nose.

Qod nodded and told Yannis, who looked much better, "You saved us. If you hadn't taken out that wizard, I think . . ."

He didn't finish the sentence, but the satyr puffed up his chest.

"All I ever hear is faun this and faun that. I figured it was time to show everyone what a *real* archer could do."

"That you did," Tulip said as she laid a massive hand on his shoulder.

"We all did good," New Guy said.

Qod had been superstitiously worried that the gremlin wouldn't survive, so he was happy to see his misgivings had been wrong.

"Yes, we did," Mac said. "But if we're done patting ourselves on the back, let's get ready. Those shit-thieving dwarves didnae leave, and knowing them, they'll be back for more."

Qod stared at the dwarves for a long moment, wondering just what drove them. Why would they march to Dark lands to kill or be killed? It boggled his mind.

Not that the why mattered, only that they were here to kill the people of the Dark.

"You heard the corporal," he told the others. "Let's get ready for the bastards."

## Chapter 34

Only, the dwarves evidently had had enough. Even from this distance, it was obvious that there was debate—vigorous debate. Eventually, one side prevailed. Dwarves started disappearing, marching along the base of the ridge, away from the battalion.

Before all of them joined the exodus, though, thirteen of them lined up, backs to the Dark soldiers. In unison, they bent over and pulled down their trousers, exposing their butts.

Before they straightened, Yannis quickly nocked an arrow and drew it back, muttering, "You're still in satyr range, assholes."

Qod lurched into motion and yanked at his arm just as he released. The arrow shot out, but it stuck in the dirt ten yards away.

His eyes flashed in anger as he turned on him, but Qod snapped at him first.

"If they're retreating, then let them. Don't give them a reason to change their mind."

The entire team stared at the two, eyes wide in shock.

Qod had never used that tone with any of them before. He met Yannis's stare, refusing to back down.

The fact that there had been debate among the dwarves—and the fact that some of them had just mooned them—meant that not all of them wanted to retreat. Qod couldn't stop the catcalls the soldiers were shouting across the grass, but other than rude gestures, the dwarves were ignoring the Dark soldiers. Hitting one of them with an arrow, though, as they were leaving, might be too much of an insult for the prickly dwarves to endure.

It wasn't worth the risk.

The two, satyr and goblin, were locked in a battle of wills for a moment before Yannis broke eye contact, and his body slumped.

"You're right, Lieutenant. I'm sorry."

It took a moment longer for Qod to relax, but then he gruffly said, "It's OK, Yannis. Just, uh, don't do it again."

Tulip's sigh of relief was impossible to miss, but it *was* possible to ignore. He pointedly turned away from the others to watch the dwarves leave.

A few moments later, a gremlin ran up.

"Sir, the lieutenant wants you."

Qod was about to ask which one, but then he spotted the two still-standing lieutenants discussing something, so he thanked the messenger and headed over.

"Good. You're here," Lieutenant Faree said. "The dwarves are leaving," she added, as if Qod couldn't see that for himself.

"But it could be a ruse. I know everyone wants to get out of this gods-cursed place, but I think we should wait until dark before we move out."

"Dwarves don't mind the night," Glascock said.

Which was true. They'd worked the mines for thousands of years, and of all the Light races, they were at home in the dark.

Qod waited for one of them to continue until he realized that they were waiting for *him* to weigh in. That was astounding, and for a moment, the shock had him speechless.

To cover that, he turned to look at the battlefield. With most of the soldiers lined up to watch the dwarves retreat, the sorting of the dead and wounded had hit a pause. The dead were the dead and could be tended to later, but many of the wounded were in no condition to start marching right away.

That was the deciding factor for him.

"We need to make sure the dwarves are well and truly away, and the wounded need time before they can move. I think we should wait until tonight to move."

Faree gave Glascock a triumphal glance and then said, "Good. It's decided. So, let's get to work."

Qod was reluctant to meet Glascock's eyes, but he couldn't help it. To his surprise, the lieutenant didn't seem angry, just resigned. He nodded to Qod, then rushed off to help Faree prepare the battalion.

A battered platoon from the Copper Dragons was kept on alert, and one of the surviving pixies flew forward to watch for a return of the dwarves while the rest worked to prepare for the march back.

An hour later, a hooded spirit appeared, and twenty minutes after that, another arrived.

"How do they know they're needed?" Qod asked Mac, his voice sounding muffled through his still swelling and now blocked nose.

"They just do, and we're better off not questioning it."

If the healers noticed that there were no living, wounded dwarves, that didn't slow them down from treating the Dark troops. They weren't miracle workers, though. More than a few soldiers passed to the beyond despite their care.

Qod had turned away from them when Pani dragged a healer to him.

"Can you take care of him?"

The healer's face was hidden in the deep shadow of the hood, but Qod could feel its gaze, and he suddenly felt guilty for taking up the hooded spirit's time. Others were far worse off.

He was about to tell the healer to go to them when it reached out, and before Qod could react, it grabbed his nose and gave it a twist.

Qod yelped and jumped back. Something had just happened, something that felt vaguely slimy and just *wrong*. He raised his hand to his nose and was surprised to feel that it was straight again. More than that, he could breathe.

The hooded spirit stood there for a long ten seconds or so before it turned and glided off to the rest of the wounded.

"Are you OK?" Pani asked.

Qod lightly pushed his nose back and forth. It still hurt, but not as much, and it could just be his imagination, but the swelling might actually be a little less.

"Uh, yes. I am."

He watched the healer's retreating back. Dulce had told him that the hooded spirits did not use wizardry in their art, but Qod had sure felt *something*.

Whatever it was, it gave him the willies, and he didn't want to experience it again. Still, his ego was somewhat relieved that his big, beautiful nose might not end up disfigured.

The activity at the battlefield slowed as the battalion waited for nightfall. Qod needed a bit of time to digest what was going on, so he pulled away from his team and stood at the edge of the marsh, looking out over the desolate landscape.

Without an active task, the image of his knife disappearing into the dwarf's back was monopolizing his thoughts. He knew he'd done the right thing, but for all the evil the Light was inflicting upon the world, that was still a living, breathing person. He had a family somewhere.

Qod wasn't even sure his blow had killed the dwarf. That didn't matter, though. He knew the . . . *joy*, he'd felt, as the blade ran home. The excitement that had rushed through him.

And now, he felt shame. Qod considered himself a good person. A good goblin. One who cared about his fellow beings. Yet how could he take pleasure in killing a sentient creature? How did that jive with his self-image?

The questions wouldn't leave him alone, and in anger, he stooped, picked up a rock, and threw it into the marsh.

*All this death, for this place?*

He realized the fight wasn't specifically for the Amenia River delta, but it just seemed like a sad place to die, so far away from civilization.

The delta was vital for the region, he knew. The water that made its way through the delta supported Offerton and cities downriver. It supplied the fertile Windy Plains, which fed a good portion of the Dark, but Qod was in a mood, filled with darker thoughts. And it wasn't just the stabbing of the dwarf. Something else was gnawing away at his mind, as well, but he couldn't quite put his finger on it.

A burst of cold wind blew across his face, and a moment later, flurries started to fall.

"Of course, we're getting a freeze. Why would I expect anything else?"

He thrust his hands in the tiny slits in his leathers, but the wind was biting his exposed ears.

Someone stepped up behind him. He didn't need to turn to know it was Pani.

"Hey," she said.

"Hey."

"You OK?"

"You already asked me that."

"That was before you decided to stand out here all alone for half an hour, staring at nothing."

"It's been that long?" he asked.

"Uh-huh."

"Just thinking," he said as he wiped his forearm across his nose, then winced.

His nose might be *healing*, but it wasn't *healed*.

They stood in silence until Pani said, "Look. Ice."

Qod hadn't noticed it, but yes, ice was forming on the water at his feet. It wasn't much, yet, but it was a reminder that the temperature was dropping.

"It shouldn't stop us," Qod told her. We've got the road and the bridges."

"And I guess the exercise will help keep us warm." She paused, then said, "I hate the cold."

Qod turned his head to look at her. She was shivering. Without thinking, he sidled up next to her. She didn't react for a moment, then moved slightly into him.

For a moment, the fight, his shame, and everything else faded away, and he was about to put his arm around her—only to keep her warm, of course—when the rest of the team approached.

"Yes, I know I've been here for half an hour, and yes, I'm OK," he said, beating Mac to the punch as he stepped slightly away from Pani. "Anything else you want to know?"

It was obvious that was exactly what Mac had been about to say and ask, and he floundered for a moment before he managed, "I guess we'll be moving out in about an hour."

"I guess so."

"Not soon enough," Yannis said. "I hate the cold. I don't see how you northerners can stand it."

"You get used to it," Pani said, belying what she'd just told Qod.

He didn't call her out on it.

"Well, uh . . ." Mac said, and an awkward silence took over.

Qod's mind started drifting again, and, more to himself than to the others, said, "That's the second time this happened."

"This is war," Mac said. "Of course, the Light will be coming for us. It was just plain bad luck that they were moving right where we were going."

And like a safecracker working a lock, that last statement aligned the mental pins, opening the door.

"I don't mean the Light. I mean General Yare," he said with conviction as a fire began to burn inside of him.

"General Yare," Nataly repeated.

"Yare. This is the second time he's tried to get us killed."

"Now, wait a minute," Mac started to say when Qod cut him off.

"No, think on it. Team Lightning. We're sent off, but somehow Thunder and Hammer are recalled, and we don't get the word?"

"It wasn't just us with Lightning," Mac said. "Yare's not going to sacrifice them, just to get you."

"Us," Qod corrected him. "The Broken Arrows and Copper Dragons. And the convicts."

"It wasn't just those three companies, though," Mac said.

But Qod wasn't listening to logic. He knew in his heart he was right.

"What about today? It isn't a coincidence that we're designated as a scout battalion, then sent off without any support."

"Scout battalions never have support," Tulip said in her gentle voice, as if explaining something to a sausage.

"Maybe not," Qod had to admit. "But it wasn't just bad luck that the dwarves were there. They were already in position when we started to climb the ridge, the same ridge we were ordered to occupy. Maybe Yare knew where they were and then sent us there."

He knew he was sounding like a crazy goblin, but Qod was positive that somehow, some way, General Yare was trying to get rid of him along with the soldiers loyal to him. He just had to figure out how he was doing it.

The others refused to meet his eyes. Even Pani, who looked stricken with worry.

*They think I've lost it.*

"You just can't see it," he said as the flame of anger was fanned into a tempest. "But I promise you this. I am going to confront the bastard."

Qod wheeled and strode off. Pani called after him, but he ignored her.

He needed to find the other two lieutenants. It was time to get the show on the road. The sooner he could confront the general, the better.

## Chapter 35

The battalion, half the size as when it marched out, crested the last rise. The Army of the Mist was spread out below them. Lazy tendrils of smoke rose from the ashes of the previous night's campfires.

Qod snarled and started to pick up the pace.

"Don't do anything stupid, small sir," Pani said as she tugged on his arm.

He jerked free.

"He tried to kill us. He tried to kill me, and he didn't care how many of the battalion died to achieve that. All those who died, they mean nothing to him."

"Listen to Pani," Corporal Mac said.

"And just let him get away with it?"

Qod had fumed during the entire march back. Every step just increased his fury. It was so obvious once he recognized what was happening. And as far as Qod was concerned, General Yare had wanted them dead.

"Don't let the 'ero shit go to your 'ead. You're still a lieutenant and 'e's a general. You won't win that battle."

Of course, the corporal was right, but Qod couldn't just stand by and do nothing. He had an ace up his sleeve.

Maybe.

"I'm not going to challenge the asshole. But I think the empress would be very, very interested in a general who murders his own troops."

Corporal Mac grabbed the same arm and held him in an iron grip.

"And you're gonna be the one to tell 'er? 'Ow you gonna do that? You think she even knows 'oo you are?"

"She promoted me. Yes, she knows who I am," Qod said stubbornly, sure of himself.

"She daena know you from a cockroach. You're a tool, nothing more. And daena you give me that butthurt look, *Lieutenant*. You know I'm right."

"Listen to him," Pani said.

"And look at all these soldiers. They'd die for you, Qod. The Mage Killer. What dae you think's gonna 'appen to them if you go and challenge the general? Or 'ears you tried to contact the empress. And 'e *will* find out."

A handful of the soldiers were close enough to hear the conversation, and they were watching to see what Qod was going to say next. But the rest, 250 strong, were trudging along, battered and weary. Twenty or thirty were wounded beyond their ability to walk on their own and were being carried or helped back to the camp.

Once again, the corporal was right. The general would put them at the point of the expected push against the Light. Twice now, he'd tried to eliminate them, so what was once more?

Qod took several deep breaths, and in a much calmer voice, said, "I won't be so obvious. When the next emissary gets here, I'll slip them a note or something."

Mac's eyes got huge, and Qod wondered what faux pax he'd just uttered now.

"You can read and write?" the kobold asked in utter surprise.

"Yes, I can. My ma taught me. Why?"

Well over half of the goblins in Yellow Rock were literate, and Qod just assumed that held true throughout the Dark races. Evidently not, though, given the corporal's reaction.

"I just . . . well, I daena expected that." He paused a moment and then said, "That might work, though. But please daena do anything until you've discussed it with—"

This time, he looked over to Lieutenant Glascock, who looked just as beat as the rest of the soldiers.

"With me," he said a moment later.

*You don't trust him.*

The lieutenant had fought like a demon, and a lot of soldiers were alive because of him, but he was an officer, an orc, and a member of one of the most powerful families of the Dark.

He probably wasn't the one to discuss this with.

"Right, Corporal. Will do."

The battalion slowly straggled into Camp Defiance. Other soldiers stopped what they were doing for a few moments to watch before getting back to their early morning tasks. Three hooded spirits left their small tent and headed toward them.

It was too late for four of the soldiers, who'd died during the march, but maybe they could save the rest of the wounded.

That was just one more thing that pissed Qod off. He didn't know how the healers organized themselves, but if a couple had been with them, maybe more lives could have been saved.

The Copper Dragon sergeant who'd appointed himself as the keeper of the wounded immediately peeled off to meet with the healers, and after a brief discussion, escorted them closer, where they started to take stock of the situation.

The path to the battalion's previous campsite took it right under the CP, where the draugr guards stared down unpassionately at them. A single major stood outside the entrance. That was it. No one else seemed to care.

At least that's what it initially looked like. As the lead elements passed, the flap to the entrance opened and several more officers rushed out and pointed.

"Yeah, look at us," Qod muttered.

"Easy," Pani reminded him.

"I'm in control. Don't worry."

And he was until General Yare emerged, along with Major Pishlyss and a handful of colonels. The general didn't come down to greet the soldiers. He stood there with a look of disdain on his face, but one tinged with . . . victory?

Pani grabbed his arm and held it fast as Qod glared at Yare. The general slowly swept his gaze over the battalion until he locked eyes with Qod, and without a shred of compassion, the Army of the Mist's commanding general smiled.

*Smiled.*

Something inside Qod broke apart. The timid, undersized goblin from Yellow Rock, the one who avoided confrontation, vanished as a wave of pent-up anger washed over him.

He spun on his heel, yanking his arm out of Pani's grasp, and started up the hill. Pani grabbed at him again, but he shrugged her off.

The general's eyes slightly widened for a brief moment before they narrowed in satisfaction, and that just enraged Qod even more. The orc was dismissing him as inconsequential when Qod wanted the general to fear him more than anything else. And if not fear him, at least acknowledge what he'd done to the soldiers of the Mage Killers.

The draugrs reacted, though. They moved to step in front of the general until the orc said something, and they hesitantly stepped back.

They needn't have worried. Qod was angry—more than that. He was livid. But he wasn't stupid. He wasn't a physical threat to the general. At best, he could make the general, and all those around him right now, feel guilty for what he'd done.

That in and of itself was a tall order. General Yare didn't seem like the type of orc who felt shame about anything. But Qod had to try. He owed it to the dead.

The hill was steeper than he'd remembered. That, or he was just exhausted by the fight and march back. Either way, he could feel hundreds of sets of eyes on him as he made his less-than-dramatic approach. He was hardly giving off the heroic avenging angel vibe.

He tried to keep from gasping for air as he climbed the last few meters and came to a stop in front of the general, who looked at him with the maddeningly mocking smile on his face.

A few of the officers had the same vulture-like look as Qod had seen when the camp commander had been escorted away. It didn't look like he was going to get any support from them.

*No matter.*

Qod pulled himself erect when another figure emerged from the CP to take her place behind the others. That gave him the slightest of pauses.  He'd developed a degree of respect for Captain k'Ree, and to see her backing up the general . . .

He shoved her out of his mind, but before he could say anything, the general beat him to the punch.

"I see you abandoned your assigned position," he said casually.

Behind him, several colonels chuckled.

Despite his intention not to let his anger take over the meeting, Qod almost lost it right there.  He had to fight to retain control.

"I believe you know why, *General*," he said, his tone when addressing the rank leaving nothing hidden.

"You were supposed to remain unseen.  I take it you failed in that?"

"How could we—"

Footsteps came up behind Qod, and he turned to see Lieutenant Glascock approaching.  But the lieutenant didn't join the command staff.  He stopped beside Qod and faced the general.

"Ah, Lieutenant.  Where is Captain Krikitos?"

"With the hooded spirits, sir.  It's doubtful he'll survive," the lieutenant said.

"Pity.  He won't be able to face the consequences of his failure."

"He didn't fail," Qod snapped.  "The Light was there waiting for us."

The general's eyes glinted, and he took a sudden step forward so that he was less than a foot from Qod, who had to fight to keep from jumping back in alarm.

He wanted to shame the general, not get him angry enough to kill him right there.

The general slowly bent over until his face was just inches from Qods, fetid orc breath washing over him.

"And how do you think the Lights knew where you were going?" he whispered with satisfaction, just loud enough for only Qod to hear.

Qod went ashen, and this time he did step back as he stared at the general in horror.  It all fell into place.  It wasn't enough to send the Qod and Team Lightning forward while pulling back their support. It wasn't enough to send the 3d Scout Battalion out into Light territory yet again. No. This time, he had to stack the deck and tell the Light what was happening.

General Yare was a traitor, pure and simple. He'd conspired with the Light to kill Dark soldiers. *His* soldiers.

His previous caution disappeared, and in shock, he shouted, "You told them where we were going!"

It took a moment to realize what he'd said, but the Mage Killers who were close enough to hear shouted out in anger.

The command staff were just as surprised at Qod's outburst, and a few of them shouted at him. The general just studied him, like a cat on a mouse.

"You . . . you . . . traitor!" He looked at the colonels and said, "General Yare conspired with the enemy." When no one said anything, he added, "He doesn't deserve to command the army, and so he has to go. He must be removed!"

And the cat pounced.

"I accept!" the general shouted with unadulterated glee.

"What?"

That wasn't what Qod was expecting to hear.

"You agree? You'll step down?"

"Tomorrow. Sunrise," the general said before he turned and reentered the CP. Some of the command staff laughed. Others just stared at Qod for a moment before they all filed after Yare.

"What's going on? He'll resign tomorrow?" Qod asked.

Lieutenant Glascock sighed and said, "You don't understand, do you?"

"No, I don't. That's why I'm asking."

"You just challenged General Yare, gobby, for command of the Army of the Mist."

## Chapter 36

"He'll be hunted down and killed," Lieutenant Glascock said. "Along with anyone else who helped him."

"We'll just have to make sure they don't find us," Pani said.

Qod barely listened to the argument. He was numb. Numb *and* angry, if that was possible. Never in a million years would he have guessed he would be facing mortal combat for command of the Army of the Mist.

And he only had himself to blame. He should have listened to Pani and Corporal Mac. Instead, he let his temper get the best of him, and so he'd walked right into General Yare's trap.

Qod was just a goblin from Yellow Rock. The gods had played their little trick, and he'd killed the elf battle mage. But the hype that accompanied that, then getting promoted to lieutenant, and finally having a battalion of soldiers expressing their loyalty to him—that was all pretty heady stuff. But had he actually begun to believe some of that? Was he being tempted with the idea that he was somehow special?

A smart little gobby--and he'd always prided himself on that—would have kept his head down. He'd have kissed the general's ass at every turn. He'd have forcefully rejected the attention of the two companies.

Instead, he'd begun to think that he could have a material effect on the war. Him. Qod of Yellow Rock.

Hubris has been the downfall of so many throughout history, so why not him?

". . . Dark and Light?" the lieutenant was saying.

"Why would the Light care about an internal fight?" Yannis asked.

"Because that's how the system works." When no one seemed to understand, he said, "The system of succession is the same for both the Dark and Light. And no one wants to change that."

Tulip scrunched her eyebrows together, but the rest were still confused. Well, Qod wasn't, but that's because he didn't care, at least for the moment.

"No one on either side wants to rock the boat on this. When a challenge is made, both sides join in an unofficial truce, but one locked into tradition. And if Qod here, having challenged the general—"

"I didn't challenge him," Qod said without any force.

"Well, you did. Even if you didn't realize it. But, as I was saying, if Qod here runs, he'll be an outcast, existing outside the bounds of either the Dark or Light. And they'll hunt him down with just as much fervor as the general will."

"But—"

"But nothing, Private Tulip. That's the way it is. Trust me on that." He paused for a moment. "Remember, too. The Light was anxious to cooperate with the general when they knew they'd be eliminating the Mage Killer."

"So you *do* think General Yare gave us up to them?" Dulce asked.

Lieutenant Glascock visibly winced. He looked around to see if anyone was within earshot, lowered his voice, and said, "Yes, I do."

Nataly kicked the ground, but no one said anything. All the lieutenant had done was confirm what they already knew.

"I don't care," Pani finally said. "I'll go with him."

"Me, too," New Guy said, quickly followed by the rest.

"And you'll be killed, just like him," the lieutenant said.

That finally roused Qod. He'd almost come to accept that he would be killed tomorrow morning, but he couldn't accept the rest of the team throwing away their lives.

"No. You won't. None of you will."

"It's our choice, Pani said.

"The hell it is," he said. And when no one responded, he asked, "What about the soldiers? They've already said they'll fight. Do you want them to die, too?"

"That's different," Corporal Mac said.

"How?"

"No, we can't let them fight. But we're your team, as in security *team*."

"And I appreciate the thought, but I can't let you do it."

"Not up to you. You're the package, not in command here," Mac said before looking pointedly at Lieutenant Glascock, who immediately threw up his hands and backed up several steps.

"I can't. No. My family."

Qod hadn't expected him to jump in, and he didn't blame the orc.

"Look, uh . . . I sympathize with you. Really, I do. And Qod, you're getting screwed, I know it. I'm not going to get in your way. I won't repeat anything you've said. But . . . no. I can't."

"I don't expect you to," Qod assured him. "I don't expect anyone to," he told the rest.

"Right," a clearly flustered Glascock said. "Look, I've got to go. Uh . . . good luck tomorrow."

He wheeled around and hurried off in the direction of the CP.

"Do you think he's going to the general now?" Nataly asked.

"No, I don't," Qod said after a moment's consideration.

"It wouldn't matter if he did," Tulip said. "Yare wants this, and he's not going to let anything get in the way of that."

"Do you think, you know, that you can defeat him?" New Guy asked. "I mean, you killed an elf battle mage, for fuck's sake. Yare's just a big orc."

There it was, out in the open. The entire team waited for the answer.

"No. I can't."

And with that came a surprisingly calm acceptance.

He looked beyond them to the battalion. The soldiers might have given the team space, but they were all watching them. If he gave the word, he was pretty sure that all of them would fight to protect him, 250 against 6,000. And after watching them in two battles, they would surprise the other soldiers. They'd fall. No doubt about that. But more than a few would go down with them. Maybe a lot of them.

Qod couldn't let that happen. After everything they'd gone through over the last few weeks, the Army of the Mist couldn't afford to lose more soldiers. That would just open the door for the Light, and a Light victory . . . well, he just couldn't contemplate that.

A brief vision of a devastated Yellow Rock, with goblin bodies littering the streets, forced its way into his mind, and he shuddered. No, he couldn't go along with anything that was going to weaken the army, even if that sure felt like surrender.

The question was whether the others would let him go. Mac said he was the package, not the commander.

He turned and looked over the valley. The sun was just reaching the far peaks, and the light seemed almost alive.

So many had died there. What was one more little goblin who'd gotten too big for his pantaloons?

"I need a little time," he told the others. "Pani, would you join me?"

Tulip rose ponderously and grabbed her hammer, but Qod said, "Just Pani. I'm safe enough here. At least until tomorrow morning."

She didn't like that. None of them did, Qod could tell.

"'Elmet and weapons," Corporal Mac said. "And if there's so much as a bird squawking, we're coming."

Which was fine with Qod. He grabbed his helmet and led his fellow goblin to a spot close to where he'd first seen her as they waited for their weapons.

"Sit with me," he said while pointing to the base of a large rock.

As small as they both were, they were out of sight from the rest of the team and the battalion. If he could ignore the low hubbub of the army in camp, he could imagine that the two of them were alone in an empty world.

Qod was not known as a goblin rake, cutting a swath through willing and eager goblinettes. Oh, he'd imagined what it would be like often enough, but in actuality, his experience was limited to what Leet and Poul had told him, and he wasn't even sure how much of that was truth.

And here he was, sitting with a rather attractive goblinette, one who actually liked him, and watching the sun set. It wasn't lost on him that in another time and place, he would think he was dreaming.

But given the situation, romance was not in the cards. Not now, and probably not ever. And that made him sad.

Still, her presence was like a warm blanket, and when she placed her hand next to his, he took it. There wasn't a shock of excitement or a rush of emotions. It was just a comfort for two goblins thrust into a world not of their choosing.

Neither one of them said a word as dusk settled over the valley. He knew Pani was waiting on him, but he wasn't ready yet. He wanted to make this moment last as long as possible.

Finally, though, long after the stars dotted the night sky, long after the smoke from a thousand campfires wafted over them, he said, "You know I have to meet Yare."

"No, you don't," Pani said, but with more hope than conviction.

"Pani, my fate's been sealed ever since that damn elf came marching down the hill."

"There's no such thing as fate. You make your own future."

Qod shook his head. She was grasping at straws now. He might have believed in free will before he was conscripted, but every single move since then had been an inevitable march to the present. Yes, he'd let his ego get the better of him. Yes, he'd imagined he was smarter than the command staff, that he could actually lead soldiers in battle. But in reality, what could he have done differently? He'd been swept up in the current with no way to get out.

The question was what he was going to do about it. He could meet his fate alone, or he could drag those who were loyal to him along. One thing was for certain, though. If he rallied his soldiers, they would share his fate. And for what?

Yare would certainly punish the battalion no matter his choice. But by leaving them out of it, some might survive to eventually make it home. And for that reason alone, he had no option.

"You know that's not true," he told Pani. "Things are too far gone for that."

She sighed and then said, "It's never too far gone until you're dead."

The words were there, but he knew she didn't believe them, either.

"And at the moment, it's just me. I can't let it be you and the battalion as well."

"No matter what you tell them, they won't let you go, though. They're not going to listen."

Qod didn't know if she meant the team or the battalion. It didn't matter, though.

"That's why I need your help."

For the first time since they sat down on the ground, she dropped his hand and turned to face him.

"My help? To do what?"

Qod held his tongue for a moment. As soon as he said the words, he'd be committed.

"You're almost the same size as me."

"I'm taller."

"Not enough to make a difference. The others, they can't tell the difference between us goblins, so . . ." he prompted, hoping she'd pick up on his meaning.

"You want me to meet Yare? I'm not sure—"

"By the Dark Mother, no! I just want you to help me sneak out. We can trade leathers, and I can take your spear. You just sit here right behind this rock and look over the valley while I sneak off."

"It won't work, and I'm not going to help you kill yourself."

"I killed the elf battle mage with a spear. You don't think I can handle a pompous orc?"

He was only being half facetious. The fact was that he had killed the elf prince, no matter the circumstances, and a tiny part of him believed that it could happen again.

"No. Yes, I mean. I just . . ."

She let out a sob and seemed to collapse in on herself. Qod slowly reached out and took her hand again.

"Pani, I don't know what will happen. Maybe I'll be killed. Maybe I'll kill Yare. But I won't know until it happens. And it has to be just me. No one else. You have to give me that."

Jonathan P. Brazee

She sat there, head down, tears dripping from her cheeks.  Finally, she gave the tiniest of nods.

"Thank you, Pani."

He looked back to make sure they were out of sight of the rest, then said, "Let's switch our leathers."

Qod removed his and put on Pani's.  Despite Qod paying for the new ones, they were not form-fitted for each goblin.  Pani's cuirass might be hanging a little low on his thighs, and his might be short on her, but they were close enough.  And with his helmet and dagger belt, she could pass for a taller version of him.

He was counting on the helmet to make a bigger difference. Qod had been issued an officer's helmet with the signature spike on top, while Pani's was the plain "soup pot" helmet issued to the average grunt.

The hardest thing for him to do was to give up his dagger.  It was a beautiful blade, and it had served him well.  Trading it for her spear seemed like he was making it harder for himself, but he knew it really wasn't going to make much of a difference.  Still, he felt a pang of regret as he handed it over.

After everything was switched, he stepped back to look at her.  She looked the part, at least, and he was counting on the darkness and that "all goblins look alike" factor to pull this off.

"Crap.  I'm going to need that," he said.

He removed the single crescent moon from Pani's collar and slipped it into a pocket.  He would need that later.

"Now, you need to sit right there where they can see you," he said while pointing to the edge of the rock.

"For how long?"

"As long as you can get away with it, but you have to give me an hour."

"Are you sure about this?"

"I am."

She shook her head and moved over to where she could be seen and sat back down.  Qod followed, but only until his head and spear were visible to the team and any of the battalion.  And he knew the team was watching.

He was a little concerned about Nataly. Vurdalaks had excellent night vision, but if she noticed anything amiss, she didn't react.

"Now point, like you're telling me to go to the CP."

She raised an arm, then dropped it.

"I . . . you . . ." he started before his throat seemed to close up.

"May the Dark Mother be with you, Small Sir," she whispered. "And come back to us."

"I'll try, Pani. I'll try."

## Chapter 37

*I guess it's real now.*

He stood to the side for a moment and studied the layout of the battalion.  Very aware of Pani's eyes on him, he refrained from giving her another look, then started to wend his way around and through the battalion.  It looked like many of the soldiers were already asleep, but there were still small groups gathered around small campfires scattered through the area.  He took a moment to spot groups of goblins.  He was going to avoid them to keep from being recognized.

*Who is going to notice a single goblin?  I'll be fine.*

He tried to keep out of the reach of the light from the campfires, and he was almost across the battalion area when a voice shouted, "Hey!"

Qod froze, his throat in his stomach, when the satyr who'd spotted him said, "Tell the Mage Killer we're with him.  He's not gonna face the general alone."

He realized his mistake. His team had black and copper leathers, and he'd gotten too close to a campfire, which lit up the copper.

Qod just waved and kept going.

*How do I deserve that?*

But if anything, it convinced him that he was doing the right thing.

There was no hue and cry, no Tulip or Mac chasing him down as he approached the CP.  He took his lieutenant's crescent moon and put it on his collar, then approached the draugr at the entrance.

"I'm Lieutenant Qod."

The draugr gave him a long look and then said, "I can't let you in with a challenge given."

After the emotional roller coaster since that morning, that struck Qod as funny, and he laughed aloud.

"Can't put the general in danger now, can we?"

The draugr didn't respond.

"Well, can you tell me where I'm supposed to go?  I'm sort of new to this."

That seemed to stump him, and he opened the flap to the tent and whispered something to someone inside.

"Wait, sir," he said before going back to attention.

A few moments later, an ogre captain came out.

"You're Qod?" the captain asked.

"Living and breathing."

"It's not morning," he said as if that was Qod's fault.

"Astute of you, sir."

"Why are you here?"

"Well, as I told this draugr here, I'm new to this. I'm not sure where I'm supposed to be to kill General Yare."

"Not here!" the ogre almost shouted.

"Then, can you tell me where?"

The captain looked back into the CP, then over his right shoulder to the hills that rose to the north.

"I guess I could show you. But don't you want to sleep? To get your rest?"

"I'm done sleeping."

The captain seemed to mull it over, and he evidently couldn't think of a reason to deny Qod.

"Give me a guard," he told the draugr, and a moment later, another one emerged.

"Follow me," the ogre said.

Qod was very aware of the draugr beside him. He warily watched the guard out of the corner of his eye, half expecting him to suddenly cut Qod down. It would be an easy way to get rid of him before the formal fight.

But nothing of the sort happened. They climbed the first hill, over a crest, then down into a small bowl. Two imperial banners were located on either side. That was it.

Qod was frankly taken aback.

"This is where we're fighting?"

"This is it."

"Where do the witnesses watch?"

"Witnesses? Where are you going with that? There're no witnesses in a challenge," he said as if Qod was a complete idiot.

"But—"

Qod had just assumed challenges were done in front of crowds of officials and citizens.

"Witnesses, he says," the ogre said to the draugr. "This won't take long."

Suddenly, he wished he'd asked Lieutenant Glascock or Captain k'Ree just how a challenge was conducted. One of the reasons he'd wanted to see and walk where the fight would take place well before dawn was to see if there was anything at all about the location that could give him an advantage, no matter how small.

The thing is, on an intellectual level, Qod knew he had no chance against a battle-hardened orc. But still, he couldn't quite accept that. He'd survived a fight with an elf battle mage, after all, with much worse odds. No matter how bad things looked, he wasn't going down without a fight. Yare was going to have to earn a victory.

But looking across the small makeshift arena, nothing stood out.

"Are you staying here?" the ogre asked.

"Yes. I'll wait for the general to show."

The ogre nodded, then signaled the draugr. They marched off, leaving Qod alone.

He spent the next hour examining every square inch of the area between the banners, but he couldn't find anything that might give him an advantage. Finally, he gave up and took a seat on the ground.

This far from the army, the night was silent, not even broken by the scurrying of small creatures of the night. Above, the stars were a firmament of light.

He settled himself in, where he would be able to see the dawn break. If this was his last night on Earth, he was going to soak up the experience.

## Chapter 38

The sun turned the sky gorgeous shades of pink and peach as it approached the horizon but filled Qod with anxiety and peace at the same time, if that was even possible. Dawn was barreling down on him, and there was nothing he could do about it. But it was beautiful, and he was just soaking in how wonderful life was.

The first flash of direct sunlight appeared over the far hills, and within minutes, the entire sun emerged as it rose. Birds awoke and greeted it, just as they had done for every sunrise for hundreds of thousands of years—and just as they would keep doing tomorrow and the next day and the next.

Birds didn't bother about the Dark and the Light. They just sang and raised the next generation. Exactly as it should be.

Qod looked over his shoulder, and his heart gave a little flutter. There was movement down at the camp, which resolved itself into the general, stripped to the waist, and followed by what seemed like the entire command staff, making his way through the watching soldiers.

*Maybe I could have had my team with me.*

But no, it was better this way. They couldn't try something stupid and get themselves killed as a result.

But the entourage stopped at the edge of the camp and spread out as General Yare continued to climb. Qod watched for a few moments, then left his vantage and climbed back to the arena, taking a spot on the east side. He shifted his position, first holding Pani's spear, then placing the butt on the ground, then holding it horizontal to the ground as he tried to figure out what looked more imposing, until he broke into self-deprecating laughter.

*Yep. That's me. Imposing.*

He let the butt of the shaft fall back and waited. He hoped he looked calm and confident, but his mind was bouncing around his brain like a songbird in a cage as he tried to come up with a plan—anything that might result in his surviving the day.

Nothing jumped out at him.

Qod was a smart goblin. He knew what was about to happen, but that didn't mean he was just going to roll over and give up. He was going to fight, and who knows? Maybe he'd get lucky. General Yare was bare-chested, and Pani's spear was five feet long. If he could somehow use that length to, as Captain **Ryys** had told him what seemed like ages ago, to "stick him with the pointy end," then he had a chance. Miracles had happened before, so why not now?

There was a sound of falling rocks, and a few moments later, the general appeared over the west side of the arena. He looked huge as he paused for a moment, the morning sunlight glistening on his oiled torso.

The orc general was clad in a plain, homespun pair of trousers that extended just to his calves. He carried a **falchion** which gleamed in the light.

Qod suddenly felt out of place in Pani's cuirass. No one had told him he had to be half-naked for the duel.

The general spotted him, gave a grunt, then strode down the rise and into the arena. He raised a hand to shield his eyes from the sunlight.

"You're a smart little gobby, aren't you?" he said. "Picking your spot like this so the sun's in my eyes. Won't do you much good, but I like the fighting spirit."

Yare oozed with confidence, and he didn't mention Qod's armor, as if it didn't matter.

That wounded Qod's pride again. The armor probably wouldn't matter, but the lack of respect was maddening.

"You know I didn't challenge you," he said as he tried to keep his voice steady.

The general shrugged and said, "It suits me to have this challenge. You were in my way."

He made a show of taking a few swings of his sword, then stretched his back.

It was theater, of course, and that just made Qod even angrier.

"Well, let's get this over," Yare finally said as he raised his sword.

He started to advance as Qod took what he hoped was a fighting stance, his spear pointing at the general's chest. He braced himself while his heart went into overdrive.

Movement to his left caught his eye, and he risked a glance. To his surprise, Captain k'Ree had appeared from behind him and was entering the arena.

General Yare looked surprised as well. He stopped, and the tip of his sword dropped.

"I don't need your help this time," he said.

k'Ree didn't respond and kept approaching.

"I think I can handle a damn gobby, Captain. You can leave."

Qod had no idea what was happening, and despite his dire position, he was intrigued by what the general was saying.

*This time? You don't need help this time?*

"I know you don't need my assistance, General," Captain k'Ree finally said.

"Then why are you here? If anyone saw you . . ."

"No one saw me, sir."

"Then why—"

The general's eyes suddenly widened, and he started to raise his sword again when the banshee sprang into motion. Impossibly quick, the captain lunged, arm outstretched. The general attempted to parry, but he was too late.

A look of shock appeared, eyes wide and mouth open. General Yare, Commander of the Dark Army of the Mist, looked down at his chest. His sword fell from nerveless fingers, and he sank to his knees.

He raised his head and gave k'Ree a look of hurt before he uttered the single word, "Why?" before he fell over on his back.

Qod was in pure panic. He wanted to run, but his feet were cemented in place.

Captain k'Ree gave the general a long look before she turned and locked her eyes on Qod, who gave a little squeak as he aimed his spearpoint at her.

She strode across the arena.

Qod waited until she reached him before he jabbed his spear at her.

The captain casually caught the shaft with her hand and yanked it out of his grip, turned, and then strode back to the prone general. Qod stared at her in confusion as she seemed to line up the spear tip to the hole in the general's chest, then pushed it home. When she pulled back, the head was covered in dark orc blood.

Captain k'Ree examined the head for a moment before she bent over and picked up the general's falchion and headed back.

Qod just stared at her as the unfathomable began to fall into place. He wasn't sure of the whys and wherefores, but the general was dead, and he wasn't. And since she hadn't killed him when she took his spear, he drew himself up as she reached him to hear her explain herself.

So he was once again surprised when, still without a word, she whipped General's sword around too quickly for him to react and hit him with the flat of the blade against the side of his head, a surprise that lasted a rat's heartbeat before his world went black.

# Chapter 39

*Pain*

Consciousness returned slowly. Qod's face was on fire, and that filled his entire being until memory flooded back. He snapped open his eyes and stared into the face of General Yare.

Qod scrambled back in panic, pain forgotten, but the general was no longer a threat. He was dead as a **troll-stomped rat.**

"Are you back?"

Qod spun around. Captain k'Ree was standing over him.

At least she wasn't holding the general's sword.

He reached to the side of his head and winced at the flash of pain. His hand came away slick with his blood.

"Why did you hit me?" was the best he could do.

"I'm sorry. I was under the impression that goblins were made of sterner stuff, and I might have acted with a little more force than was warranted."

That made no sense to his muddled brain.

"But why?"

"No one is going to believe you defeated General Yare and came out unscathed."

"But I didn't defeat . . . oh."

Things were becoming clearer now, starting with the captain inserting Pani's spear into the wound she made. What wasn't clear was why.

Positions of authority for orcs had always been settled on personal combat, and that tradition had been adopted—at the orcs' insistence—when the Dark had come together to fight the Light invaders.

The concept was sacrosanct, as much as anything was across the races. The fact that Captain k'Ree had broken the Dark compact—and taken from the general's own words, not for the first time—was a lot for Qod to take in. Whatever the reason, he didn't think it boded well for him, and he was uneasy as to what was coming.

It wasn't just uneasy. Qod was not an orc, of course, but still, he felt guilty. Dirty. It went against all he considered honorable and righteous.

"You have to hurry. They're waiting. Pick up your spear and return to the camp," the banshee captain told him.

"But I didn't really defeat him. You did. You cheated."

The captain snorted in amusement.

"You'd rather he won?"

When she put it like that . . .

"No. I'm happy to be alive, of course. And I thank you."

"Don't thank me yet," she said with a snort.

"Why? What do you mean?"

"Forget it," she said, all business again. "You just march over the berm and back to camp. When you're challenged, just say, 'The past is defeated. It's time for a new beginning.' You got that?"

"The past, uh, is defeated. It's time for a new beginning," he repeated.

"The past is defeated. It's time for a new beginning," she said, correcting him. "It's vital you say it exactly like that. Again, say it."

"The past is defeated. It's time for a new beginning."

She didn't seem convinced he could say the words correctly, which got under his green skin more than a bit. He was in shock at the turn of events, but he could manage a simple sentence, even if it didn't make any sense.

The captain glanced back over her shoulder toward the camp as if expecting a posse of orcs and ogres to appear, then turned back to him.

"They're going to ask you questions. Lots of questions. Ignore them. Do not answer. Understand?"

"Yes, ma'am," he said.

He was giving her only twenty percent of his attention at the moment. His mind was racing as he tried to grasp the real situation here.

"Go directly to the CP. I'll be waiting there."

He was aware enough to know that since she snuck in, she would want to get back unseen, but so much had happened over the last few minutes that he didn't question her ability to be back waiting for him by the time he got there.

Qod glanced one more time at the prone body of the dead orc. He still felt guilty for breaking tradition, but he felt nothing for the orc.

*Let the worms have him.*

"OK, Captain. I get back to the CP. Then what? And what happens to me?"

This time, she laughed out loud.

"What happens to you? I should think that even a goblin from Yellow Rock would know the answer to that. You killed the general. So you are now in command of the Army of the Mist."

## Chapter 40

Qod climbed the slight rise until his head almost crested the top. His heart was pounding in his chest. His palms were wet and clammy.

"Are you sure—" he started while turning around, but Captain k'Ree was gone.

He wasn't sure how she'd managed that. There was no cover in the arena at all.

With a sigh, he turned back. He transferred Pani's spear to his left hand, wiped his right against his thigh, then hefted the spear again. The tip was coated in dark orc blood that seemed to suck in the morning sunlight.

He took a deep breath, then stepped into view of the gathered crowd below. There was a moment of silence, as if all the air in the region was taken in at once, before those waiting erupted in shouts so loud that Qod took half a step back.

*Get a hold of yourself.*

He marshalled up the will, then stepped forward to begin the long walk down to the edge of the camp. Individual shouts reached him as they asked questions. Keeping the captain's orders—

*No, not orders. Advice, I guess, if I really am a general now.*

He sure didn't feel like a general, though.

Keeping her *advice*, he ignored them all. He tried to keep a stern countenance as he approached them, but in truth, he thought he probably looked more like a pouting sausage.

The crowd didn't come to meet him, as if they were being restrained by an invisible wall instead of mere tradition—that and maybe the line of draugrs in front of them. That was until he got to about 150 yards away, and someone broke free to rush at him.

Someone small. Goblin-sized.

Qod didn't need his goblin-eyesight to know who she was.

"Small Sir! I knew you would win," Pani said as she collided with him, almost knocking him off his feet.

Her hug released the relief that had been building up. Tears flowed onto her chest.

"I didn't—" he started to sob before realism hit.

He was awash in guilt for how the general was killed, but he knew that if he valued his life, no hint of what happened could leak out. And the only way to ensure that was for no one to know. Even Pani.

"I didn't know I could win," he changed his confession.

The shouts were getting louder. A few looked like they were going to ignore protocol and charge forward, too. And with the evident anger among some of them, Qod didn't want to see what they'd do to him away from all the rest.

"We have to keep moving," he told Pani.

She pulled back.

"You're bleeding," she said in a worried tone.

"I was in a fight," Qod said, hating to lie to her. "He didn't go easily."

"Battle wounds," she said.

She reached up to his face, but instead of touching the blood, she carefully wiped the tear tracks running down his cheeks, like a goblinette soothing a sausage, then went from mothering to soldier as she pulled herself up and took a position one step to his left and one behind.

Her eyes lingered on the orc blood on the spear tip—*her* spear tip—before she said, "Let's do it, Small Sir."

It probably would have been better if she'd waited, given the commotion ahead, but he was glad she was with him. She gave him a sense of grounding that settled his mind and let him actually think ahead instead of just being caught up in the tsunami.

It looked like most of the command staff was waiting just behind the line of draugrs and in front of the gathering crowd, and as he'd noted, more than a few were angry. Qod didn't relish just walking into that scrum, but he wasn't alone here, and he didn't mean just Pani.

It wasn't hard to spot Tulip, over toward the right. And once he had her, he could see the rest of his team. Qod immediately veered in that direction and made a beeline toward them.

The main group saw that, of course, and with a hive mind, started shifting over en masse. Tulip saw that and reoriented her body, offering them her broad back. Qod knew that not even a troll could hold back a mob, but with the pack of bodies already there, it might be enough to give him the break he wanted.

Corporal Mac also saw what was happening, and he was taking over, placing the rest of the team so that Qod and Pani could slip into their embrace. But how long could they hold?

"Pick up the pace, Pani," Qod said.

He didn't break into a run, but he came close. It seemed like forever, but it probably took twenty or twenty-five seconds before the two goblins slipped past the draugrs and joined the team.

"Where to?" Mac asked as he scanned the press of soldiers.

"The CP. I have to get there."

"Dulce—" Mac started to say, but she beat him to the punch.

"I'm on it. Follow me."

The sprite darted into the air, quickly picked out a route, and pointed.

"Private Tulip," Lieutenant Glascock shouted as he pushed past the soldiers.

*What now?*

That was all Qod needed, an orc officer whose motives were murky.

But he told her, "Break a path to the CP. Everyone else, get on Tulip's ass."

Corporal Mac looked like he was going to protest, but then he bit back whatever he was going to say. They could use all the help they could get, and having an orc officer, who seemed to still be in security mode, could only help.

"And you," Glascock told Qod. "You stay on *my* ass. We've got to get you into the CP until things calm down." Then, "Sir," he added almost as an afterthought.

He drew his falchion and held it at the ready as the team started pushing itself through the crowd. The lieutenant had many foibles, but the orc could fight, and when threatened, he carried himself as a warrior, something no one could miss. Whether it was that or Tulip's bulk, the mass of soldiers slowly parted out of their way.

Soon, it was evident that things weren't as bad as Qod had feared. There were angry shouts, and many of the questions thrown at him were pointed. But more of the crowd were seemingly confused or just in shock. And the farther they got, the more small folk were in the mix.

Shouts of "Mage Killer" started overwhelming the angry ones. And like a snowball rolling down a hill, more and more small folk seemed to be attaching themselves to the team, forming an ever-growing entourage.

Qod started to feel the tiniest stirrings of confidence. He still hadn't come to terms with the fact that he was now the commanding general, and he couldn't begin to fathom why he was, but with so many supporters, he began to have hope that he might get out of this with his skin intact.

*Probably not, but there's at least a chance.*

Qod could see some of the command staff running along the periphery as they tried to beat him to the CP, but as more soldiers started converging on them, their going wasn't exactly clear.

A gremlin ran under Tulip's legs, and the lieutenant grabbed Qod and pushed him behind him.

The lieutenant maneuvered to skewer the soldier, but the gremlin hugged Pani and said, "May the Dark Mother bless you!" before taking Pani's hand and holding it to her forehead.

And then just like that, she was gone.

With all that had transpired, it took Qod a moment to realize that the goblin anonymity had struck again. Pani was wearing his leathers, and he hers. So, despite the difference in height, the gremlin had mistaken her for him.

"You might want to change back as soon as we get there, sir," the lieutenant said.

Far from the stress of the fight and then making his appearance, there was almost a festive mood when they reached the CP.

Qod eyed the draugrs at the entrance warily—he'd supposedly just killed their protectee, after all. But they signaled for him and the lieutenant to enter.

Not the rest of the team, though, despite Corporal Mac's protests. For a moment, Qod was tempted to try out this whole general thing and order them to let the team in, but he knew he shouldn't push things until he knew exactly where he stood.

Tulip looked like she was going to push past the two draugrs at the entrance, although Qod wasn't sure how she thought she would fit inside. She'd have to bend over double. What concerned him more was that even at less than half her size, Qod had a feeling that the draugrs would be able to easily handle her.

"Just stand by, Tulip. And all of you. I'll rejoin you as soon as I can."

The big troll didn't look happy, but she nodded and stepped back a couple of paces.

The entrance to the CP was quiet, something he'd never seen. That didn't last long, though. A few moments after they entered, an ogre major came from the back. He gaped as he took in Qod and his bloody face, all while avoiding his eyes. He opened and closed his mouth a few times before he focused on Lieutenant Glascock.

"Get him into the conference room."

"Follow me," the lieutenant told Qod. "And if you want my advice, don't say anything yet."

Qod frowned. If he really was the new general, then why was he and the captain telling him to be quiet? The fact that both of them had warned him to keep his mouth shut didn't carry good implications.

It was probably smart advice, though.

The two walked through the main operations section. There were only a few soldiers there, each, except for the major, somewhat junior enlisted. All stood at his entrance with varying degrees of shock on their faces.

The command staff started arriving as the lieutenant almost pulled him into the conference room. Captain k'Ree was already there, looking cool, calm, and collected. She pointed to the chair at the head of the table, then turned to stand with the lieutenant to face the entrance. Qod took a seat, but he was a small goblin while the general had been a large orc. With only his eyes above the edge of the table, he looked like a year-old sausage eating with the adults for the first time.

He chose to stand, instead, and hoped that his beating heart wasn't visible to the command staff as they began to fill the space. Not just the senior staff who'd been there the first time Qod had been at a meeting, but at least three times that many along with six draugrs.

No one directly addressed him, but they weren't shy about expressing their feelings. Most were along the lines of "How in the Light hell did he defeat Yare?" or "This is impossible."

More concerning was the animosity that too many were exhibiting, and the comments of "What are we going to do about it?"

To be honest, aside from the fact that he wasn't qualified, Qod didn't *want* to be the commanding general. He wondered if he could just offer a bargain to step down and quietly go back to Yellow Rock. Well, maybe he and his team, if they wanted.

*Crap. What about the Mage Killers?*

Judging from what he was overhearing, if things went wrong, they'd suffer, too, especially if they protested. Maybe he could protect them by making a deal, but probably not. There were too many of them to ignore.

It was best to keep taking Glascock's advice and see which way the wind was blowing before trying anything.

Despite the crowding, there was a bubble of space around Qod, as if he was ill with the skin rot—that is, until Major Pishlyss slipped beside him. The kukudh still made Qod uneasy, and he shifted his position slightly so he could see if the major was suddenly going to try and remove their embarrassing predicament.

"Where is he?" a voice shouted.

The pack of officers parted, and General Tillmus, the assistant army commander, pushed his way forward. He scanned the room, whipping right past Qod, not noticing him until his second pass.

"You."

Qod tried to look confident. He didn't think he was pulling it off.

"How did you defeat Yare?"

In Qod's hearing, all officers had referred to the dead general as "General Yare." Never just "Yare." It was pretty evident to Qod that Tillmus didn't give a dwarf turd for the departed former commander, and things gelled in his mind.

He ignored the question and quickly scanned the gathered officers. Some were angry. Some were confused. But more than a few exhibited naked avarice. Qod would bet his last rat crack that they were trying to figure out how they could take advantage of the situation.

That put a new, and decidedly more dangerous spin on things. Qod had assumed that the orcs, in particular, would be angry that a goblin had killed their general. But if the senior officers were scheming to take command themselves, then Qod was in more trouble than he'd assumed.

"I asked you how you defeated Yare," the general repeated.

Qod looked to k'Ree, then Glascock for guidance. Neither caught his eye. He then casually placed Pani's spear on the table, the orc blood even darker in the light from the wizard balls hanging from the ceiling. All eyes were locked on it.

"Well, he did kill the battle mage," someone said quietly.

"We don't know that," a familiar voice said. "It was just another orc who said it, and you know orcs lie," Colonel Manticoz, Qod's first commander, said.

Hisses greeted the ogre officer.

"No insult intended, but you know it's true," he added before he stepped closer to Qod.

"I mean, it beggars belief. An elf battle mage? And then Yare? He might have been an asshole, but Yare was a warrior who'd survived six challenges. So *this* defeated him? I didn't see it. None of us saw it."

Qod gulped, and he feared his face would be blushing orange. No one saw it because he didn't actually kill the general. The colonel was right.

"Easy, Colonel. You're treading on dangerous ground, there," General Tillmus said.

"Oh, so you want a gobby to lead the Army of the Mist? May the Dark Mother protect us," he said, dripping scorn.

All eyes swiveled back to the general.

"No, that's ridiculous. But we can't impugn the sacrality of the challenge ring. There are other ways to take care of this."

*How?*

"I want to protect the ways," Manticoz said. "And my honor refuses to let this creature besmirch them." He looked around. "Do any of you believe that a gobby killed Yare?"

There were a lot of head shakes in agreement, but not by everyone. Many still had that calculating look in their eyes.

"And I won't ruin the honor of the Army of the Mist by having a sniveling gobby as our commander. And if you won't take action, by the devil' short hairs, I will."

He spun while pulling out his mandinka, the short blade favored by ogre officers, and lunged for Qod, who gave a small squeak and jumped back.

But Manticoz stopped after one step. Qod watched in confusion as the colonel's mouth dropped open, his eyes wide. He looked down at eight inches of steel that was suddenly protruding from his chest.

The spike disappeared, and the colonel dropped to his knees, revealing the draugr lieutenant, bloody sword in his hand.

Shouts of surprise and anger filled the tent, and the draugr gave a flick of his wrist. In an instant, Qod was surrounded by the bodyguards.

There had to be forty or fifty officers in the conference room and only six draugrs, but no one seemed to want to take them on. An ogre checked on Manticoz, but it had been obvious that the draugr lieutenant had known what he was doing.

"You always were a hothead, Manticoz," the general said as he stepped over the body.

He held his hands up to show the draugrs that he was not about to attack Qod, whose heart was still pounding in overtime, before he turned to face the rest.

"Manticoz was right, though. We cannot, in all honor, be commanded by a gobby. But we must do this by the procedures passed down over generations and ratified in the accords."

Qod had thought General Tillmus to be something of an afterthought to Yare, quiet and without a presence. But with Yare dead, the ogre spoke with authority and command.

And he knew what the general was going to say next would have grave consequences to him. Qod's future was at stake.

"But there is a right way and a wrong way to go about this. Manticoz did it the wrong way. I will do it the right way."

He turned around and locked eyes with Qod, the way a cat locks on a mouse. And like a mouse, Qod froze.

"Private Qod, I hereby challenge you for command of the Army of the Mist."

*So that's how they're going to do it.*

The conference room erupted into shouts. Most were cheers. Qod wasn't going to find succor from them.

Qod didn't believe in fate. He had expected to die facing Yare, but a strange set of circumstances had saved him. But if fate was a thing, it wasn't going to be denied, it seemed. One way or the other, his time on Earth was going to end.

"This afternoon, gobby," the general said with a look of satisfaction that couldn't be denied.

Major Pishlyss, who was still standing beside Qod, cleared his throat.

"I'm sorry, General Tillmus. But you can't do that."

The general rolled his eyes and then said in a condescending voice, "If you insist on being a stickler, Major, we can wait until tomorrow morning."

"I'm afraid that won't be possible either, sir."

The general was getting angry, but he asked, "Pray tell, why not?"

"General Qod has not been confirmed by the empress yet. Until then, he is only the acting commanding general, and his position is not eligible for challenges."

Qod felt a sudden flash of hope. He had no real idea how the challenge system was set up. But if the major was right . . .

But Pishlyss was a major, and Tillmus a general. Majors didn't win battles with generals very often. Qod's only hope was that the draugrs sided with him and not the general.

An orc leaned into the general's ear and whispered something. Tillmus's eyes narrowed, and he whispered something back. The orc shook his head.

Now, the general stared daggers into the unflinching draugr lieutenant.

"Of course, Major Pishlyss," he said, forcing the words out through gritted teeth. "We will, of course, honor the accords and follow them to the letter."

He spun on his heels and stalked out. That seemed to be a signal. Slowly at first, then in a rush, the conference room started to empty.

"Captain k'Ree, Lieutenant Glascock, will you please remain?" the major said.

Pishlyss worded it as a question, but it was clear he wasn't asking them. He didn't address the draugrs, but they weren't going anywhere.

"Thank you," Qod told the lieutenant.

The draugr didn't change expression, but he gave Qod the tiniest of nods.

The major, k'Ree, and Glascock huddled together as the last of the officers filed out.

Qod just stood there. His knees were weak, and he was mentally and physically exhausted. His life had been on the line, but he'd done nothing. He'd said nothing. He'd been a mere ornament while others decided his fate.

He didn't know how long it would take the empress to confirm—or possibly deny—his position. For all he knew, he'd be facing General Tillmus tomorrow, and he couldn't count on k'Ree to bail him out again.

But he made a vow to himself.  He wasn't going to be a mere spectator going forward.  He was going to have a voice in his future, however long or however short that future might be.

"The past is defeated. It's time for a new beginning," he said, even if he was the only one listening.

# Chapter 41

"Do you have any questions?" Captain k'Ree asked?

*By the Dark Mother, damn right I do. Like, why did you save me, for one?*

But Qod knew that was a question that had to be left unasked, at least for now. He might be the general—*acting* general—but he had no illusions that he was really in charge. His best hope for survival was to reveal nothing and hear everything.

"No, ma'am," he said instead.

The corner of her mouth quirked upward just the tiniest amount. "That's *Captain* k'Ree, sir."

*That's going to take some getting used to.*

"Right. *Captain*."

"Then with that, I'll leave you alone." She hesitated a moment, then added, "If I may be so bold, I'd recommend you stay in your quarters for now."

She didn't have to expound on her reasoning. Despite the sporadic chants of "Mage Killers" spreading around the camp, wandering around could be dangerous. Challenge rules or not, the Light wasn't the only group to employ assassins.

"Understood, ma—Captain."

She nodded and stepped out. A moment later, one of the draugrs opened the flap.

"Private Mud Geyser requests an audience, sir."

"Yes, yes, of course. Let her in, please."

The draugr—Qod made a mental note to get all of his bodyguards' names—stepped back, and moments later, Pani stepped in, without her spear, and stopped dead in her tracks before she gave out a low whistle.

"*These* are your quarters, Small Sir?"

"Right?"

Qod had been in the commanding general's quarters for several hours now, first with Major Pishlyss, then with Colonel Piminta, the army's Chief of Staff—who looked like he wished he was anywhere else—and then Captain k'Ree. He'd been just as shocked at the utter opulence as Pani was. It was hard to imagine that they were in a corner of the CP out in the field and not somewhere in the Imperial Palace.

Elaborate silks hung from every wall. Pads cushioned each step. The bed was huge, large enough for an entire goblin family, and it looked extremely inviting. wizard-powered lights hung from the ceiling, and air warmed by **wizard balls** flowed gently through with no visible fans.

She slowly walked through the quarters, picking up pieces of art, then setting them back down before moving to the next one. When she got to the bed, she pressed down on the mattress with her hand.

"Can I," she asked hopefully.

"Sure."

Pani giggled and jumped, twisting in the air to land on her back. Qod had to laugh at the tough warrior turning into a three-year-old goblinette.

She lay there for a long moment before she sat up and sheepishly slid off the bed and back on her feet.

"I'm sorry. I just . . . I mean, I never in my life . . ."

"I know. Me neither."

She suddenly quieted and gathered herself.

"Forgive me, General. I forgot myself for a moment."

"I'm still Qod, Pani."

"With all due respect, no, you are not."

Qod started to argue, but he had to stop. He wasn't Private Qod from Yellow Rock anymore. No matter how it had happened, he was in at least temporary command of the Army of the Mist.

The thing was, he didn't want things to have changed between them. With any of his team. That is, if they were still his team. He had draugr bodyguards now.

"How is everyone?" he asked.

"They're outside the CP, waiting. The lieutenant, he doesn't know if we're being disbanded or what. So, the others, we sort of decided that I should try and see if I could talk to you, to, you know, find out."

That gave Qod a warm and fuzzy. The team was his anchor in a tempest sea.

"There's nothing to find out.  You're still my security team."

"But the draugrs—"

"If I really am the general, I think I can decide where my friends are going to be."

She relaxed ever-so-slightly, gave out a little sigh, and said, "They're going to be pleased."

Qod was never too good with goblinettes, but maybe the two full moons on his collar gave him superpowers.

"What about you, Pani?  Are you pleased?"

"Of course, General" she said with a tiny smile as she avoided his eyes.

*In for a penny . . .*

"Pani, when we're alone, you don't have to do all this general crap."

"But you are a general, she protested.  And I'm a private."

"Look, I'm kind of alone here.  Tillmus is a general, too, but he wants to challenge me.  I need someone I can talk to.  I need a . . . a friend."

She just stood there, still averting her eyes.

"Can, you know, you be that?  My friend?"

"If you want, General," she said, her voice a mere whisper.

"That starts with this 'general' thing.  This is me, Pani. Not General Yellow Rock."

"If you want, Small Sir."

Qod laughed out loud.  He'd been angling for "Qod," but he'd almost gotten used to "Small Sir," so that would do for now.

Baby steps.

He stood there awkwardly, not quite knowing what to say, when he was saved by Captain k'Ree barging into his quarters.

That relief vanished when the banshee said, "Sorry for the intrusion, General, but you need to come to ops now."

"Why?  What's going on?"

"The faeby bastards are on the move."

"They're withdrawing?" Qod asked hopefully.

Rumors were that the Light had suffered so many casualties that they were going to give up and leave.

"They're formed for battle, sir. They're heading right for us."

# Chapter 42

Captain k'Ree paused at the entrance, and Qod strode past her and into ops, which took up most of the CP. The place was a beehive of activity. General Tillmus was there, conferring with Colonel Kyss, the operations officer. Kyss was a ghoul and the senior-most officer in the Army of the Mist who was not an orc or ogre.

Qod steeled his nerve and marched up to the general.

"What's happening?" he asked him.

The general turned his head and looked down his nose at Qod, then returned to the colonel.

If that was intended as a dismissal, it was working. Qod hesitated, unsure of himself.

*What now?*

"Establish yourself," Captain k'Ree whispered so quietly that Qod almost missed it.

He gave the banshee a quick look and wondered if she knew exactly the limit of goblin hearing.

Qod cleared his throat and then said, "I asked you what's happening, General."

This time, Tillmus rolled his eyes and said, "I don't have time for this."

Captain k'Ree started to whisper something else, but Qod didn't need it. Anger flared again. He'd promised that he wasn't going to just be a spectator, and by the Dark Mother, he was going to keep that promise.

"You *will* answer me, General," he said so sharply that half of ops stopped what they were doing to stare at him.

"Or what?" Tillmus asked, finally turning to face Qod.

"I gave you an order. Are you going to disobey it?" Qod asked before pointedly turning to look at the two draugrs standing post at the entrance.

Qod didn't know exactly what would happen if he ordered the bodyguards to take General Tillmus, but he guessed it wouldn't be good.

He must have guessed right, given that Tillmus visibly quailed as he shot his own look at them.

"Of course, not, uh, sir. I'm just trying to work on a response with Colonel Kolor here."

As soon as the words were out of his mouth, the colonel took half a step back as if not wanting to get blood splattered on him.

"Maybe, uh . . ." he said as he scanned ops. "Maybe Major Foan can get you up to speed?"

Qod's ego wanted Tillmus himself to get him up to speed, but if the Light forces were approaching, then those two were probably the most qualified to come up with a plan to counter them. His pride was outweighed by the needs of the contingency.

"Of course, General," he said.

Tillmus gave one more apprehensive glance at the draugrs as a slightly overweight orc rushed forward.

He didn't look happy as he guided Qod and k'Ree to the sand table in the middle of the space. Qod had never seen one before. He'd never seen a map, for that matter. It took him a moment to orient himself before the representation became clear in his mind. The table represented the entire Fanciful Highlands, and glowing wizard lights in the shape of various races represented the disposition of Dark and Light forces.

The major jumped right in and spent the next twenty minutes giving him an update on the enemy situation. It was worse than Qod had feared. The last he heard, the Light forces had been building fortifications in the Whispering Forest, where they would presumably hold out until they could be reinforced with troops from the far south.

With reinforcements so far away, the urgency of the situation had gone down a few notches. However, either those new troops had marched incredibly quickly, or the Light Forces were still at much higher numbers than had been previously estimated. It looked to Qod that their building the fort had been yet another ruse to lure the Dark into complacency.

The good news was that Dark scouts had spotted the Light army on the move. The bad news was that their numbers somehow exceeded the numbers of surviving Dark soldiers, who had been so depleted during the current campaign.

At the moment, the main Light body, composed mostly of centaurs and elves, was heading south, toward Offerton, moving quickly over the low ground so as to cut off the Army of the Mist from any reinforcements from Offerton and points beyond. The feeling was that they'd bend back around to reach the Army of the Mist's rear, then attack.

Another smaller force of what looked like dwarves was moving through the mountains toward the Long Caldron and beyond that, Camp Defiance. Major Foan said that the assumption was that they'd conduct a two-pronged pincher movement against them, but Qod thought that he detected a hint of doubt in the orc's voice.

Without prompting, the major jumped right into what General Tillmus's response was going to be, which seemed to be remaining essentially in place, "holding the high ground" until such time as they could hit the Light forces with waves of infantry.

Qod winced when he heard "waves." The Dark commanders had a habit of throwing bodies at an enemy, hoping to overcome the Light by overwhelming them. It didn't work out that way very often, and even when it did, it came at a huge cost. Qod had already seen the devastation these tactics caused. Gremlin, kobold, orc, ogre, troll, and yes, goblin families across the land would never see their loved ones again.

"Doesn't a frontal assault require an advantage in numbers?"

"Well, yes, sir," the major said.

He gave the dwarf lights a long look before asking, "How many dwarves does each light represent?"

"I . . . I don't know, sir. I think it depends on who's powering the sand table."

"Find out," Captain k'Ree said, the first time she'd opened her mouth since the brief started.

With a lot more alacrity than he'd shown with Qod, and despite outranking her, he said, "Yes, ma'am," before hurrying off.

Qod could tell that most of the command staff were well aware of him, even if they were going about their tasks. None seemed close enough to hear him, though.

"Any suggestions, Captain?" he asked under his breath.

"You're the general, sir."

Qod snorted his rejection of that.

"But if I were to step in and make a mistake, I might just have an accident, right? One before the draugrs could react?"

She didn't answer, which was response enough for him. Not that he blamed her. He still didn't know what game was being played, but he was sure that if he put the Dark at risk, the game would be chopped short at a quick end.

"So, the safest thing would be to just sit back and let General Tillmus run the show."

Once again, she remained silent.

The problem was that Qod had a very uneasy feeling about the plan as explained by Major Foan. It wasn't just the difference in the size of both forces. It wasn't that the mass attacks that the Dark military seemed to favor didn't seem to work. Something else seemed off, and he didn't have the formal military training to recognize it.

Qod was not about to march over to Tillmus and wrest control of what was left of the Army of the Mist, but maybe he could spot something that was being missed and bring it to the general's attention.

It wasn't as if he had anything else to do.

Foan returned with an ogre wizard.

"This is Lraine. He's powering the sand table."

Unlike the first wizard Qod had seen, the gremlin, the ogre was not wearing a robe and pointy hat. He was in a simple smock like Dulce wore and a worn leather cuirass.

"You have a question for me, General?"

"Each one of those dwarf figures. Do they represent a specific number of dwarves?"

"Not exactly," the wizard said. "My powers are not that precise, but each one should be around one hundred and forty-four of them."

Qod did a quick calculation. There were nine flickering dwarves, so there were about 1,300 of them heading over the mountains. He'd actually expected more. It was still a significant force, but not insurmountable.

What worried him more was the much larger number of Light soldiers in the main force.

He turned to the major.

"Back to the plan for a frontal assault. If what Lraine says is right, then they outnumber us."

"But we'd be going downhill, sir. That gives *us* the advantage."

Qod frowned. He understood that theoretically, holding the high ground was a good thing, but that wasn't absolute. The Light had held it at the Battle of Long Caldron and lost. They'd held it during his second battle, where he'd killed the battle mage, and they'd lost then, too. They had the high ground at Mossy Ridge, but that had resulted in a draw and their retreat. The Light had killed huge numbers of Dark soldiers, but they had still lost the battles.

It wasn't as if their present position was the highest ground. Yes, it looked down the Upper Anemia River Valley and the northern approach, but it was surrounded by even higher ground.

"What's to keep the main body from climbing into the hills here?" Qod asked, pointing to the northwest of their position.

"Well, nothing, sir. But they're heavy with centaurs and elves, and that's pretty rough terrain."

When Qod didn't respond, the major added, "Centaurs don't like mountains much. Neither do elves, what with their long legs," he said, lifting up his own right leg in emphasis.

*Yes, and dwarves like the mountains. I know.*

The fact that the two forces seemed to be split by races, though, begged the question as to why. So far, the Light had surprised the Dark at every turn, using tactics and magic, even with the battle mage dead, to fool the Dark. Qod didn't think they were suddenly about to start adhering to Dark expectations.

Then a thought hit him, and he asked the wizard, "During the battle here, the Light wizards hid their troops that were ready to roll rocks on us. Could they be messing with what our scouts detected?"

"Yes, they could be."

"Well, can you, you know, get through that, to make sure of their numbers?"

He'd been told the main force was the one taking the valley route, but the dwarves in the mountains confused him, and he really wanted to know their actual numbers.

"I'm afraid not, sir."

"Of course, you can't," he muttered. "Why have the gods given the most powerful magic to the Light?"

It was a rhetorical question, but the ogre drew himself up and said, "Counterspells take much more power than an initial casting."

Qod didn't like the ogre's defensiveness, and he snapped, "That battle mage had no problem with the gremlin wizard who burnt up the arrows in my first fight."

The wizard's eyes clouded over, and he drew back.

"I apologize, General, that we have no mages with the Army of the Mist. Master Will was lost at Thundershoot Corner. But our wizard class has the same capabilities as the Light's."

"Then why haven't I seen it. Other than the gremlin—"

"Wonto. He was the gremlin wizard who burnt the arrows. Which revealed him to the battle mage and got him killed, may the Dark Mother bless his soul."

One of the closest orcs, who hadn't seemed to be listening, quickly bowed and touched his forehead.

Qod lowered his voice even more and said, "All I've seen you wizards do is pass messages and create some lights. Why no more zapping arrows or anything else?"

"Altering the physical world takes power. Wonto had it, but he couldn't stand up to a battle mage. Altering perceptions is much, much easier."

"Then why haven't you been doing that?"

Wizard Lraine's face went stony, losing all expression.

His voice went to a whisper that even Qod had trouble hearing.

"We offered, but we are not totally trusted by the command. Practitioners in the Arcane Arts have never been fully accepted by the warrior class. We taint their honor, so they say."

This was something unexpected, and it took more than a few moments for it to sink in. He looked around the ops center, which was using wizardware. The illumination consisted of two dozen wizard lights. Heat balls warmed the CP, keeping out the encroaching winter cold. The sand table used wizardry to indicate positions. Even communications with **Taxian** were accomplished with magic.

If wizardry was so widespread, why would the orcs and ogres shy away from it if it could help win battles? Heck, Lraine here *was* an ogre. And the greatest hero in Dark history was General Ptolomon, who was also a full-fledged mage.

There was so much about the world that Qod didn't understand, but he had a sneaky suspicion that politics and power were at the bottom of it. And, now that he thought of it, it explained why, since General Ptolomon, wizards and mages were not actually part of the military. That was for another place and time, though. Right now, the Light was marching on them, and nothing would matter if they couldn't be turned back.

He needed more information. Dulce had explained, at least in part, how magic worked. But he needed practical knowledge now.

"So, you're saying that you, and I mean all of our wizards, can do much more than I've seen so far."

The ogre drew himself up, showing just a bit of pride. "Yes, sir."

"Interesting. And how many wizards do we have with the army?"

"There are fourteen of us, General."

There was a distinct tone of hope in his voice now.

Qod glanced around the ops center. The orc who'd touched his forehead was openly watching him now. In the corner, General Tillmus and two new colonels were deep in discussion.

"You know Sergeant Tark?" he asked the wizard.

"Yes, sir. The armorer."

"I want you to gather all your wizards and meet me there in twenty minutes. And tell Dulce to have my team there, too. You got that?"

"Yes, SIR!" he said. "We'll be there!"

"Then go."

The wizard drew himself upright and, despite his civilian status, saluted Qod, the first time anyone had done that. It caught Qod unprepared, and he fumbled one in return.

Qod watched the wizard hurry out. He didn't have a plan. He didn't know if he would be able to come up with a plan. But at least he wasn't standing on the sidelines watching the war march past him.

He looked up at Captain k'Ree, who was silently staring at him.

"Well, are you going to be taking me out before I screw something up?" he asked in jest.

Mostly in jest, at least.

"We'll see, General. We'll see."

## Chapter 43

"It's clear, sir," Lieutenant Helvig, the draugr shift commander, said.

"Thank you, Lieutenant," Qod said.

"If there's anything you need, sir, you just tell me," Sergeant Tark said. "I'll be right here outside."

Tulip turned and faced outboard without a word, hammer across her chest. She didn't seem happy to be left out, but there was no way she could fit inside. The rest of the team and the wizards followed Qod into the welcome warmth of the forge.

Qod hadn't thought about the heat when he'd told Lraine to gather the wizards and meet him there. He just wanted an inside location outside the CP and with relative privacy so they could talk. And with it still being a temporary camp, choices were limited. But he'd noticed that Tark had erected a shelter made from scrounged materials around his forge—Corporal Mac had said it was so he could more easily maintain a constant forge temperature—and he'd decided to use that.

He wasn't the only one to appreciate the warmth. There were more than a few sighs of pleasure as gloves were removed and collars loosened.

It wasn't full winter yet, and the temperatures were hovering around freezing, but the cold, moist, and never-ending wind was a harbinger of the coming winter snows to the Fanciful Highlands.

There was some chatting as folks introduced themselves to each other, and Qod let it go on for a few minutes before he started the meeting.

"Thank you for bringing all the wizards here, Lraine."

The wizard gave a slow, non-ogre-like nod.

Qod noted that and briefly wondered if that was a general wizard thing or if Lraine was simply an odd ogre. But there was time to explore that later. Hopefully. What he needed now was a quick, but complete concept of what the wizards could accomplish.

"Dulce has briefed me on some of the basics of wizardry, but I've got some questions."

Another calm nod.

"And I'm going to jump right in. First and foremost, why are the Light wizards so much stronger than you guys?"

There was a brief flash in Lraine's eyes, and Qod wondered if there wasn't more of the ogre temper in the wizard than he'd thought.

The other wizards looked at Lraine for him to answer.

The ogre took a long breath, then with measured words, said, "It is true that only the Light, specifically elves, has produced battle mages. But I can assure you, General, that other than that, Dark wizards have the same potential as those from the Light."

Qod frowned. "Then why haven't you done anything in our bat. . ." he started to say before the "potential" sank in.

All of the wizards, including Dulce, started to bristle.

"Let me rephrase that. I saw the gremlin wizard burn arrows in flight."

"That was Wonto," Lraine said.

"Yes, Wizard Wonto. But other than that, we've got the typical wizardware. Wizard lights in the CP. Heat balls. We use wizardry to communicate with Taxian. But except for the lights Dulce created above the Long Caldron—"

"Dulce, Bomot, and me," a kobold said.

"Excuse me?"

"The three of us, General. It was a meld. Dulce realized she needed the power boost, so Bomot and I provided it."

That was news to Qod. He'd assumed that the lights were all Dulce.

"OK," he said. "The three of you. But to my point, the faeby wizards were able to hide soldiers from us, for one example. Why can't you?"

The wizards all exchanged looks that Qod couldn't interpret, except that it seemed they had opinions but didn't want to be the one to voice them.

Dulce cleared her throat and said, "I did hide Tulip at the barricade."

Qod nodded, and the silence returned.

Finally, Lraine spoke.

"With all due respect, sir, magic is magic. It doesn't care if the wizard is Dark or Light. It's just power, part of nature. Mindless."

Which didn't answer the question, in Qod's mind.

When Lraine didn't go further, he asked, "So, why haven't you hidden our soldiers, if the faebies are doing it? You said, a moment ago, that you have the same potential. Is that the reason?"

"No, sir. Well, yes, in a way."

He was clearly uncomfortable, so Qod said, "Go on."

"I told you, sir, that the command doesn't think that wizardry is honorable."

"I don't feel the same way, Lraine."

The other wizards perked up at his words.

"And I appreciate that, sir, but wizardry, it's like anything else. It takes practice to become proficient."

He paused a moment, then turned and swept an arm to encompass the others.

"All of us have varying degrees of inherent talent. But we could all be stronger in the arts if we were allowed to train and practice."

"Tell him about the academy, Lraine," the kobold who'd spoken up about assisting Dulce said.

"The Light, they scour the population for anyone who has a hint of talent, and then bring them to their Wizard Academy on one of the southern isles. There, they are taught to maximize their skills and practice them to increase their power."

"I take it we don't have an academy?"

The wizard shook his head.

"And if we did, all of you would be the match of the Light wizards.

This time, all fourteen of them nodded.

Qod took it one more step. "And the reason we don't have an academy is because we, as in the Dark, think your arcane arts are not honorable. Except for creature comforts," Qod said, glancing at the wizard light hanging from the ceiling.

"That's right, sir," Lraine said.

Qod considered that. He looked at his team to see if any of them had something to say or ask, but from the way they were looking back at him, they were waiting for him to come up with something.

*Three weeks ago, I was a new private, knowing nothing about warfare. And now, I'm supposed to have all the answers?*

In a sane world, that would be impossible. But as unbelievable as it was, that was the position he found himself in. And if there was anything he could do to contribute, then he was going to do it.

"Lieutenant Glascock," he said. "I know you've been in the CP, *listening* to what was going on."

He'd almost said "spying."

"What is the disposition of the Light forces?"

"The last report has the main body closing in on Offerton. We expect them to raze the facilities there to isolate us from supplies or potential reinforcements. The dwarves advancing through the high ground have slowed down, but are still moving."

That's what he expected about the main force. The Army of the Mist should have traversed the Anemia Delta and defended Offerton, but once again, the Light army had gotten the jump on them.

Offerton was lost. He just hoped the people there had managed to escape.

The dwarves in the mountains bothered him, though. Their route made no sense, especially with only something over a thousand soldiers. General Tillmus was sure fixated on them, though, and his plan revolved around their presence.

Maybe it didn't matter. There would be time to react to the expected assault by the main body, and Tillmus wanted to be in position to repulse the dwarves first, if they attacked.

*But why would they attack before the main body?*

What he didn't know always made Qod more uneasy than what he did know. For each battle, the Light had managed to surprise the Dark. So what was it this time?

He stood there silently for a long moment. Pani stepped up to his side, but no one else said a word.

*I have to know what's really going on.*

"You told me that the dwarves could be using wizardry to hide what they're really doing," he told Lraine, who nodded. "Could you, using your powers, be able to tell what's going on with them?"

"It shouldn't be too difficult," he said.

"OK, then. When we're done here, I want you to figure that out. Once we know that—"

"I'm sorry, sir. But that won't be possible."

"Why? You just said you could."

"If they were here or I was there. It would take proximity to accomplish. And even if I knew exactly where they were, just getting there would be problematic."

Qod grunted. He hadn't considered that, or even known it had to be considered. Ogres were strong and could fight, but they were not as mobile as orcs. Lraine was obviously older than most, and hiking the up and down terrain wouldn't be the easiest thing.

He would need someone who could move quickly over the mountains. Qod swept his gaze across the wizards before the choice was obvious.

"Dulce, do you have the abili—"

"Yes, sir," she almost shouted as she flew two feet into the air. "I can do it!"

A pang of regret swept through him. Dulce was his friend, and sending her out to scout would come with extreme danger. The thought of losing her struck fear into his soul.

The rational side of his mind said that Dulce's life was no more important than any other life, and if the information was needed, then he had to send her. But this was Dulce, not some nameless soldier he didn't know.

*Be strong.*

It took an extreme force of will to say, "Then, as soon as we're done here, I need you to go investigate. We need to know exactly what we're facing."

She beamed with pride, which made him swallow the bile that had come up his throat from fear that he was sending her to her death.

"Lieutenant, how long do we have before the enemy gets here?"

"The dwarves? As little as a day and a half. But with them slowing down, two days."

"And the main body?"

"No one knows. If they want to destroy Offerton, three days to do that and come up the river. If they don't loot the place, maybe two days, according to our Intel."

*Yeah, with their track record of bad analysis?*

Qod took a deep breath. What did he really know about warfare? Nothing. Why was he acting like he was a real general?

The easiest thing for him to do would be to thank the others for briefing him, then let them go. Then he could return to the CP, sit in the corner, and let the real soldiers do their jobs.

If Dulce found out something out of the ordinary, Qod could tell Tillmus. If she didn't, well then no one would have to know she'd even gone out.

Except . . .

Something told him Tillmus and the command staff were missing something, something that could have drastic consequences. He didn't know why he felt that way, only that he couldn't shake off the feeling. And he knew he couldn't ignore his gut.

*Oh, by the Dark Mother, screw it.*

"Worst case basis, we've got two days, then. Wizards, I need to know what you can and can't do. Then together, we're going to come up with a plan of attack."

# Chapter 44

"The Third Scouts. They've actually seen the dwarves," General Tillmus protested.

Qod tried to hide his frustration.

"I told you. Dulce was able to pierce the Light's transference. There're not more than thirty dwarves approaching from across the mountains."

"But she's just a pixie," General Tillmus said.

"A wizard."

The general couldn't hide his sneer. "You can't trust wizardry."

Beside him, Colonel Kolar nodded in agreement.

*As we sit here in wizard light and heat.*

"And what is this transference thing?"

Qod gave a mental sigh. He hadn't quite grasped the nuances of the wizardry, but he had to give it a shot.

"That's when a wizard is able to shift the image of something over distances. So the images the scouts saw were actually farther away. Like around Offerton."

"No. That's dwarf shit. Why am I only hearing about this now? I don't think you can just send what you see somewhere else."

*You're only hearing about it now because you won't let the wizards wizard.*

"Look. We can get messages all the way from Taxian, right? What someone, like the empress, says there is heard here," Qod said.

"That's not the same. And that's only if we have a wizard here."

"And maybe they have a wizard to receive the images? With, say, twenty dwarves for security?"

The general exchanged glances with the colonel.

An unspoken message crossed between them, and the general said, "No. That's just a theory. And if we ignore the dwarves, it would be to our peril."

*It's not a damn theory.*

Qod looked from the general to the colonel and back at Tillmus.

"I didn't want to take this step, but I am the commanding general. What if I just order you to obey?"

The answer was quick and blunt.

"Then I will kill you right here and now."

Qod took a reflexive step back. Maybe it wasn't such a good idea to meet with the two alone, without his draugrs.

"You do know that the empress will order your execution if you do that."

At least, that's what Lieutenant Glascock told him, and Qod really hoped that was true.

"Yes, I do."

Qod stared at him in surprise.

"Then why do it?" he asked.

"Because my life means nothing if the Dark falls," he answered with more emphasis than he'd shown so far. "You want us to abandon this position on the high ground, which is at least somewhat defensible, and meet a larger faeby force down in the open. Not just open, but marshland. That's suicide."

Qod stared at the general, and something about the way he said it convinced him that Tillmus was serious. He would kill him and face the consequences after the fact.

That made him far more dangerous. Qod had to figure out some way to convince him.

"But I told you, with the wizards—"

General Tillmus waved him off.

"That's another thing. You have some faeby-cursed plan to use wizards, of all things, to even up the sides? Really? Wizards? None of whom we have left are much better than party magicians. What are you going to do? Have them raise pretty lights?"

"It's not that. I told you what we're doing."

The general snorted. "Fairy tales."

*You're blinded by your prejudice, Tillmus.*

"Listen to me. You do acknowledge that the Light's main force is in Offerton, and that they're coming here next, right?"

Both the general and colonel nodded.

"And there're more of them than there are of us."

"Which is why we need to be in a defensive position. Let them come to us."

At least he believed that, which was good, Qod had to admit. Unlike Yare, who believed the only way to win was to throw waves of soldiers at the enemy.

"Colonel," Qod said, turning to the Operations Officer. "Yesterday, you said that this position was going to be tight."

"Yes, sir. We'll be packed in. But that makes it easy for our reserve to react to breaks in our line."

Qod purposefully ignored that last point.

"But having more breathing room would make us less vulnerable to the Light, right? Remember the battle mage and what he did to the Black Smokes?"

Both officers winced.

And before either of them said that the Light forces facing them didn't have a battle mage, he said, "Let's look at the reality. General Tillmus, you don't control the entire Army of the Mist."

The general started to protest, but Qod kept going.

"No matter what you say, no matter what you do to me, I have two battalions who are loyal to me, and if anything happens to me, they will take action."

The general stood as anger took over, and Qod held out a hand, palm outward.

"I won't tell them to do that. We can't afford to fight among ourselves. Not with the demons of the Light wanting to dance on our bones. Correct?"

The general's eyes were glowering, but he controlled himself and nodded.

"So, what about this? I'm taking those loyal to me, and we'll do what we can to attrit the Light army."

The moment he said it, the little goblin from Yellow Rock wanted to take it back. But General Qod from Yellow Rock knew it was the right thing to do.

"If you take your two battalions to face them, they'll run right over you."

"Not before we kill some of the bastards, which means you'll be dealing with fewer of them."

The general stared at him for a long moment, then asked, "Why would you do that?"

"You're not the only one who is willing to die for the Dark, General Tillmus."

This time, the general didn't bother to look at the colonel. He was still standing, but he strode purposefully around the table to Qod, who stood to meet him, wondering if he'd miscalculated. His hand itched to reach for his dagger.

But General Tillmus stuck out his hand instead of a sword. Qod hesitantly reached out to take it.

"I think we can accept that, General Qod, and may the Dark Mother guide you and your soldiers."

# Chapter 45

Qod stepped gingerly out on the ice and tamped down with his foot.

"Will this  hold their weight?" he asked Dulce.  "It still looks pretty thin."

Dulce motioned to one of Qod's draugrs, who unhesitantly strode out on the ice.  It sagged slightly, which no ice Qod had ever seen had done, but it held.

A day ago, when Team Blizzard arrived in the delta, a very thin sheet of ice had formed along much of the marsh. There was even open water.  But led by the head wizard, nine of the strongest Dark wizards had "melded," to use their terminology, and with their combined effort, convinced the water to crystallize to a greater degree.

Qod knew "convince" was not the right term for the wizardry they'd managed, but for his understanding, it was as good as anything else. The way Lraine had explained it, with the ice on the verge of forming on its own, it took relatively little power to induce the heat molecules to migrate away— which was the same basic concept they used to make the heat balls—and make the ice crystals join tighter.

An elven battle mage, like the one Qod had killed, could transform the marsh, even in the height of the summer sun, but with the temperatures hovering at freezing, this was a gods-given gift to the Dark forces.  It took far less power when all they had to do was 'nudge" the marsh into cooperating.

"Wizard smart, not wizard strong," Lraine had told him when they came up with the plan.

It was good advice, and not just for wizards.  Team Blizzard was much larger than either he or General Tillmus had expected.  Both the Copper Dragons and Broken Spears had miraculously grown as soldiers came over on their own, and, to Qod's amazement, a Black Smoke battalion had joined them as they marched out of camp.  Qod didn't know if they did that on their own or if Tillmus had relented and sent them, and he didn't ask.  He was just grateful for their presence. Even with them, though, Team Blizzard couldn't match the brute power of the Light force facing them, so they had to use their brains to even the playing field.

Qod hoped the plan they'd developed would do that. With the Light army advancing out of Offerton, they'd find out soon enough, something that both excited Qod and made him want to throw up on the icy marsh.

"And it will hold up under the weight of centaurs?"

"It should," Dulce said, but not sounding too sure of herself.

Qod turned toward the ring of wizards sitting on the ground, hands linked to each other. Their eyes were closed and they concentrated to keep the power flowing. He'd have felt better if they were up on the slopes above the valley floor, out of sight in the trees. But the farther away they were, the more power they had to exert. He'd already demanded they freeze too much territory, so handicapping them more could bring the entire operation crashing down.

The civilian kobold workers had done their best to pile brush to block the view of the wizards from downstream, but any Light-cursed pixie flying by would spot them.

*Thank the Mother for the civilians*, Qod told himself for the hundredth time.

When they'd descended from the camp, they'd encountered a steady stream of refugees fleeing Offerton. Some of the stories they told of the atrocities the Light were conducting brought alternating tears and anger among all who heard. If there was any doubt about what faced them, that was gone, and they were even more determined to crush the enemy.

But the big advantage was that with the Dark ready to make a stand, hundreds of civilians paused their flight to assist the preparations. The kobold engineers, in particular, were a godsend.

The original plan was simply to freeze the water spanning the entire delta. That left the two roads untouched, but doing something about that was beyond their ability to address.

As soon as the fleeing kobolds understood that, they got to work. Nine hours later, the roads might as well never have been there. They'd been taken down enough so that the water had covered them and then frozen. Not only that, but by some skilled engineering, there looked to be roads where there weren't any.

The two highways would take some work to repair, but Qod thought the price was one worth paying.

In addition to the engineers, close to two hundred former soldiers joined them. A few had weapons, both old military swords or spears kept as souvenirs or everyday tools. Twenty more had been armed when a human trader refugee, of all things, had donated the weapons he'd scavenged before hurrying on. But it was a grim fact that soldiers would fall today, and their weapons would then be free for the taking.

Perhaps the biggest surprise was the eleven trolls who'd been part of the Offerton police force. They'd been ordered by their captain to leave, something they were wracked with shame about, and this gave them an opportunity to erase that.

The stream of refugees had slowed to a trickle, and each time one or two came around the bend, civilians stationed in the trees rushed out and pulled them into hiding along the slopes. Qod didn't want anyone caught on the ice when the Light army advanced.

Qod stepped off the ice and motioned for Tulip to pick him up. It had been embarrassing at first, but with all the work being done, they both were past it by now. Perched on her shoulder, he could survey the area.

A few kobolds were putting finishing touches here and there. The Black Smoke detachment—half of the battalion's strength—along with the eleven troll police were in a loose formation on the first sizable piece of dry land where the river started spreading out into the marsh. In the manner of soldiers since time memorial, they were gabbing in small groups, smoking, or stretched out on the ground asleep.

They were the key. The first key of many that had to go right. If they didn't grab the Light's attention, the entire plan could be stillborn. There was dry land on either side of the marsh, after all, something that Qod tried not to think of.

Major Joon, the Black Smoke battalion commander, who'd chosen to make her stand with the bait, caught his gaze, and she gave him a slow salute. Qod self-consciously returned it.

On either side of the marsh, just inside the tree line, was the rest of Team Blizzard, military and civilians alike. Eight hundred goblins, gremlins, ogres, orcs, pixies, trolls, vurdalaks, satyrs, brownies, banshees, gryphons, and even a selkie from the southern oceans. Win or lose, this was truly a Dark alliance.

"General?" Lieutenant Glascock said.

Qod turned to look at where the orc was pointing. A single harpy was gliding down from the peak at the bend in the river.

She flared her wings and came to a halt at Tulip's feet. Four sprite heads hung from a string around her neck—Light scouts who'd ventured up the river before the Dark was ready.

"They're almost here, General," she said. "They're passing Mossy Ridge and should be in view within half an hour."

Ice threatened to freeze Qod's gut. It had been one thing to rush the preparations for the battle. But it was something else to realize the time had come. One way or the other, this was going to be decided before the day was over.

The last time he'd been in the area, as part of the 3rd Scout Battalion, they were ambushed at Mossy Ridge by the Light. If the world were a fair place, this time the Dark would be doing the ambush.

Unfortunately, fair had nothing to do with it. It was up to them to fight for the win.

"Very well, Sergeant. Thank you. Go find a post where you can watch for any Light surprises."

"I can fight, sir."

"I know you can. But you can do us more good up at the heights."

Qod had pixies stationed all along the high ground, but a harpy in full attack dive was much faster than they were.

"Dulce!" he shouted.

A moment later, she was hovering in front of his eyes.

"Are you ready?"

"Yes, sir."

"Get it done."

She flew off to join the other two remaining wizards. The slopes above the marsh were clear of Dark soldiers downriver from where Qod was. The troops were crammed into the more limited slopes closer to the orcs and trolls acting as bait. Too many soldiers in too little space, which meant they could be easily spotted. The Light might feel confident and still advance if they were spotted, but Qod didn't want to take the chance.

That's where they were taking a page from the Light battle book. Dulce and the other two would try to shield them from view like the Light wizards did at the Long Caldron.

Qod was sure he'd forgotten something. Many somethings. But there wasn't much he could do about it now. The cards had been dealt.

From his perch on Tulip's shoulder, he looked down on his team, which for him now included his draugrs.

"I don't have any rousing words to say, and I know you don't need them," he said. "But I *can* say that I'm proud to be serving with you. And with that, let those faeby bastards come."

# Chapter 46

"Don't worry, Lieutenant," Qod told his draugr commander, who kept trying to fall back. "It really doesn't matter where I am. If we lose, we're all going to meet the Dark Mother today.

Big words, and he hoped he was sounding confident, but in reality, his heart was pounding. This was it. His plan was about to be tested, and his imposter syndrome was in full swing.

What made him think he could command an army in combat? He was just a goblin from Yellow Rock, not a professional soldier. And he knew his plan was risky. Putting his life on the line meant nothing in the big swing of things, but he'd put his soldiers' lives on the line, too. More than them. If they fell, the Light rampagers would have a free shot to sweep through the Anemia River basin and points north.

Lieutenant Helvig bit his lower lip, but he didn't argue this time. Qod hoped he'd given up. Every ounce of him wanted to pull back, and he didn't need the temptation.

The draugr officer had a point. Qod didn't have to be there with Major Joon and her Black Smokes. He could observe the battle from a safer spot above the valley floor, but something made him position himself where every Dark soldier could see him. And he hadn't been blowing smoke up Helvig's butt. If this plan fell apart, he wasn't going to survive the day, no matter where he was.

"There they are," Tulip said.

Qod's pucker factor jumped tenfold as the first of the Light army appeared, coming around the bend.

"Centaurs," Qod said.

"That's what you wanted," Lieutenant Glascock said.

That was true. Centaurs were headstrong, confident of being able to handle anything thrown their way. Qod wanted them to see the orcs and trolls formed up and ready to repulse them. Hopefully, they'd be overcome by a killing frenzy and not notice that the ice under their feet wasn't quite normal. If the elves were in the vanguard, wily bastards that they were, then Qod's plan could be revealed before he had a chance to put it into operation.

It might still come to naught. Centaurs were the heaviest of the Light soldiers, and Qod worried that his wizards were not going to be able to keep the ice solid under their weight.

*If that happens, just deal with it.*

The shift in the centaurs was visible across the delta as they spotted the bait. A claxon call reverberated over the icy marsh, and the centaurs surged forward. That was exactly what Qod was counting on, but images of them at the barricade kept flashing through his mind. If they reached Joon, even with the trolls, Qod feared it would be a massacre.

He stood on tiptoes on Tulip's shoulder as more of the force came into sight. And more of them. And yet still more. Elves with pikes in perfect formation. Dwarves.

"Fauns," he said, almost in a curse.

Elves were extremely effective archers, and some of them would have bows, but Qod feared that the fauns could be the difference. Archers had taken a front seat in his mind, but while he'd taken steps to address the problem, he just didn't have as many satyr bowmen as he wanted.

*We don't have enough of anything.*

Qod was still bitter about General Tillmus's obstinacy. With the rest of the Army of the Mist, he would be far more confident that they could prevail here on the Anemia delta. Let thirty dwarves have the highlands. What could they do from there?

He had been continually second-guessing his not pushing the issue, but as Pani pointed out, if the Dark army had clashed for control, then even the winner would have been so weakened that they'd be just a speedbump to the Light advance.

"They're about to reach the edge of the wizardry," Lieutenant Glascock said.

Lraine had explained that the farther they stretched their efforts, the less effective they'd be. And even with a shorter reach, there wasn't a firm line to where their wizardry would start working. But eight hours after the wizards went to work, the civilian kobolds had pulled down a large bristlecone as a marker at the edge of where ice seemed to be growing and where the northside road had been dug out.

Qod held his breath as the quickly advancing centaurs reached the tree, and the enemy, with no road to follow, started to spread out. For a moment, nothing changed. The enemy was still advancing. Then, to his dismay, several centaurs broke through the ice and started floundering.

"It's not holding," Nataly said.

But the rest of the centaurs kept going, and the ones who'd broken through managed to climb out and follow the rest. If any of them thought that wizards were at work, it certainly didn't seem to slow them down. If anything, the freedom to spread out seemed to motivate them. Qod didn't need goblin ears to hear their war shouts as they advanced.

The orcs returned the shouts. Most were frankly both obscene and physically impossible. Qod didn't think that the centaurs could make out what the orcs were saying, but they didn't have to. They could guess.

As the centaurs dispersed, more of the rest of the Light could be seen. Two things became clear. There were fewer centaurs than had been expected, but far more elves.

Qod should have expected that. Many of the centaurs had been killed in previous battles, including at the barricade, but the elves, when faced with a strong position, had retreated. It was obvious that far fewer of them had been killed than Intel had reported.

"It doesn't change anything," he muttered.

Still, Qod was a creature of his upbringing, where, as a tiny sausage, he'd been told tales of the evil elves who preyed on misbehaving goblins. He was inordinately apprehensive of the leaders of the Light, and he'd just as soon face about anyone else.

But it wasn't just the elves that were revealed. There were many more dwarves as well, fauns, and, to his surprise, large numbers of Light small folk: brownies, gnomes, and fairies, all with gleaming white armor. Qod was worried that some of the soldiers who weren't as headstrong as the centaurs would realize something was amiss, but it was as if the centaurs were the head of the spear that was already launched, pulling the shaft of the rest of the force along in their wake, whether they liked it or not.

But not everyone was following in trace. With the force spreading out, some were leaving the bottomland and heading into the trees.

"Dwarf shit!" Qod said.

His team swiveled to look up at him.

"They're disappearing!"

"What do you mean?" Lieutenant Glascock asked.

But Tulip immediately understood.

"Some elves are moving into the trees, and they are disappearing from sight."

Qod was kicking himself. This should have been foreseen. Dulce and her team's visual shielding did not recognize friend or foe, so just as the Light army couldn't see the Dark soldiers on the tree-covered slopes, neither could Qod. And it was logical that when faced with a visible foe, the Light would send forces into the trees for flank security.

Now, one of two things could happen. The rest of the enemy would notice that their elven scouts had disappeared, and they'd know the Dark was using wizardry. Or, they'd run into the westernmost troops Qod had emplaced.

Either was bad news, with only a third of the Light force firmly in the iced area.

Qod turned on Tulip's shoulder to where the wizard ring was fighting to keep the ice strong.

"What is it?" Major Juun shouted at him.

"Elves moving up the slopes and disappearing."

"SOP," she said with a nod. "Don't worry. They've got another two hundred yards before they run into anyone."

Which was right, he realized. But that didn't take into account that someone would notice their fellow soldiers vanishing.

Except . . .

He looked back at the enemy. They were spreading out and pushing forward with the centaurs leading the charge. If they kept going at this rate, the first of the centaurs would clash with the orcs in three minutes, maybe four. Along with

Jonathan P. Brazee

signal flags and horns, the Light used fairies as the Dark used pixies for battlefield communications, but even if they wanted to, could the Light commander stop what was now a full-out charge?

*Maybe yes, maybe no.*

In any other circumstance, Qod would be hoping for something to slow down and blunt an enemy assault. Now, he mentally urged them on while he constantly tried to estimate how much of the enemy force was on the ice. More were pushing forward, but he couldn't see the end of them.

One thing was certain. Qod had been hoping Intel was wrong as to their numbers. And they were, but not in the direction Qod had wanted. There were more Light soldiers than Intel had estimated.

The distance between centaurs and orcs (and Qod) kept shrinking, and, as Major Juun started to form up her soldiers, with the troll police on either side. The insults in native centaur and Lingua were now clear, and if anything, the centaurs became more enraged, and several of the ones in the front broke into a sprint as they told the orcs what they would do to them.

"General?" Lieutenant Glascock asked.

"Not yet."

Qod was very conscious of the glances being sent his way. But he held fast. Not enough of the Light soldiers were in the kill zone.

A clash sounded in the northern slope, followed by the blast of a Light **gjallarhorn**. Some of the second wave started to slow and turn in that direction, and still Qod held off. The Light soldiers in the rear kept pushing forward.

An arrow arched out of the elves, which Qod ignored until Pani shouted, "Tulip!"

A massive hand reached up to cover Qod a split-second before the arrow sank into her palm.

"They're targeting you!" Pani shouted at him. "Get down."

"Just a little longer," he answered as he watched the charge.

The seven centaur greyhounds came to the end of the ice.

"General! You've got to give the signal!" Glascock yelled.

The centaurs charged across the dry land straight at the orc center, which braced for the impact. But the trolls closed in on the sides. Stopping a warrior centaur was not the same thing as arresting a drunk ogre, though, and the first troll was immediately dropped before the others could engage. The charge was blunted, but the next group was almost to the dry land.

He couldn't wait any longer. Qod raised the small red flag that he had stuck in his belt and shouted, "Now!"

A ghoul, tall enough to see over the screen of vegetation, raised a hand in acknowledgment and turned away.

Qod shifted back to the kill zone and held his breath. And nothing happened. Several more centaurs reached the dry ground, and in a moment, it would be a torrent.

"Get him out of here," both lieutenants shouted in unison, and Tulip started to leave.

Qod yanked on her ear and shouted, "Wait."

The big troll hesitated when a single crack reverberated across the entire valley before the entire ground seemed to break open as Lraine's wizards released their hold on the spell.

Centaurs crashed into the freezing water, then got mired in the cold mud as their weight drove them down. Elves, fauns, and dwarves, the latter laden with their heavy armor, broke through.

Five blasts on an ogre ram horn, repeated by others stationed on both slopes, rolled over the delta. Dulce and her team cut their screen, and a moment later, volleys of arrows reached out from the slopes to rain hell on the trapped soldiers. Fauns and elves tried to return the fire, but with almost impossible footing and Dark soldiers taking cover, their fire was ineffective. Not just that. Their arrows fell short, and Qod pumped a fist in the air.

Archers were extremely careful with their bowstrings, which they kept in beeswax-wrapped leather pouches. Get them wet, and they lose their effectiveness. Already, Qod could see fauns struggling to pull out replacement drawstrings, but while struggling in the frigid water and mud, that was going to be difficult. Meanwhile, they were targets.

Unfortunately, Qod couldn't take full advantage of that. His satyrs were dealing death to the enemy, but he just didn't have many of them left. So, he had armed gremlins and ghouls under the theory that put enough arrows out there, some would strike flesh.

He was correct, but not to enough of a degree.

A spear whistled through the air—not too close, but close enough so that Tulip grabbed and lowered him to the ground. Immediately, he was surrounded.

"I can't see!" he protested.

But he could. Through Tulip's legs, a wave of mostly kobolds, all trilling their *uran* and clad in light leather cuirasses, was sweeping out of the trees.

Getting them out of their armor had almost caused a mutiny. They were as attached to it as were the dwarves to theirs.

But out in the delta, dwarves were drowning in the deep spots. Where elves might be chest deep in places, some dwarves had fallen into holes and were completely underwater. And with their armor, they had no chance unless they could manage to get out of it, which for dwarves, took some doing.

The kobolds, armed with pikes and billhooks, came to the edge of the water, ready to spear any Light soldier who'd managed to pull themselves close enough. Without their armor weighing them down, they could even dart forward to strike a blow.

The centaurs were almost completely incapacitated. They were immensely strong, but they were also extremely heavy. With legs that were not designed for mud, they quickly became mired. After throwing their spears in anger, they became immobile targets for Qod's soldiers.

For several minutes, the devastation wrought upon the Light was terrible, and Qod let himself hope that his plan might actually work. But only around half of the Light army had been in the kill zone, and across the area, some were able to extricate themselves without Dark opposition.

Particularly the Light small folk. Brownies, sprites, and gnomes, lighter to begin with and without heavy armor, were able to crawl or swim, if necessary, and emerge cold but unscathed.

And they were mad and looking to fight.

The biggest threat, though, was from the huge number of soldiers who'd never been in the kill zone. They'd been along the edges or at the rear of the force when the spell had been released.

It took several minutes for them to reorganize, but soon, they were moving up both sides of the marsh. Major Juun had fallen, but her soldiers hooked up with the remainder of the battalion to assault forward on the south side of the marsh, and they made progress. But further downstream, goblins, gremlins, and kobolds were being cut down. The banner for the Copper Dragons fell, was raised again, then dropped once more.

On the other side of the marsh, Elves—the security who'd gone into the trees—emerged. They quickly pounced on the Broken Spears on that side, scything through them. Qod's heart almost burst as he watched his soldiers die.

"General, you need to retreat," Lieutenant Helvig said. "We'll cover you."

Then to Lieutenant Glascock, he said, "Stay off the highway. Take him cross-country and get back to General Tillmus."

Glascock stepped forward and took Qod's arm, but the smaller goblin yanked it free with strength he didn't realize he had.

"No!" he shouted.

"You have to—"

"Mac, raise my banner."

The kobold corporal smiled, pulled it off his back, and handed it to Tulip.

"Wave it."

She hesitated a moment, then nodded, came to her full height, and started waving it around.

Qod searched among the orcs until he saw a signaler. "You! Corporal. Sound the rally."

The orc's eyes widened in surprise as he looked at the banner for a moment before he realized what it meant, then back at Qod. A wicked smile crossed his face. He reached into his pack, removed his ram horn, and blew the rally call.

"Again!" Qod ordered.

"Once more, the discordant, grating, and wonderful call floated across the marsh. Almost immediately, Dark soldiers started to break contact and sprint to Tulip and the banner. The break was so abrupt that it caught most of the enemy flatfooted.

Not for long, though. They began to chase down the Dark soldiers, slaughtering the slow and wounded.

The Black Smokes arrived first and started forming a circle around Qod, parting to let more in as they arrived. Dark soldiers of all races reached them, then turned to face the enemy.

A group of dwarves was so intent on running down their hated kobolds that they might not have realized what was standing in their way. They crashed into the line and were stopped cold.

The survivors pulled back and screamed insults when they were ordered to retreat.

"What's happening?" Pani asked. "Why have they stopped?"

"They want to plan this out," Qod said, and Mac nodded.

The entire Light assault had seemed piecemeal, something very un-Light-like. Qod figured that someone had decided to take over.

It took almost thirty minutes before that someone surfaced. By that time, any Dark soldier who was going to make the rally was there. Qod figured he had three hundred soldiers and four of the troll police. They had their backs against the water, which meant no one was behind them.

It also meant there was no retreat.

In a semi-circle around them were at least nine hundred soldiers of the Light. No centaurs—which made Qod perversely happy—and heavy on the small folk, but it was more than enough to simply overrun his soldiers.

It was just a matter of when, not if.

The only thing Qod and his soldiers could do was to make sure they took out as many of them as possible before they fell. Leave fewer for General Tillmus to face.

Qod met with Captain Coonin, who'd taken over for Major Juun and the two surviving lieutenants to see if there was any way out of this. They could try and fight their way through, but that was a fool's errand. They could try to cross the muddy marsh, but the Light could simply march to the other side and beat them there.

No, it looked like it was going to be a fight right here. Once that was accepted, Qod and his team—his original security and the draugrs—waited under his banner.

"Do you regret it?" Pani asked him.

Qod actually had to think about it before he said, "No. This was our only chance, and, by the Dark Mother, we almost pulled it off."

"Gave the bastards a bloody nose, we did," Mac said.

"Yes, that we did."

"Here comes someone," Tulip told him. "Two someones. One with a white flag."

Around him, he could feel the soldiers alert.

Qod stepped forward. Striding across no man's land was a faun, carrying a white flag, followed by an elf with almost as much gold on as the battle mage he'd killed was wearing.

The colonel stepped around the faun and stood, hands on his hips as he sneered at the Dark soldiers.

"Is the one they call the Mage Killer here?"

Pani grabbed his arm, but Qod stepped forward.

"Colonel, I am General Qod."

He'd almost said "General Qod from Yellow Rock," but he'd stopped that just in time. There was no reason to give this guy an excuse to find and raze the village.

That obviously surprised the colonel. It was only then that his eyes locked on the full moons on Qod's collar.

Evidently, the thought of a goblin general was so strange to him that he'd never bothered to notice his rank insignia.

The elf seemed to recover. He snorted, then said, "So it is true. The Dark has sunk so low that they have a gobby leading them."

Anger flared in him, but before Qod could answer, Mac said, "He killed your elf battle mage."

A tiny cloud passed over the elf's eyes, but his sneer quickly returned.

"Propoganda lie."

"Somebody killed that idiot, seeing as he's not here," Mac said.

"This is between officers, *Corporal*," the colonel said with disdain. "Even a gobby officer."

"Ooh, got his goat," Nataly said.

"As I said, I'm General Qod, otherwise known as the Mage Killer. There is no reason for further bloodshed, Dark or light. I will offer myself to you if you let my soldiers withdraw."

Pani said, "No!" and the colonel laughed.

"You think I came here to ask for your surrender?"

*No, but I was hoping.*

"If you continue with your attack, many of your soldiers will die, too."

"They will always die. That's what soldiers do."

The faun holding the white flag's eyes flinched, but that was all.

"No, I just wanted to make sure the so-called Mage Killer was present. I want to be the one to personally kill you."

Without another word, he wheeled on his heels and strode off. The faun was taken by surprise, and he was a half-second late following.

"Such a sweet guy," Nataly said to the elf's retreating back.

"Well, I guess we'd better get ready," Captain Coonin said.

He started to turn away but paused.

"General, I just wanted to say, it's been an honor. We almost did it. *You* almost did it. It was your plan, and it would have gone down in the annals of the Dark as one of our greatest battles."

And with that, he was gone.

"Wow," Pani said. "I never would have thought an orc would say that to a goblin."

Qod was rather gobsmacked, too, and he felt a warm flow of pleasure. Unfortunately, it was short-lived. As soon as the colonel returned to his soldiers, there was movement as they were reorganized.

They watched the shifting to try to understand what was coming next. It looked like a massive frontal assault on the three sides. No archers, which meant their drawstrings were unusable, but more likely, the colonel wanted this to be brutal hand-to-hand, which was fine with Qod. They'd be able to kill more of them that way.

And he had archers. Nineteen satyrs and twelve of the gremlins and ghouls. Not many arrows left, but they'd account for some of the Light attackers.

As the Light changed positions, one of the dwarves shouted, "Kobolds. Meet us!"

Dwarves and kobolds were close to the same size and temperament, and they occupied many of the same economic niches. They were also mortal enemies. The Black Smoke orcs, who were the anchor for the defense, shifted to let the kobolds face the dwarves.

Qod didn't think ancient rivalries should dictate his force, but given the situation, what difference did it make? If that's where his kobolds wanted to be, he owed it to them.

He gave Mac a quick glance to see if he wanted to join, but the corporal avoided his eyes.

Finally, the Light was set. It looked like this was going to be an initial probe. Most of the Light had backed off, many climbing partway up the slope like spectators of a featherball game. All of the elves were with that group. Directly facing them were dwarves, gnomes, brownies, and sprites—all small folk except for the dwarves.

The numbers facing them were only somewhat more than Qod had.

"Why are they limiting it?" he asked.

Mac answered, "Typical elf shit. The way we're set up 'ere, they can't bring all their numbers against us at once. So they use the fodder to cut our number, rough us up before the elves get their 'ands dirty."

Qod looked out at their attackers. If they thought they were fodder, they didn't show it. Instead, they were yelling their hate and slapping their chests with their weapons.

"Don't be caught unawares," Captain Coonin called out. "The elves might be coming in right on their asses."

*Crap, he's right.*

The Light had fooled the Dark often enough, and here he was simply accepting what he was seeing. It would take nothing for the elves and the rest to charge down the hill and join the fray.

The high, clear, beautiful, horrible tone of the dwarven **gjallarhorn** cut through the din, and like attack dogs unleashed, the Light soldiers burst into a charge with a deafening roar. Qod's soldiers had only moments to lower their pikes and raise their weapons.

Arrows flew out, dropping attackers, but the Light soldiers smashed into the line almost intact.

Pikes skewered dozens, their dead or writhing bodies blocking the others. It devolved into individuals maneuvering and reaching to try to strike an enemy. Many blows only wounded the target, but others hit home with fatal effects. Qod, his dagger drawn, started to move forward only to be yanked back by Private Riss, one of his draugrs.

"No, General. You stay here."

Qod was tempted to order the private to let him go, but one look on her face, and he knew that order would be ignored.

Bodies started to pile in front of the line. Dark soldiers fell, too. Many of the kobolds. But the Black Smokes were more than holding their own, and the police trolls were able to reach over the heads of the defenders to smash down the attackers.

The fight raged for several minutes. All the while, the spectators watched. Finally, a single note sounded, and the survivors retreated.

Qod hadn't struck out in anger. He hadn't done anything. But he was breathing hard as if he'd been in the midst of the fighting.

"Close it up!" Captain Coonin shouted. "Fill in the gaps."

*That's what I should be doing instead of sitting here like a precious gem being protected.*

He bolted forward, surprising his draugrs. With them in hot pursuit, he started running up and down the line, ordering soldiers into position, getting the wounded and the dead pulled back. His team and the draugrs, once they realized he wasn't about to singlehandedly attack the Light, joined in.

And there was a lot to do. Too many had been killed, especially among the kobolds. But the dwarves had paid the price, too. The dead and wounded were piled high. Some were still alive. A gnome with her intestines hanging loose was climbing over dead bodies as she tried to drag herself away.

The Dark soldiers let her go.

*Let her fellow faebies deal with her.*

Qod was everywhere, encouraging soldiers, giving hope to the wounded. This was something he could do.

"Looks like they're not going to wait any longer," Mac said while Qod held the hand of a dying goblin.

He looked up. The elves were filing back down. A few fauns were readying their bows, and it looked like all the combat-ready soldiers were going to be part of this push.

The goblin convulsed and died right then. Qod looked at him, numb to the sorrow. He didn't even know his name or where he was from, and at that moment, something inside of him broke.

There was no fear anymore. No imposter syndrome. No doubt. He was General Qod from Yellow Rock, and, by the Dark Mother, that was how he was going to die.

"Tulip, up!"

She raised him to her shoulder, and he shouted to his soldiers, "This is where we make our history. You have one more task in front of you. Before you die, take four of the bastards with you to be your servants in hell!"

His soldiers erupted into cheers. "Mage Killer" became a chant. Out beyond their position, the elves watched in silence.

One of the fauns raised his bow, and Qod just stared at her, but another faun reached over and pushed the bow toward the ground, then pointed toward their colonel.

Qod didn't even care. Now or five minutes from now. Death was coming for them all, so it didn't matter when.

"Down," he told Tulip, who lowered him to the ground.

One more time, the **gjallarhorn** trumpeted over the battlefield, and with a roar, the Light started collapsing on the Dark.

The last battle had begun.

# Chapter 47

The clash of Light and Dark made the ground shake. Faun and satyr, dwarf and kobold, brownie and gremlin—races so close to each other that it was hard for Qod to tell them apart—came together with the sole purpose of killing one another.

The elves, most of whose white armor was still clean from the mud that besmirched the others and egged on by the orcs, arrowed in on their historical foes.

The Dark archers exhausted their remaining arrows within seconds, dropped their bows, drew their blade weapons, and joined their Dark brethren.

Utter chaos reigned. Qod was everywhere, urging his soldiers on, his team with him. Lieutenant Glascock went down after a hit to the side of his head, but the flow of the battle pushed Qod away from him.

A section of kobolds collapsed, and dwarves started pouring through, and he had to pull every other ogre to retake the gap. Even that wouldn't have been enough without the three remaining police trolls, arrows sticking out of their bodies like porcupine quills, rushing to reinforce them.

The line held for the moment, but barely, and the pressure was immense. Pure numbers of the Light pushed the line back as the half-circle shrank, step by step.

Qod's draugrs tried to form a protective shield around him, and the Light archers, who stayed beyond the battleline, noticed. Lieutenant Helvig took an arrow through the throat and fell. Within a minute, Private Riss was hit in the thigh with a spear.

"Spread out," Qod told Sergeant Aamaw, the detail second-in-command. "You're making yourselves targets."

The sergeant ignored him until Qod took a different tack and said, "You're making *me* a target!"

He wasn't really concerned about himself, but he didn't want his bodyguard to be obvious targets for the fauns. If they were so closely surrounding him, then they were obviously protecting something and while the one faun archer declined

Jonathan P. Brazee

to shoot, he thought most faun archers would jump at the chance to eliminate them.

The sergeant let that sink in as an arrow whistled past his face before he nodded in understanding and pushed his draugrs out several paces. It wasn't perfect, but it gave Qod a little more freedom to move.

But move where? One of the police trolls fell with an anguished scream, swarmed under by gnomes. That opened a small gap, but one large enough that a dozen elves vaulted over the bodies and into the center of the defense.

"Tulip, Nataly, go!" Qod ordered.

He'd been holding them back as a small reaction force.

"Finally," Tulip said as she rushed the elves, who seemed surprised to be facing her.

They didn't quail, though, and rushed to meet her. But with their focus on Tulip, they forgot about the others. Nataly took one down from behind, but their biggest mistake was getting too close to the draugrs.

Sergeant Aamaw gave the order, and as quick as striking copperheads, half of his team darted in, struck, and retreated back to their position. They left all the elves and one of their own dead, and Tulip, wounded and blood streaming down an arm, looking for more enemies to engage.

Qod's mouth dropped open. He'd seen how quickly they could react when Lieutenant Helvig had killed Manticoz in the CP, and he knew they were deadly, but he hadn't seen them in actual combat before.

A faun arrow thudded into the ground at Tulip's feet. Yannis darted forward, snatched it with one hand while unslinging the bow off his back, and with one smooth move, nocked, drew back, and let fly. The arrow caught an elf in the mouth as he leaped over several kobold bodies.

That was when Qod realized that the incoming arrows were now few and far between. Up on the slope, the few fauns that had working bows were now starting to descend with drawn blades.

One weapon in the Light armory might have been depleted, but they still outnumbered the besieged Dark defenders. And as he watched, more of his soldiers fell, and their position was becoming untenable. With the soldiers in hand-to-hand combat, their focus was on staying alive long enough to kill the faeby in front of them, so the individual soldiers didn't see the gaps opening on either side of them.

Qod, in the center of their position, though, could see what was happening, and he had to shrink their perimeter to close the gaps caused by the fallen.

"Pass the word. We need to pull back," he told his team.

Nataly, Yannis, New Guy, and Tulip rushed to obey, but Mac and Pani hesitated.

"Go! I have my draugrs."

With Tulip physically yanking soldiers back, the line started to contract. Qod knew that it would only buy them some time, though. The end result was inevitable.

Before the gaps were closed, though, a phalanx of elves, all clad in immaculate silver and gold armor, burst through the line. One spotted Qod and pointed. They charged. Sergeant Aamaw gave the order, and the draugrs met the charge.

This time, though, they'd met a tougher foe. The elves were whirling harbingers of death. Many of them fell to the draugrs, but they acted in pairs, in threes, even fours, to take down Qod's bodyguards. Qod wasn't just going to watch. He darted forward, his dagger ready. Two draugrs were engaged with Private Riss, who was now bleeding heavily from a slash on his arm. As they maneuvered, one of the elves' back was toward Qod. He darted forward and struck, but his blade skittered up the armor. The elf wheeled around, swinging his sword. Extended and out of balance, Qod knew he couldn't get out of the way. This was finally it.

But the elf saw who it was and deflected the blade at the last instant to swish over Qod's head. The elf looked down at him, which gave Riss the opening he needed. After dispatching the other elf, he plunged his blade through the back of this one's neck.

"Thanks, General," Riss shouted before he wheeled to face three more elves charging him.

Qod stared at the dying elf for a moment.

"Why did you hesitate?" he asked.

The elf just gurgled, golden-tinged blood pulsing out of the side of his neck. His eyes glazed, and he was gone.

Qod shook his head to clear it and looked for someone else he could help. But Riss was the last draugr standing, and a moment later, he was bowled over.

Only five of the now bloodstained elves were still alive. His draugrs had killed three for each one of them, but they had needed to kill four.

Qod raised his dagger. Maybe he could wound one. But they didn't attack. Instead, they parted in the middle, and standing calmly in the midst of the battle was the elf colonel.

"Well, gobby. If you really did kill our battle mage, then you shouldn't have any problem with me now, should you?"

Qod just shook his head in disgust. This colonel let his elite soldiers die just so he could claim a personal victory by killing the Mage Killer?

The elf commander misinterpreted his shake, and his eyes got bigger.

"Do you really believe that? You poor, besotted fool. Well, it's time. You and me. Commander to commander, as it should be."

It was only then that Qod realized that at least twenty of the elves streaming into the position weren't fighting. They were standing behind their commander, just watching.

Qod knew about challenging for leadership. He'd never heard of enemy commanders battling it out. And maybe after he won, the elf would let his surviving soldiers surrender.

*Probably not.*

His soldiers were going to fight, and the elf wouldn't let any of them go anyway.

He raised his dagger above his head. The colonel gave him a short nod, then started forward . . . until his head disappeared in a cloud of **gold** mist. It was gone. The body remained upright for a second, not knowing it was dead, before it collapsed, and blood pulsed out in spurts.

There was a roar of outrage from the elves, their anger aimed at Qod. That allowed Tulip to bowl them over as she ran to pick up the hammer she'd just thrown at the colonel and then back up to protect Qod. Mac, Pani, Nataly, Yannis, and

New Guy slipped beside him. The team was back, facing what Qod suddenly realized must be the Light's command staff.

Staff or not, they were armed, and they were angry. One of them suddenly charged, yelling a battle cry. A casual backhand from Tulip broke him in two, the body tumbling back several yards before sliding to a crumbled stop.

There was a bubble of shocked silence amidst the ongoing fighting.

Then a major stepped forward, faced his peers, and said, "You saw what they did to the colonel, violating *a'saan*. We need to avenge him!"

Others stared at Tulip, then at each other. Several started to pull additional fighting elves from where they were battling.

"Cowards," Mac said. "Always getting the grunts to do their dirty work."

The battle was getting to the end stage. Pockets of Dark soldiers were still fighting, but the Light was surrounding them and whittling away at their numbers. And with more unengaged soldiers, the command staff was able to pull more of them in. Without Tulip, they'd have already moved, but with her, the elf major obviously wanted overkill.

Qod and his team closed up, their backs against the water, as they waited.

"Given the situation, do you think you can finally call me by my name?" New Guy asked.

"What is it?" Mac asked. "I forgot."

"It's Castor," Qod said.

"OK, Castor it is."

Finally, it looked like the major was satisfied as he brought his fighters on line.

"About time," Mac muttered when a warbling, out-of-tune, *beautiful* call swept over the battlefield.

The Light recognized it, too. Everyone, Dark and Light alike, swiveled to stare at the slope above them. Like a swarm of locusts, hundreds of arrows darkened the sky as they plunged on the massed Light soldiers outside the Dark's position. Bodies fell, and screams sounded.

Another volley of arrows wreaked havoc on the Light before at least a battalion of Black Smokes emerged from the trees like avenging angels. The major, who had been hesitant to charge the seven of them, was a whirlwind as he tried to reorient his troops to the threat, but Qod's soldiers wouldn't disengage. They switched from defense to offense, and while their numbers were few, the Light troops had suffered a mental one-eighty.

Some of the Light on the fringe of the force started to run, but others managed to get into some semblance of order to meet the charge. Laudable, but futile. The Black Smokes hit the Light hard, sweeping the mostly small folk out of the way. And it wasn't just the Black Smokes. More and more Dark soldiers poured out of the trees.

"It's the rest of the damn army," Mac said in wonder.

And leading the second wave was none other than General Tillmus, screaming loud enough to put a banshee to shame.

"What happened?" Qod asked. "Why did he come?"

"Thank the Dark Mother that he did," Mac said.

The reversal of fortune was too much for the Light to overcome. They were mentally defeated, despite the numbers still being slightly in their favor. But the Dark soldiers were not to be denied.

Several Light soldiers turned their fear onto Qod and his team, and New Guy—Castor—took a spear in the side, but they managed to stay alive until the rest of the draugrs cut through the mass of fighting and reached them.

Captain Sveto glanced at his downed draugrs without a change of expression.

"Are you OK, General?" he asked.

"We're alive."

"And you will stay that way," he said as his bodyguards surrounded them.

With the draugrs there, no one else decided to try and attack them. Qod had a front row seat observing the battle. He felt guilty about being protected there while Dark soldiers were fighting and dying, but when he suggested that they join the battle, Captain Sveto flatly refused to let him go.

The outcome was obvious, but the Light, with their retreat cut off, was not going to make this easy. Dark soldiers were killed as the Light fought tooth and nail. But more of the Light left the mortal plane.

Some might have escaped, but the vast majority were killed. No prisoners. No wounded. Qod knew it was necessary, but he avoided watching the cleanup, and he tried to ignore the cries of the wounded before they joined the ranks of the dead.

"What a victory," Castor said. "I'll be telling my grandkids about this someday."

Nataly put her arm around his shoulder. "If you need me to tell them it's all true, you just ask."

The others were happy, almost jubilant. Qod was numb. It might be a victory, but he had to guess that at least six hundred soldiers—his soldiers—had been killed. Killed because of his plan. It had seemed like the right thing to do, but without Tillmus arriving, it would have failed.

And that was on him. He'd let his hubris convince himself that he understood warfare.

"General? General Tillmus's coming," Captain Sveto said.

That raised Qod from his dark thoughts. General Tillmus, with his black and grey armor, now dented and bloody, was striding purposefully toward them with a single orc . . .

"Look. It's Glascock," Pani said. "I saw him getting killed."

Mac grunted. "Bastard's too tough to die."

Qod felt a warm rush of relief. He'd thought the lieutenant was dead, too. But there he was, missing his helmet, a bloody ear, but with the cocked assuredness that had become comforting to Qod over the last month.

He drew himself up and stepped forward to meet Tillmus. His team started to follow, but he waved them back.

General Tillmus had saved the day, and he was probably going to want to take the credit—and command.

And at the moment, Qod was willing to let him. He'd had enough of the killing—Dark and Light.

The general marched up to him, and to Qod's surprise, saluted.

"It's good to see you alive and well, General," Tillmus said.

"Uh . . . you, too, General."

Tillmus looked over Qod's head out into the marsh. Bodies were everywhere.

"So, that's where it happened," he said.

*I guess you'll need to know when you tell the empress how you defeated the Light army.*

"Yes. There. And here."

"Of course."

When Qod didn't respond, he asked, "What are your orders now, sir?"

Qod sure didn't expect that question.

"You mean, you don't want to take command?"

That seemed to surprise him even more.

"I can't challenge you. You haven't been confirmed."

*Saved by a legality. For now.*

Somehow, that just deepened his mood.

But then, General Tillmus said, "But even if you were, I wouldn't challenge you."

"But you wanted to," Qod blurted. "You tried to."

Tillmus shrugged. "Yes, and I'm ogre enough to admit that I was wrong. Look at this. I never could have come up with such a . . . an *audacious* plan."

Qod was pretty sure he'd been about to say something else instead of audacious. Something profane.

"And if I were commanding the Army of the Mist, we'd be either dead or scattered to the wind now, with the faebies ravaging the entire Fanciful Highlands.

"I don't think you can be so sure—"

"Begging the general's pardon, I *am* sure. Please give me credit enough to see what's right in front of my face."

He paused and looked out on the marsh again.

"How many do you think died out there in the water?" he asked. "Six hundred? Seven? Looks like all of the centaurs."

Qod didn't offer a guess. It could be seven hundred, but he really didn't want to think of death at the moment.

"And you used wizards, of all things."

*Wizards! Shit!*

Qod spun around and shouted to Mac, "Go find the wizards. Now!"

He was mortified that he'd forgotten about them now that the battle was over. For all he knew, the Light had found and slaughtered them.

He turned around, and General Tillmus was giving him a puzzled look.

"We need to gather the wizards up," Qod mumbled.

"I should say so." He paused a moment, then looked at the ground.

"If you don't mind me saying, and I mean no disrespect, but I would have never in a million years have thought that it would be a gobb—a goblin—who would be our next great general."

"I'm hardly a great general," Qod automatically said.

"I can see the proof right here, sir. I may not be the smartest ogre in the pack, but give me credit for seeing that you might just be the next Ptolomon. You are destined for great things, and if you'll allow me, I'd like to be at your side as you do them."

Qod just stared at him for a moment. His imposter syndrome had been raging since the day Captain Ryys had told him to just stick the pointy end of his spear at any charging elves. He'd just been caught up and in a torrent of improbable events far out of his control.

But this was an ogre general, a professional soldier. And if he was telling him that, was it possible there was some truth to it?

He cleared his throat and tried to sound confident as he said, "Your expertise and experience are invaluable, General, and I'd be honored have you at my side as we defend our people from the Light.".

## Chapter 48

"We would have lost without you," Qod said inside the darkened tent.

The wizards were lying on cots. Most of them, that was. Vikky, the orc wizard, hadn't survived the effort.

Food and water were available, but it didn't look like the food, at least, had been touched. Qod made a mental note to refill their water jugs.

"It was close, sir," Lraine said. "I wasn't sure we could hold it when Vikky died."

"But you did hold. And that saved us."

"We're just glad you gave us the chance."

He paused, then gave Qod a shy glance.

"We really did do OK, didn't we?"

"More than OK, Lraine. All of you did."

Qod glanced around the tent, darkened because it helped the wizards recover from their splitting headaches. He'd seen Dulce before after a spell and how long it took her to recover, but he'd never realized that wizardry could be this exhausting to the point of debilitation.

*Big spells have big consequences, I guess.*

Vikky had died under the strain of holding the ice steady after the Light army advanced over it. The entire battle plan almost came to an end right there, according to Lraine. Their spell came close to collapsing before the others could rally their power.

Qod shuddered when he was told that, and frankly, he was glad he hadn't known until after the battle was won.

Dulce, who was sitting on her cot and watching the two of them, and her team were relatively well off. Their spell hadn't been as draining. But Lraine and his team were on empty. They hadn't even known how the battle had gone. The ghoul who had relayed Qod's signal said that as soon as they cut the spell, they had gone catatonic.

She actually thought they were dead, and checking Vikky only confirmed that. She left them to join the fight.

Tracks around them confirmed that the Light had reached their wizard ring, but by the Dark Mother's grace, they'd been left alone, where they stayed unconscious until they were recovered after the battle.

"General?" a voice called from outside the tent.

Qod reached over and put a hand on Lraine's knee. "The empress will be told what you wizards did. We . . . the entire Dark, are in your debt."

He nodded at Dulce, then left the tent, blinking in the bright sunlight. It was cold, but the kind of invigorating cold that made someone glad that they were alive. All around him, soldiers were carrying on with their chores—sharpening weapons, cleaning gear, eating, and just gathering in groups and celebrating their continuing journey through life.

Not enough of them, though. Too many were missing, which dampened the mood.

"Do you have the figures?" he asked Major Pishlyss.

"One thousand, four hundred and thirteen," he said. "Still a viable force."

Qod waited for more, and when the major shifted his weight from foot to foot, he prompted, "And the dead?"

"Over fifteen hundred."

Qod just stared at the kukudh, who was visibly wilted.

"Over fifteen hundred? What does that mean? Sixteen? Two thousand? These soldiers died for the Dark. I want an exact number, and I want a list of names. Every single one of them deserves to be honored."

"Sir, we're still trying to recover bodies. Some ended up in the water."

"It's simple, Major. Subtract the number of living from our strength before the battle. Wa-la, we have the number who were lost."

Now, the major was even more obviously ill at ease. He refused to meet Qod's eyes, shifting from staring over his head to the ground between them.

"We . . . uh . . . we don't know exactly what our strength was, sir."

That shocked Qod, and his mouth dropped open.

"We don't know."

"No, sir.  We never do.  With so many, you know, coming in and out . . ."

"I bet you know exactly how many Black Smokes we had," he muttered, just loud enough for the major to hear.

Pishlyss didn't refute that.

Qod knew that the command considered the small folk as expendable supplies, no different than a spear or a sword.  But what hurt was that they probably knew the exact numbers of spears in the supply chain.

*That's going to change*, he vowed.  *If the empress confirms me, that is.*

"And the wounded."

The major looked up, smiled broadly, and eagerly said, "Eight hundred and six, sir. The hooded spirits say that only forty-one are still in mortal danger."

Then he seemed to realize that his happiness at having an answer was probably out of place, given the subject.

"We are making the wounded comfortable," he said in a more somber voice.  "They've all sacrificed for you."

"For the Dark, Major."

"Of course, General.  That's what I meant.  Forgive me."

Qod contemplated the kukudh for a long minute.  Not too long ago, the major might have held Qod's life in his hands. If he'd advised Yare differently, Qod might be long dead and forgotten.

The officer had seemed like the pinnacle of efficiency and knowledge, sure of himself.  Now, his deference was almost shocking.  Qod wondered if it was a true sea change or an act of some kind.

There was something about the major that Qod didn't trust, but he had long realized that Pishlyss was far more powerful and far more vital to the army's functioning than any other major—or maybe any other officer.

The kukudh still gave him the creeps, but he knew enough that he needed the major's full dedication and capabilities for the good of his command.

"The Light?" he asked in a more neutral tone.

This time, the major's dead eyes—well, didn't light up, but became "less dead."

"I don't have exact numbers. They're still pulling bodies out. But at least three thousand. Probably more."

It was Qod's turn to be surprised. "Three thousand?"

He hadn't expected nearly that number. Surely a lot of them had escaped.

"How many got away?"

"None. Well, almost none. Colonel Oh blocked their retreat."

Qod had been told that the colonel had led a force down the high ground between the battlefield and Offerton. Evidently, Qod still had to find out more about what had actually happened.

He knew the basics. General Tillmus had kept his force in place, but Qod's insistence that the dwarves were a mirage had kept eating at his mind. Finally, he ordered the Second Scouts to initiate contact but be ready for an immediate retreat.

The Scouts found thirty-two dwarves, not an army.

He immediately realized that once again, the Light had sucked him in, and he'd played the fool. And by doing so—still not believing Qod's plan could work—he thought he'd sentenced Qod and his troops to an almost certain death.

He momentarily considered remaining in place to meet the inevitable Light attack, but his conscience wouldn't allow for that. Fearing he was too late, he rushed the army over the range and down toward the Anemia delta. The gjallarhorns sounding gave him hope, and he pushed the troops into an all-out charge, which arrived in the proverbial nick of time.

What Qod didn't know were the details. He didn't know which soldiers rose above and beyond, and he wanted to somehow recognize them. Any soldier, not just the officers. He made another mental note—one of about a hundred since the end of the battle—to make sure he got as many of those details as possible over the coming days.

Then something Pishlyss said sunk in.

"They're still pulling bodies out of the water? We've got our soldiers doing that?"

The Light army facing them might have been destroyed, but who was to say there wasn't another army out there? With relatively few combat-ready soldiers, he didn't like the idea of them being separated in two groups.

"No, sir. The humans are doing it mostly. Scavenging, you know. It's like a Samhain morning for them with everything they can steal."

Disdain dripped from his voice, which matched what Qod felt when he heard the words.

"Which we'll have to buy back from them," Qod said.

"That's the way of the world, General."

"General?" a voice called out.

Qod turned to see Captain k'Rhee striding over to him.

"Yes, Captain?"

"Colonel Dan requests your presence."

"What about?"

K'Ree pursed her lips, then said, "She and Colonel Wonoponot are having a difference of opinion on the priority for pike resupply."

Qod just raised his eyebrows.

"We don't have enough for more than one of them, and with Offerton burnt to the ground, we won't get a resupply for some time now."

"Can't General Tillmus handle it?"

"If you order him to handle it, yes, he can."

"What the captain is saying, sir, is that perhaps this is a time to cement your, uh, leadership with, if I may be so bold to say, Colonel Oh," Major Pishlyss said, reverting back to his behind-the-scenes advising.

Qod looked at the captain, who gave him the slightest of nods.

*Why did I think this would all be over after the battle?*

He was getting the feeling that winning the peace was going to be a much bigger task.

"Lead on," he said with a sigh.

# Chapter 49

"I don't like this, sir," Lieutenant Glascock said as Qod removed his armor.

The leathers were only slightly worse for wear, and a big part of him wanted to show up in the village in full kit. But the real reason he was doing this was with all the upheaval he'd experienced over the last—was it only a month?—he wanted to reconnect with his roots. He wanted to capture at least something of who he was—the nerdy, unassuming bookworm who wouldn't hurt a fly.

Well, that and one more reason that wasn't as commendable.

"I can't very well come in with a company of soldiers now, can I?"

"Why not? You're the most powerful person in the Fanciful Highlands right now. You can do what you want."

Qod shook his head. "You can watch me in case the Light has secretly infiltrated Yellow Rock in a plot to kill me. Fly in Dulce if that will make you feel better. But these are my folk. Simple folk. A company of soldiers would be traumatizing."

"But—"

"No buts. If I can handle a battle mage, if I can handle Yare, then I think I'm safe enough in a small village of goblins. And the draugrs are in position."

"But—"

"It's settled. You're staying here. That's an order."

For a moment, Qod thought Glascock was going to refuse. Qod wasn't officially a general yet, even if he was wearing the two full moons on his collar. But he kept his mouth closed.

"Keep the company back beyond the hill," Qod said gently. "Remember, we goblins have pretty good eyesight."

The lieutenant drew himself up and gave Qod a curt nod before turning away.

He muttered, "The major's going to be royally pissed," probably forgetting that goblins had excellent hearing as well.

Qod gave a wry smile. Glascock was worried about Major Pishlyss, not General Tillmus nor any of the colonels. Despite the success in the last battle, Qod knew that many of them would just as soon see Qod wander off into a company of elves and disappear from the scene.

"I don't know why I can't come with you," Pani said in a pout. "I'm a goblin, too."

Qod was tempted. Pani was an impressive figure of a goblinette, and for him to come waltzing in with her on his arm would certainly turn some heads. But for reasons he wasn't quite sure of, that just seemed icky to him. He didn't know what his relationship with Pani was anymore, and being a general now sure complicated things. One thing was for sure, though. He didn't want to use her for a mere ego boost.

"This is something I have to do alone," he gently said.

He turned to Lieutenant Sean, just recently promoted from sergeant to take Lieutenant Helvig's place.

"Your draugrs are in place?"

"Yes, General."

"And you're sure they can't be seen?"

"No one can see us if we don't want them to."

"Well, then. I'm off."

He left his team and climbed to the top of Ragweed Hill. It wasn't the season for the pollen, but his nose twitched in memory. The hill was a grandiose designation for what was really just a small rise. As he climbed, his heart started racing. And when he crested the top, and Yellow Rock was in sight, he let out a sigh.

*Home.*

He took a moment to search the surrounding area, but the draugr lieutenant was as good as his word. Fifteen of the bodyguards were surrounding the village, but he couldn't spot a single one.

Qod took a deep breath and cut down to the Rocky Highway, another grandiose designation for the dirt road that led to Deerhorn Rapids and parts beyond. The army, the battles, his current position—all were forgotten as he hurried into the village.

Cuddy was the first to see him. The old goblin was sitting under his eaves, sucking on his long pipe.

"The war's over?" he asked.

"No, Cuddy. Not yet."

"You desert, then?"

"Just here for a quick visit. Then I'm heading back."

The old goblin shrugged, then tilted his head back and closed his eyes.

Qod didn't know what he expected, but that was a little disappointing. He ran into Voxi and Rap, who nodded their greeting before getting back to their One Off game, before he spotted Kassy.

"As I live and breathe, it's Qod," she said. "Good to see you, son, and in one piece."

Kassy was the village's teacher and one of Qod's favorite goblins. She held up a hand for him to wait and darted back into her hovel. A moment later, she reemerged with a small muslin bag that she handed to him.

"Are these . . ." he started as he quickly untied the top.

A heavenly smell rose.

"Your rat cracks!"

Besides being the village teacher, Kassy was an excellent cook. Qod couldn't wait. He grabbed one and bit into the greasy deliciousness. These were the real deal, not the poor army copies.

"Oh, by the Dark Mother. You don't know how much I've missed these."

He closed the bag, afraid he'd eat them all, and he wanted to share them with Pani.

"Anything for our soldiers, Qod. Umm . . ."

Qod finished off the cracker and then asked, "Umm what?"

"That's a pretty fancy tunic there, and it doesn't look like a uniform."

Qod glanced down. It *was* a fancy tunic, better than anything he'd ever owned. And as underwear, it didn't have military markings. He'd gotten it before the last battle. Rumor was that the cloth used for the senior officers was even elf-woven.

"This is nothing.  Just what we wear under our leathers."

"Where are your leathers?"

"Uh . . . being repaired from the last battle. That's why . . . uh, that's why I had a chance to come visit.  The army's only over there, an hour's walk," he said, pointing over Ragweed Hill."

"I guess the army's changed since my day, giving privates such nice gear."

Qod raised his eyebrows.  He had no idea that Kassy had ever served, which meant he had to be even more careful in what he said.

He needed to change the subject.

"How's my home?" he asked.

Her eyes clouded over, and all she said was, "Juut."

Anger blossomed.  This was the darker reason Qod had wanted to see his village. He had figured Juut wouldn't wait for the full year before taking over Qod's hovel, but to hear it from Kassy lit a fire under him.

"Thanks, Kassy.  For the rat cracks and for that information."

Kassy just nodded as Qod wheeled about and marched across the village.  A dozen goblins greeted him, but he ignored them all.  He reached his home, hesitated a moment, then flung open the door.

Eight sausages were playing on the floor.  Wyr spun around from where she was preparing lunch, and her face paled when she saw him.

"You!"

"Yes, me!" Qod said, his voice almost a shout.

Wyr backed up against the wooden counter.

"Pan, get your pa," she said.

One of the sausages ran out the door.

"What are you doing in my home?" Qod asked, his voice as sharp as ice.

"Juut, uh, he said you were dead.  Fighting the faebies."

"As you can see, I am very much *not* dead."

Wyr was frightened, Qod could see. And that didn't make him feel proud, but this was his home, and it was the only thing he had left from his family.

"Where are my manners, Qod?" Wyr asked in a wavering voice. "Would you like some thistle tea?"

He started to refuse. He didn't want her to be nice. He wanted her to argue and fight. But to refuse tea. That was something a civilized goblin didn't do.

"Why yes, Wyr. Thank you."

She was trembling as she prepared the tea. His anger flared again when she turned back to him and handed the tea in a fine ceramic teacup—the teacup his father had bought years ago to woo his mother and the highest quality item Qod owned.

He bit back a comment and sipped the tea.

"Are you a ghost, Mr. Qod?" one of the sausages—Qod didn't know their names—asked.

"No," Qod said.

"My pa said you got killed, so you must be a ghost," she said with little sausage logic.

"Hush, Anny," Wyr said. "You leave Qod alone."

But Anny wasn't done. She grabbed his hand.

"If you're alive, are you going to take our home away from us?"

Wyr gasped, and her siblings all stopped playing to stare at him.

"It's not your home. It's my home," he said.

"Oh. OK," Anny said in a resigned voice. She dropped his hand and stepped back. "It's a nice home. I'll miss it."

Qod stared at her for a long moment, then took in the hovel. It wasn't a nice home. It was merely adequate. It might not be much, but it was his home, not Juut's. He'd just stolen it from him. Planned the whole thing, too, Qod was certain.

Except . . .

It wasn't just Juut. The other sausages were staring at him with wide eyes, and Wyr was standing, hand in front of her mouth, her body tense as if she thought he was going to attack her.

345

Anny looked up at him with sad sausage eyes. No anger toward him. Just resignation.

*Oh, dwarf shit.*

"Come here," Qod told her as he knelt.

"Anny! Get away from him," Wyr said in fear.

The little goblinette ignored her mother and stepped closer.

"I won't take your home," he said in a quiet voice.

Wyr gasped behind him.

"But you have to be a good sausage, you hear? Take care of your littermates."

"I can do that."

"I know you can."

He reached over and patted her head, then stood and faced Wyr.

"Not this," he said, holding the teacup. "This, you're going to put away. No one uses it, and when I come back, you'll give it to me."

"You'll let us stay in your home?" she asked with both doubt and hope.

"The teacup. It's mine."

"Yes, yes, of course."

She darted forward and took his hand, but Qod yanked it back. He was sure she knew what they had done was wrong. She was part of it.

He took one last look at the sausages as he mentally berated himself for being a softhearted fool. Didn't he have to be harder if he was going to be a general?

But he just couldn't turn them out. The sausages weren't at fault, only the parents.

He spun around and back out through the door. Wyr called after him, but he blocked her words.

Now, he wondered why he'd come back. This had been his home, but not anymore. His family was dead, and Qod from Yellow Rock was dead as well. He was someone else now.

"Qod!"

He turned to see Juut, followed by little Pan, running after him.

*Great. Just what I need now.*

"You're not taking back your house!" Juut screamed.

Goblins started to gather at the commotion.

"I already—"

"Are you a deserter? They'll kill you, and I'll make sure they know where to find you."

Something inside Qod finally broke.

"Just like you got me conscripted Juut? So you can steal my home?"

"I . . . it's like this . . ." Juut stuttered, then changed to, "That doesn't matter. You're a deserter now, and that means you can't take my home!"

Without thinking, Qod charged Juut and grabbed the larger goblin by the collar and yanked him down until they were face-to-face."

"I am not a deserter," he said with enough venom that Juut tried to jerk back. "And I've already given my home to your little Anny and the rest of your sausages. But by the Dark Mother, if you so much as open your mouth one more time, I'm taking it back!"

Confusion transformed Juut's face, and his mouth did open, but in shock as he stared over Qod's shoulder.

"What's the matter with you?"

Juut just pointed.

Qod turned around. Lieutenant Glascock and his team were charging toward him. The draugrs who had surrounded the village were converging as well.

"General! You need to come with us," the lieutenant shouted, still twenty-five yards away and closing.

Qod, still holding Juut's collar, asked, "Why? What's happening?"

"The empress. She just arrived. And she wants to see you."

"The empress? She's here? And she wants me?"

The team slid to a stop in front of him.

"Yes, sir. Please put on your leathers and come now."

Pani and Natayla handed him his armor.

There was a gasping sound. Qod turned to see Juut struggling to breathe. Qod was cutting off his air.

"The teacup's mine," he said as he released the goblin, who fell to his knees.

Goblins who had started to gather to watch Qod and Juut were now slowly backing away.

He quickly put on the leathers, which seemed to put him back into a military mindset. He gave one more look at his fellow villagers before turning back to the anxious lieutenant.

"Well, we'd better not keep the empress waiting," he said as he marched off, leaving Yellow Rock behind.

# Chapter 50

"Hurry, sir," General Tillmus hissed. "She's been waiting too long."

The assistant Army of the Mist commander, who had met them at the edge of the camp, was nervous.

Extremely nervous.

And that was infectious. Qod knew his off galivanting around in Yellow Rock was probably not a good look for the army commanding general, but he hadn't thought too much about it. Now, though, with Tillmus looking like he was going to have a mental breakdown, rumors about the empress's volatile temper and her penchant for removing those who displeased her started running through his mind.

*But we won the battle. She has to be happy about that.*

If he was trying to convince himself that he wasn't in trouble, it wasn't working. If the empress had any of the orc prickliness that Yare had, then she could easily see having to cool her heels waiting for him as a personal affront, and that could have drastic repercussions.

It wasn't just keeping her waiting. That wasn't even his most pressing concern. He didn't need Captain k'Ree to tell him that by winning the battle—maybe *especially* by winning the battle—he could now be conceived as a threat instead of a convenient, controllable figurehead. He wasn't about to challenge the empress, but did she know that? And for all the lip service given to the challenge tradition, he now knew politics was still a very real part of the Dark throne.

If the empress decided that Qod was any sort of bump in the road to her plans, then she could use any excuse to simply take him out of the equation.

Surrounded by his team and draugrs, he hurried down the slope toward the CP. It seemed that the entire army was standing around, silently watching them.

Not entirely silent. A few muted cheers rose from the crowd, but without the usual degree of enthusiasm. Every soldier knew the significance of the situation. The empress just didn't fly around to the far reaches of the Dark lands on social calls.

As they got closer to the CP, the crowd became denser, culminating with the Mage Killers packed around the CP itself.

Sergeant Tark broke free and tried to approach, almost getting skewered by a tightly wound draugr.

"Let him through," Qod ordered.

"We don't have time for this," Tillmus whispered.

Qod ignored him and waited for the armorer.

"Sir, I just wanted . . . we just wanted you to tell you that if, you know, something happens and you need us, we're here. You just give the word, and we'll come running."

Qod looked beyond **him**. All eyes were locked on him. Not just the Mage Killers. Soldiers from other units, including some Gray Ghosts, and even some junior officers, were nodding their agreement as well.

Pride—and gratitude—welled up from his heart. Qod knew that the Army of the Mist couldn't stand up to the total might of the Dark. The empress was just too powerful. But the idea that they would take action to protect him was humbling.

He wouldn't let them, of course. Dark fighting against Dark was inconceivable when the Light would certainly be taking action to avenge their recent defeat.

"Nothing's going to happen, Tark," he said, patting the kobold's shoulder. "But thank you."

He started to walk past Tark, who reached out to grab his shoulder. Qod had to wave back the draugrs who leapt into action.

"Really, sir. The empress. She could—"

"Pass the word, Tark. No matter what happens, no one does anything."

The armorer reluctantly nodded and stepped back.

"Was that smart, Small Sir?" Pani stepped up beside him and quietly asked. "You might need them."

Qod took a moment to glance at his entourage. The normally expressionless draugrs looked agitated. General Tillmus was positively beside himself with worry. His team was nervous, and Lieutenant Glascock had a determined look while he ran his hand over the pommel of his sword.

He briefly wondered if he should just turn the group around and leave. He had the feeling that they would go along with it. But to what end? The empress had long arms, and refusing to meet with her would only add fuel to any misgivings she had about him.

"Let's get this done," he said as he pulled himself to his full height, puffed out his chest, and started walking.

They passed through the crowd until, about thirty yards out, the press of soldiers abruptly ended, leaving a clear buffer around the CP. It wasn't hard to see why.

The first thing Qod saw was the palanquin. It was smaller than he expected, and somewhat plain-looking in black with red trim. But the eight gryphon bearers captured his attention.

Qod had never seen a gryphon before, and they were frankly magnificent as they sat on their haunches, still in their harnesses, as if everyone around them didn't exist.

Almost. As soon as Qod and his group emerged from the crowd, a single gryphon turned to stare at him with golden eyes. Qod had no idea what it was thinking, but his reptile brain knew a predator when he saw one, and a shiver ran the length of his body.

Harpies could fly people if necessary, but only the empress had a team of gryphons. The notoriously difficult beasts were reportedly always just a moment away from erupting into violence. The fact that the empress flew them with abandon was just one more example of her power.

Qod felt more than heard his draugrs alert, and it was only then that he pulled his gaze from the gryphons to the imperial guard. Those draugrs, clad in armor so black that it seemed to suck in all the light around them, had drawn themselves up as soon as they spotted Qod and his team.

The tension in the air was palpable, which took Qod by surprise. Draugrs were draugrs, right? Was there something he was missing here?

"Is everything OK, Lieutenant Sean?"

"Yes, sir. We know our duty."

*You're not answering what I need to know.*

He wanted an explanation. It sure looked like his bodyguards were up for a fight.

"Just calm down, Lieutenant. We don't need to instigate anything."

"Yes, sir," the draugr said, but he didn't relax any.

*I hope this doesn't blow up on us.*

He felt that he was in a tsunami that had swept him up and was taking him inexorably forward to a fate out of his hands. It pissed him off to feel powerless again, but he sure didn't have an exit ramp that he could see.

So, he let the flow carry him. They reached the CP, where a draugr captain in the Imperial Guard stopped them.

"Only General Yellow Rock is to enter."

Lieutenant Glascock and Sean both protested, but to no avail. The captain ignored them.

"It's OK," Qod said. "You stay here."

Sean was locked onto the Imperial Guard captain, and he looked like he wanted to argue with Qod.

"I'm serious. I don't want a fight here," Qod said.

The nod was almost imperceptible, but Qod thought his draugrs would comply.

Pani grabbed his hand and whispered, "Make sure you come back, Small Sir."

He gave a wry smile. Here he was, about to meet with the Empress of the Dark, and he was still "Small Sir" to Pani.

"That's my intent," he said as he gently removed her grip.

He gave his team one last look. Tulip was gently shifting her weight from one foot to the other with Dulce perched on her massive shoulder. Yannis was softly stroking his bow, his eyes clouded and unreadable. Nataly and Castor were angry. Only Mac was smiling, and he gave Qod a big thumbs-up.

"Hey, cheer up. Maybe she's going to give me a medal," Qod said with a forced joviality. "We did win the battle, after all."

He turned, took a deep breath, and started to remove his blade, but the captain shook his head.

The fact that the draugr wasn't taking his weapon was not a measure of respect, Qod realized. It was a sign that he posed no threat to the empress.

"I did kill the Battle Mage," Qod muttered.

If the captain heard that, he didn't react. With a small sigh, Qod brushed by him and entered the CP into relative darkness. And quiet.

The wizard lights in the outer area were off. Some daylight got in through holes and seams, enough to see that the place was empty, something Qod had never seen. There wasn't a soul around. It was eerie.

*Now what?*

The only light was coming through the flap to the conference room, so he headed there, stopping at the flap when he heard subdued talking inside.

"Uh, hello? It's General Qod. I mean General Yellow Rock," he said with an embarrassing quaver in his voice.

The talking stopped before a voice said, "Come on in, General."

Qod pushed open the flap and blinked in the brightly lit space for a second before he could see clearly.

The empress was sitting at the head of the conference table, and she was . . . *impressive.* Tall and thin, she exuded pure power coupled with typical orc assuredness. Whereas Yare had been a brute of an orc, she was all whipcord and sinew. Yare might have been no pushover in a challenge, but the empress had won more challenges than Qod could count. Supposedly, no one had even tried for almost four years now. Looking at her, Qod had no doubt that she was death in orc form.

She was dressed in full, impeccable black and red leathers trimmed with fur, which oddly caught his attention. The weather had warmed up considerably after the battle, but maybe she needed the extra protection while riding in the palanquin.

*Who cares, Qod? Pay attention.*

"You may leave," she said in a soft voice.

"What?"

But she wasn't speaking to him.  It was only then that Qod noticed Captain k'Ree standing off to the side.

"Yes, Your Majesty," the captain said as she bowed her head.

When she raised it, she gave Qod a penetrating stare for a few moments.  He didn't know what it meant, if it was good or bad.  She broke the stare without saying a word and left the room.

Qod watched her leave for a moment.  He didn't think it was very common for a mere banshee captain to be having a private audience with the Empress of the Dark.  But then again, captains weren't supposed to interfere with challenges, either.

"She's your agent.  Here, with the army," Qod blurted without thinking, then immediately regretted it.

"I'm sorry, Your Majesty.  I didn't mean—"

The empress waved him silent and gave a slight chuckle.  "She said you were quick on the uptake."

Qod didn't respond.  It had been obvious that k'Ree was more than she seemed, but he should have figured out before that she was the key to everything here with the Army of the Mist. His mind started racing as he tried to remember if he'd done anything to piss her off.  Probably a lot.

"Sit, Qod from Yellow Rock," the empress said, bringing him back to the here and now.

He noticed that she hadn't used his rank, but he couldn't figure out if that was good or bad.

*Not great, I'd guess.*

He started to the other end of the table when the empress said, "No.  Here, near me, so we don't have to shout."

"Yes, Your Majesty."

Qod took the seat next to her.  Something was off, though, and it took a moment for him to figure it out.

Orcs had a certain body odor.  Bitter, like dried chicory. The empress, on the other hand, smelled like jasmine.  She smelled more like a troll than an orc, and that bothered him.

She was the empress with more resources than anyone in the Dark, and she could certainly bathe herself with perfume, but why, way out here in the Fanciful Highlands with the Army of the Mist.

He had a feeling that her choice was purposeful, almost as if she wanted Qod to forget he was dealing with an orc.

*Won't work. I won't forget who you are.*

He tried to keep his expression neutral as he waited for her to speak.

Which she finally did.

"What am I going to do with you?"

"Your Majesty?"

"I think the question is pretty clear,"

"I . . . just let me be?"

She chuckled again, this time louder.

"I bet you'd like that. But, you see, things are a little more complicated than that."

Qod had been hoping for praise for winning the battle. He feared her coming in aggressively in attack mode. He hadn't imagined her just casually sitting there, smelling like jasmine and having a relatively calm discussion.

"I did win the battle, Your Majesty. I served the Dark to the best of my ability."

She looked down her hooked nose at him before asking, "Just to where does your loyalty lie, Qod from Yellow Rock?"

"To the Dark, Your Majesty. To all of the Dark races."

The complacent eyes flashed for the briefest of moments, and Qod caught a quick glimpse of the fabled viciousness that had enabled her to rise to the top of the Dark.

*Did I just screw up?*

He probably should have said he was loyal to her, but he'd reacted naturally. For a moment, he thought about changing his answer, but no, he wasn't going to do that. He wasn't going to lie. If he was going to be purged, then let it be for telling the truth, and the truth was that his loyalty was to the entire Dark, not just the empress.

Just as quickly as her anger had flashed, it was gone.

"So you're not a faeby agent, as the departed General Yare reported back to me."

Which was news to him. He had no idea he'd been accused of that.

"No!" he shouted. "Never! I'm not an anything for the Light bastards!"

"Too bad. That would make my decision easier."

"Decision?"

If she was here to decide something, Qod thought that the chances were that she'd flown all this way to give him a medal were nil.

"Surely Captain k'Ree told you that your generalship is temporary. I have to confirm or deny it."

"She told me, but she didn't say you would be coming to do it in person."

The empress gave him a grudging nod before saying, "I wasn't going to. But after this last battle, I decided I needed to come in person to see what I had in you instead of relying on third parties."

Qod felt a surge of hope.

*If our battlefield victory changed her calculus, then that has to be for the good, right?*

Then he thought, *Except for that ugly little fact that I might now be considered a threat.*

"I am just a goblin trying to do my duty, Your Majesty."

To that, she laughed out loud. "You are anything but 'just a goblin,' Qod from Yellow Rock."

He didn't know how to answer that.

"Tell me, why did you decide to use wizardry to fight the faebies," she asked.

The change of gears confused him a little, and he was flustered when he answered, "The Light uses magic, and we almost lost the Battle of the Long Caldron because of it."

"The Light is evil, and they use evil means."

"Wizardry isn't evil or good," Qod protested before he remembered he was speaking with the empress.

"I mean, it's the use that's evil or good," he added in a more controlled tone.

She shrugged and said, "All my generals and ministers seem to disagree with you. Magic is inherently evil, and using it for battlefield victory lacks honor.

Qod felt the world closing down on him. So this was the problem. He'd used his wizards in the battle, and that had somehow brought dishonor to the Dark.

"Losing the battle lacks honor, too," he muttered.

She didn't disagree, so he pushed further. "We use magic every day. To see," he said, pointing at the wizard lights. "To communicate. To heal our wounded."

"That's the hooded spirits who do that."

"It's still magic. And during my first battle, we had a wizard who burnt up the incoming arrows."

"In defense."

Qod knew he wasn't going to convince her. It was hypocritical, in his opinion, to use magic in so many ways but balk in others.

"I've been briefed on the battle. One thing isn't clear. You'd already lost your strongest wizards. I don't see where you had the power to freeze the marsh."

Qod debated what he should say before coming up with, "The temperatures were close to freezing anyway. It only took them a little power to shift the heat away and for the water to freeze."

"Them?" she asked, for the first time sounding like she was surprised.

*Crap. What did I just do?*

"Yes, Your Majesty. We used all of our wizards to link up, which allowed their power to multiply to where they could freeze the marsh, then hold it steady under the weight of the centaurs."

"Link up?"

*Surely, she already knows about that.*

She scrunched up her brow for a moment.

"Yes, that's an odd use of a link, but it could work." She thought about it for another moment, then said, "Who was the focal point?"

Qod felt his heart sink. She'd asked that question too casually, almost as an afterthought, which meant that she really wanted to know.

And he didn't want to reveal that. He didn't want Lraine to have crosshairs painted on him.

"Focal point?" he asked, hoping that the empress would assume he knew nothing about that.

"Never mind," she said, brushing him off. "I'll send someone to investigate."

Before he could breathe a sigh of relief, she continued. "But the ice alone didn't swing the battle, from all reports. The tactics were yours or Tillmus's?"

"Mine, Your Majesty. Mostly. But without the small unit leaders, none of this would have happened. It was their reactions that held the day."

"But you put it all into motion."

"In my first battles, all we did was charge the faebies and waste soldiers. There wasn't an attempt to outsmart the Light, just overrun them. I just decided we were going to do to them what they were doing to us."

The empress gave a wry grin. "Yes, Yare. Undefeatable in the challenge ring, but a bad tactician." She shook her head and said, almost to herself, "He had to go."

Qod just stared at her. He'd wondered exactly why Captain k'Ree had killed Yare. The empress might have just answered that question. Not why Qod was chosen, though, unless he was in the right place at the right time for her to move forward with her plan.

He'd ignored the fact that both of them knew he hadn't killed Yare during the challenge, but he thought it was time to clear the air on that. Before he could ask, though, a chant of "Mage Killer" reached them.

They both listened for a few moments before the empress said, "And therein lies the problem."

Qod winced. This was bad timing for him.

"Your Majesty? The problem?" he asked as if it wasn't obvious.

"You've got fifteen hundred soldiers in the Army of the Mist. If you gave the order, I'm sure they would happily overrun my Imperial Guard and kill me."

"NO, Your Majesty. I would never do that!"

"I almost believe you, but that doesn't matter. What does matter is that their loyalty is to you, not me."

"Their loyalty is to the Dark, not me."

"Dwarf shit, Qod from Yellow Rock. It's to you. Listen to them."

It was both with pride and fear that he heard the chants. Each one of them was another nail in his coffin.

"We're down to fifteen hundred surviving soldiers, Your Majesty. You have hundreds of thousands. We're hardly a threat to you," he tried.

"Movements grow. Your name will only shine brighter."

"I'm a goblin. A gobby. No one cares."

"Now you're being naïve, and it doesn't become you," she said with a scowl. "You're even more dangerous because you're a goblin. The small folk will rally to you."

Qod was done. He didn't have any other arguments.

The empress leaned back in her chair and faced the ceiling.

"You killed Viwsam. I still don't know how, but you did it. You removed Yare and the elf bitch Elisia, and I don't know which one was the bigger thorn in my side."

*I didn't remove Yare. You did.*

"You've shown a knack for leadership and sound decisions. But you are also a threat to the Dark. To me."

She paused, still staring at the ceiling. Qod stared at her exposed throat. He still had his blade. If he could draw it without her hearing him, he might be able to jump and stab her in the neck before she could react.

His hand actually started to drift to his dagger when he shook his head and stopped. Even if he did somehow manage to kill the empress, it would be outside the challenge ring. Murder. And he didn't think the Imperial Guard would take too kindly to that. And his soldiers would react as well. They might very well overcome the Guard, but it would be a bloodbath.

"The smartest thing for me to do would be to remove the threat now and be done with it."

Qod sighed. He'd been half-expecting this ever since he knew she had arrived. That didn't make it any easier to accept.

Hopefully, there was still one thing he could do, and that was to ensure that he would be the only one to suffer. There would be no reprisals against his followers.

He cleared his throat to speak, but the empress suddenly sat up, looked him in the eye, and said, "I'm not always the smartest orc in the litter, General."

"Your Majesty?"

"I don't always make the smartest decisions. I hope this doesn't come around to bite me in my ass, but I'm confirming your generalship, Qod from Yellow Rock."

Qod was speechless as he stared at her. He heard the words, but they didn't make sense.

"You can thank me now, General."

"Uh, thank you, Your Majesty."

"Hardly the most enthusiastic statement of gratitude I've heard."

"I'm . . . I'm just surprised. I thought . . ."

"You thought I'd make the logical choice. I thought I would, too, when I first came here. But I don't know. The Light is building up. This campaign here in the Fanciful Highlands was just the first phase for something bigger."

That caught his attention. His entire world had been limited to the north, and her words were a reminder that the fight between Dark and Light was much bigger than that.

"You've shown a knack for outmaneuvering and outwitting the Light commanders, and I've got a feeling we might need a fresh look when the final battle commences."

*Me? A goblin from Yellow Rock?*

It was inconceivable.

"I'll do whatever you need me to do, Your Majesty."

"I know you will. For now," she said. "I'm leaving Tillmus in place for now. You're going to have to deal with him on your own."

General Tillmus had seemed to have lost his animosity toward Qod, but the ogre had ambition, and Qod knew he still didn't completely believe that Qod had killed both the battle mage and the previous commanding general. At some point, his confidence would grow, and he'd make his move.

"What should I do?"

"You're a general now.  You figure it out."

Which meant Qod was largely on his own.  The empress wasn't going to use her power to protect him.

"Just see that you don't make me regret this," she said as she stood.

"Now, escort me out to my palanquin.  I've got a long flight back to Taxian."

His mind was spinning as he fell one step behind her.

At the flap, she paused and turned to bend over him.

"Just remember, gobby, that if you move against me, I will crush you like a cockroach.  You and every one of your followers," she said, her voice as cold as ice, her eyes as hard as diamonds.

Qod quailed. There was no doubt in his mind that she was absolutely serious.

"Nuh . . . no, Your Majesty.  Never."

"Maybe you think so now, gobby, but things change. Except my vow to you if you move against me. That will never change."

"I understand, Your Majesty."

"Good," she said as she straightened.  "Now smile and follow me out."

## Chapter 51

Relief and fear fought with each other as Qod followed the empress through the dark and empty ops center.  He was alive, and it seemed he would be for the near future, at least.  But her warning had hit home.

Like it or not, Qod was still a pawn in a much bigger game, one where he wasn't sure of the rules.

Captain k'Ree was waiting near the entrance.  She looked from the empress to Qod and back to the empress as they passed before she turned and disappeared back into the depths of the CP.

"I said smile, General," Empress Almavoy told him as she pushed open the flap.

Both groups of draugrs jumped at her appearance, and for a moment, Qod thought they were going to clash, but the empress said, "Everything's fine, Captain Kallio."

The Imperial Guard started to relax, but Lieutenant Sean waited until Qod nodded before he gave some unseen signal and his draugrs took it down a few notches.

He caught Pani's anxious eyes.

She mouthed, "Are you OK?" and Qod gave her what he hoped was a reassuring nod.

The sun was setting in the west, casting a golden glow on the camp.  The empress stopped outside the CP, her body perfectly posed in the light, and faced the mass of now silent soldiers. Qod was certain that she was completely aware of the image, and that it would burn into every soldier's memory.

"Soldiers of the Army of the Mist," she shouted, her voice carrying farther than it should have.

*I guess that magic's OK.*

"You have won a tremendous battle against the Light here in the Fanciful Highlands, and you should be proud of that."

The soldiers burst into cheers, but more muted than Qod would have expected.

"Your bravery and sacrifice have blunted the faeby invasion, saving countless orcs, ogres, banshees, trolls, kobolds, pixies, and gremlins."

"And goblins," a voice shouted from the mass.

"Yes, and goblins," the empress said before turning and holding out a hand to Qod.

He wasn't sure what she wanted, so he stepped up a few steps. She motioned him closer, and so he came alongside her.

The empress took his hand, then lifted his entire arm, almost pulling his shoulder out of its socket.

"Especially this goblin. So, I am pleased to announce that I have confirmed Qod of Yellow Rock as the commanding general of the Army of the Mist!"

This time, the roar was deafening. Chants of "Mage Killer" filled the camp.

And it wasn't just the small folk, even if they might be the loudest. Orcs and ogres, infantry and Black Smokes, enlisted and officers alike, were celebrating.

Only his draugrs were silent, but it wasn't his imagination that their chests were puffed up a little more as they scanned for any potential threat to him.

The empress waited until the chants died before she spoke again. "I wish I could stay, but duty calls me back to the Misty Throne. You may have blunted the Light up north, but the enemy isn't defeated everywhere. They're planning their next attack. When they do, I know I can count on the Army of the Mist to run back into the fray to protect the people of the Dark."

The soldiers cheered again. The empress gave a small signal and her draugrs moved into formation around her, then together, they started to head to the palanquin.

"Go with her," Captain k'Ree, who suddenly appeared at Qod's side, said.

Qod hurried on his short legs to keep up.

The gryphons were stirring as they approached. The empress stopped, turned, and waved to the soldiers, who cheered yet again.

"Bow," she told Qod through clenched teeth, the smile never leaving her face.

Qod quickly stepped forward, went to one knee, and bowed his head. When the empress extended her hand, Qod kissed her ring.

Half of the soldiers cheered, mostly orcs and ogres.

The empress gave the slightest of frowns, then said, "Now kiss my cheek."

The empress was tall, and Qod was short, so she had to bend way over for him.

"Pay attention to k'Ree," she whispered. "She speaks with my voice."

Which he'd already realized.

"Yes, Your Majesty. I understand."

The empress took his hand again, raised his arm, and they both faced the soldiers once more. This time, she seemed pleased with the cheers, which were much louder.

Either the cheers or the nearness of the empress seemed to excite the gryphons. They started pacing in their traces. Two gave out what seemed to be half growls, half yowls.

The empress didn't seem to notice.

"Remember, don't cross me," she said out of the side of her mouth before she turned and approached the palanquin.

She gratefully mounted the platform, then took her seat in the center. The gryphons stepped outward until their harnesses were taut.

The empress waved once more to the soldiers, then snapped her fingers. As one, the gryphons leapt into the air, so smoothly done that the harnesses never slacked. The palanquin swayed, though, which caused the empress to clutch at her seat.

Still, it was an impressive sight to see the eight gryphons beat the air into submission as they rose into the sky.

The moment the palanquin left the ground, the Imperial Guard fell into formation and began to run toward the southern route out of the highlands. A moment later, what looked to be a company of pixies rose from the nearest hilltop and converged on the empress.

The guard didn't seem concerned, so the pixies must have been expected. Qod hadn't even considered the Imperial

Guard. In retrospect, they couldn't have flown in with the empress. So, either they'd run a very long distance all the way from Taxian, or they were staged somewhere closer.

He made a mental note to find out.

His team converged on him as the empress headed south. No one said anything as they watched. Qod let the silence reign. Too much had happened to him, and it was going to take time to come to terms with everything. But as he watched the palanquin get smaller and smaller, he felt a moment of pride.

The Dark faced an existential threat from the Light. But somehow, by a series of miracles, he'd been thrust into a situation where he could be part of the fight. He wasn't fated to be an observer in Yellow Rock, letting good battle evil without him.

"What now, Small Sir?" Pani asked as the empress slipped past the far peaks and out of sight.

Qod turned to look at the soldiers. His soldiers. Most were drifting off, back to whatever soldiers did when they weren't fighting. They came from every race belonging to the Dark. But they were together for a common cause. Whether orc or pixie, ogre or goblin, they were all part of the same team. Brothers and sisters in arms.

Over where the officers were breaking up, he caught Captain k'Ree's eyes. She gave him a nod before turning and disappearing among the others.

Then there was his team, who were looking at him, waiting for his answer. Troll, pixie, gremlin, satyr, vurdalak, kobold, and orc. Soldier and wizard. They were the family he'd lost. And with family, he knew he could do anything.

"What do we do now? We get ready, Pani. The Light is coming for us, and by the Dark Mother, we're going to be ready for them."

Thank you for reading *The Goblin General.* I hope you enjoyed it, and I would welcome any feedback on any of the review sites.

If you would like updates on new books releases, news, or special offers, please consider signing up for my mailing list. Your email will not be sold, rented, or in any other way disseminated. If you are interested, please sign up at the link below:

**http://eepurl.com/bnFSHH**

## Other Books by Jonathan Brazee

### <u>Gemini Twins</u>
Gemini Twins
Gemini Rising

### <u>Werewolf of Marines</u>
Werewolf of Marines: Semper Lycanus
Werewolf of Marines: Patria Lycanus
Werewolf of Marines: Pax Lycanus

### <u>The United Federation Marine Corps</u>
Recruit
Sergeant
Lieutenant
Captain
Major
Lieutenant Colonel
Colonel
Commandant
Legacy Marines
Esther's Story: Recon Marine

Noah's Story: Marine Tanker
Esther's Story: Special Duty
Blood United

Coda

Rebel (Set in the UFMC universe.)

Behind Enemy Lines  (A UFMC Prequel)

The Accidental War (A Ryck Lysander Short Story
Published in BOB's Bar: Tales from the Multiverse

### **Ghost Marines**
Integration
Unification
Devotion
Fusion

### **The Navy of Humankind:  Wasp Squadron**
Fire Ant
Crystals
Ace

### **The United Federation Marine Corps'**
### **Grub Wars**
Alliance
The Price of Honor
Division of Power

Jonathan P. Brazee

## Women of the United Federation Marine Corps
Gladiator
Sniper
Corpsman

High Value Target (A Gracie Medicine Crow Short Story)
BOLO Mission (A Gracie Medicine Crow Short Story)
None Left Behind (A Gracie Medicine Crow Short Story)

Weaponized Math (A Gracie Medicine Crow Novelette, Published in The Expanding Universe 3. Nebula Award Finalist)

## The Return of the Marines Trilogy
The Few
The Proud
The Marines

## The Al Anbar Chronicles:  First Marine Expeditionary Force--Iraq
Prisoner of Fallujah
Combat Corpsman
Sniper

## Call to Arms Capernica
Conscientious Objector
POG
Veteran

Soldier

Animal Soldier:  Hannibal

To the Shores of Tripoli

Wererat

Darwin's Quest:  The Search for the Ultimate Survivor

Starship in a Bottle

## Short Stories

Venus:  A Paleolithic Short Story

Secession

Duty

Semper Fidelis

Checkmate (Published in The Expanding Universe 4)

Recon Pilot

The Bridge

Silent Hero

## Sentenced to War (with JN Chaney)
Seeds of War
Children of Angels
Song of Redemption
An Uneasy Alliance
A Broken Alliance
An Alliance Reforged
When Worlds Fail
What Lies Behind
Gods of War

United We Kill
Marines Never Die
Nexus of Chaos
Exiled to Perdition
Into The Void
Brave New Dawn

## Undead Marine (With JN Chaney)

Undead Marine
Proof of Concept
Mission Creep
Marine Corpse
A Meeting of Minds
Dead to Rights

## Seeds of War (With Lawrence Schoen)

Invasion
Scorched Earth
Bitter Harvest

# Non-Fiction

Exercise for a Longer Life

The Effects of Environmental Activism on the Yellowfin Tuna Industry

# Author Website

http://www.jonathanbrazee.com

# Twitter

https://twitter.com/jonathanbrazee